Native Storiers: A Series of American Narratives

Series Editors   Gerald Vizenor   Diane Glancy

Elsie's Business

Frances Washburn

University of Nebraska Press

Lincoln & London

Set in Enschedé Renard. Book design by R. Eckersley.
Library of Congress Cataloging-in-Publication Data
Washburn, Frances.
Elsie's Business / Frances Washburn.
p.   cm.   – (Native storiers)
ISBN-13: 978-0-8032-9865-1 (paperback : alkaline paper)
ISBN-10: 0-8032-9865-x (paperback : alkaline paper)
1. Indian women – Fiction. 2. Rape victims – Fiction.
3. Dakota Indians – Fiction. 4. Indian reservations –
Fiction. 5. Standing Rock Indian Reservation
(N.D. and S.D.) – Fiction. I. Title. II. Series.
PS3623.A8673E67 2006   813'.6 – dc22
2006000848

For all of my relations

Elsie's Business

January 16, 1970

Anukite

If you want to know more about Elsie's story than just the official
reports you have to ask one of the grandfathers, because they know
all the old stories as well as the new ones, the latest gossip, and sometimes it's all the same stories happening over and over. Someone just
changes things up a little bit, a name here, a place there. Elsie's story
could go any which of a way. Ask Oscar DuCharme. He can tell you
all the stories. No one else seems inclined to tell you much of anything.

Oscar could live in the newest tribal housing project; he qualifies,
but he doesn't want to. Instead he lives in the little white frame
house just off Main Street, where there aren't any sidewalks, and the
view is the back of The Steak House that faces onto Main Street. He
and his wife, Ruby, dead now for years, bought the little house years
ago, not on the time payment plan, but with one big chunk of money
they'd saved up from the lease payments on their land allotments.

Bigger towns touch the gossip one day, one week, maybe one
month, and then they reach out to some newer story, but in Jackson,
a story as big as Elsie's happens rarely, so it gets handed around for
weeks and months. It's been a little over eleven months now since
Elsie died, and people have fondled the story so long that they've
worn the bumps off it, smoothed it with loving words, polished it
with lies, half truths, and omissions. Now it just sits there on the
shelf with all the other stories, something that you look at now and
then and say, "Oh, yes, that one. Really interesting. I can't remember
all the details, but if you really want to see it like it happened, go ask
one of the grandfathers."

You walk down the slight hill from Main Street, turn right on
First Street, and halfway up the block on the left, there's Oscar's

house, smoke rising from the chimney telling you that he's home and got his wood stove going. The early January snow, six inches deep, hides the packed earth of his front yard. In front of the skeletal Chinese elm that he planted twenty years ago, a snowdrift finger angles across the yard, pointing its icy tip towards the southwest like a contrary compass. You notice that the bottom right side of the front door has the white paint scratched away in fresh parallel arcs. Oscar must have another dog, you think, and when you knock, a yapping from inside tells you that he has indeed found a replacement for Tiger, his mutt that they told you had died last summer when you asked if he had a mean dog.

The door opens and Oscar stands there, his dark eyes, deep set in heavy wrinkles, blinking a little at the glare of sunshine off the snow. He's dressed in old khaki pants and brown cloth bedroom slippers, a navy blue sweater with a ladder run falling from a half-torn-off little alligator patch on the left side of his chest. The sweater is tight over his big belly. The tail of a faded green plaid shirt hangs in a drape below his sweater front. Cowering behind his leg, a brown ratty dog yaps a high-pitched sound.

"*Hau*," he says, and then he makes a sharp downward motion with his right hand and the dog hushes. "Come in."

"Hello," you say, and you start to explain who you are, but he stops you before you get more out than your name.

"Know who you are," he says. "Word gets around." He doesn't ask what you want from him.

The room smells of brewed coffee, beans and ham cooking in the kitchen, damp dog and cigarette smoke.

"It's a good day," he says. He snaps brown, bent fingers, points behind the sofa and the dog disappears behind it. "But it's cold. I don't like winter so much anymore. You know, I used to like ice fishing, but not anymore. How about you?"

"No. I like summer fishing."

He hrrumps in agreement. "I have coffee just made. I'll get us some."

You sense that it isn't time yet for you to ask about Elsie's story. Perhaps there are matters of politeness to attend first.

He starts for the kitchen door, taking slow, shuffling steps. The dog darts out from behind the other end of the sofa, dashes ahead of him, toenails clicking on the worn linoleum floor.

The living room is small; walls once painted white are yellowed by the smoke from the old man's cigarettes, festooned here and there with greasy, gray cobwebs that he probably never notices. A battered lumpy sofa in mud brown tweed sits against one wall, an orange velour rocker next to it and in between, a small table with a lamp, an overflowing ashtray and a mostly eaten bologna sandwich. Opposite the sofa, a small television with a coat hanger for an antenna sits on top of a larger console television. Both are switched on to an afternoon game show with the picture in black and white visible on the smaller one, and the sound coming out of the console set. Waist-high stacks of books stand like three wise men beside the television. Here and there on the walls, Oscar has thumbtacked up color pictures torn from magazines – Niagara Falls, a mountain view that could be anywhere in the world, a group of kangaroos shown against a red barren landscape.

He hollers from the kitchen.

"Sit down. Be comfortable. I don't have that powder cream stuff for the coffee. I got that can milk, the kind with the flowers on the label."

"That's fine," you say. "Just a dollop. I don't take sugar." You push aside the newspapers on the end of the sofa and sit.

He returns in a moment bearing two thick tan mugs of coffee. The dog follows, gives one short territory-defining yap at you before it disappears again behind the sofa. Oscar lowers himself into the orange velour chair, and the springs in the seat relax and cup his weight so that he looks like he is wrapped in a moth-eaten trade blanket.

You sit and sip in silence for a few minutes, and then he talks about the weather a little more. Finally, it is time.

"Grandfather, I heard that Elsie Roberts was your niece," you say.

He puts down his coffee cup on the table, fishes in his sweater pocket for a moment and brings out a pack of no-filter cigarettes.

3

Instead of having only that one end of the pack torn off, the whole top is ripped open, right across the seal. He takes out a cigarette, leans back and struggles with his hand in his pocket until he has extracted an old scratched silver Zippo lighter. He lights the cigarette, draws deeply and exhales, his eyes squinted.

"Elsie was everybody's niece," he says. Then he explains. "You know, it's the old kinship way of thinking about people. We are all related in that way, so Elsie was my niece in that Indian way, but not white man way. Indian way that makes her your cousin, everybody's relative – cousin, niece. Indian way, makes me your grandfather, and everybody's grandfather. How do you feel about that?" He isn't challenging you; he's smiling. For one time in your life, you feel included. He goes on.

"See, calling everybody cousin or niece or whatever makes us feel close, family, but it also makes it damned hard to find a mate if you have to think of everyone you meet as a cousin or a niece or some other family member. Some rules must not be broken. Elsie came to be as the result of broken rules, and then she broke some herself, and that's the heartbreak of it all."

You don't have anything to say to that since you are part of the rule breaking yourself, so you just sip your coffee and wait.

Then he begins the story, and you sit still and listen.

"Elsie's mother was from here, but Elsie wasn't born here. She was born at Marty Mission School, where her mother went after her husband died. Elsie's mother was a one only. You know that expression, 'one only'?"

You don't, but he explains.

"It means a woman who marries only once, no matter what happens after that. It's old-fashioned as hell, and women these days don't pay it any mind, but back in the old days, a one only woman could be one of those demons the Christians talk about, and she would still be respected by her own people, revered even, no matter what else she did, just because of her devotion to a dead man."

Burning tobacco smoke curls around his head, defines the air currents in the room, floats towards you carrying the words and the feelings.

4

"Elsie's mother – her name was Mary – anyways, she didn't have family anymore, just her husband's people down here, and six to seven months after he died, she left. Went back to Marty Mission, where she'd been raised up and went to school come from. So Mary goes up there, and after Elsie is born, she moves off to Mobridge and she takes jobs cleaning houses for people, just like she used to do here. Mary's kind of odd, kind of stays to herself, but she does good work, so people don't care. They don't have much to do with her, but they know she's a one only, so, like I say, she gets a lot of respect. Maybe not friendship, though, you know? That's a different thing. So anyway, Elsie gets raised up there in Mobridge. They're kind of outcasts from everybody, just the two of them all alone. But from what people say, they were making a way for themselves, you know, a living. They say."

His eyes take on a far away look and you know he's right there, up at Standing Rock, where the official story says it happened, but doesn't make you feel like it's real. It's like Oscar is right there in Elsie's pocket on the night it happened. Like he's right there watching, but he can't stop any of it. He just had to be there. Somebody had to tell the story.

Oscar folds his hands over his big belly and he starts a different story, a story that you think doesn't have anything to do with Elsie.

So one day, Inktomi, the Spider was going along
And he was thinking heavy.
All the people were busy going about their business and
Inktomi had no business to go about.
Whenever he tried to work with the people, they told him
To go away and mind his own business.
But he didn't have any business to mind.
So, Inktomi, the Spider was just going along
And he walked by the lodge of the first man and first woman,
Wazi and Wakanka.
Inktomi noticed that they were just sitting there,
not doing anything.

5

They sighed real big from time to time, and they didn't look happy.
So Inktomi stops.
"What's wrong?" he asks.
"Oh, it's nothing that you can fix," Wazi says.

"How do you know that?" Inktomi replies. "Ask me."
"Go mind your own business," says Wakanka.
"Let me help! I can make your business be my business," Inktomi says.
Wazi and Wakanka just sigh again and look unhappy.
"As it happens, my business is all caught up. Let me help!"
Now Inktomi is begging.
So Wazi and Wakanka look at each other and then Wazi says:
"Our beautiful daughter, Ite, is married to the Wind God, Tate.
And now that she is gone from our lodge, we have no one to boss around.
Tate has honored our daughter, but she is still only human, and so are we.
We want to be gods."
Inktomi considered.
"If Ite could be made a god, would she then make you gods?"
Wazi and Wakanka exchanged glances.
"Yes, but how could that be made to happen?"
Inktomi rubbed his hands together. Here was some business!
So, people didn't want him around, huh? So the other people wouldn't let
him help with their business, huh?
He could make them look foolish, and they might think twice before they
told him to mind his own business.
"Give me your consent and I will make it happen."
Wazi and Wakanka smiled and agreed.
Inktomi went on then, and went to Ite, and while
she was sleeping,
He whispered in her ear.
He whispered, "Anpetu Wi, the Sun, has much power.
He has more power than your husband, Tate.
And you are beautiful. If you smile at him

Just so
If you dip your chin and look up at him through your eyelashes

Just so
And turn away slowly, looking back
Enough times, he will not be able to resist."
So, on awakening, Ite followed Inktomi's suggestions until all the gods
were talking, but nobody was talking about it to Anpetu Wi's wife,
Hanhepi Wi.
"I am secure now," Ite said to herself. "I can be the god wife of Anpetu Wi,
when I want to."
Just then, Anpetu Wi decided to give a feast.
At the feast, Ite looks around, bold.
Boldly, she walks over and sits down in the place reserved for Anpetu Wi's
wife.
Hanhepi Wi enters just then, and she sees the situation and she demands
She demands that something be done.
Now Anpetu Wi looks around at the little smiles on the gods' faces.
He looks at Hanhepi Wi's angry face and
He looks at Ite, lowering her chin and smiling up at him through her
lashes.
He does not see Inktomi, peeking from the corner.
Anpetu Wi looks and his eyes are open.
Anpetu Wi points his finger and half of Ite's face turns ugly.
He points again and Ite is banished to the earth and ever afterwards,
The people will call her
Anukite

The Double Faced Woman.

Oscar sits still for a minute. Then he heaves himself up out of the chair and he says, "Let me get you some more coffee."

2

March 21, 1967

A 1967 Black Camaro

The road runs deep and narrow between the winter accumulation of aging snowbanks, shoved to the sides by the county snowplows. Car tracks make muddy ruts in the slushy depths that freeze at sundown into lumpy chunks alternating with smooth, slippery places, long and narrow skating strips frozen black in the shallow tracks. Elsie Roberts hurries along, climbing the snow cliffs at the roadside whenever yellow headlights reflecting off the black ice and the low growl of a motor tell her that a car comes, and she has to get out of the way or get run over. She hurries because it's dark, and because her mother, who has been in St. Mary's hospital for weeks, will be expecting Elsie during visiting hours.

Behind Elsie's careful, fast walking a motor growls and tires crush ice beneath them. Headlights shine cockeyed, one reflecting sparkles from the black ice, the other shining yellow light on the right side snowbank, catching the quick movement of Elsie's overshoes, buckles jingling as she scrambles up the snowbank and out of the way of the oncoming vehicle. Her dark olive green coat flaps black in the evening backwash of frosty air from an old pickup, passing, crunching the snow and grumbling and going on. She jumps from the snowbank back into the narrow roadway, overshoes slipping and grabbing for traction, arms flung out to balance her tall, awkward body. She hurries on, tying her worn, brown woolen scarf closer about her dark, pinned-up braids.

She passes two houses set back off the road. The snow has been shoveled from narrow driveways branching off the main road, arteries connecting those snug houses to everything else. The snow removed from the driveways is piled on top of the snowdrift alongside the road making the tunnel of the main road deeper, darker in these places on either side of the driveways. From both houses comes a faint glow of electric lights behind black traceries of bare cottonwood and elm branches. Smudges of low-growing pine and cedar soak up light, hovering broadly on the light, starlit snow. These houses are familiar to Elsie in daylight of all seasons, when she sometimes does housecleaning and laundry for the people who live within, but on this early spring night, even the dogs – familiar tail-waggers and face-lickers in other seasons – bark at Elsie as she crunches past. Elsie hurries on, not bothering to call a soothing "hush." At the hospital, her mother waits.

Elsie's strong shoulders, arms, and upper back ache from this long day's work of early spring housecleaning for Mrs. Swensen, always the first of Elsie's day employers to throw out the winter. On the walk to work this morning, Elsie had heard the geese going north, crying their greeting as they passed. This chorus was Mrs. Swensen's annual sign to begin the cleaning out, but Elsie hoped that Mrs. Swensen wouldn't hear the geese. She wanted to spend the day at the hospital with her mother. Dr. Weston told Elsie that her mother might die at any time, her lungs so scarred from tuberculosis that she can scarcely breathe, and pneumonia is eminent. But Mrs. Swensen heard the geese.

Another car comes fast behind Elsie and she jumps at the snowbank. The toes of her overshoes catch in the lumpy ice and she stumbles, flings her arms out for balance, and scrambles up the cold wall as a dark car blows past flinging loose flakes of snow. Fiery taillights, oblong with a bite off one corner, stare at her through flying snowflakes. She knows this car, a brand new black 1967 Camaro. They say that Bobby and Billy Mason's dad went all the way to Denver to buy it for the twins' high school graduation coming up in May. The twins drive it to school from their parents' ranch thirty miles south and west, down on the Moreau River, and then they drive it too fast around town, chasing dogs and cats that happen to wander into the streets, slamming on the brakes so the car spins donut circles on the slick spots, narrowly stopping in time to avoid hitting old people slowly crossing the slippery streets. When people complain, the boys say they can't help it if their new car is light in the rear end and has good brakes. And usually these twins have their friend Paul Johnson with them, and he is even worse when they let him drive. He rolls down the window and shouts obscenities, but no one reprimands him because he only shouts his suggestions at Indian girls, following them along the street until they escape into a store, or around a corner, or behind a group of wrinkled brown grandfathers who sometimes stand talking to each other, shoulders hunched against the cold, hands in pockets, on street corners.

Now Elsie jumps down from the snowbank, hurrying, slipping on the ice jumbles, but she stops because that new Camaro car slows and slides a little sideways and those taillight eyes get brighter; the motor roars, and the car begins to back up very fast, going side-to-side in the narrow roadway. She jumps for the snowbank again, slips down on one knee, feeling the jagged ice cut. She gets up and scrambles again, up the crumbling snow as the car passes beneath her, close enough so that she sees the mud scum, lighter color on the sides of the black car.

The car slides to a stop, the back end bumping the snowbank opposite so the car is canted sideways and the headlights hit Elsie in the eyes. She presses her body against the cold, rough snow. Beneath her coat, a trickle of blood runs from her knee into the top of her overshoe, blotting itself on the top of her sock.

She hears the car window squeaking a complaint in the cold as someone rolls it down. The door opens slightly and the dome light turns the car interior yellow above the heads of three people whose faces are indistinct in the dark. She sees one person sitting in the back, but leaning forward over the front seat, and two others in front. She knows them even in the dim light because she recognizes the car. She is one of the Indian girls that they follow down the street. She remembers the boys from school, too, in those days before she turned sixteen and quit, even though they were in a class four years behind her. Trouble goes before them, travels with them, follows behind them like a bad smell.

"Hey, guys, look at this, we almost hit a deer!"

"Oh, dear!"

The laughter rolls from the car window, and one of the boys slaps the side of the car and hollering, "WOO, woo, woo, woo! WOO, woo, woo, woo!"

The sound is clear and profound in the narrow, cold tunnel of the road, and from the house just past, dogs respond with a continuous bark BARK bark bark bark. BARK bark bark bark.

Elsie turns her face to the snow, away from the bright headlights, closing her eyes, but still seeing pinwheels of light and color behind her closed lids. She hears muffled conversation and more laughter, hears the car door open, the crunch of heavy footsteps on the road. The car motor growls softly, and she smells the exhaust hovering blue in the crisp, black air, and then the voices inside fall silent. Footsteps come closer and then, *scrunch*, she hears, as one of the feet press toe-first into the snowbank beside her leg. A hand tugs the wool scarf tail, pulling the under-chin knot tight against her throat, cutting off her terrified breathing. She resists, and the hand lets go suddenly, slaps the back of her head hard, forcing her face into the snow. She feels the hard, cold ice crystals against her cheek. Snow crumbles beneath her overshoes, and she feels herself sliding down. Her mittened hands try to hold onto the snowbank, and just as she finds a solid place to plant her feet, the hand jerks the scarf again pulling her head back and up so she sees the Big Dipper in the dark sky, watching, impassive and unfeeling. She feels warm breath on her ear through the scarf, and she hears the whisper.

"What are you doing out here all alone?"

She tries to jerk away, her hands digging and clutching at the snow, her head drawn backwards by the hand pulling the scarf, her feet scuffling, her bloody knee scraping against the snow until she falls backwards onto the road, jerking the scarf from the boy's grasp as she goes down.

The boy falls beside her. "You goddamned slippery whore!"

His hand comes out of nowhere, slapping her in the mouth, crushing her lips against her teeth.

Now laughter comes again from the car, and the horn hoonks,

hoonks, hoonks, hoonks, long, drawn-out sounds, and one of the boys screams so loud his voice becomes hoarse on the end, "*Towee! Toweeeeee!* Hey skindian, wanna suck my dick? Come on baby, you know you wanna!"

Another boy hangs halfway out the car window, flapping his arms and making loud kissing sounds with his mouth. Sitting safely on his own front porch two hundred yards away, the dog begins barking again, a coward's bark, inquisitive, nervous.

Elsie rolls over to her side scrambling to stand up, her coat and dress rucked up and her bare upper thigh scraping against the icy road. The first boy – it's Paul, she sees his flashing teeth in his grinning mouth, smells the alcohol on his breath as he braces a hand against the small of her back, grinding her down so he can stand up easier. He stands, breathing hard, with the car lights behind him and his cap knocked off. Elsie sees his hair as the wind rises and ruffles it so that it stands straight out from his head, and his body looms over her, and she sees the black blob that is his boot coming fast at her face. She rolls away. The boot toe catches her in the left ear instead of the face, instantly exploding pain, a black blanket of agony that passes between her eyes and the stars overhead. Pain flashes circle from her head to her toes, down and back, a tornado swirl that gathers in her lungs, travels up her throat, bursts screaming from her bloody mouth.

"God DAMN dirty bitch! Bust my ass on the ice, will you?" Paul kicks again at Elsie's crumpled body, the blow catching her in mid-throat with a mushy crunch, and she is gone off into herself. Somewhere in a tiny space in her head, she walks along the creek bank in spring, touching gently the celery green tree leaves of the willows, while a million miles away she hears the barking of cowardly dogs.

He laughs as he bends over and grabs the back of her coat collar. "Will one of you guys stop laughing long enough to help me load this squaw in the car?"

She is breathing heavily, her nose, an overripe plum swelling squashy on her face. Blood bubbles come from the corner of her mouth with each breath. She is a deer, wounded and run to earth, not dead yet, but waiting for the final shot.

"What the hell for?" Billy asks. "Nuh-uh, man, I'm not hauling some dirty old skin in this car."

"I'm thinking we could have some more fun with this one," Paul says. He drops Elsie, stoops and retrieves his cap, adjusting it on his head.

"Our old man finds out we had a squaw in the car and we're dead," Billy said.

"Your old man would be damned proud that you finally got a piece of ass, even if it is red meat," Paul shouts, now dragging Elsie towards the car.

"Billy, you're a chickenshit, and you know it," Bobby says.

"I am not. Who's the one that chased those two drunk Indians up on the sidewalk today? Huh?"

"Oh, that ain't nothing, especially since you got the hell out there when that old white woman shook her cane at you, big brave Billy."

"Cut it out asshole, you know that old woman is Kathy's grand-mother."

"So you're afraid to piss off your girlfriend's grandma? Pussy!"

"Shut up!"

"Both of you shut up!" Paul yelled. "Will you little titty babies help me load this cow or do I have to do it all by myself?"

Bobby opens the car door and steps out.

"I don't know," Billy says. "What do you have in mind?"

"Just what the hell do you think I have in mind? Do you want to be a sheep fucker all your life?"

"Hey, our old man raises cattle, not sheep!"

"So? Your girlfriend is Kathy, and her old man raises sheep. Are you after her or the sheep? Baaa. Baaa."

"Oh, all right, goddamn it!" Billy emerges from the driver's side of the car.

A mile past the river heading east, those boys drive that new black Camaro car off onto a small side place where five or six mailboxes perch on posts, a row of mouthpieces, each one waiting for the mes-sage. Billy and Paul get out of the front seat and tug at the heavy inert body while Bobby in the back seat pushes until a dark heavy

13

bundle emerges full-grown from the womb of the vehicle, flopping limply like a newborn onto the icy ground. The figures move quickly, speaking little, gruffly, word smoke in the below zero air. Paul goes back around and gets into the car, long scratches on his left cheek illuminated and hidden again in the dark night as he slams the car door. Billy stands in the road looking down at his hands, smeared darkly shiny and sticky.

"Christ!" Billy walks to the edge of the ditch, squats and scrubs his hands with snow. Across the ditch the wind has swirled snow into graceful shapes, now a little shiny from the daytime above-zero temperature melt, a snowy meringue atop chocolate pie earth. He smells the velvety dark hot chocolate, the lightness of sugar and egg white on top, sees it, enthroned in the middle of his mother's kitchen table, tastes the little bit of sweet meringue pinched from the edge when her back was turned.

From the car's back seat, Bobby leans forward and yells out the driver's side window. "Hey, Billy! What the hell are you doing? Let's go!"

Twenty feet away, beyond a four-strand barbed wire fence, a dozen white-faced red cows shift their feet, watching.

"What the hell are you staring at!" Billy yells at the placid white faces. He stands, shaking the snow from his hands, drying them on his brown one-hundred-percent down-filled western-cut coat, and he looks down the highway, watching as a pair of yellow eyes appear, moving towards him. He stares at the distant car lights, marveling at how far light shines on a dark night.

"Billy, we got to get out of here! There's a car coming!"

He looks up at the Big Dipper, those stars sending light from billions of miles across the vast emptiness of space. He looks down at the lights coming up the road.

Bobby and Paul burst from the car, grab him by the sleeves of his one-hundred-percent down-filled western-cut coat, hustle him forward, fling him into the back seat, slam the doors shut. Bobby slams the car in gear. It starts forward with a jerk and a bump and he slams it into reverse, spins the wheel, and hits – something. The car lurches.

Paul shouts, "Fuck, fuck, fuck!"

The car roars forward accompanied by a thumping bumping dragging.

"Christ, what the hell?" Bobby slows, opens his car door and looks back. Elsie is following, her clothing caught on something, some part under the car.

The yellow eyes of the approaching car grow bigger.

Bobby stops the car, jumps out and tears the body away, jumps back in.

That new black Camaro, 1967 model, all the way from Denver roars away into the night, flinging gravel behind that pings off the mailbox mouths perched on posts waiting for the message.

Elsie stops beside the creek, kicks off her worn, old shoes and wades into the shallow water, feeling the squishy mud. The dogs have stopped barking.

The driver of the oncoming car is watching the fast disappearing red taillights, so he sees the big dark bundle on the road barely in time to avoid it. He slows, stops, and backs up.

3

January 17, 1970

Sinte Sapela Win

Oscar hands you a second cup of coffee and you take a sip, and you don't make a face even though its been sitting on the back of the stove simmering for too long now, and gone thick with a burned flavor beneath the evaporated milk taste. Little black flecks of grounds float on top.

Oscar settles himself again. The dog pokes his head from behind the sofa, giving short, one-word-sentence barks.

"Yap. Yap. Yap."

Oscar flings a book at him.

"Lowan, shut up." He smiles. "I call him that because he sings all the time."

You want to know the rest of Elsie's story, but you wait for him to tell you in his own time. He tells you a different story.

Oscar talking now, he says, "Remember Anukite, the Double-Face woman, who tried to steal Hanhepi Wi's husband? Well, the Deer Woman is kind of like Anukite.

"See, there's two kinds of deer. Black-tailed deer and white-tailed deer. It's Sinte Sapela Win, the black-tailed deer, that men got to watch out for."

> *One time there was this man out hunting, they say,*
> *And he came across this beautiful woman out far away from camp*
> *Where she shouldn't ought to be, because a woman of good morals*
> *Just doesn't go wandering off alone very much.*
> *But she is beautiful and she smiles at him boldly.*
> *She touches his arm, and she says*
> *"Stay with me."*

This man, he already has a good woman, but this one, this
Beautiful woman, it's like she has some specialness.
So, this man, he sits down beside her and he lets her touch him all over
And then he has her in that way, and he goes to sleep.
When he wakes up, the woman is gone, and
He looks, but he only sees a black-tailed deer standing at the edge
Of a little woods.
He jumps up and he chases her, but she runs away and loses him.
He goes back to camp, but he can no longer think of his good woman.
He thinks about the deer woman all the time.
He goes out looking for her everyday, but he does not hunt.
His family begins to starve.
They live only because others see that they have no food
And share their food with the man's family.
But he doesn't eat. He can't sleep
And one day, he goes out looking for the deer woman and
He doesn't go back.
Others go looking for him, and a long way from camp
They find him, dead.
He has been trampled to death by a deer.

"There's lots of those old deer woman stories," Oscar says. "Well, it's just about supper time, and there's plenty. Why don't you eat with me?"

So you follow him into the kitchen. He's got this old table that has chrome legs that curve a little bit out where they connect to the table, and there are three chairs with red plastic padded seats and backs to match the tabletop. Two of them have gray duct tape stuck over rips in the padding.

"Take a seat," he says, and he opens the door on one of the old-fashioned white metal cabinets and gets out plates. He brings silverware, puts a folded green towel on the tabletop and sits the pot of soup in the middle with a big serving spoon.

"Help yourself," he says while he fetches half a loaf of bread from the top of the refrigerator and puts it, still in the plastic wrapper, alongside your plate. "It's not fancy, but it's filling."

17

He sits and motions with his chin towards the pot. You take the spoon and start to dip some of the steaming hot soup onto your plate.

He says, "No, no," and grabs your wrist. "Dig down DEEP. There's puppy in the bottom." He drops your wrist and laughs at the expression on your face.

Finally, he stops laughing and he says, "I was just kidding. It's beef, really. But you know," and he reaches for the spoon to fill his own plate, "I hear puppy is pretty good eating. Some of the old folks say so. I keep promising myself I'll try it some time, so next time you come to visit, you better make sure Lowan is around and singing."

Lowan is around right now. He's right under the table, scratching at your pants leg whenever Oscar doesn't drop bites of food fast enough.

Oscar eats two bowls of soup, burps politely and urges you to eat more. You push back your plate and say you couldn't possibly eat another bite – you're stuffed. You are, and it was good. Oscar's lips curve up in a bit of a smile.

"Come back, tomorrow," he says. "We'll eat leftovers and tell more stories."

The sun has set and a thick layer of clouds hide the stars. You walk back up the slight rise in the street to Main Street and turn right, walking along the short two blocks of the business district, passing The Steak House on the left. It's open, but the supper hour is just past, only three men sit at one table, drinking coffee before they go home to their families. A waitress stands behind the counter, arms folded across her pink uniformed chest, waiting for them to hurry up and leave so she can sweep up. Out of the window, she sees you coming up the sidewalk and she rushes to the front door, locks it, and flips the sign over.

CLOSED.

You wonder if she knew Elsie. You wonder if Elsie walked along this same street, looked in this same window the night she died. You wonder what that waitress remembers of Elsie. Was she just another Indian, a silent shadow that once appeared out of nowhere without form or substance and disappeared the same way, leaving only a slightly darker hole in the night? Or was she someone this waitress talked to every day, someone she spoke with as you would a friend?

You walk on, past the one-story brick courthouse that people have bragged about to you, modern when it replaced the old white frame building fifteen years ago, but looking now like the goods you see in old catalogs. Serviceable, but cheap and dated. You think about all the Indians that have gone through those doors to appear before the Justice of the Peace. Drunk and disorderly. Driving without a license. Assault. The building looks so small, you wonder how anything so small could be the center of events that affect so many people's lives.

Pellets of sleet drop, ice seeds from the heavy clouds, driven by a rising wind. You turn up your coat collar, tuck your hands in your pocket and walk quickly down the street to the Dakota Inn – third room on the left, just past the alcove where the soda vending machine and the ice maker sit, silent, unnecessary, waiting for summer. Three cars hunker in the parking lot like faithful dogs curled up on the doorstep, waiting for their masters to return, and through the lobby window, the clerk sits idly turning the pages of a magazine with one hand and twisting a bit of her blonde hair with the other hand. It's only eight o'clock, but it feels later. Too late.

4

March 21, 1907, to March 21, 1967

One Hundred Years of Waiting

Klaus Schmidt and his bride stepped off the boat at Ellis Island after years – it seemed like *years* – in steerage class, crowded with hundreds of others into spaces where they couldn't stand erect without bumping their heads, where they couldn't move without bumping into someone else, where they breathed in smells of vomit and sweat, feces and urine, desperation and hope. It was raining in the United States, and they lifted their faces and let it wash them. They endured the long lines snaking down corridors, up steps and around corners. They passed the watchful eyes of those looking for the halt, the lame, the ones who coughed incessantly, the ones whose eyes were runny. They passed before the inspectors sitting at desks, acting as if they were only sorting apples, choosing the best ones to polish and the rest to trash. They passed.

They walked the confusing streets of New York City to the train station, through the hurrying crowds of people, crossing streets littered with horse manure, inhaling the smell of the shit mingled with the people sweat and the spicy odors of food cooking that emerged from family-owned restaurants and stalls along the street. They were jostled aside and pushed forward. Klaus stepped up to the ticket window in the train station and in his broken English, asked for two tickets to South Dakota, slowly counting out the unfamiliar paper money and coins.

Somewhere crossing Illinois, after nights spent sleeping in their seats, Emma turned from looking out the window and she said to Klaus, "*Mein Gott*, it is so big!"

In South Dakota, just south of Mobridge, they homesteaded their one hundred and sixty acres. The land was beautiful. The land! It rolled on endlessly, a great ocean of grass, green waves of it. A man could drown here on these endless prairies over a thousand miles from the sea. There had been two wet years in a row. Klaus built a small house, dug a well, broke the prairie, so tough with centuries of grass roots that at times he had to use an axe. And as soon as he could, he planted two trees just feet from his front door. He watered them every day.

The season turned and the weather did, too, and the second year was drier, but Klaus harvested his first crop, and Emma was pregnant. Then, the rains ceased as if the gods had turned off the faucets. The child failed to thrive, withered, and died like the grain in the fields, and Emma, too, grew frail and gaunt, skin browned by the sun, hair roughened by the wind. A second pregnancy and a third and a fourth ended in miscarriages, as no rain fell from the brassy sky, and the seeds Klaus planted in the earth came up unevenly, peppering the rows green for a few days, then browning off and dying. Klaus hauled water from town, saving precious quarts for his two trees, even pouring the urine from the night slops onto the dusty ground at their trunks, an offering of himself, the only water that he had to give, even as he worried that the salt and urea in the urine might kill the trees, but it didn't.

In the end, it was not enough. He sent Emma back to New York, where a distant cousin had followed them to this new country and set up a bakery. Another year he planted, and another year did not rain, until one day when the wind wouldn't cease to blow, Klaus got a letter offering him a job in the cousin's bakery. He took it, but before he left, he blessed the tree, the one tree that survived the drought, the bitter winters, and Klaus's urine. The new county road made a sharp curve to the left just at the Schmidts' property line and not twenty feet farther, the tree, with its roots firmly established, grew and thrived, surrounded by the brittle, tan bones of horse weeds and the seer grass creeping slowly back over the broken sod.

Those boys tug Elsie away from that black car, roll her away, drive away, and leave the yellow lights of the oncoming car diminishing in the rear view mirror. That boy Paul, sitting in the front passenger

21

seat, he laughs then, a nervous laugh of relief. He turns around to Billy, curled up on the backseat.

"Hand me up a beer," he says.

Billy doesn't answer.

Paul reaches between the seats and pokes him.

"Hand me up a beer, man."

Billy says, "Get it yourself."

Paul half crawls between the seats, pummeling Billy, and Billy puts his hands over his head and moans.

Bobby grabs Paul's coattail, pulls him back.

"Let him alone!"

Paul snarls and lashes out at Bobby with a fist, catching him on the neck, just below the ear.

Bobby's arm jerks the steering wheel and that black Camaro veers across the yellow line and back, rocking as it goes.

"Goddamn it, settle down! You're going to make me wreck!"

Paul leans into the backseat, fumbling on the floor, and turns back with a can of beer in his hand. Settling in his seat, he pops the top and mutters to himself, "Goddamned pussies."

He drinks the beer down in one long gulping chug, rolls down the window and pitches the can, but it's blown back by the wind of their passage, hitting in the road, bouncing.

"Let's have some music," he says, "lighten up you guys a bit." He pushes the black button on the far right, turns up the volume knob and the jingle for KOMA Oklahoma City comes through the speakers, followed by some fast-talking announcer who couldn't possibly be from Oklahoma giving announcements about bands playing from Texas to Kansas. Then a song comes on and Paul drums his fingers on the dashboard keeping time. He stops and stretches his left arm out, way out, bumping Bobby lightly on the chin.

"Hey, Bob," he says. "Got you a little, huh? Didn't you? Huh?"

He turns around and leans between the seats.

"Hey, Billy. Guess what, old son? You ain't a virgin anymore. How about that? Let's drink to that!"

He reaches under the front seat and pulls out a bottle of vodka, half empty, screws off the cap and takes a long swig.

"Whoooeeeeee!" he hollers.

Bobby starts growing a little smile, and then he's laughing too.

"Give me a drink of that." Bobby takes a long drink and then he holds the bottle back over the seat wiggling it from side to side. "Here, Billy, you got to have a drink. Come on."

A couple of minutes pass and then Billy sits up and takes the bottle. Now they're all three laughing, teeth glowing in the green fluorescent dash lights, as they come up on the road curve that goes around the old Schmidt place.

Billy is sitting up now, leaning between the seats and he sees it first.

"Jesus Christ!"

There in the road in front of them is a deer, a big deer, antlers branching everywhere, biggest deer they've ever seen, and Bobby screams and slams on the brakes and that black car slides, but it's too late. The car crosses Klaus Schmidt's former property line as if pulled by a string straight to the tree, and the front end smashes dead into the trunk, and the momentum brings the back end up so the car is almost standing perpendicular, and it falls again back to earth and rocks and is silent. Steam rises from the broken radiator, and in a few minutes the broken engine tick tick ticks as it cools in the cold night air.

Elsie is a child again, remembering. She walks along the creek bank, touching the dark green willow leaves, smiling to herself a little. Whenever she can, she comes here to the creek just behind the little frame house that she and her mother share on the outskirts of Mobridge, and now that her school is let out for the summer, she comes often. She is tall for as second grader – oh, third grade now that she has passed – and the skirt of her last year's summer dress falls just below her knees. Once a bright white and pink flour sack print, it has faded to a soft pastel, the fabric softened from many rub-bings on the washboard.

The snow has gone, turned to water, filled the creeks, and receded again leaving, alongside the creek banks, a three-foot-wide slick, dark gel that records the tracks of animals going to and from the brown water. Elsie stands very quietly. Then – there! Look! Skittering across the mud, three – no, four or five – tiny turtles, a little bigger than a large black beetle, but round, the size of a quarter or smaller.

Elsie steps slowly forward to the edge of the mud, positions herself just so, there where their trail to and from the water leads into the grass. She sinks to her knees in the grass, spreads her skirt, scraping mud over the edge of it to make a kind of ramp into her lap, and she waits. Somewhere behind her, hidden in the tall prairie grass, a pheasant rooster issues a challenge that goes unanswered, and overhead, a pair of meadowlarks sky dance along the creek, tumbling over and over in midair. The sun rises higher. Elsie's legs go prickly and then numb, but she still sits.

Out of the water, a tiny greenish brown head emerges and then another and another and another, like a small school of sticks suddenly rising to the surface as the quick moving creek water ripples around them. Elsie sucks in her breath sharply. The tiny creatures emerge from the creek, running across the mud, their momentum swinging them a little side to side, tiny claws digging in. They run straight for Elsie, straight into her cloth skirt snare, scrambling their claws for purchase on the worn fabric.

"Elsie! Elsie!" her mother calls her from somewhere behind her over the lip of the creek bank.

Elsie gathers her skirt around the captives; they're in the bag of her skirt and she hollers, "Yes!"

She wads the skirt tail tight, so much of the scanty skirt that her worn underwear and her brown, mosquito bitten legs show beneath. She stands, but her bloodless legs cave beneath her and she falls sideways into the mud, sliding down the slanted bank and into the water, gasping with the shock. She's sitting on her bottom in the squishy creek bed bobbing gently in the shallow water, but she holds tight to the skirt-tail bag.

"Elsie!"

Her mother pushes aside the willow branches and stands laughing, her broad body shaking.

"Elsie, get out of that muddy creek, right now! Look, you've spoiled your dress and we have to leave in a few minutes. Remember? I'm cleaning the Smiths' house today, and you can't stay home alone."

"*Ina*, help me."

Elsie's mother takes a long step into the mud, reaches down and, grasping Elsie by the back of the dress, swings her dripping from the water and onto the grass. Elsie sits there smiling, both hands clutching the wadded skirt.

"*Ina*, look!" She looses her grip on the fabric, and there inside are three tiny turtles.

Slowly, the sun fades to a murky dusk, and Elsie hears her mother calling her, far away and weak.

"Elsie. Elsie."

She tries, but only one eye opens, only a little way. The dim light through that narrow slit punishes her, and she closes it again. There's a smell – disinfectant, antiseptic – similar to the smell of soap that she used just this morning on her hands and knees scrubbing the corners of Mrs. Swensen's linoleum floored kitchen. Why is it so dark?

"Elsie. Elsie."

Fingertips stroke her hair, gently as a bird. No, her mother shouldn't touch Elsie's hair. She'll get all muddy. Then she tries to sit up.

Her body screams with pain. She is encased in concrete, pinning her flat, and she can't breathe, except through her mouth, but every breath that goes down pokes red hot pins in her throat, punishes the so-slight movement of her chest. She cannot lift her arms. She moves one foot, side-to-side, and it brushes against a smoothness with a tiny swishing sound.

"Elsie." Her mother continues stroking her hair.

She turns her head just an inch or so towards the hand, and her throat screams in pain, but she cannot make a sound.

A door squeaks open and the room explodes in light, brighter than a dozen suns, blazing on her closed eyelids.

25

"Mrs. Roberts, what are you doing out of bed? I know, I know. You want to help your daughter, but you won't help by making yourself worse. Here, let's get you back into bed."

The nurse half carries the frail, older woman across the short tiled area between the two beds.

"She needs me," Elsie's mother says.

The nurse arranges the pillows, fusses with the sheets.

"Yes, and that's why we've put her in the room with you. So when she comes around, you will be here with her, but she won't come around any faster with you standing there. You're just going to weaken yourself and then you can't help yourself, let alone your daughter."

"I need to touch her. She's awake."

"No, no, you're mistaken, Mrs. Roberts. Elsie is heavily sedated."

Elsie moves that foot again. Swish. And again. Swish, swish.

Mrs. Roberts's eyes go to Elsie, and the nurse hears the swish of Elsie's foot against the sheets.

"Oh, you're right! I'm going to get the doctor. I'll be right back."

Elsie can't see the doctor, only a white blur, but she feels every touch of his hands, every cold steel thing that touches her skin like an electric shock. As he touches, the doctor talks, half to Elsie, half to himself with a rough voice.

"You might not remember what I'm going to tell you," he says, "but I'm going to tell you anyway. You've got a simple fracture of the left tibia, three broken bones in your left hand, broken left ulna, dislocated left shoulder, broken ribs – you're lucky none of them punctured a lung – broken nose, severe concussion, crushed larynx. And that's just the big stuff. I've also put more stitches into you than I can count and cleaned off the places where you have no skin left. You're going to live. You're going to walk again, but you'll probably have a hitch in your get-along for the rest of your life. I don't think you're going to talk again, but you'll be able to make some sound. I don't know, you could fool me there, but I wouldn't count on it."

He stops talking while he listens to her heartbeat, pulls the stethoscope from his ears and sticks it half hanging out of his coat pocket. The nurse pulls the sheet back up over Elsie's chest.

The doctor pulls up the metal side rail on the bed, and looks down at Elsie's half open left eye.

"I want to know just as soon as you can tell me somehow, some-way, just who the hell did this to you because I want to kill the son of a bitch with my own two hands. I also want to know when you goddamned Indians are going to quit trying to kill each other."

"Doctor – " The nurse starts to speak.

The doctor waves his hand at her.

"Yeah, yeah, yeah, I know. Why the hell I can't get a transfer out of this hellhole, I don't know."

He starts for the door, and the nurse pulls the examination curtain back from Elsie's bed.

He turns back.

"Push these two beds together, will you? I think Mrs. Roberts should be as close as possible to her daughter. Be good for both of them."

"But, doctor, that will make it harder to tend to the both of them," the nurse protests.

"You'll manage," he says.

The door opens a little and a man in a brown sheriff's uniform, brown Stetson hat over a florid face peers into the room.

"Doctor, can I have a word with her?"

"I TOLD you," the doctor says. "I told you, she can't talk, can't say a damned word, her larynx is crushed."

Sheriff Earl Peterson steps into the room.

"No indication? Nothing?"

"Nothing, zero, not a peep. She's alive and that's about it. And even when she's healed, she may not remember a thing after she was ten years old. She's had a hell of a concussion, amongst a few other not so minor problems."

"Was she drinking?"

"No. Blood test shows no alcohol in her blood stream."

"I want to know who did this," Peterson says.

"Well, for Chrissake, that makes two of us, but I doubt like hell we ever will."

Elsie's foot swishes against the sheets again, unheard over the voices. The nurse is pulling Mrs. Roberts's bed out from the wall, the wheels squeaking on the hard waxed tile.

"Been a hell of a night, ain't it?" Sheriff Peterson comments, taking off his hat and running his hand over his thinning hair. "Elsie, here, then those kids smashing their car. Dead, just like that." He snaps his fingers.

"Whoever said nothing happens in small towns, ain't never been here," the doctor says.

The nurse positions Mrs. Roberts's bed and steps over to move Elsie's bed. Elsie swishes her foot, harder, faster.

"Doctor," the nurse says, "she's doing something funny here with her foot. Maybe a seizure."

The doctor returns to Elsie's bed. She stops moving her foot.

"Probably just muscle spasms," he says, "but that would be pretty unusual considering all the morphine we've pumped into her." He puts his hands on either side of her head, and Elsie squeezes that one eye shut, open, shut, open.

"Hello, what have we got here," he murmurs. "Elsie, you trying to tell me something?"

He takes out a tiny flashlight, shines it into the eye that isn't swollen completely shut.

Elsie squeezes her eye shut, open, shut, open.

The sheriff steps up by the bed.

"What you got here, doc?"

"I don't know, but I think she's trying to tell us something."

Elsie is back in the creek, clutching a skirt full of turtles, but she's drowning this time, and she's calling for her mother, but it isn't her mother's name she's trying to say. She's not calling, *Ina, Ina*. She's pulling her breath into her lungs, she's pulling the water into her lungs and it hurts, it hurts, and she's forming a sound with her smashed mouth beneath that swollen nose.

"Mmmmm,"

"Shh," the nurse says. "Doctor, it's just the pain, I think. Can we up the morphine?"

"Mmm. Mmmaaa."

28

"Elsie, Elsie, quiet," the nurse says. "Don't try to talk. Your mother is right here, right next to you. I'm moving your beds together."

"Mm. Mmmaaaaas."

Sheriff Peterson shifts from foot to foot, holding his hat in his hand.

"I don't think she's trying to say 'mother,'" the doctor says. "Elsie, what is it? Are you trying to say who did this to you?"

Elsie squeezes that eye shut, open, shut.

"MMMMM. MMMmmaaaaas. On. MMMmmmaaas on."

"Mason?" The nurse looks at the sheriff. "Does it sound like Mason?"

"MMMmmmaaason." The turtles are escaping, swimming away, swimming away into the brown creek water, and she's never going to have them, the three that she named Tom and Dick and Harry. She's never going to feel their tiny claws curve over the tip of her finger, never going to feel that scratchy turtle finger hug.

"We didn't say any names just now. Did we?" the sheriff asks.

"No, we didn't," the doctor says. "Elsie, no more trying to talk. I know you can hear. Are you trying to tell us who did this to you? Close your eye twice if you are."

Elsie's eyes shut, open, shut, open.

"Okay, now, Elsie, I understand. Now, this is important – it's very important. Are you trying to say Mason? Is that who did this to you? Those Mason boys and that boy that always runs around with them?"

Elsie's eyes open, shut, open, shut, open, shut, open, shut, and the turtles turn in the stream, floating brown stick heads swim towards her and Tom, Dick and Harry crawl up her arm, perching on her shoulder.

The doctor's eyes lift from Elsie's face and meet Earl Peterson's gaze.

"Jesus H. Christ."

5

January 18, 1970

Talking and Walking

You and Oscar walk south from the main part of town to the intersection where Highway 18 crosses Country Road 73, stop briefly to check for nonexistent traffic, cross, and continue south up the hill and past the county hospital. It's a warm day for South Dakota in January. You and Oscar are both walking along with your coats unzipped, flapping a little in the light breeze. Lowan runs now ahead, now getting left behind as he stops to follow some scent off the road into low snowdrifts, big white warts on the earth with weeds rising through them like coarse hair.

"They say this is good for me, this walking business," Oscar says, interrupting his story. "I don't know if my heart knows that, though. I like the old Lakota way, when a big belly meant you were old enough to have achieved wisdom and deserved respect. Nowadays, this belly just means I eat bad and have high cholesterol. White people change everything."

He points at the hospital with his chin, and you know he's referring to the doctors that work there.

"So, that hospital, that's where she died?" you ask.

"No, no. You're getting it all confused. She was dead when they brought her to this hospital, but this isn't the hospital she was in after that rape and beating. That was at the hospital up in Mobridge, before they moved her down here. A lot of stuff happened between that place in Mobridge and the time when she died down here. See, it's like this:

"Elsie wasn't supposed to talk, you know. Those boys thought she was dead when they dumped her, but they were wrong. They were the ones who were dead, were dead before they ever hit that tree. The one that was in the back seat, Billy, well, he was alive when they found the wreck, and he kept mumbling about hitting a deer, a giant of a deer, but if there was one, it was never found. Lots of deer hang out around that corner because there's a field right across the road where they forage in the winter, and then go back across the road and nest up during the day in the weeds and brush around that big old tree. Everybody up there knows that. It's the first place hunters go in the fall hoping to get a big rack to put on the wall. Of course, no one ever gets a deer there. The first shot from the first gun and those deer, they're gone until the season is over along about Christmas. Then they go back. It was spring, so there were deer around there, though. Those boys could've seen one. They should've known to look out, but they were drinking and driving too fast. Anyways, Billy died in the ambulance, so who knows? Maybe he just thought he saw a deer. Like pink elephants, you know?"

Elsie's mother is in the bed next her daughter, and she lies facing her, as close to Elsie as she can get, reaching out with her hand now and then, touching Elsie's hair, unbraided and washed clean of mud and lying in long black twisted skeins on the white pillow. Just in case Elsie is awake, she hums a little tune from time to time. Her mother remembers when Elsie was little, she ran away to the creek bank every chance she got. She remembers when Elsie was a baby, lying close to her at night, and earlier still, before Elsie was born, a tiny turtle herself floating in the water balloon beneath her mother's heart. And back before that.

Mrs. Roberts was married just before her husband went off to that war somewhere over there across that water that was as wide – wider – than the prairie. She was an only child, her parents and the rest of her family dead from influenza, raised at the mission boarding school where she met her husband. They were so young then, and he was so old when he came back after code talking his way through that war. She believed that the man who came back left the better part of himself over there, across the ocean, while she spent four long years living with his family. The after years, after he came back and both of them lived with his family, were the long ones, the hard ones. He never stopped drinking, it seemed to her, and whatever she did to make him stop, his family undid. That was when she started working back there in Jackson, cleaning houses for the white people, one day a week here, one day a week there, cleaning burnt-on grease off kitchen ranges, scrubbing floors, washing clothes and hanging them outside even in the winter when they froze stiff as corpses. Then that spring came when her husband froze to death, passed out drunk in the alley behind the B and B bar on Main Street. She thought he looked just like a pair of those pants that she pried off the winter clothesline – empty and frost rimed, a cold sack long ago emptied of his soul. Mrs. Roberts just went on working, cleaning houses, and stayed with his family. What else was she to do?

That next summer when the seasonal workers came through harvesting the wheat, she found herself the object of attention from all those men coming though on the harvest crews with no wives, the men who expected to be in Bennett a few days before going on to another town just like it farther north, then another, until the fields were bare from Texas to the Canadian border, then they'd go back south like the wild geese. Mrs. Roberts was still young, still pretty with strong muscles from hard work, and she was lonely. Then there was that one night when it was too hot to sleep, even outside on the porch, and she sat on the steps with her thin nightgown clinging damply to her body, and the night was so quiet she could hear herself sweat. That night a man, a lone man came walking, walking along the street. She didn't see him until he was right there in front of the house and he spoke.

"Mighty hot night, isn't it ma'am?" he said, and she jumped, startled, but he acted like he didn't notice, like they might have been sitting in a park in broad daylight. "Feels like home, down in Mississippi," he said.

She drew up her knees and pulled her nightgown tail down over them.

"Yes, ma'am," he went on, "sure enough feels like Rolling Fork, Mississippi. I don't guess you ever been there." He stopped and laughed. "Ain't many people ever been to Rolling Fork, Mississippi, tell you the truth. Ain't much to look at there, either, but it's a good place to be. You got good delta dirt, grow most anything, and this time a year the living is good with all that okra and tomatoes and corn coming in out of the garden. And it ain't too far from the old Mississippi herself, you know. You can get a mess of catfish to go along with that okra for supper. And the nights – nights is just like this. Hot and heavy." He stopped again and laughed again. "I guess you can tell I'm pretty homesick. Shouldn'ta let my brother talk me into coming on this wheat harvesting business. You can bet, I won't be doing it another summer."

Elsie's mother didn't say anything.

"Well, ma'am, I'll be going on now. Daylight coming on pretty early in the morning and I'll be heading out for somebody else's field."

He walked off up the street, but a hundred feet farther on, in that sweaty dark night, he turned back and said, "My name's George, ma'am. George Washington. No relation to the original." Then he laughed again and walked away.

That July was hot days, too, when the clouds piled up in the west and the farmers and harvesters prayed that the rain would hold off until the wheat was harvested. Their prayers were answered. The clouds grumbled, lightning flashed at sundown and into the early evening and died away again, and the nights smoldered and steamed, but it didn't rain.

That man walked the streets by night when it was too hot to sleep, stopping to talk to Elsie's mother every time, until one night, she came down from the porch, and walked with him. She told him her name. She put her hand in his, and she walked. She saw his hand in the moonlight, joined dark skin to darker skin, the sweat mingling between them, a slippery glue binding two strangers in that July night that was so like Mississippi and so far from it.

Just after Christmas, Elsie's mother was changing clothes when her mother-in-law saw that Mrs. Roberts wasn't just getting fat. She put her out. Mrs. Roberts hitchhiked back to the boarding school at Marty Mission where the nuns welcomed their prodigal daughter, except they didn't know about the prodigal part until the child was born.

Sister Agatha gave Mrs. Roberts the form to fill out for Elsie's birth certificate and under the part where you list the father and his occupation, Mrs. Roberts wrote:

George Washington.
Rolling Fork, Mississippi.
Farmer.

Elsie was born on Holy Thursday in April, and on Easter Sunday, Mrs. Roberts rose from her bed like Christ from his tomb, bundled Elsie up and climbed into the car that took her to Mobridge where a good Catholic woman donated a little house on the creek for Mrs. Roberts and Elsie to live in. Then, when Elsie was two weeks old, Mrs. Roberts started her rounds of cleaning the white people's houses in Mobridge. It amused Mrs. Roberts that the Indians in Mobridge honored her as a one only, a widow who never remarried. She cleaned for others, she took care of Elsie, and she kept herself to herself. She made a little extra money tanning deer hides that hunters gave her, scraping the skins, removing the hair, softening them, sewing them into moccasins and bags that she sold at local stores. She had a fine eye for beadwork, too, and the designs on the leatherwork were unique and beautiful in the traditional colors – white, blue, yellow, red, black.

Elsie was her treasure, and she guarded her treasure strictly. There was no one among the children at the public school for Elsie to befriend, no one interested in her, and Mrs. Roberts refused to send her child to boarding school. Elsie's friends were her turtles, Tom, Dick, and Harry. When she quit high school at sixteen, a decision her mother deplored, but couldn't prevent, Elsie's life changed very little, except now she helped her mother full time with house cleaning, until her mother got sick. Then week by week, month by month, Elsie did more and Mrs. Roberts did less.

Now, Mrs. Roberts strokes Elsie's hair gently, and she wonders what will become of her daughter.

The nurse sits in the hospital lunchroom eating a sandwich brought from home and thinking. She's thinking her way through what she knows and what to do with that knowing. She wads up the waxed paper from her sandwich and tosses it at the trash can, misses, and gets up with a sigh to pick it up. On the countertop, there's a steel bedpan with two inches of water, an upturned saucer in the middle, and two turtles sitting on the saucer munching a piece of lettuce from the nurse's sandwich. They are about the same size – three or four inches across – except the back of one is painted red and one is painted yellow. There is a black letter on the back of each one, a *T* on the red one, a *D* on the yellow.

The door opens and Sheriff Peterson comes in.

The nurse just looks at him.

"Well?"

He makes a grimace, pours himself a cup of coffee from the pot on the countertop beside the bedpan.

"Elsie's turtles?" he asks.

"Yeah. Two of them. I stopped at their house on the way in this morning. The third one was frozen into the ice of the pan she kept them in. Dead as a doornail. That one was painted blue."

He pokes at the red one.

"That paint probably ain't good for them," he says.

"You didn't come here to discuss turtle health, did you? What did you find out?"

"I just came from the boneyard behind Lew's Chevrolet. That's where the wrecker took the boys' car."

He pours sugar into the styrofoam cup and stirs.

"And?"

He sets the coffee down on the countertop, reaches into his pocket, and pulls out a muddy scrap of dark olive green wool fabric.

"Here."

The nurse takes it, turns it over in her hand.

"That was caught underneath the car. Look familiar?"

The nurse walks to a locker across the room, opens it and pulls out a paper bag stuffed with clothes. She dumps the contents on the table: black buckle-up overshoes, brown lace-up oxford shoes, brown socks with a hole in the toe of one and the cuff of the other one stiff and dark, a bloody, muddy dress that might once have been navy blue, shreds of a ragged brassiere held together in places with safety pins, and a dark olive green coat. She lays the coat out on the table and they stare at it. Pieces are torn off here and there, but the piece she holds in her hand matches the coat.

"Now, what?" she asks.

Peterson walks over, sits half on the edge of the table, one black booted foot dangling. He takes off his hat and rubs a big hand across his hair.

"I don't know," he says.

The nurse stuffs the clothes back into the bag.

"Those boys are dead," the sheriff says. "I don't know if it would serve any purpose to have it all come out now. You can't try dead men, and it wouldn't do Elsie a bit of good anyway. Do you think Jack Mason is going to stand still for an investigation into what his boys and their friend were up to just before they got killed?"

"So you're going to let them get away with it?"

"They didn't get away with anything. They're dead. What the hell am I supposed to do?"

The nurse stares at him.

"I'm up for reelection next fall," he continues. "Jack Mason is not going to support the man who sullied his sons' names."

The nurse pinches her lips together.

"What about justice?"

"What about justice? What about justice?" He slams his foot on the floor and stands up. "For all practical purposes, justice has already been served by that damn deer that stepped in front of those boys' car, if there ever was a deer in the first place. Did they deserve to goddamn die for what they did? Fuck if I know, but I do know that I got a wife and three kids to support and I need this goddamn job, even if I hate it like hell sometimes."

"What about Elsie?"

"What ABOUT Elsie? I can't do anything about Elsie."

"Listen, Elsie's mother died an hour ago. Everett's Funeral Home should be here any minute to pick up the body."

The sheriff shuts his eyes and cringes.

"I'm damn sorry about that," he says, "but she had tuberculosis dammit, she would've died anyway no matter what happened to Elsie."

"Yes. That's true. But now, Elsie is in no condition to work. How is she going to support herself?"

"I don't know, welfare, whatever the rest of these damned Indians do. How the hell should I know?"

The nurse is silent for a minute and then she says, "Earl, you're a good Catholic aren't you?"

"So what is that, a philosophical question? What are you asking me here? Am I supposed to be the Good Samaritan and take this Indian girl into my home? Put her up along with my wife and kids?"

"No, just listen for a minute! Your wife is active in the church, too, isn't she? Doesn't the two of you know somebody in some other parish, somewhere away from here?"

"I don't know."

"Well, you can ask, can't you?"

Peterson smashes his hat onto his head.

"All right, all right. I'll see what I can do."

He swallows all his coffee in one gulp, smashes the styrofoam cup, tosses it into the trash can.

"You owe me one," he says.

After he's gone, the nurse takes the bag of clothes out behind the hospital and stuffs it into the incinerator.

The three of you, Oscar and Lowan and you, have walked on past the hospital a little ways to the graveyard. You walked through the unlocked gate to the back, where the newest graves are. Faded plastic flowers – yellow and pink and red – are testimony to remembrance, but there are no flowers on the grave Oscar has brought you to see. There is a small square headstone, bought by the county, Oscar tells you.

"See, the county don't ordinarily buy headstones for the indigent. They just put up a wooden cross marker, but there was a sort of collective guilt about this death, so the commissioners voted the money for the headstone."

There is no sentimental saying, no hearts and flowers, no Biblical quotation, only the name and dates of birth and death:

JOHN CAULFIELD
Born September 15, 1940
Died January 6, 1969

37

"Not bad for the town drunk, huh?" Oscar smiles. "Maybe better than he deserved, but then, I don't know. He could be a pain in the ass, begging money off people when he was drunk and getting belligerent with people that wouldn't give. Most folks didn't give. This is a pretty religious town, you know, at least on the surface. What goes on underneath ain't nothing that Jesus man would appreciate. But John was a good-hearted man, too. When he was sober, he'd give the shirt off his back if he thought someone else needed it more than him."

"And what did this John Caulfield have to do with Elsie?" you ask.

"Plenty. Or so some people think," Oscar says, and says no more for now.

The two of you walk over to another part of the graveyard, and there is another small county-bought tombstone on Elsie's grave. You've seen it before, the first day you got to town.

ELSIE ROBERTS
Born April 17, 1948
Died January 4, 1969

The sun is going down, and the wind is coming up. You zip up your coat and turn up the collar, stuff your reddened hands in your pockets.

"Let's walk back to that Steak House," you say. "I'll buy."

Oscar pats his belly.

"Walk it off, put it back," he laughs.

Lowan trots through the door behind you, and instantly the waitress is pointing.

"No, Oscar, NO! How many times do I have to tell you, no dogs in here."

Oscar smiles and spreads his hands wide. "But, he's a seeing eye dog! I need him."

"Horse shit," the waitress says and points again. "Get him out."

Oscar sighs and pulls his coat off. "Come on, Lowan."

Just outside the front door, Oscar pulls his coat off and places it

38

under the scrubby bush that's supposed to be landscaping but just looks like trying too hard. He pats it and makes kissing sounds. Lowan whines but settles himself on the coat, and Oscar pulls it up around the dog, crossing the sleeves on top like a hug. He comes back in, rubbing his arms briskly. The waitress slaps two menus down on a table near the door and walks back to the kitchen.

"Some folks think that only people are alive," Oscar says.

6

April 24, 1967

Moving

Mary Margaret Nancy Hoskins Marks was named for her two older sisters, Mary and Margaret who had died in infancy, and even though her parents called her Nancy, she knew the stories of her two sisters who preceded her, and she felt that she could never be just herself, Nancy. She felt like one of those old medieval manuscripts written on sheepskin where two previous works had been scraped off, but not completely, so that the new words written on top showed through in places, intruding themselves into whatever came after. It did not help that after Nancy, her mother could have no more children to take her mind off Mary and Margaret and Nancy – well, Nancy was an afterthought. It did not help that Nancy's mother had two larger than life portraits of Mary and Margaret (painted in oil from photographs after the children's deaths), hanging on the wall above the bed in the master bedroom, a macabre shrine where she worshiped every night as she refused sex with Nancy's father. There could be no children; sex was only for procreation; there could be no procreation – a closed circle of sacrifice and self-torture. Nancy lived her life for *them*, all the others, born and unborn, as well as herself.

Pregnant at seventeen, she married her lover, Donald Marks, and felt that she was now inscribed with another life to live, that of Mrs. Donald Marks. Maybe she should have felt relieved when she miscarried Donald's child, relieved of yet another life, but she did not. She grew thin and frowsy from the burden of living for so many others. Then, when she discovered that, like her mother, she could not bear another child, Nancy could not stop grieving. She had hoped for two children at least, so that she could transfer the lives she carried, one each, onto her offspring. Here's one for *you*, that's Mary's; here's one for *you*, that's Margaret's. And then, there could be a third child that could be new and blank and it's own person, unencumbered by the past. She even had a name picked out for this child who would never be born – Joy. She never considered that it might be a boy.

Donald, unable to comfort Nancy, and unable to understand her refusal to heal, turned away, sought solace for himself among the Indian women in and around Jackson. It wasn't that he found them more attractive than the white women, or more willing. He found them more convenient. As for the Indian women, they appreciated a man who bought them nice things, even if the things he bought were small, but more than that, they appreciated a man who wasn't still mourning the generations of lost warriors before him like so many of their own men. Donald Marks had his own ghosts, but they were of his own generation and not of a history that he couldn't change.

The Indians and the whites in Jackson occupied congruent spaces, but lived separate lives. While the Indians knew all about the white world, had to know for their own survival, events in the Indian community – gossip – seldom crossed from the Indian world to the white world. A one-way valve existed at the rare points of intersection between the two communities. Rarely, information leaked back, when the valve failed for a moment.

For sixteen years of her marriage, Nancy stayed out of the back-wash. There was no direct information, but there were inevitable signs of Donald's infidelity that she ignored, investing herself in the bake sales at Our Lady of the Sacred Heart Catholic Church, the spring rummage sale, and the building fund drive. At home, she tended a huge garden, filling jars and jars with green beans and toma-toes, making piccalilli and jelly and sweet beet pickles until the shelves of the dusty cellar bent with the weight of the preserved food. One year, when she found herself with still too much time to think, she sent off to the Norfolk Hatchery for fifty chicks, fluffy yellow peepers, straight run, and then she continued the practice every year. She named them, and in times of desperation, she called them interchangeably – you are Mary, you are Margaret, and you are Joy.

Nancy was naturally the person that Father Horst relied on whenever anything needed doing, so he turned to her when the call came from the sheriff's wife in Mobridge, about finding a place for Elsie. Father Horst's housekeeper, a devout widow who lived in the cottage behind the church, had gotten too old for the job and went to live with her son in Denver six months earlier. Father Horst didn't really need a housekeeper, being by nature a neat sort of person who regularly picked up after himself and did his own laundry and cooking and frankly, enjoyed not being fussed over. But, he was a kind man as well who considered personal sacrifice as part of his calling. He would welcome Elsie as the new housekeeper, Catholic or not, but could Nancy make the arrangements to get Elsie down to Jackson? Nancy suggested to the sheriff that he bring Elsie halfway from Mobridge and she would meet him to collect Elsie, but he insisted they he bring her farther, all the way to Kadoka, and Nancy didn't argue.

She left a covered plate of food in the refrigerator for Donald's lunch – potato salad, two pieces of fried chicken, a generous serving of green beans, topped with a thick slice of homemade bread (already buttered) – and a chocolate cake on the kitchen counter. She plopped her old straw cowboy hat on her head and set off in her faded, blue pickup to meet the sheriff and Elsie at Kadoka. As she bounced down her rough driveway to the main road, a pair of meadowlarks, dressed in yellow vests marked with a black V, circled and called in that distinctive five-note call, "go see the PREACHer." Or maybe it was "wee Willie WINKie." She had heard it both ways. She passed growing fields of green wheat and thought, as so many others before her had thought, that they looked like green oceans with the breeze rippling waves across them. It was a good day to be alive, a good day to be on her way to meet Elsie Roberts. Such a tragic story. She winced at the thought of what Elsie had endured, what no woman should have to endure.

Coming into Kadoka from the south, Nancy turned right, passing businesses strung out alongside the road like bits of trash tossed out randomly by motorists, on the way through to the Black Hills to see president's heads popping up out of a mountain, bodies and feet permanently planted in land not their own. She pulled into the agreed upon meeting place, a Texaco station. He was already there, sitting in a cop car, another figure beside him in the front seat.

"You the sheriff from Mobridge?" she asked tentatively through the window.

He touched his hat brim, opened the door and got out. "Yes, ma'am. Earl Peterson. You must be Nancy Marks."

She put out her small, strong hand and shook his firmly.

"Yes. Happy to meet you. So how's our Elsie?"

"To tell the truth, Mrs. Marks, I don't really know. She hasn't spoken a word all the way down here," he said. He kept his voice low. "She can talk, you know, I've heard her say a few words, but it sounds pretty strange. I'd guess she thinks it puts people off, but then, I hear she never was much of a talker before – well, before."

Nancy walked around and opened the passenger door and leaned over.

"Hi, Elsie. I'm Nancy Marks. It's nice to meet you."

Elsie glanced quickly at Nancy and then away. Her large hands moved in her lap as if she wasn't sure whether she should extend one for a handshake or not. She wore a black floral printed house dress, hair in braids pinned up on her head.

"Let's get your things in my pickup, and then we'll get a bite to eat before we start back. You must be hungry. Do you need help?"

Elsie didn't move until Nancy extended her hand, and then she moved abruptly, drawing away from Nancy's hand and stepping out of the car. Nancy was surprised that Elsie was tall with good muscles even though she was thin. She had expected a little person, maybe even smaller than her own five-foot-two height. This woman was beautiful in a young Amazon way. She carried a cloth bag, home-made looking and plain brown that hung from one shoulder, and an opened bottle of pop in the other hand.

The sheriff opened the trunk of his car, lifted out two paper bags and a large cardboard box and put them in the cab of Nancy's truck. Elsie stepped up into the pickup, calf muscles flexing like elongated

43

dark hearts pulsing slowly one-two. She tucked her dress tightly around her legs as she sat down.

Sheriff Peterson closed his car trunk, walked back to his car with Nancy.

"Think she'll be okay?" he asked.

"Sure," Nancy answered. "I expect it will take some time. Want to grab a hamburger with us? It might help her to have someone familiar around for a few minutes. Just while she gets to know me a bit."

"No, no. I'd best be getting back." He jingled his keys from hand to hand.

"All right, then. Thanks, sheriff."

He looked down at his black booted feet.

"It's the least I could do. The only thing I could do," he said. He looked up at her pale blue eyes. "Do you think I'm doing the right thing?"

Nancy clasped his forearm. "Absolutely."

"Well, all right. Give me a call if there's anything – you know."

"Sure. Don't worry about her," Nancy said, letting go of his arm. "Elsie is going to be just fine."

Peterson raised his voice and hollered at Elsie.

"You take care of yourself, Elsie, all right?"

Elsie stared straight ahead through the windshield, but she raised and lowered the fingers of one hand slightly from where they rested on the frame of the open truck window.

"Good-bye, Elsie."

Nancy climbed into her pickup and banged the door.

"Let's see if this town has a McDonald's, shall we?" she asked.

Elsie said, "Do you want to see my turtles?" Her voice came out raspy and hoarse. Some of the words broke in the middle abruptly changing pitch from low to high. She pulled the cloth shoulder bag around to her lap and reached inside.

"I'd like that very much," Nancy said.

Elsie pulled out a slightly less than palm sized, pinto turtle – red paint flaked from its olive back, legs pin wheeling.

"He's Christmas!" Nancy took him and held him up in front of her face.

"No. He's Tom," Elsie said.

"Oh, I didn't mean his name was Christmas. I only meant – well, he's green and red. You know, Christmas colors."

"He's Tom," Elsie insisted.

"Hello, Tom," Nancy said. She touched the turtle's nose with a forefinger. Instantly, head and all four legs withdrew into the shell. She handed him back to Elsie and took the second turtle, colored yellow paint and green shell.

"Now this one has John Deere tractor colors," Nancy said, and then hastened to add, "but I know that isn't his name."

"Dick," Elsie said. "His name is Dick."

Nancy rubbed her finger over the smooth shell of the turtle's belly. They're nothing like a cat or a dog, or a chick, not soft and cuddly, she thought. You can't hug a turtle, and they can't hug you back.

"I had another one. That one was called Harry, but he's dead," Elsie said. She said it straight out, as if the turtle had held no special significance, but was like a pretty rock that you pick up one day from a roadside and then discover later in the washing machine, wonder why you bothered with it, and chunk it into the trash.

"Harry was blue," Elsie said.

"I'm sure that Harry was a lovely turtle, too," Nancy replied, as she handed Dick back to Elsie, who kissed both of the turtles' backs before she put them back into her bag.

"These are chrysemys picta marginata turtles," Elsie went on. "There are other species of chrysemys in the United States, but this one is common up here in slow moving creeks and marshy places. See, I know Tom and Dick are males because they have elongated fore claws and a thicker, longer tail." A little smile turned up the corner of Elsie's full lips.

"Elsie, how did you know that?" Nancy was surprised. She had been thinking that Elsie was pretty simple, childlike, and wondering if she had always been that way, or if maybe the ordeal she had been through had damaged her mentally, and now, she wondered if Elsie might have guessed what she was thinking.

"I read books," Elsie said.

45

"Well, I should say you do," Nancy said. She wondered what other knowledge Elsie had stored in her head, and what might come out of her mouth.

"Would you like this?" Elsie held out the bottle of pop.

"No, thank you. But what about that hamburger?"

Elsie still held out the bottle of pop, so Nancy took it, noticing that it was warm as slop. Peterson must have bought it for her without knowing that Elsie probably never drank the stuff. Nancy took the bottle, opened the door and poured it outside onto the warm dirt, put the empty bottle behind the pickup seat.

They ate hamburgers and French fries in the truck as Nancy drove south across the stretch of badlands that crossed the highway. Wind driven sand, rain and the action of frost had carved fantastic shapes from the soft sandstone – mushrooms and knobs, gullies and caves in the cliffs.

"This is the badlands," Nancy said when she noticed Elsie's interest.

"How can land be bad?" Elsie asked.

Just past the WELCOME TO JACKSON sign at the outskirts of town, Elsie asked, "Is there a newspaper in town?"

Nancy was puzzled.

"Sure. The *Jackson Messenger*. It isn't much more than a slander sheet, but its what we have."

"Do they have want ads?" Elsie asked.

"Sure. Are you looking for something?"

"No. I want to put an ad in."

"An ad? For what, Elsie?"

"Work. For work."

"Elsie, you don't have to work for anybody but Father Horst. Didn't the sheriff explain to you? You keep house for him, and in return you get your own little cottage to live in and a little money every month for groceries and what you need."

"It won't be enough work," Elsie said, her jaw set. "I need more work."

"Well, I don't know, Elsie," Nancy argued. She didn't know how

46

delicate to be with the woman. "Maybe you should wait a little. It might be too soon."

Elsie bunched her skirt tail in clenched hands, lowered her chin.

"I need to work," she said.

"All right. I can show you where the newspaper office is, and you could go up there later this week."

"Could you show me now? Today?"

"Well. All right."

So few people were on the streets that the town seemed dormant, dozing beneath the warm Midwestern sun, but it was Tuesday. Tomorrow would bring people into town for the weekly auction at the stock barn on the outskirts of town next to the fairgrounds, even though there wouldn't be many animals exchanging owners. Calves were weaned and sold off in the late fall, but there would be a few head of dry cows, canners and cutters passing through, a few head of hogs, maybe a novelty beast or two like a Shetland pony who had thrown his kid owner one too many times and could only benefit from a good selling. No matter how few the animals going through the stock barn, the country folk came to town. They would wait to buy any necessaries until Wednesday when the women could gather at The Steak House and talk over iced tea with the gossip biddies who worked in the courthouse. Their men folk would sit on the built-in wooden benches rising in an amphitheater from the shit-stained white-pipe-and-sawdust-floored center pen of the stock barn, exchanging lies and talking about the weather reports over the patter of the sweating auctioneer singing the praises of some scrawny old brindle cow with cancer eye and no calf.

Nancy turned left at the high school, drove past the low red brick courthouse, turned left again and parked in front of a white painted cement block building. A neatly lettered sign above the door read: Jackson Messenger.

Elsie made no move to get out.

"This is the newspaper, Elsie, right there through that door."

A man in old jeans and a dirty gray striped shirt sat on the sidewalk, legs stuck straight out in front of him, chin on his chest asleep.

Or passed out. A bottle neck protruded from a brown paper bag between his legs.

"Do you want me to go in with you, Elsie?"

Elsie reached for the door handle, popped the door open.

The man's head came up an inch or so, dropped back onto his chest.

Nancy noticed Elsie's eyes on him.

"Oh, sweetie! You're afraid of – oh, don't be afraid. That's just John Caulfield. Look, he's too drunk to move. He won't hurt you. I'll come with you." She opened her door, but Elsie put out her hand.

"NNOooo." Elsie's voice burbled up and down the scale.

"You sure?"

Elsie got out and stepped up on the sidewalk.

John Caulfield's head came up and he stared at Elsie, only half seeing.

"HEY, who are you?"

Elsie stopped dead still.

"John Caulfield, you behave yourself!" Nancy yelled at him.

"You gonna make me!" he hollered back in her general direction.

"I'm warning you, John, I'll haul you up off that sidewalk and whip you myself and THEN I'll have you thrown in jail!"

Caulfield was silent for a minute, and then he mumbled, "Yes, ma'am," and his head lolled back on his chest, while his fingers fumbled for the paper wrapped bottle.

"It's okay, Elsie. He won't hurt you."

Elsie walked cautiously past Caulfield and into the newspaper office.

Elsie was gone only a few minutes, came back out, edged around the sleeping Caulfield who didn't move this time, and got back into Nancy's truck.

Nancy drove down the street to the church, easing her truck into the narrow tree-shaded driveway between the Our Lady of the Sacred Heart Catholic Church and the low white house where Father Horst lived. A narrow sidewalk went between the two buildings, and on either side the earth was packed hard as concrete and sterile of any living thing – no grass, no flowers. The cottage that would be Elsie's was half-hidden behind the priest's house, and he sat there on the stoop at his back door, looking up from the book on his knees as Nancy turned off the pickup motor. His yellow tabby cat that he called simply Cat wound back and forth across his legs, ignored. A pipe held in his left hand had gone out long since, or maybe he had forgotten to light it in the first place.

He stood up. He was young, blond, and blue-eyed and handsome as a movie star. Nancy always smiled when she saw him, wondering if he had any idea that half the women in the parish believed it was a sin against womankind that he had chosen the priesthood. She doubted if he was aware of it. He lived in his head and not his body.

She got out and walked around to Elsie's door and opened it.

"Father Horst," she said, "Meet your new housekeeper."

7

January 18, 1970

A Meeting

A skinny waitress wearing faded jeans beneath a white polyester smock, bra strap looping out below a sleeve, takes the plates, emptied except for a brown steak sauce smear, and sets down two saucers of bread pudding. The puddings are leftovers from the lunch special dessert.

Oscar leans close to his and looks at it, snags the pocket of the waitress as she's walking away.

"Umm, could I have a little more whipped cream on this?"

She rolls her eyes at you behind his back, but she juggles the dirty dishes into one hand and takes back his saucer.

He sits back and surveys the restaurant, while you dig into your own dessert.

There are only three other occupied tables and Oscar gives you the low down on who they are – one older man, a gray-faced, exhausted-looking traveling salesman on his weekly run through Jackson, one insurance business owner who isn't married and has no one to cook for him, and a pair of teenagers having a quiet spat in a corner booth. The rest of the town eats quietly at home.

"Lucky kids," Oscar says pointing with his chin at the teenagers in the corner booth.

"Because they're fighting? Doesn't seem so lucky to me. They look pretty miserable," you answer.

"They're still young enough to fight," he says.

The waitress sets the saucer of dessert heaped with whipped cream on the table with a bang and stalks back to the kitchen. She returns with the coffee pot and refills your cups.

"She's sure in a happy mood," you comment.

Oscar shrugs. "She's got her own problems," he says. "That's John

Caulfield's sister," but he doesn't elaborate further, so you ask about John himself.

"John grew up here," Oscar says, wiping a bit of whipped cream from the end of his nose. "His family lives out east of town on a small farm. They're good people, just getting by from one harvest season to the next like a lot of smaller farmers around here. Mrs. Caulfield, John's mother, works at the courthouse part time. There's another sister, too, married to a small-time farmer a couple of counties over. The trouble with John was he thought too much, and he couldn't stand his own thoughts. He was always too big for Bennett, but he couldn't make himself leave, either. He hated farming, but he was an only son, and his dad couldn't afford hired help, so he put John on a tractor when he was barely able to see over the steering wheel. Doesn't take a lot of concentration to run a tractor around and around a field. You got a lot of time to think."

You push your dessert plate away, take up your coffee cup and sip, and Oscar's story spins around the room, mingling with the smoke from the insurance man's cigarette.

"John did all the things kids around here do – played Little League baseball, went ice skating on the creek in the winter, went pheasant hunting in the fall. His dad was no slave driver; he gave the kid a lot of leeway, but John just never took hold of anything. Except football. He loved the game. 'Course, there wasn't any of those Pop Warner football teams for kids around here. There just ain't enough kids to make up teams, but John started playing a little in grade school. He was a big kid, bigger than most of the other boys and quick, too, and that's not usual to have both in the same person. He played a little basketball, too, but football was what he loved. By the time he got to high school he was the star, and he could play any position – quarterback, wide receiver, tackle – the years he played for the Jackson Warriors were the best years the high school team ever had. He got a lot of attention, and he liked it. I got to say that it never went to his head, either. His dad kept him humble with plenty of work and responsibility.

"The fall of his senior year, he was being scouted by a couple of the big colleges – Nebraska and Oklahoma came looking at him, and it seemed like everything was set for him. Then he had an accident. He had just quarterbacked the best game of his life against Philip – scored two touchdowns in the last quarter, rushed for over one hundred and fifty yards – as a quarterback, mind – and he had an appointment to talk with the football scout from Nebraska. On the Sunday morning after that game, his dad sent him out to the barn to grind feed for the hogs. Well, he was probably thinking too much and not paying attention, but anyway, he got his pants leg caught in the power takeoff on the tractor and he couldn't get loose. By the time his dad heard his screams and got out there, John's leg was tore up so bad that it took three operations on his leg and it never was right again. That ended his football career.

"He graduated from high school, but his grades never were that good and, of course, there wasn't any football scholarship to get him in to college. He just worked on the farm with his dad and got more sullen. And he started drinking. By the time he was old enough to drink legally, he was already an alcoholic. When he started getting abusive during his drinking bouts, his family just couldn't handle it anymore, so they kicked him out. So, John moved into town and started doing a little work here and there to support himself. He'd work at a gas station for awhile, and then he'd get drunk, not show up, and they'd fire him. He's a good worker when he's sober, though, so whenever someone got shorthanded, the livestock auction barn would put him on, or one of the gas stations would take him back. He spent a lot of nights locked up in the city jail.

"I guess he must have been, oh, somewhere around thirty when Elsie came to town. He was too drunk to remember that first meeting, but they met again not more than a couple of weeks after she got to Jackson. In a town this small, you can't help but run into each other."

After Mass at Sacred Heart on Sunday, a Mass that Elsie didn't attend even though Father Horst had made a point to invite her, two women knocked on Elsie's door and introduced themselves to Elsie as Mrs. Packwood and Mrs. Kemper and said they had come about Elsie's ad in the *Messenger*.

Every morning after that, Elsie tidied Father Horst's quarters, a chore that took only a couple of hours, except on Wednesdays when she changed the linens, and did his laundry. On Mondays and Thursdays she spent the rest of the day at the Packwoods' and on Tuesdays and Fridays at the Kempers'. The Packwoods – Mrs. Packwood was Wilma – owned and ran The Steak House, not all that demanding of a job in a town where you only get busy for three weeks or so when the custom harvesters are in town, and after Friday night football games in the fall. Still, the job required the presence of either Mr. or Mrs. Packwood at all times, so Mr. Packwood took the six to two shift and Mrs. Packwood took the two to ten, which meant that Elsie saw Mrs. Packwood first every morning and then Mr. Packwood when he got home from his morning shift, smelling of scrambled eggs and the cinnamon rolls that he baked fresh every morning. Mrs. Packwood, a dumpy little woman who enjoyed her husband's baked goods too much, lived in her own world, going from home to work to church and back again with no awareness of other people's lives, except when it confused her own routine. She was dumb as a doorknob.

Mr. Packwood was smooth, slick even. Men liked his hearty manner, but it just made women nervous and with good reason. More than one teenaged waitress working the night shift at The Steak House had gotten her bottom pinched by Packwood, although he seldom went farther than that. Or so they say. But they also say that some of those girls didn't mind having their bottoms pinched.

The Kempers owned what everyone called the dime store, but it had more than the usual bric-a-brac because the Kempers had opened up the upstairs part of the building and put in a line of clothing. You could sort through a limited selection of women's dresses, kids' play clothes and men's work pants and shirts on the racks, all fiercely illuminated with new fluorescent lighting, while the thirtyish clerk, who was also the town whore (so the gossipers said), hovered nearby earning her minimum wage pay. Kemper himself was a huge man, fat as well as tall, and so gentle and shy that he couldn't look customers in the eye but stuttered greetings to them while looking past their shoulders. People wondered how on earth he had ever managed to propose to his wife, who was tiny and delicate and as outgoing as Kemper was not. Everyone speculated that she had proposed to him.

On Elsie's first day, Mrs. Packwood laid out a work plan that would ensure Elsie kept moving from the time she crossed the threshold until the time she left, but Elsie was experienced in working for women with ambitious plans for everyone but themselves. She had her own rhythm of steadiness, progressing from one job to another to another, and what got done was done well, and what didn't would be there another day. Her first day, she did a general cleaning of the entire house, putting things in good order, so that after that it would only take a small part of her working day to keep it so, and she could tackle one deep cleaning job every day after that.

Elsie was aware that Nancy Marks thought she wasn't ready yet to take on heavy work, but after her first week, Elsie felt tired but restored to her old self in an odd way. She took satisfaction and pleasure in the simple task of cleaning a floor on her hands and knees and seeing the shining result, clean and separate from human meanness. A clean floor just is.

The big job on her second day of the second week was the garage, cluttered and piled with boxes of dry food stuffs that there was no room to store at the restaurant, bags of clothes that Mrs. Packwood no longer needed but couldn't bear to part with, and the general people clutter that seems to grow and reproduce itself. She opened the heavy garage door first, flooding the space with bright northern summer light that sought out the darkest corners. She separated the contents into three piles – Things To Be Saved, Things That Could Be Tossed Out, and Things To Ask Mrs. Packwood About Before Tossing Out.

Within three hours she had worked her way from the door to the back of the garage with the piles of the three varieties of Things behind her growing higher, when she came to the last corner, a workbench of sorts piled high with tangled coat hangars, light bulbs purchased on sale still in the brown store bags, old newspapers, an iron with a burned off cord, and almost empty paint cans with permanently stuck on lids. Her back ached a little from stooping and lifting. Dust and cobwebs stuck to her sweat damp skin, and she considered stopping to get a drink of water, but decided to finish the last bit before taking a rest. On the bottom shelf beneath the workbench back in the farthest corner, she came upon a stack of magazines of a kind that she had never seen before, certainly not on the racks in the Mobridge Public Library.

She sat down on an upturned paint bucket and looked. They made her remember things, brutal things, dark things that should never see light, and she shivered in the heat and filth in the garage. Then she put the magazines back where she found them, closed the garage door and went back into the house. When Mr. Packwood came home, Elsie told him she needed to leave early. She picked up her bag and walked out, leaving him standing in the spic-and-span kitchen thinking that Elsie was indeed an odd one.

She walked down to the corner and there, beneath the branches of a Chinese elm tree, her knees failed her and she sat on the curb and put her head on her knees. A couple of cars passed, slowing to stare at her and going on. She didn't notice. She was listening to footsteps crunching on snow, seeing car taillights with one corner pinched off, feeling hands grasping, slapping. And the laughter and the smell of beery breath.

"Hey. You all right?"

Elsie's head snapped up.

John Caulfield stood leaning on a spade in the yard across the street.

"Whoa, be easy," he said as if he were talking to a skittish horse. "I'm just doing a little yard work here. I was in the back, but now I got to thin out this iris bed. You okay?"

Elsie nodded her head slowly, but she sat with a tension about her, watching.

John dug the spade into the flowerbed, loosening the dirt, lifting the green plants out onto the grass. He talked on without looking at her.

"You were just sitting there so quiet. I thought you might be sick or in trouble. You're new in town, ain't you? Name's Effie ain't it?"

Elsie cleared her throat. "ELSIE."

John smiled a little bit.

"Oh, yes. ELSIE. Elsie, Elsie, Elsie. Can't think of anything that could be short for. It's a nice name just all by itself. You take my name. John Caulfield. Now, John is so short people can't make it any shorter, so some people make it longer, or just substitute another short name. Johnny. Jack. Ain't that just like people? They always gotta mess with things and change everything around, can't just leave well enough alone."

He went on talking to her, but low as if he were carrying on a conversation with himself, and he never looked at her, but just kept digging in the spade, loosening the dirt, laying the plants on the grass.

She watched him performing that simple task, and gradually his words and his work lulled her. The tension eased and she sat, just sat and waited.

When the flowerbed was empty of green, he dug the spade into the ground and left it standing upright like a stop sign, pulled a faded red handkerchief from his back pocket and wiped the sweat from his face.

"Doesn't look like hard work, but you'd be surprised," he said. "I'm just going to go get my water jug." He walked around the corner of the house and came right back carrying an old glass bottle with burlap sewn around it, soaked with water.

Elsie watched warily as he came across the yard slowly and eased himself down on the curb across the street. She watched him lift the jug and drink, his throat moving as he swallowed.

He started to screw the cap back on, then he looked at her and held out the jug.

"Oh, you thirsty? There's plenty. I promise I ain't got any germs."

She looked at the damp jug in his hand, looked at his face. She stood up and gathered herself as if she were leaping the Grand Canyon, and then she walked across the street and took the bottle from his hands. In that moment of crossing from one side to the other side of that street, the lives of the two were joined, not like in a marriage, but like two fibers in an old blanket twisted together so strongly that when one would break the other would, too. When Elsie had drank and handed the bottle back, he patted the curb beside him and she sat, three feet farther away from him than he had indicated, and he talked while she listened. Then she spoke a little, haltingly at first, and he listened.

"We're a lot alike, Elsie, you and me," John said. "Mostly, people don't see us. We're background, like trees and sky, we're just there, being what we are and doing what we do. Most people only notice a tree when the wind blows it down, or see the sky when rain or snow is falling out of it, but the tree and the sky, they see each other."

When she got up to leave, he called her back again.

"There's another thing, Elsie. I'm harmless as a fly, just ask anybody, when I'm not drinking that is, and usually I just get too stupid drunk to move. It's my medicine, Elsie, and it takes a whole lot of it to make me believe I'm somebody else. But sometimes, when I'm drinking, something just comes over me. Then I forget that I used to have a family. So when you see me on the street, and I've been drinking, walk on the other side."

He began picking up the dislodged, flat green fans of plants and shaking them apart. Elsie walked away.

The waitress has cleared all the tables, filled the salt and pepper shakers and the catsup bottles, swept the floor, and now she's standing back by the swinging doors to the kitchen with her arms crossed staring out the window.

You want to ask Oscar how he could know what John Caulfield said to Elsie Roberts, but you have a feeling he wouldn't tell you or maybe he couldn't tell you how he knew, but you believe he knows.

It's late, and the story rests in your gut along with the steak, both needing time to digest. You push back your chair and stand up, and the waitress rushes to the cash register to take your money for the meal. When she hands you your change, you notice her enlarged knuckles, the chapped and reddened backs of her hands, cold fingertips brushing yours. She follows you to the door and locks it after you have walked out, a solid permanent sounding click.

Outside, the air is so cold that you feel the moisture inside your nose freezing with each breath you take. Lowan has been waiting, curled into Oscar's coat. The dog smells the scraps of fat from the steak that Oscar carries wrapped in a paper napkin.

"Thanks for keeping my coat warm," Oscar says. He pulls on the coat tucking the small dog inside, zipping the coat up as far as it will go. He thanks you for the meal, waves goodbye and walks off down the street with Lowan muttering dog songs, blues about being left out the cold.

8

Mobridge, 1949–1950

Learning Tradition

Men who see the deer woman go crazy, but women who see her are rewarded with the ability to make beautiful things – maybe beadwork or quillwork. Mary Roberts, they said, had met the deer woman, and been gifted. If that were so, it was small compensation, small indeed, for the absence of joy and satisfaction in her life, an absence that, except for her daughter, might have been unbearable.

It began when Elsie was still a baby. One day, a deer hunter, a white man with a red complexion and an awkward, shuffling way about him appeared at the little cabin among the trees at the edge of town. He stepped out of his muddy pickup, took another step, looking around as if at any moment he'd change his mind, get back behind the wheel, and drive away. Then, a dog roared around the corner of the cabin, rushing between him and the pickup door, and he called out to the house.

Mary stepped out of the door, wrapping a shawl closer about her shoulders and called the dog. He descended to his belly and crawled to her. She patted his head, snapped her fingers, and he sat at her feet, an uncertain scowl for the man.

"Yes?" Mary said.

The man hastily snatched off his cap, held it tightly against his leg in his big hand, as if afraid she would bite him.

"You people know how to tan hides," he started, and then stopped. "I mean, you know, turn them into leather."

"Yes," she answered, but she didn't know how, raised as she was at the boarding school, with no access to forbidden old ways.

"Well, uh, ma'am, I've been thinking. See, every year I get a deer and so do most of my friends. We eat the meat, but the hides just goes to waste. I was thinking, that's a damned shame. I was thinking about that and what good shoes – like maybe moccasins – could be made out of those hides. If they were tanned right, you know. My granddad had a pair of moccasins some squaw – some woman, an Indian woman, made to measure. They were soft as gloves and beaded pretty on the toes. He wore them until they fell off his feet, but never could get anyone else to make him another pair. So, I was thinking, maybe you'd tan the hides and make me a pair of moccasins in trade."

It was a long speech for a shy man, and now that he'd given it, and she still stood there silently staring at him, he thought he crossed that forbidden boundary between them and him. He looked down at the cap crumpled in his hand.

No, she didn't know how to tan hides, had only done a little beadwork, taught by her mother-in-law in those happy early days of her marriage. But she had heard older women talk about tanning, and if she tried and failed she lost nothing. She would need stretcher frames, she knew, and if she was to tan them in the old way, the way she had heard of, brains to cook and rub into the hides.

The dog whined, half stood up and settled again at her feet.

"Sorry to have bothered you, ma'am," the man muttered and turned abruptly. The dog, sensing retreat, gave a growl and stalked after the man.

"Shush," Mary said to him, stepping forward and grasping the dog by the ruff.

"How many hides?" Mary asked.

The man turned back, so relieved that he spoke too quickly, urgently as if now that the proposal might be accepted, he was anxious to conclude the business and go, and maybe forget about it and not come back.

"I have three good hides right here," he pulled half frozen bloody lumps out of the back of the pickup. "I didn't know about preserving them, I mean, until you could start tanning, so I just rolled them up like carpets and left them out in the cold. You think that's okay?"

Mary didn't know, but it sounded reasonable.

"I need stretcher frames," she said.

"What's that?"

Mary described them, what she thought they should look like, what size.

"I can make those," he said. "Anything else?"

"Brains," Mary said. "What did you do with the brains?"

His face bore a puzzled look. "From the deer, you mean?"

"Yes. I need brains to tan the hides."

He was at a loss, thinking that was the end of the matter.

"I could use beef brains. I suppose," Elsie said.

"Oh," he said, a smile of relief on his face. "Grocery store has that in the meat case. I always wondered who would buy that, figured it was dog food. I can get that."

"All right, then," Mary said. "Three hides, stretchers and brains. Two pair of moccasins."

"Naa, naa," he protested, now in a bargaining mood. "Since I'm making the stretchers and supplying the brains – " He paused and chuckled a bit, "well, in a manner of speaking, I'm supplying the brains – I think I should get four pair of moccasins. That ought to last my lifetime."

Mary saw, not just a one time transaction, but possibly, a continuous source of income. She bargained back.

"Two pair of moccasins. And a purse for your wife."

He thought about that. It would be a unique gift for Christmas, coming up in just over six weeks.

"All right, but done by Christmas. Can you promise?"

Mary crossed herself in the Christian way and said, "Yes."

And so it began. The next day, the man delivered the frames, showing them off proudly, solid two-by-four construction with slots in the corners fitted with bolts and washers, a construction that allowed the frames to be expanded or contracted to accommodate different sizes of hides. He sat them under the big elm tree in the yard, and then handed her a grocery sack with the brains wrapped in white butcher paper – five pounds of them, squishy through the paper.

"Is that enough?" he asked.

"Yes," she said, pretending that she knew.

When he had left she took the hides to the creek, washing them in the ice cold water, rinsing them over and over until her arms ached from the effort. She put the brains in a pan with water to stew slowly while she sharpened her best butcher knife, laid the hides, hairy and soggy, out on the dry grass.

Not slits for the lacing, she thought, they would tear as the hide stretched. Carefully she cut small holes around the edges of each hide, and then began lacing them to the frames with lengths of clothesline rope. The dog grabbed one hide and began chewing it. She yelled and slapped at him with the end of the clothesline rope. He retreated, looking wistful, but she could see a problem. With the sharp knife, she cut a tag from one side of a hide and pitched it to him. He caught it in midair, and disappeared under the house with it. That would satisfy him for now, but what about later, when it got dark and she went into the house for the night? It wasn't just her dog, but all the other dogs in the area that would be drawn to the smell, not to mention cats. She had heard about tanning hides, but no one had mentioned the stink. She sat back on her heels to think, her eyes traveling up the trunk of the elm tree. There, about fifteen feet off the ground a branch, eight inches thick grew out at a right angle from the trunk.

Hours later, interrupted by frequent breaks to check on Elsie napping in her crib, she had done all she thought she could for the time being. The hides were laced into the frames, scraped free of clinging bits of flesh and smeared with the brains that had cooked into a paste. She had scraped her arm as well, on the tree bark when she climbed to the limb to fling ropes over it, but the frames with the laced-in hides hung in the tree, far above the reach of hungry animals. She pressed her hands into the small of her back and leaned back against the pressure, easing the ache.

Elsie was fussing in her crib, but stopped abruptly when Mary picked her up, the child's small face suddenly screwed up in something like disgust. Mary sniffed her own sleeve.

"Phew! You will have to wait then," Mary said, placing Elsie back in the crib, where she promptly resumed wailing, while Mary poured hot water from the tea kettle into a pan to wash.

Mary worked the hides over the next few weeks, fitting the work in between the days when she cleaned house for the white ladies, always careful that she had washed all traces of stink from her hair, her body and her clothes before she presented herself for work.

The first batch of hides was trial and error. She managed to remove all the hair and clinging flesh, to work the hides into some degree of suppleness, pulling them back and forth around a fence post, but still, they smelled, and it wasn't the pleasant smell of the shoe and saddle store. That man's wife would not want a purse that smelled like hamburger left too long in the sun. Finally, Mary had to approach one of the Lakota women whom she had seen on the streets, one of the older women who, if not friendly, had at least not turned her head when Mary walked past.

"Soak them in your water and wood ashes," the woman said. "Then smoke them."

"In my water? Smoke them?"

The woman's lips compressed as if she didn't want to say it plainer, as if the words could not escape her mouth.

"You know," she said finally. "When you make water? Mix it with wood ashes, like a thin paste. Then smoke them."

"How much – umm, of my water and how much ashes? Smoke them over a fire?"

But the woman would speak no more.

Mary didn't understand how the stink of urine and ashes could kill the stink of rotting flesh, but it did, after soaking and more rinsing in the creek water, though the hides still did not smell like the saddle and shoe shop. After the process, she smoked them over a slow fire, smoking herself at the same time, eyes stinging and lungs burning when the wind swirled the smoke just wrong. The problem then was that the leather smelled like barbecue without the sweet overtones of sauce. She was desperate, but hanging the hides in the tree for a few days diminished the smoky miasma to a light aroma, noticeable only if you put your nose close and breathed deeply. She pulled them back and forth around the fence post some more, and finally, she laid the best hide out on the scrubbed pine floor and carefully cut out the pieces for the two pair of moccasins using the pattern she had made from a paper sack. She smiled, remembering how the man had sat on the upturned washtub in the front yard while she measured and marked down the numbers, drew around his foot on the paper with a pencil.

Before she sewed the pieces together, she did the part that she already knew how to do: she beaded rosettes in red and black on the toes of one pair, and on the other, a geometric design in blue and yellow and white. After the beading was done, she stitched the pieces together, pulling the leather thongs so tight that they bit deeply into the leather, into her hands as well, but her hands were strong and would mend. The handbag was a simple design, just a bag with a drawstring around the top, but the beauty was in the beadwork – rosettes again, but in black and white with just a few dots of turquoise beads that stood out against the somber colors like tiny jewels. She believed that the man would be happy with moccasins no matter how they looked as long as they were comfortable, but the wife must be impressed, for Elsie had a plan. If the wife liked the bag, then maybe her friends would like one, too, and maybe she could make them and sell them.

When the man picked up the bag and moccasins just before Christmas, he smiled at her and thanked her and told her the work was beautiful, and she dropped her head and could not answer. She did not know that his wife thought the bag was tacky and touristy, that she left it lying half out of its wrappings on the hall table for days. But then, her friends came over to play cards one cold night just before New Year's, and they saw the bag, and they wanted it. The beaded Indian bags became a local phenomenon. Mary made five more bags from the hide and a half she had left, and several tiny ones for coin purses and promised more next year, when deer season came again.

The Indians in town saw the bags carried around by the white women. They heard who had made them, and they looked as close as they could whenever they had the chance at the soft creamy leather, the beads firmly attached, the patterns and color that were variations on old designs, but uniquely Mary's own.

She has seen the deer woman, it was said.

Elsie couldn't remember when her mother hadn't tanned hides and beaded. It seemed to her that every fall, the big elm tree grew clusters of tanning frames, the stink of the process clung to the house, the neighborhood dogs sat beneath the tree howling and fighting over the prizes they couldn't reach. Throughout the rest of the year, Elsie watched her mother cut and shape the leather, bead them in bright patterns and sew the pieces together into saleable items. Naturally, Elsie learned and tried her own hand at the beading. Although the first efforts came out lopsided and awkward, by the time Elsie was twelve years old, she was contributing more than a little to the work. Between them they added a goodly sum to their income, and Elsie was beginning to be more than a little help with the house cleaning jobs, too.

9

June through November, 1967

Just Following Tradition

Elsie threaded her way through the summer in Jackson, working, always working, minding her own business and ignoring the events and the stories, both true and false, that concerned those events. Most of the happenings were minor, things that fell under the category of mischief, not crime.

That summer, a group of high school boys spent their spare time devising ways to hide their friend's Volkswagen, a car that seemed incongruous, foreign, and tiny in a town full of pickup trucks and family sedans. Wherever the owner of the Volkswagen parked it, he could never be sure it would be there when he returned. Once he found it hidden in the bushes behind the Episcopal Church, two blocks from where he had parked, and another time he recovered it from where it had been parked on the fifty-yard line of the high school football field with a sign stuck to the trunk that read KICK ME. After a while, the joke wore thin with him; he told his friends to stop or else, and when they continued, he did "or else." He reported the incidents as malicious mischief to the Sheriff Parker, who had a talk with the boys. Everyone was upset with everyone for awhile, but after some days the friendships resumed. In small towns, you can't easily exchange one set of friends for another. There just aren't enough people in the potential friends pool.

The gossip burned hot for a while about the sixteen-year-old whose parents had suddenly hustled her out of town. They said she was pregnant, sent to have an abortion. They said she was pregnant, sent to a relative's house in California until she could have the baby, give it up for adoption, and return. They said the parents didn't want her to marry her boyfriend, that he was too immature, with no prospects. Then a few people said that it wasn't the boyfriend's baby at all. The girl was a waitress at The Steak House, and the rumors said she stayed later than she needed too many nights when she worked the two to ten shift. The girl's family switched their loyalty from the Episcopal Church, where the Packwoods also attended, to another church across town. People went around looking askance at Mr. Packwood, and the atmosphere when Elsie went to clean for them was decidedly cool. Then the Episcopal pastor preached a sermon about not judging others and the scandal quieted.

The usual high number of Indians were arrested for drunk and disorderly, public intoxication or just GPV – general principals violated. Most of them were unable to pay their fines, so, as usual, they worked it off by laboring at five dollars a day (less the cost of their two scanty meals per day) serving as helpers for the city garbage collection. Except for the Indians themselves, no one else talked about the Indian arrests. It was too commonplace. They did chuckle about the time just after the Fourth of July, when the mayor was so drunk he couldn't walk up the steps out of the basement of the American Legion Club, but lay on the steps trying to look up the skirts of women passing up and down. Sheriff Parker had come and collected the mayor and took him home to his wife.

The custom harvest crews rolled into town; it rained too much and they had to stay longer than usual waiting for the mud to dry up so they could get into the fields, but soon, they and their giant mechanical insect machines moved on. The county fair came and went with the parade down Main Street led by the high school band, sweating in their heavy wool uniforms, complete with the vest-like overlay, in the August heat. There was the annual rush to buy school clothes and supplies, and then the air turned cooler, and those who attended the Friday night football games wore jackets and saw their breath while they stood on the sidelines cheering on the home team in between talking about their neighbors.

Elsie gained weight, lost that awkward scarecrow look. Some might say she got fat. She had a weakness for sweets, but more so for fruit, especially oranges, and she was observed at least twice a week carrying home from the Red Owl Grocery Store a net bag full of oranges and other groceries piled in a kid's old red wagon that she had acquired for hauling things, and that brown cloth bag containing her turtles, Tom and Dick, hanging over her shoulder.

When she first came to town, the white people speculated about her origins and why she had come, but Elsie refused to be drawn into talking about it. Then, Nancy Marks put out the story that Elsie's mother had died in Mobridge and she had nowhere else to go, a story that satisfied the curious and was, after all, true. Nancy urged Elsie to attend church, join the altar society, but when Elsie was noncommittal Nancy didn't push it. She came to Elsie's little house behind the church a couple of times a week, just to talk, sometimes bringing fresh vegetables from her garden or a glass or two of just-made chokecherry jelly. Elsie seemed to enjoy Nancy's visits, although she didn't talk much. She listened while she held Tom or Dick, or she knitted. She always offered Nancy coffee and sometimes an orange or a plate of cookies.

The white people of Jackson thought Elsie was strange, always carrying those turtles around with her, but she was industrious and never caused trouble. She became that necessary person in every small town – the odd single woman, while John Caulfield was another necessary person – the town drunk with a tragic past. The Indian people steered clear of Elsie, remembering her mother and the oddness of Mary's past in the town. It wasn't that they were unkind to Elsie, but that they were a little afraid of her, being as she was, the embodiment of past transgressions, living proof of what happens when people upset the social order of things.

It was the children – both Indian and white – who took to Elsie, and no wonder. She spoke to them as if they mattered, listening to their childish stories with a seriousness of expression that conveyed genuine interest. She showed them her turtles, allowing them to play with them. Sometimes she let the children hold races between Tom and Dick on the sidewalk in front of the grocery store while the mothers watched Elsie, clapping her hands and laughing at odd moments, such as that time when Tom veered off the curb, turned upside down allowing Dick to win the race. They saw Elsie as harmless, a simpleminded woman whose intellect was not much higher than the children's, but the woman who worked at the county library suspected there was more to Elsie than what seemed obvious. Elsie was a reader. She went to the library often, usually sitting and reading books there, although she sometimes checked out books about turtles or birds or South Dakota history. The librarian watched Elsie read, and after Elsie had stowed the books back on the shelves and left, the librarian tried to remember the color of the binding and where the book was shelved. She figured out – or thought she did – that Elsie had eclectic tastes in topics – general interest medical books, herbal remedies, biographies of historical figures, but never novels, never popular fiction or the romance novels that were the main interest of many library patrons. The librarian only suspected that Elsie wasn't as simple as she seemed, but John Caulfield knew it because Elsie talked to him.

In the course of their daily business, they passed each other on the street, met in line at the grocery store. Sometimes they sat on a bench in the park and ate their noonday lunch, scattering bread crumbs for the birds, while they talked, not of people or things, but ideas. John began calling Elsie the Turtle Woman Philosopher, a term that made her laugh in that odd way, the sound bubbling up and down the scale in a way that most people found discomforting, even creepy, but John thought endearing and uniquely Elsie. People stared at them but didn't talk to them, perhaps, as John said, they weren't noticeable, but only present like the sky and the trees.

"We're quite a pair, aren't we," John said often. "The town drunk and the town crazy woman," which made Elsie laugh again.

Always though, Elsie remembered what he had told her, and if he appeared to be drunk, she avoided him, going around the block or entering a store to finger fabrics and fumble through knickknacks without buying anything until she was sure that he had passed on down the street. A couple of times John ended up in jail for harassing someone for money when he was drunk. Once he even hit a farmer, a harmless roundhouse swing that barely grazed the man's shoulder as he jumped back. John was ashamed when he heard of what he had done, but not ashamed enough to give up drinking.

Halloween came with the country kids brought into town by their parents to trick or treat, and the usual outhouses of Indians tipped over, hay bales dumped in the middle of Main Street and lit afire. As late fall came on, Elsie and John's lunches in the park ceased. It was just too cold to sit still that long.

Deer season came, and every male person over the age of twelve and some females went hunting. The successful ones returned, deer draped over the pickup hood or heaped in the box, head and antlers hanging over the side to best display advantage, and made the traditional drive up and down the streets to show off before taking their kills to the meat processing plant just on the edge of town. The plant processed local cattle, hogs, a few sheep, but their busiest time was during the peak of deer season. It was called Jackson Locker Plant because the owners not only processed the carcasses for other people and sold meat, but they also rented individual freezers to store meat for folks who didn't have a home freezer, or didn't have room in the one they had. It was owned and run by the Kolcek family, headed by a stern, red-faced little Pole who beat his wife, not too severely, you understand, on alternate Saturday nights and attended church on the opposite Sundays. The general consensus about the reason for the beatings was that Mrs. Kolcek had born no sons, only five strapping daughters, mostly grown, any one of whom could have downed their father like a pole-axed hog, gutted him, and ground him into sausage had they chosen. They didn't choose to do so, out of some odd sense of duty to the father, perhaps, but maybe because they didn't know their own strength, believing that their father, who could yell louder, was automatically in power. The older two girls had married meek men that allowed them to be the boss at home, and that appeared to balance the power in the girls' eyes. Besides, it made Mr. Kolcek happy because his sons-in-law worked in the business. Generally speaking, everyone was happy except for Mrs. Kolcek.

On one of those November days when the gray clouds roll back, when the sun shines, and you can anticipate the crunch when you bite into a Jonathan apple, Elsie walked out to Jackson Locker Plant.

70

Packwood's pickup was in the parking lot, probably there to pick up his weekly meat supply for The Steak House, so Elsie waited around the corner until she saw him leave. The building ran back deep and narrow to the pens in the back, but the front part contained the store smelling of fresh blood and animal flesh, pink sawdust sweeping compound inches deep on the wooden floor.

The eldest Kolcek daughter, Kate, was behind the counter weighing up pork chops for a local housewife. Elsie waited until the transaction was completed and the woman had gone, tinkling the bell above the front door.

"Yeah, can I help ya?" Kate leaned muscular arms on top of the meat counter, chewing gum. "Got a special on the pork chops this week."

"NoOoo, thank you," Elsie said. "I was wondering what you do with the hides."

Kate popped her gum and stood up straight. "Huh? What hides?"

"From the animals, you know."

"The beeves and the hogs and such you mean? Dad sells them to a dealer out of Omaha. Comes in every month or so to collect 'em. Why you wanna know?"

Elsie shook her head. "NooOO. I mean the deer hides."

Kate snorted. "Oh, them. Nobody wants 'em. They go to the landfill. Why?"

"Do you suppose," Elsie said but her voice came out too harsh and raspy. Kate stared at her, impatiently popping the gum.

"Well?"

"Do you suppose," Elsie began again, "that I could have some of them."

"Whatever for? They ain't no good for anything. A lot of 'em is so full of bullet holes you could strain tea through 'em. People around here call themselves hunters," she snorted again. "Most of the hides is pretty mangy, too."

"I would like to have a few of the good ones," Elsie said formally.

Kate turned her head part way and shouted towards the back. "Dad!"

71

And then to Elsie, she said, "You can ask him," and she took a pan of soapy water that smelled strongly of bleach and began washing down the counter behind the meat case.

Elsie waited, staring at the colored diagrams on the wall of how to cut up beef carcasses. In a few minutes Mr. Kolcek banged open the door from the back of the plant, yelled, "What!"

Elsie jumped at his loud voice, grew perceptibly smaller when he turned his eyes her way in response to Kate's pointing finger.

"She's asking about the deer hides," Kate said.

Kolcek wiped his hands on his bloody apron, stood staring at Elsie with his hands on his hips. "Yeah?"

"Umm, I was wondering," Elsie said. "Since you just throw out all the deer hides, if I could just pick out a few of the good ones."

Kolcek stared. "What the hell for?"

"To tan."

"What do you do with the leather?"

"I make things," Elsie said.

"What things?"

"Moccasins, handbags. Stuff like that."

Kolcek didn't answer for a minute. Then he said, "I'll let you have all the hides you can work, if I get one tanned hide out every two you do."

"Six," Elsie counter offered. "One out of every six."

Kolcek narrowed his eyes. "Six! That's robbery! Think you can get the best of me in a bargain, do you?"

Elsie just waited. A late season fly sailed drowsily around the room, repeatedly buzzing Kolcek's head. Kolcek swatted at it leaving a bloody streak on his cheek.

"One out of four," Kolcek offered.

Elsie shook her head. "No."

Kolcek considered,

"All right, all right, one out of five, but that's my best offer."

Elsie nodded. "Yes."

"All right. Well, come out in the back here and pick out your hides."

Elsie went through the door into the cold back butchering room, and Kolcek started to follow. Kate caught his sleeve.

"What are you going to do with tanned deer hides, Dad?"

"Hell if I know," he said, "but you can't let people have something for nothing, now can you?"

On the vacant lot behind the church, a big cottonwood tree stood sixty feet tall with a couple of sturdy branches coming off at right angles. It was surrounded by weeds and lilac bushes gone wild, some seven feet tall that masked the area around the tree from view. Getting stretcher frames had not been a problem.

Elsie drew a sketch and asked John Caulfield to make them for her. He was curious, but she only smiled at his questions, and so he agreed. He bought the lumber and put them together for her, delivering them after dark as she had asked, along with several lengths of sturdy rope, and some lighter-weight clothesline cord.

"I don't know what you're up to, Elsie," he had said, "but I guess it doesn't matter. I can't get into anymore trouble than I usually do."

"I'll make it up to you," she said.

She had only taken five hides for the first batch, choosing the biggest ones with the least amount of damage from the hunters' bullets and the processing of the carcass for meat. She put them to soak in her bathtub on a Sunday night, knowing that Nancy wouldn't come by for her weekly visit until Thursday. By Wednesday, the hides were scraped, laced into the stretcher frames and hanging in the cottonwood tree. The dirt, hair and flesh had been cleaned out of the bathtub, and the whole room disinfected with bleach. By the time she put the second batch of hides to soak, two weeks later, the first ones were ready to be pulled and worked into pliability with a soft, suede finish. Then the second week in December the weather turned unseasonably warm.

Snow from a few light early storms melted and ran in the streets; a light breeze dried the ground out and sun shone from an empty sky. People wore their winter coats unbuttoned in the mornings, shed them at noon and carried them home over their shoulders at the end of the day.

"It feels like spring," they said, and some folks who fancied themselves prophets, added, "but we'll pay for this later, you bet. We're going to have a hard winter when it hits and a cold, late spring."

Elsie did not enjoy the pleasant weather. The day the snow began to melt, she was suddenly ill, barely able to stagger over to the rectory to inform Father Horst, who informed the Mrs. Packwood and Mrs. Kemper, who were not happy and barely sympathetic. Christmas was coming on with all the extra baking and cleaning that they would now have to do themselves with Elsie down sick.

Nancy came bringing orange juice and soup and thinking that her remedies wouldn't do much good because Elsie didn't appear to have a cold or the flu. She tried to convince Elsie to go see the doctor for a diagnosis, but Elsie refused and Nancy worried. Elsie had lost weight, her face drawn, her bones beginning to protrude again. But, as Nancy told Father Horst, they couldn't simply drag her off to the doctor, and probably it was only a serious stomach virus, but she worried that it might be something caused by the original trauma at Mobridge.

Some days later, Elsie seemed to have stabilized. With the snow all gone, and the sun warming the air, one morning Father Horst took his pipe and a book to sit on the back stoop on the south side of the rectory. He had just tamped his pipe, lit it, and opened his book when a light breeze lifted his corn silk hair, bringing an odor from across the fence behind the lilac bushes.

Father Horst sniffed the air.

"Must be some dead cat or something," he thought and dismissed the odor, relaxing into his book. An hour later, the sun warmed his face and the breeze came up again and the smell rose, too.

"Whew!" he said, putting his book down and walking over to the old leaning fence. The smell was stronger, and he pressed down the top wires of the fence, stepped over and pushed his way through the lilac bushes. The smell hit him like a charnel house. He looked up at the five stretcher frames strung in the tree, swaying gently on their ropes in the breeze.

"What on earth is going on here?" he asked himself. He stood and stared at the frames, at bits of deer hide and hair scattered on the ground, and he knew.

"Oh, Elsie," he sighed, and went back over the fences, across to Elsie's little house and knocked on the door.

The curtain on the door window twitched, Elsie's face appeared and disappeared, but she didn't open the door for a couple of minutes, and when she did, she opened it only a few inches.

"Elsie, I know this isn't the best time, but I have to talk to you," Father Horst said. "Can I come in?"

She opened the door and stood aside, motioning him to the table to sit. She was dressed at least, instead of wearing the old nightgown that she had been wearing, and she seemed a little stronger. Her hair had been combed but not braided in her usual way, and it hung down around her shoulders. Father Horst thought it made her young and very vulnerable. He regretted that he had to talk to her.

"I have coffee," Elsie said and started to the stove to turn on the burner.

"No, no, Elsie. Thank you, but no." He sat with his hands in his lap wondering how to put what he had to say. The kitchen was clean and neat, no dishes in the sink, the worn linoleum floor scrubbed, but he smelled or imagined he still smelled the odor of rotting flesh. "You should sit down, Elsie," he said.

She pulled out a chair from the table, perched on the front part of the seat, her back very straight as if she were a school girl about to be punished by the principal.

He cleared his throat.

"I found your – ah, your tannery in the cottonwood tree. The smell led me to it. Elsie, you just can't do this. I'm sorry, but we have neighbors, and they will be complaining about the stink. Why did you do this? Didn't you think about the mess it would make?"

Elsie fumbled with her hands.

"We've always done this," she said. "My mother and I. We make leather, and then we make things from the leather and sell them."

He started to take her hand, and then thought about the smell that seemed to linger on himself and didn't.

"Elsie, what do you need more money for? If you need more, the parish can pay you a little more. We can't have you not getting enough to eat. There are ways – "

"No," Elsie said. "I get enough to eat. I just like to have a little extra money. It's a way."

"But, what about – I mean, can't you just buy leather already tanned?"

Elsie shook her head, stood up and went to the stove to turn on the burner under the coffee pot. She seemed to walk slowly, a little weak and indecisive in her movements. Father Horst felt like a mean spirited penny pincher.

The blue flame leaped under the coffee pot, and Elsie straightened and looked at him.

"Cow leather is too stiff," she said. "And thick. It's hard to push a needle through."

"Isn't there someplace to buy tanned deer skins?" His brain scurried here and there looking for an answer that would serve.

"Not the same," Elsie shook her head. "Commercial tanning with chemicals. I tan in that old way. I use brains."

Oh, God, he thought, brains – rotting internal organs of dead game animals. He felt like retching. Again, he imagined the smell had followed him into the room.

"How much longer before those ones in the tree are done?" he asked. "Is the stink going to get worse?"

"No, they are almost done. The stink will go away now."

He ran his hand through his hair, looked at his hand and wiped it on his pants leg.

"You don't have any more stashed somewhere around here do you?" He looked around the spic-and-span room, at the clean countertops, the calendar from Smith's Feed Store hanging on the wall, the red-and-white plaid dish towels neatly folded and draped over a cabinet door, the weeds? herbs? hanging on a string over the south facing window drying in the sunshine.

"No. That's all. I was going to go get another batch, and then I got sick."

"DON'T – don't go get anymore, Elsie, please. We'll find some way to get you the right kind of leather."

The smell of boiling coffee rose with the steam from the pot on the stove, masking the other smell.

"Promise me, Elsie," he said. "You just can't do this sort of thing when you live in town. It just won't work. The neighbors will complain, and we will have dogs and cats coming around."

"I promise," she said, reaching into an overhead cupboard and taking out a pair of cups. "Would you like coffee now?"

He sighed in relief, and said, "Yes, please. That would be nice. But only a half cup. You need to rest. I'm sorry I had to bother you about this right now, but – "

"It's all right," Elsie said.

"You sure the stink will go away pretty soon now?"

Elsie poured steaming black coffee into the cups, set the sugar bowl and a can of condensed milk on the table.

"Yes," she said. "But it will be better if it gets cold again soon."

When he had gone, Elsie put the cups in the sink, and then she went into the little bedroom and lay down on top of the old chenille bedspread. She was very tired, but she smiled a little as she drifted off to nap.

10

Christmas, 1967

On Christmas Day, Elsie was one of several guests at the Marks' house. She didn't want to go, but Nancy kept insisting, and finally Elsie gave in. She rode out to the Marks' farm with Father Horst, who made cheerful talk about the beauty of the Midnight Mass, the church decorated with evergreens that mingled their piney smell with the incense, the candles, the voices of the choir floating over the church from the balcony. Christmas was his favorite time of the ecumenical year.

The sun shone from a partly cloudy sky, but the wind whipped color into Elsie's thin face as she and Father Horst walked from the car to Nancy's back door. The house was old, a 1930s white clapboard that Donald had spent a lot of time and no inconsiderable amount of money on upgrading the plumbing and the wiring and adding additional insulation. Nancy continuously redecorated.

Now, she welcomed Father Horst and Elsie into her overly warm kitchen, heavy with the smell of turkey, sage dressing, homemade bread, and apple cinnamon pies. As usual, all her guests were in the kitchen, helping cook or just observing, and there were plenty of guests, some neighbors, some town folks, a good mix of old folks and younger families with kids including the sheriff, Ed Parker, and his wife, Janet, and their two teenaged daughters. Ed, being the good politician that he was, tried to rotate holidays, spending one at this constituent's house, the next at another's. His wife hated it, but his daughters hated it more. They wondered why their dad should worry about keeping a job that nobody else wanted anyway. Ed replied that maybe no one wanted to run for the office, but if he got fired, someone else would be glad to be appointed. Ed didn't always agree with his fellow sheriffs in the State of South Dakota, but on this one point, he and the sheriff from Mobridge were in complete accord. You got to keep friends in high places.

Dinner was served in the dining room for the adults while the kids ate at the breakfast bar in the kitchen, which meant their mothers had to make several trips to the kitchen to clean up dropped broken glasses and settle kid disputes. When it was finished, the men retired to the living room television, while the women went back to the kitchen to clean up the dishes and put away the leftovers.

Elsie found that by burying her arms to the elbows in soapy dish water, she could keep her back to the room, lessening her discomfort at being surrounded by women she barely knew, except for Nancy. When the dishes were done, Elsie dried her water-wrinkled hands and went with the other women to see Nancy's latest quilt project, and then they all joined the men in the living room. Elsie sat on the bench in front of the piano, watching the hands turn slowly on the cuckoo clock behind the sofa, but shortly, the children came to her, asking to see the turtles, and Elsie was talking softly to the children about the eating habits of turtles, about the different kinds that there were. The children exclaimed with delight when they touched the turtles noses and watched them pull back into their shells.

Father Horst was telling a story about Steve, an old Swedish farmer who had lost an arm in a tractor accident, but was still one of the best fishermen in the county.

"So, Steve is telling me about his fishing trip up to Angostura Dam last summer," Father Horst was saying. "And you know, he's telling me about the one that got away. He says he had it almost into the boat and then it slipped the hook and before he could catch it, it was gone. He tells me, it was THIS big." Father Horst puts one hand behind his back, holds out the other hand, palm perpendicular to the floor, making a chopping motion.

"And I say to him, well Steve that doesn't tell me much, cause I don't know where you're measuring FROM!"

As the room roared with laughter, Nancy noticed Ed beckoning her from the kitchen door.

"What do you need, Ed?" she hollered above the laughter.

"Can't find the cider," he said.

"It's just there, in the pan on the back of the stove."

He disappeared, and hollered back, "Where?"

She sighed and got up.

Ed stood in the kitchen, a cup of steaming cider in his hand.

"I found it," he said, "I just needed to speak to you in private. Sheriff Earl Peterson from Mobridge called me yesterday."

Nancy was puzzled.

"So? I'd think he probably calls you pretty regular about this and that."

"Oh, sure, sure. But this wasn't about the usual. Seems he got a funny phone call himself call from a rancher up in Mobridge name of Jack Mason."

"Oh, shit," Nancy said.

"Now, now, don't get in a dither yet. Just listen."

Nancy noticed that the pan of cider on the stove had simmered dry. She turned off the burner and put the pan in the sink. Already, it smelled a bit burned.

"Quit fussing and listen now," Ed said.

"Alright, already, just tell me what Mason wanted." She dreaded what he might tell her.

"I'm trying to. Mason asked Sheriff Peterson up there if there was a woman living down here name of Elsie Roberts, and the sheriff had to say yes, and why would Mason want to know. Mason said that he'd been hearing rumors. Some folks, especially the Indians, up in Mobridge are saying that his boys and their friend were up to no good with Elsie the night they got killed, and he's pretty hot about that. Says he can't believe anybody would take the word of an Indian squaw over decent white folks."

"A squaw! And what's that about decent white folks? Those little criminal bastards couldn't be called decent white folks by any stretch of the imagination! And why is this all coming up now, after all these months? I'd have of thought people would have something else to talk about by now."

"Wait, wait," Ed said. "There's more. Mason wants Peterson to look into what Elsie is doing down here. He thinks that she's accusing his boys of – of – well, you know, and he's saying that between the two of us, we'd better put a stop to it or he will."

"That son of a bitch!" Nancy stamped her foot, starting to pace the brown and white tiled floor. "That bastard! Elsie just wants to live in peace, that's why the sheriff up in Mobridge got her out of there."

"Well, is she talking about it?" Ed asked pointedly.

Nancy glared at him.

"Hell, no, she's not, and if you had any sense, you'd know that. She barely speaks two words to anybody, even me, and why the hell would she go talking about the most painful thing that ever happened to her to a bunch of white people that she doesn't even know?"

Ed leaned against the sink, turned the faucet on and ran water into the burned cider pan. The telephone rang, and Nancy moved to the wall phone but somebody in the living room picked it up.

"Well, is she saying anything to the Indians? I gather that's where the story is coming from up in Mobridge."

"No! No, she's not. The Indians in town act like Elsie doesn't exist. You'd think they were afraid of her or something. Damn it, she's the wronged person here, and you'd think she led those boys into sin and then killed them for it. What the hell is the matter with Mason? For that matter, what the hell is the matter with you? And Peterson?"

Nancy was outraged that Sheriff Peterson gave up Elsie's whereabouts so easily.

Parker put up a defensive hand.

"Hold it, a minute, here. I'm just checking things out. I wasn't accusing Elsie of anything."

Nancy's eyes were narrowed and she was breathing hard.

"Mason made serious threats against an innocent person. And even if Elsie was talking – which she isn't – Mason wouldn't have any right to retaliate against her. Did the good sheriff of Mobridge say anything to Mason about that? And what are you going to do about all of this?"

"Nothing, nothing. Well, Peterson didn't say he was going to do nothing, he just told Mason he'd check it out. That's when he called me."

81

"Well, now you've checked it out," Nancy said. "So, I can assume that you're going to report to Peterson, and he's going to tell Mason that Elsie isn't the one doing the talking? If, in fact, anyone at all is talking."

"Sure, sure. But you just make sure that Elsie does keep quiet."

Nancy was close to hitting him.

"Goddamn you! I TOLD you she isn't saying a word, and why would she? I wish to hell she would talk about it! This isn't just about an Indian girl being assaulted by white boys, it's about an ugly crime that men have been committing against women since time began."

"Ah, Nancy, don't turn it into that old argument," he said, and then realized he was pushing her too far. He stepped back, turned and looked out the window. The winter bare, dark branches of a young elm tree rattled and swayed in the rising wind. Clouds had moved in and the sun was fading behind a thick wall of gray.

Nancy would not be calmed.

"What's Mason going to do about it anyway? What the hell does he mean, 'put a stop to it'? There's nothing to put a stop to! And if he was any kind of 'decent white folks,' he would have put a stop to his sons' behavior," Nancy said.

Ed turned back to face Nancy, hands held up in front of him as if to ward off her words.

"I'm sorry," Ed said. "I didn't come across like I meant to. I only meant to warn you. Hell, far as I can see, Elsie is harmless. She just keeps in the background and minds her own business."

"Yes, she does!"

"Nancy, I'm just trying to keep things calm and smooth, you know. That's my job. And according to Peterson, Mason knows a lot of the big local ranchers down here. I guess he's the president or head of some state ranchers' association."

Nancy thought his voice sounded too high, pleading, and not at all like his political speeches when he kept his voice pitched low and confident.

"Worried about reelection, are you Ed?"

"Nancy, that isn't fair. I – "

Father Horst came into the kitchen, buttoning up his coat.

"Sorry to interrupt," he said. "That phone call was from the hospital. Old Mrs. Dubinski came in with a heart attack, and she's pretty bad off. I have to go, but, Elsie – I hate to make her leave the party. Could you – "

Nancy patted his arm.

"Go, go," she said. "Someone here will give Elsie a ride home."

"Thanks," he said back over his shoulder as he went out the door, lowering his head against the wind.

Nancy looked at Ed.

"Since you appear to have some good old boy connection with Sheriff Peterson why don't you get him to check out Mason's story up in Mobridge? You don't even know if there are really any rumors going on up there, or if Mason just got to thinking about it and decided to shut Elsie up *before* she said anything!"

"Well, I was going to call up there, but I thought I'd talk to you first. Find out if Elsie was talking, you know." His voice had lost the pleading quality, regained the deeper tone of authority and confidence.

"Elsie does talk, and it's a miracle she can after what she's been through, but she isn't talking about *that*."

She stared at him, but he wouldn't meet her eyes.

"I think our discussion is over," she said.

The younger guests took their exhausted, cranky kids and bowls of leftovers and went home, hollering their thank yous back through the cold evening air. The rest of the guests organized a couple of tables to play whist, and Nancy managed to get Elsie off the piano bench to play.

Elsie quickly caught on to the game and with Nancy as her partner, came close to winning a couple of rounds, losing because of the turn of the cards and not lack of skill. Nancy looked at Elsie across the table, at her dark face, thin and elegant with broad cheekbones, her full lips compressed as she concentrated on the cards she held in strong hands, hands with short nails.

Elsie should have been born to two parents who cared for each other, Nancy thought. She should have grown up with younger brothers and sisters to play with, to teach and watch over. She should have had boyfriends and then lovers who told her she was beautiful, who appreciated her industry, her shy smiles, her strength. She should have a husband, a home, children of her own, but instead, Elsie was a woman with something broken inside, something not physical. Who will love her, Nancy wondered. The Indians ignored her, so there was little chance of any romantic attachments there, and the white men considered her beneath them. Besides, could Elsie ever trust any white man, let alone love one?

Nancy remembered another Indian girl, much younger, named Loretta. Both Nancy and Loretta had gone to a small country grade school with all eight grades taught in two rooms, less than twenty students total. Loretta had been enrolled when Nancy was in the fifth grade, the only fifth grader, and even though she was four years older, Loretta was placed in fifth as well. Nancy was glad for a fellow student, someone to discuss the lessons with, but Loretta was not conversational. The only Indian student in the school, Loretta was ignored by the other students, but Nancy tried to befriend her. She sought Loretta out on the playground, when the others were engaged in a rousing game of tag and Loretta stood by the far fence, looking away, plucking idly at a sunflower.

Nancy had no idea why she pursued a friendship with an Indian girl who didn't seem the least interested in her or any of the other students, for that matter. Maybe it had something to do with an article she had read in a teen magazine about making newcomers feel welcome, even though the article was written about newcomers in a big city school with hundreds of students. Maybe it was because of old Father Trent's sermon one Sunday about doing unto others, about Jesus saying that if you do something unto the least of his children, it was as if it was done unto Him. Maybe it was her own feeling of isolation as an only child whose parents expected more than she could give.

Loretta stood out among the fair skinned, light haired students descended from German or Irish or Scandinavian immigrants. When the sun came through the south classroom window, blue highlights shimmered in Loretta's black hair that hung loose down her back. Nancy did not understand how Loretta could be so seemingly ignorant of her own exotic beauty, her long muscles showing beneath the sleeves and skirt of the dresses she wore – pink dresses, yellow dresses that set off her skin.

Then one day while Nancy was outside raking leaves, a chore she liked because it allowed her to escape her mother's dour, looming presence, Loretta appeared at the gate. She had walked across the field from her home a mile and a half away. They talked little, but sat on the step and smelled the burning leaves, went inside for spice cake that Nancy's mother had just taken out of the oven. Nancy's mother accepted Loretta without prying questions or surreptitious looks, and Nancy was grateful. It was as if Nancy's mother was aware that Loretta was like a fragile butterfly, prepared to sail away if approached too abruptly. After that, Loretta came occasionally, not often, and slowly began to talk more and more.

On the day of the annual school Easter egg hunt, Loretta came to school dressed up in a sky blue dress, white shoes with little high heels, and hose. She had matured overnight into a beautiful young woman, Nancy thought, while she herself remained locked in childhood, unchanging. Loretta's family was going to New Mexico, she told Nancy, and just shrugged when Nancy asked how long they would be gone, would they be staying with relatives or what. Loretta found one lavender egg and then sat down on the step, dress tucked primly around her knees.

When the hunt was over and all the children were counting their eggs and bragging over who had found the most, a shiny Ford station wagon with several adult Indians drove into the school yard. Loretta ran to the car, climbed into the back seat and the car drove away.

"Well, I never," the teacher said. "She didn't even ask permission to leave."

That was the last time that Nancy saw Loretta. She never returned to school, and two years later, Loretta and her younger cousin, Ernest, were killed in a one car accident. The newspaper account said that Loretta was speeding on a back country road, missed a wide turn, went off the road and over an embankment, where the car rolled several times. The picture in the paper made the wrecked car looked like a crushed egg. Loretta had not been drinking.

Now, looking across the card table at Elsie, Nancy wondered why young Indian women seemed the center of so much tragedy. What was it? Accident of birth? Or had God just singled them out to be designated shit catchers? But she couldn't blame God for it, and it wasn't just Indian women who attracted tragedy. Look at her own mother, dying to be a mother, not just once but three times over and the joy of it denied her, except for Nancy. And what about herself? She glanced at Ed's two daughters sitting on the sofa, one idly leafing through a magazine, the other indolently licking a candy cane. The candy cane licker was severely overweight, and Nancy thought she'd fix that if the girl were hers. But she wasn't.

"Nancy! Nancy, it's your play!" Ed's wife, Janet, who was also his partner in the game, was talking to her, and Ed was nudging her arm.

"Oh, sorry," Nancy said, and hastily chose a card and tossed it into the play, which brought a delighted crow from Ed.

"You can't trump a queen with a jack," he said as he raked in the pile.

"Sorry, Elsie, I blew that one," Nancy apologized to Elsie, who smiled and touched Nancy's hand. "I guess I'm just tired."

When the hand was played out and the points totaled up, the players sat back and yawned. The other table of players had given up and wandered off to graze on a bit more turkey and dressing, or another piece of fudge.

The cuckoo clock was just striking eleven as the guests gathered up their pans and dishes in which they had brought their food contributions, now filled with leftovers, hunted their coats out and prepared to leave. Nancy fetched her own coat preparing to drive Elsie home.

Donald removed the coat and hung it back up.

"You got up to put the turkey on at three a.m.," he said, "and you said you'd come back to bed, but you didn't. You've been running ever since, so why don't you just relax? I'll take Elsie home."

Nancy briefly leaned her head on his chest.

"I do feel a headache coming on," she said.

Donald gave her a little squeeze.

"I'll be back before you know it," he said.

Sunshine coming through the east windows awakened Nancy early the next morning, confusing her for a moment because there were no east windows in her bedroom. It took a few moments for her to realize that she wasn't in her bedroom, but had fallen asleep on the living room sofa. Even though she had pulled the afghan down over herself in the night, she was chilly. Groggily she rose and turned up the thermostat, went to the kitchen and started a pot of coffee, but as she stared out the window waiting for the water to fill the pot, she noticed something missing – Donald's blue Ford pickup was not parked out front. The old familiar feeling of dread and anguish and betrayal climbed from her belly to her throat like a bad case of heart burn. She knew better, but she hoped that maybe his truck had broken down, and he had walked home.

She poured the water into the coffee maker, put in the grounds and switched it on. She knew he wouldn't be there, but she checked the bedroom just in case, and there, still laid out on the bed, was the quilt she had been showing the women the night before, on top of the bed, unslept in.

Maybe there had been an accident and this time he was dead. Maybe he had been in an accident with Elsie, and she was dead, too!

Nancy ran to the phone and dialed Father Horst's number. It rang five times, ten, twelve before Father Horst's sleepy voice answered the phone.

"Hello?"

"Father, this is Nancy. I know it's too early to be calling, but I wonder if you know if Donald got Elsie home all right last night."

A sleepy silence, and then he said, "Can't you ask him?"

"He isn't home," Nancy said with an edge in her voice.

Again a short pause, and then Father Horst's voice came on again, calm and strong and very awake now.

"I'm sorry, Nancy. I haven't seen Elsie this morning, but it is early. I got in late last night – at the hospital with Mrs. Dubinski, you know. I never paid any attention to whether or not Elsie's lights were on. Tell you what, let me get dressed and I'll go check. Okay? I'll call you right back."

"Yes. Okay. Thank you, Father."

Nancy hung up the phone and poured herself a cup of coffee. She forced herself to sit at the kitchen table instead of pacing, still shivering because the house hadn't warmed up yet. She cursed herself for not suspecting Donald's motives in volunteering to take Elsie home. It was just an excuse to get away from home, to go on one of his drunken chases around the reservation with who knew which of the women he dallied with. She knew, had even got him to admit it a couple of times, when he was in a particularly remorseful mood, when she had accused herself of being the cause of it all.

"It's me, isn't it?" she had said. "If I could have had kids, it would all be different."

He had grabbed her shoulders and looked into her eyes.

"No," he said. "It's just me. It wouldn't matter if we had a dozen kids. It's not your fault, it's mine. I just – I just can't help myself."

She'd pleaded with him then.

"Is it the drinking or the women? What can I do to make you happy?"

He turned away shaking his head. "I don't know."

She should have known last night what he was up to, she thought. It had been three months since his last binge – a three day absence when he returned smelling of alcohol and sweat and sex, a rough growth of dark beard mingled with a few gray whiskers, and eyes that looked like burned holes in blanket. He'd stumbled in late in the afternoon, while she was making up the last of the summer tomatoes into piccalilli. Even above the smell of hot tomatoes and peppers, vinegar and spices, she could smell his guilt. He didn't look her in the eye, tried to hug her and she pushed him away, didn't speak. He had started out of the kitchen, turned and stood staring at her back; she felt his red eyes on her.

He did the usual. Showered, slept for twenty-four hours, and then threw himself into work on the farm, speaking to her gently even when she didn't answer. As usual, her silence was broken by the presence of visitors, neighbors came by to borrow Donald's forge to repair a broken piece of equipment. Nancy's pride wouldn't allow her to exhibit her marital problems in front of friends, so she resumed speaking to Donald in front of them and naturally carried it over after the company left.

He had been so good since that last time, she told herself, but she had always known deep inside that it couldn't last, that the day would come when she least expected it that he would take off again and not come home for a day or two or longer. She never knew what precipitated his wanderings, could figure out no pattern, except that he ran around more in the wintertime when the workload on the farm was lighter. He was just there and all was well, then he was gone, and everything was wrong. Sometimes she secretly hoped he would be killed in a car accident. It might be better than this living uncertainty, and the knowledge that even though the neighbors didn't talk to her about the situation, they certainly talked among themselves, and worse yet, she felt their unspoken pity.

She jumped when the phone rang. It was Father Horst.

"Hi, Nancy. I just talked to Elsie. Woke her up to do it, but she says Donald brought her home and then left. She said he stopped at the M & M package store and bought a bottle before he dropped her off. She thought he was going right back home. That's all she knows."

Nancy sighed. So Elsie was safe – good – but Donald was off again – not good.

"I'm relieved that Elsie is okay," Nancy said.

"Yes. Me, too. Sorry I don't know anymore about where Donald is. I expect he's okay wherever he is. Well, not really okay, but you know what I mean."

"I know. Thanks, Father," Nancy said and started to hang up. "Oh, how is Mrs. Dubinski?"

"She passed away early this morning," Father Horst said. "The wake and rosary will be held tonight and burial mass on Friday." He cleared his throat. "I know you might not feel like supervising the kitchen for the family dinner after mass, so . . ."

"Oh, no. I'll be glad to do it, Father. It – it helps me keep my mind off things."

"All right. If there's anything I can do for you?"

"No, no. I'm fine."

She wasn't fine. She was numb.

11

January 20, 1970

How the Crow Got to Be Black

You sit in Oscar's orange velour chair, Lowan asleep on the floor at your feet, having decided after your constant visits that you are no threat to his position. It is too hot in the room for the long underwear you have put on beneath jeans, flannel shirt, work boots. Your armpits are damp, forehead beaded with sweat. Outside, the wind howls, picking up handfuls of snow flakes, fine and hard as sand, flinging them against the windows and the walls with harsh rattling sounds. You wonder why anyone would choose to live in a place with freezing cold winter blizzards and broiling hot summer heat. North. There's nothing good about it. You wonder what the weather is like now down South, but you know: cool cloudy days with cold nights that send damp chill to the bone, alternating with unseasonable warmth when the sun and the sky conspire to make you believe it is spring when it isn't. Soon, the camellias and the hibiscus will burst into red and orange and fuchsia pink, that color that always makes you think of a woman, a bad woman, a woman who opens her fuchsia in the darkness of night, sweet and full bloomed. But, now, here, outside is a blank white page forecasting emptiness.

Oscar sits on the sunken end of the sofa, head tilted back, snoring softly, his cup of coffee cooling on the table beside him.

A gust of wind raises a shingle on the roof, finds a pathway beneath and raises a whining howl, eerie, a live spirit wailing for entrance.

Oscar stops snoring, blinks and raises his head, wiping a bit of drool from the corner of his mouth.

"It's a good day to sleep," he says, as his hand fumbles for his coffee cup. "It's a good day to remember and tell stories."

He wants you to ask for a story, you think, but you are preoccupied with other matters, and the story you want to hear isn't the same as the rest of the one you need to hear.

"I wonder. Why does everything official take so much longer in small towns?" you ask.

Oscar takes a long noisy sip of cold coffee before he answers.

"Everybody sees themselves as lots more important than they are," Oscar says. "And everybody wants to show everyone else that they're the most important. No sense of hurry. Hurry means that someone else is directing you, pushing you, and you lose importance. So they slow down, make people push them, make people wait. You have to pretend that there is no hurry, if you want something done fast. Because then whoever is in charge thinks they can move fast because they want to. It's a game. We got a name for those people that work in the courthouse. We call them the lightning people, cause, you know, they move so fast. But you know what follows, lightning, right? Thunder! Thunder beings going to punish those courthouse lightnings someday."

Lowan wakes, glances up at Oscar, stretches and resumes his position.

"It's just lazy white folk," you say. "I just want to get this business tended to and go home."

Oscar motions towards the window.

"Look," he says. "Nobody with any sense is going anywhere right now. There are some who say that Waziye, the old wizard of the North, brings storms to punish us, to make us suffer. I say that's wrong. Maybe that's what Waziye thinks, too, but if you just don't fight the storm, then it's a gift. Children are free from school, adults are free from work. Don't fret about what you can't do. Enjoy the time Waziye gives to be with your family at a time when you wouldn't usually get to. Relax, think. Remember. Eat good food. It's a time out from time, when you don't have to be doing anything, and ain't much anybody can do to you."

Family. Well, you don't have any here, that's for sure.

He catches your eye, and probably your thoughts, because he says softly, "*Mitakuye oyasin.*"

92

All right, you think, whatever he means. If he says so. You look out the window at the snow swirling in the wind, knowing that the courthouse is closed, the officials are home, and even if they were at work, they would not hurry, but smile at you, hand you one more form to fill out, tell you some story like, it has to go before the judge for a decision, but he is out of town visiting his son in Arizona and when he gets back . . . maybe, then. Or some other bureaucratic excuse for doing nothing.

"Long time ago," Oscar begins, and you know you're going to get a story whether you want one or not. You just hope that it isn't one about patience because yours is about run out, and you don't want to hear about your own faults.

"Wait," Oscar says. "We need more coffee for this one." He takes your cup and his to the kitchen and returns with steaming cups, slopping a little because he hasn't left room for the evaporated milk.

He puts the cups down on the end table and sits heavily, licking the coffee spill from his hand. He takes a deep breath, slaps both hands down on his thighs.

"Well, now, it begins. Long time ago, crows were all white."

He chuckles a bit and looks at you. "You're gonna appreciate this one," he says in an aside.

"They say that all crows were white originally, you see. This was before the people had horses or guns, but still we depended on the buffalo for everything. They were our food, our clothing, our houses, all. Hunting them was hard, very hard. We had to creep up on them, silently, and then LET FLY with our stone arrows. Many times, the buffalo, they would be wounded but not die, and in their fear and pain, run away, and the people would have no food, they say. But sometimes, the people didn't get a chance to shoot their arrows, because of the crows who were friends with the buffalo. When the crows would see the people coming for the buffalo, the crows would fly high and say to the buffalo, 'CAW CAW. The hunters are coming! The hunters are coming! Run!'

"And so, more and more the people could not get close enough to kill buffalo. The people grew weak and were starving, they say. So the people held a council. They talked and they decided that the crow that warned the buffalo the most often was the biggest, whitest crow of them all. The people decided upon a plan.

"The warriors gathered their weapons and began to creep up on the herd, except for one warrior who covered himself with a buffalo hide and quietly mingled himself with the herd. Of course, the biggest white crow saw him and flew over the buffalo screaming, 'CAW CAW CAW. The hunters are near; the hunters are coming. Run!'

"The buffalo all ran away except for the warrior who had disguised himself as a buffalo. The big white crow flew down to him, shouting, 'Why aren't you running? Didn't you hear me warn you?'

"The warrior beneath the buffalo robe did not answer but went on pretending to eat grass. The crow came closer, shouting louder.

"Then

"QUICKLY the warrior beneath the hide GRABBED that big crow's legs and tied them with a piece of sinew.

"That crow, he was shocked, but he didn't know what to do or say, so he just went on crying, 'CAW CAW CAW.' As he shouted, he flapped his wings but he couldn't get loose.

"So the warrior took the crow to the council so they could decide what to do. The warriors talked and talked but couldn't decide on a plan. Then, one of the young warriors, angry about the waiting, he grabbed that big white crow and flung him into the fire. And pretty quick the fire burned through the sinew and set the crow free. But his feathers were singed and all covered with soot, and ever since crows have all been black."

You wait for more of the story, but Oscar has stopped.

"But," you ask, "did the crows still warn the buffalo? How did the people keep from starving?"

Oscar looks disgusted. "It isn't about *that*," he says. "It's a story about how the crow became black."

"Yes," you say, "but I still want to know about the starving people."

Oscar holds out his arm and says, "Feel. Go on, touch me."

Not understanding, you touch his arm, his skin feels old and papery.

94

"See?"

"No," you say.

He rolls his eyes. "The people didn't starve! I'm here, we're here, that's proof we didn't starve."

He's getting annoyed with you now, but you still want an answer.

He sighs.

"Some people can't figure out their own answers," he complains. "Gotta have it all explained for you."

Lowan sits up and looks at you, as if he too, is embarrassed by your ignorance.

"Horses!" Oscar says. "We got horses, and then it didn't matter if the crows warned the buffalo, we could ride our horses fast enough to catch the buffalo when they ran."

You feel pretty silly, for not discovering the obvious answer on your own.

Oscar senses that, and he lets you off the hook. He slaps you on the knee.

"Come on," he says. "Beans are about ready. Let's eat."

After the last pink bean heart, the last drop of soup and tiny chunk of ham has been wiped from your plates with a bit of bread, you sit back a minute and think about the pleasure of a full stomach and a warm room with pleasant company, maybe not family, but what answers for family now, while the wind howls outside. When the dishes are washed and put away, and you are thinking you're ready for more of Elsie's story, but that Oscar has decided, like the courthouse officials, to make you wait for the rest of it, he beckons you back to the living room, sits, and with his hands crossed over his full belly, he begins.

"Right after Christmas Elsie went back to work, and for a while, there weren't any more phone calls from Mason up in Mobridge. If he showed up around here, nobody knew anything about it. The winter got bit off piece by piece. Elsie gained weight and went back doing what she had done before, except that she started working up the hides she had tanned into things she could sell. She made handbags like her mother had done, big ones of softened buckskin with beadwork in bright blues and reds and yellows. She beaded belts, and made a few dolls like her mother had made for her with their own tiny costumes of soft deerskin and beaded eyes and noses and mouths. She took them down to the co-op down on the main highway. The manager at the co-op bought the items figuring he could sell them to the tourists going through on their way to the Black Hills. Course, there weren't any tourists yet, but there would be. The manager said he was 'building his inventory.' A few were even bought by local people, people who wanted a novelty item to send to relatives back east.

"When she had used up all the tanned hides she had, she went to Kolcek and offered to buy the ones that he'd taken for his share. Since he didn't know what do with them anyway, he sold them back to her.

"And then she made herself a pair of moccasins, soft creamy leather with a turtle beaded on each toe in black and green and white, with red beads for the nostrils. A natural colored turtle, not a painted one.

"And Nancy Marks saw Elsie's moccasins."

12

January 16, 1968

Moccasins

It was one of those January days when the air feels like a deep freeze, and the sun shines out of a clear blue sky like a billion-trillion-volt light bulb. Nancy's boots crunched on the frozen snow as she walked up the sidewalk and knocked on Elsie's door. The curtain on the door window parted briefly; Elsie smiled and opened the door.

"Elsie, I can't stay but just a few minutes," Nancy said, stamping the snow off her boots before she stepped onto Elsie's clean floor.

"There's coffee," Elsie said, waving at the bubbling pot on the stove. "Just fresh."

"Well . . . you talked me into it," Nancy said. She took off her coat and draped it on the back of a chair and sat. She didn't have any purpose in coming to see Elsie, but she had just come from Sheriff Ed's office where she learned there had been no more phone calls from Mason, not so much as a peep. She was relieved, and just wanted to see Elsie, to reassure herself that Elsie was truly all right.

Elsie brought cups, canned milk, and sugar to the table and poured the hot, rich-smelling coffee into the cups.

"I got gas at the co-op this afternoon and guess what? That bag you made with the red and black beading? It's sold! The stuff may be all gone before the tourists even start coming through."

"Good," Elsie said. "I have leather left, so I can make more. Look."

She stuck her feet out to show off her moccasins, creamy leather with a turtle beaded on each toe.

"Oh, Elsie, they're beautiful! And you've put turtles on them, too."

Elsie held up her right foot.

"See, this one is Tom."

Then she held up her left foot.

"And this one is Dick."

"But you've not colored them red and yellow. They look like regular colored turtles. But, how do you know which is which?"

"Tom's on the right, and Dick's on the left."

She took them off and handed them to Nancy to be admired.

"You know, you should make moccasins to sell, too, Elsie," she said.

Elsie shook her head.

"NoOOo. I don't know about sizes and things like that. I have to measure the person's foot."

"Too bad," Nancy said. "These are so much nicer than those commercial ones you buy in the store." She had a thought.

"You can make them, though, I mean, if you can measure the person's foot, like you say?"

"Sure."

"I was trying to think of a present for Donald's birthday next month. A pair of these moccasins would be perfect. Do you think you could make a pair to fit if you had a pair of his shoes to go by?"

Elsie wrinkled her forehead and thought.

"I don't know. I'd be afraid to try that."

"Hmm. Well, I guess it wouldn't have to be a surprise present. I could get Donald to come by so you could measure his foot. Would you make a pair then?"

Elsie nodded and smiled.

"Okay then. How about if he came by on Saturday? But don't put turtles on the toes, okay?"

Elsie laughed.

"One time," she said, "This man had my mother make him a pair of moccasins and he told her he wanted a bullhead beaded on each toe. So my mother made them, and when he came to pick them up, he was maaadd!! See my mother thought he meant bullhead like the fish, you know? So there was a black leaping fish on the toe of each moccasin. He wanted a cattle kind of bull head, you know?" Elsie made horns with her fingers beside her head.

"Oh, no!" Nancy laughed. "So, did he take them anyway?"

"Yes, after a while, he thought it was funny, too." Elsie said. "Then my mother got orders from a few fishermen to make bullhead moccasins for them."

Nancy shook her finger at Elsie.

"No bullheads on Donald's moccasins – neither fish or nor cattle. Maybe, I don't know, could you do a sheaf of wheat?"

13

January 22, 1970

Oscar's B & B

It's the kids' laughter that woke you, and you smile thinking about growing up with your brothers and sisters and cousins and the Sunday rowdies with all of you climbing over and under and around and pilfering through everything in your grandma's house, while their mamas and aunties shake their heads and yell, "No! I said you don't touch that! If I have to get up from here . . ."

But then you open your eyes and it's like no place you remember, and the kids' voices are all wrong, and you see your breath floating in a tiny fog above your mouth, a little cloud that hides where you are and how you got here, and even who you are. You turn your head towards a dim light coming from the side and there's a window covered with a blanket outlined by a tiny rim of light. The air smells of dark earth and old leather, dust and ancient perfume, distant. Not home. No. You are in a wrong place in a wrong time and just before the panic bubbles up like bile from your gut, you remember.

You are in Oscar's spare bedroom. Well, he calls it the spare bedroom. Just yesterday, seems days ago, as you were about to go back to the hotel through the snow that swirled like it was flung out of a central point in the air right in front of your eyes, Oscar said, "Do you feel like a round trip?"

You didn't get it, wondered if this was the punch line to another one of his stories that you didn't want to admit you didn't understand.

"If you don't mind the double walk, why don't you go get your stuff and come back here. Stay with me. I got a spare bedroom. Company may get a little boring, but the food's good. And it's free."

You think about the dwindling money in your wallet and feel like now you can close the zipper on it, or at least have to open it less often. You think about how comfortable Oscar is to be with, and even that you don't mind Lowan's yapping. Much.

"I've always been good at walking," you say. You look out the window, knowing night is coming on, not like getting dark, but more like the slow lowering of a heavy down curtain.

"I like to walk at night."

Oscar squints out the window.

"You need a hand with your stuff?" he asks.

"No, I can get it all in one trip."

"Good," he says, slapping you on the back. "I hate night walking in the cold. I'll keep the fire going."

Forty-five minutes later you are back at Oscar's carrying your single bag, chilled to the core, cheeks numb beneath the scarf you've wrapped over the lower half of your face.

The door to the spare room sticks and resists as if Oscar welcomes you, but the house doesn't. He puts a shoulder to it, and it gives suddenly so he falls inward, stumbling as he does on something half across the doorway.

"Dammit," he says. "Forgot about the potatoes."

There's a hundred-pound sack of potatoes, open and partly spilled right there.

"Spuds keep in here pretty good in the cold. Don't grow those fat wormy whiskers all over before I get them eat up."

Oscar flicks the light switch, but nothing happens.

"Hmm, bulb must be burned out."

He flicks his Zippo, and the room is lit like a voodoo queen's consulting room, dim objects of unknown entity lurk here and there, blurry photos and pictures on the wall of unknown people and places and things. Oscar begins heaving things to one side, pushing boxes and things that make skreeking noises as they resist movement on the cold linoleum floor. It's not a spare bedroom, you realize, it's the storeroom for Oscar's life.

"Here, wait. I got a flashlight," you say. You set your bag down on the floor, rummaging.

The light is tiny, not one of those new jobbies that light up a space like airport landing lights, but in the smallness of the room, it is enough. There's a bed with a black cast-iron head and footboard, a faded pattern of roses painted on the panel at the head. It's mounded up with clothes as if a giant sleeping body reposed upon it. Oscar starts grabbing armloads of the clothes and piling them on top of the full cardboard boxes that are stacked against the opposite wall. You position the flashlight on top of what appears to be a bureau, step forward to help, feeling the softness of the fabrics, so cool and smooth to the touch that they feel wet. You realize they aren't Oscar's clothes, but the clothes of his dead wife that he has never sorted out to give away. Beneath the heaps of clothes, there's a sway-bellied mattress on the bed with a quilt in a star pattern of blues and greens and purples, wrinkled in places as if some giant's body had pressed its life into the fabric.

"*Waste yelo.*" Oscar says.

He half closes the door revealing a sturdy hook on the back, dark heavy clothes hanging from it like a dangling body. He lifts up on them, as if to save them the choking death, carries them to the pile and places them lovingly on top.

He points back at the hook.

"Your very own closet," he says.

"Thank you," you say.

He shrugs his shoulders.

"We can leave the door open at night so some heat can come in here."

You think he could leave the door open forever and the place would still be as cold as a refrigerator. Already your toes and even your butt feels chilled, your nose a little runny, but then you think about the money flying all by itself out of your wallet and into that little box behind the clerk's desk at the Dakota Hotel.

"This will do me just fine," you say.

"Good. I thought you'd think that," he says. "Meals are when I feel like fixing them. If you get hungry in between times, help yourself, just don't touch the brownies on top of the refrigerator without asking first. My daughter makes them special for me."

"Wouldn't dream of it," you say. "Never been a brownie toucher."

Now, as you come awake more, you know that it wasn't the kids' voices in the living room that woke you, but the absence of sound beneath their voices, and you look towards the window again. The storm is over, no snow pelting the windows. It's quiet outside. You start to get up, but it's a labor, piled up as you are with heavy quilts like a bear in a den.

You glance through the partly open doorway and peer through the kitchen into the living room where you can see the blue-jeaned knees of someone sitting on the sofa, and two kids, maybe six and eight years old, darting back and forth like – like – the phrase comes into your head – like wild Indians. You smother a laugh, and step into the living room.

"*Hau, kola,*" Oscar says.

"Good morning," you answer.

"I said, *hau, kola.*"

"How, cola," you repeat.

Oscar chuckles at the stout, dark-haired woman on the sofa.

"I'll make an Indi'n out of him, yet."

The woman's full mouth curls down in disgust, and her hands go down to touch the shoulders of the two kids – boys – who have become suddenly motionless at her feet, their big eyes looking up at the stranger.

"Looks too close to midnight to me," she says sourly.

Oscar's face is a mask, but he says pointedly, "You're about half an hour to midnight yourself."

"All right, Dad, I know I need to learn to be more polite. That's what you're always telling me," she says to Oscar, and then to the boys, "That pan of brownies is on the table. You can have one each, now."

The boys leap up and run past you, one on each side as if you were a post in their river of motion.

"My daughter, Irene. We say *cunksi,*" Oscar says indicating the woman with his lips.

"Pleased to meet you, ma'am," you say and step forward to take her smooth warm hand. Her fingers are long, the palm and fingers calloused and hard. She looks into your face, seriously, as if she expects to find something there and isn't sure if she should welcome it or kill it.

"Better get some coffee," Oscar says. "Irene brings news that needs caffeine to smooth it down."

Irene stands up.

"I'll get it," she says. "I could use a refill." She takes her cup and Oscar's and walks to the kitchen. She wears baggy jeans, a worn sweatshirt, old cracked leather shoes that look wet, as if she walked through snow in them, and you know that she did. You wonder if Elsie looked like Irene.

"No," Oscar says behind you. "Elsie was bigger. Irene is a few years older, too."

You turn sharply and look at Oscar.

He points a finger to his temple and says, "Kidneys."

"Hey, hey!" Irene yells out in the kitchen. "I didn't say you eat half the pan."

There is a mumbled response, then the sounds of slaps and scuffling and laughter.

Irene bears the coffee cups back, the three steaming cups tripoded between her fingers. She hasn't put any cream in, but you decide not to say anything.

"Disrespectful little whelps," she says.

Oscar sighs.

"You weren't raised like that," he says to her. "Nobody hit you kids. That ain't the Indi'n way."

Irene settles herself on the sofa, and you sit perched on the edge at the other end.

"Well, maybe it's the new Indi'n way," she says. "Times change."

There is a moment of silence as you all three blow on the hot coffee to cool it, and the kids giggle in the kitchen.

"Irene works at the hotel," Oscar begins.

You look at her in surprise, not remembering seeing her there, wondering if she is one of those silent maids, like the unseen wife who always makes sure the bed is made, the laundry done, floors swept, and trash taken out.

"I work at the Wayside Hotel," Irene says. "The new one down on Highway 18."

You wonder what that has to do with anything, but you can tell by the tense way that she and Oscar are sitting that it is something, something important that you had better pay attention to.

"Yes?" You take a sip of the coffee, trying not to wince at the bitter blackness of it, the lack of the usual evaporated milk to take the bite away.

"Night before last, just before the storm came in?"

Is she asking you if that's true? That the storm came in? But you nod.

"A man came in for a room, a man I didn't know."

"That's not right for this time of year," Oscar says. "Not tourist season."

Irene stares at him as if to say it's her story, and she's going to tell it.

"We get salesmen on their regular route you know, but this guy wasn't anybody I knew. You can't be too nosey, you know, can't look too close at the name on the check-in card, at least until after the people have gone on to their room. But then I looked. His handwriting is real good. He wrote his name as Jack Mason from Mobridge."

"You mean – "

She nods.

"Yeah. Those Mason boys from Mobridge. It's their dad."

The coffee hasn't gotten any better tasting.

"You're sure?"

"Well, I guess Jack Mason is a pretty common name, but, I mean, South Dakota doesn't have a very big population, and Mobridge is pretty damned small. I don't think there's another Jack Mason in Mobridge."

You're looking at the black coffee in the cup, and everything else is just as dark, dark as a tomb, dark as a grave, dark as – well, that's just plain stupid, you tell yourself. But maybe not. Didn't Jack Mason threaten Elsie? Well, not directly, but the threat was there, just because he *thought* that *maybe* she talked about what happened. And nobody ever asked him where he was on the night that Elsie died. They just assumed – or maybe they didn't assume. Maybe they knew something. Well, you ask yourself, and who the hell is *they*? What *they* are we talking about here? But you know the answer to that one, too. The *they* who thought they had the answer, thought they knew who killed Elsie, and later on, if it turned out wrong, well, that was a mystery, and had nothing to do with Jack Mason, or if it did *they* didn't want to know about it. She was dead and buried and forgotten. Forgotten, that is, until you took your savings out of the bank and came to Jackson, came to Jackson with a mouthful of questions and a face that stood out in Jackson like a raisin in an oatmeal cookie.

"Well, maybe he's here for a what-do-call-it? A rancher's convention or something?" You're reaching for a reason that isn't going to be there, and you know it.

Oscar looks down at his feet, wide old man's feet in thick socks stuffed into those old, worn slippers of his.

Irene gives that little twist of her head, rolls her eyes up at the cobwebbed ceiling.

"No. And, yes, I'm sure of it. In a town this size, your neighbor knows you farted before the stink can even get over to their house. If there was anything going on in this town besides time and the rent, I'd know about it. There isn't any convention," she says.

He can't be here because of you, that's just too – too – too Hollywood thriller movie.

"Maybe he's here to visit friends."

"Uh, uh," Irene says. "If you go to visit friends, you stay at their house, not in a hotel."

She's right. Oscar isn't really your friend, or well, he's pretty new for a friend, and yet, you're staying at his house and not in a hotel.

"Besides," she goes on, "Jack Mason doesn't have any friends, just suck-ups, and suck-ups go to him for the leavings, or he summons them. He doesn't drive almost all the way across the state in a storm just to offer favors to suck-ups."

So, there's no way around it.

"Who's the suck-up in this town?" you ask.

Sharp voices come from the kitchen; the boys are in a fuss.

"*Wastepi!*"

Whatever she said has no effect on the fight in the kitchen, but she ignores it. Lowan gets up and runs to the kitchen, as if he's been seconded to referee.

"Somebody I been talking to at the courthouse," you guess aloud.

Oscar raises his eyebrows.

"Everybody you been talking to at the courthouse," he says. "If you talk to one of those biddies, you've told everyone. Word gets around faster than the moccasin telegraph. Well, maybe not *quite* that fast."

"But, I'm not doing anything, not asking those people to tell me anything about Elsie," and then you remember who you're talking to now, who you've been asking questions.

"No," Oscar says quietly. "I'm a member of the moccasin telegraph, but I don't tell any of my stories to *wasicu*, not the important ones, anyways."

You're ashamed for your thought, but he won't let you be embarrassed for long. From the battered little side table, he picks up an empty cigarette pack, wads it up and pitches it at you.

"Don't be flattering yourself," he says. "Ain't no way you'd ever pass for a *wasicu*."

The balled up cigarette pack bounces off your chest, lands in the middle of the mud-tracked linoleum. Lowan dashes back from the kitchen, mouths the wad of paper, and trots behind the sofa with it.

"Won't the nicotine on that make him sick?" you ask.

"Shee-it," Irene says. "That dog should've died of secondhand smoke two months ago, just like the first one did."

"No, no," Oscar says. "Tiger, well, I don't know what killed him. But Lowan, he's smart. You know, that little bit of nicotine on that pack? It's like he's self-medicating. A little bit at a time and – " he snaps his fingers, " – all of a sudden, he's immune. Sort of, hair of the dog that bit him."

His shoulders shake, and Irene slaps him on the shoulder.

"Aww, Dad!"

It's a moment of lightness, a moment that ends in silence that stretches like a rubber band, close to the limit of its tensile strength.

"I can't leave her now," you say.

"No," Oscar agrees. "We left her. We left it alone when we shouldn't have. But I'd get done what I needed to and get out of town if I were you."

The boys are back, sliding cautiously around you, pulling on Irene's arm.

"Mama, let's go. We want to go sledding down the church hill," the littlest one says.

"It's a snow day," she says, pulling her arm away. "They let school out, so if they see you sledding, they'll think you could have been in school. Then next time it comes a storm, they won't cancel school. You want that?"

"That's crap," the bigger one says. "They cancel school 'cause the country kids can't make it into town. They don't care about town kids. Come on, Mama, let's go."

Irene sighs and grabs her coat off the back of the couch.

"All right, all right."

"I get the sled first!" the little one hollers.

"Nuh-uh," the bigger one shoves him, and the little one reels backwards, bumping into the stacked televisions. The top one rocks a little.

"Don't be doing that," Oscar admonishes quietly. "That's priceless entertainment value."

"I think I'm doing something really nice for them, saving up to get them a sled for Christmas. But they fight over it every time it snows. Just ruins the whole idea of it," Irene complains.

She finishes buttoning her coat while the kids fling on their own wraps and run out the door.

Oscar reaches up his arms, and she leans over and kisses his cheek.

"*Cunski*," he says.

You stand up, and she looks you up and down, but she must have decided that you're all right because she rests her hand lightly on your shoulder for a minute, turns away, and then the door closes behind them leaving a chill from the outside that lingers and the silence of their absence.

"I like your daughter," you say to Oscar.

He smiles, a big wide smile.

"She's a good one," he says. "Now, Charles, that brother of hers!" He shakes his head.

You've started it now, and you've already spent half the money that you took years to save up, so you tell yourself you might as well finish it, no matter how it turns out.

14

January 23, 1970, Morning

Red Tape

It's one of those days so cold that the moisture inside your nose freezes as you walk to the courthouse, but that isn't all that's cold. There's this even colder icy spot right between your shoulders where you imagine that Jack Mason's bullet is going to go. The traffic is pretty heavy for a small town, everyone come to town to replenish their larders after the storm and to stock up for the next one, but also to share stories with their neighbors about how they made it through the storm, how the cattle are doing, and who has the deepest snow. The chains on the pickup trucks and cars crunch on the snow-packed Main Street, jingle as the tires go around. The air is still with blue exhaust hanging in the air, not even rising to the low gray cloud ceiling overhead. You wonder if that new blue Ford is his pickup, or maybe that black one. You wonder if the license tag on his vehicle would be different than the ones here in Jackson. A different prefix maybe? Or not? You wish that you had asked Irene for the tag number. Maybe the hotel clerks don't write down guests' vehicle tag numbers here. She would have said if she knew, wouldn't she? It's only three blocks from Oscar's house to the courthouse, but it feels like miles. The pancakes he made you for breakfast have adhered to the inside of your stomach like a thick layer of tar, and you can't get any relief by belching, though you try to make yourself and just get air in your stomach, so it feels worse.

The courthouse is open; a few people besides the workers are inside, but it appears that they don't have much business to do. They stand around talking but hush up when you walk past, heading for County Coroner Staley's office. There's no one behind the desk when you walk in, which isn't surprising since the coroner is also the only undertaker in town and probably has other business to attend to. Usually, though, there is a secretary or someone standing around. You take a seat on one of the olive green naugahyde chairs, put your hat on your knee and prepare to wait. Again.

The sun comes through the south-facing window, slowly brightening like a light bulb on a rheostat. The room is small and warm for an old building and you feel safe here among the old furniture, the bulletin board behind the desk with flyers, and notices thumbtacked up three deep in places, it looks like. Your toes are thawing out, and you wonder if they will soak your socks.

"Hello! Oh, excuse me, I didn't mean to startle you," the red-haired woman says. She's cheerful, too, like they say all fat people are, which you know damned well isn't true for most of them.

You stand up and reach to take off your hat, remember it was on your knee but has now rolled over and rested itself up against the front of the desk.

"Ma'am. I just came to see the coroner. I'm – "

She waves her hand to stop you.

"Oh, I know who you are. How could I miss you?" There she stops herself abruptly, then stammers on.

"I mean, well, I mean, how COULD I miss you? I mean you're in here practically every day, now aren't you? Not that we mind, you see – " Her face is as red as her hair.

You give her a break, leaning over to pick up your hat.

"Ma'am, I was just checking to see if the coroner has signed those papers yet."

"Oh, yes," she says, relieved to move on. "Um, yes. He signed them and everything is all set."

"So, when can I expect the body to be exhumed?"

"Oh, well, I don't really know about that," she says, stepping over to the desk to straighten an already neatly stacked pile of papers. "You'll have to talk to the coroner himself about that."

"And when would he be coming into the office?"

She moves on to another stack of papers.

"I'm really not sure," she says. "He has a couple of clients in to prepare for funerals. Of course, you know that has to take precedence."

"Yes, ma'am. I would assume so. But doesn't he have any helpers to take over for him? I just need to see him for a few minutes, you know."

"Oh, I know. It's just that I don't know. I mean, I don't know how long that takes."

"Well, once that's done, I'd assume he would have some time before he has to attend to the burials themselves, wouldn't he?"

"Oh, there won't be any burials. Not yet, anyway."

"What?"

She stops fussing with the papers and points out the window.

"The ground is too frozen for burials. There's a heater thing that thaws out the ground enough to dig the graves, but even that doesn't work very well until the temperature gets above ten below zero. So, I expect that will be a few days."

A few days, you think. If they can't dig a new grave, then they can't dig up an old one, either. More bureaucratic red tape, courtesy of South Dakota weather. You never expected to take a two week – or maybe even longer – vacation here in the middle of a hard winter.

"Well, when do you think I ought to check back?" you ask.

The woman's rings sparkle in the brightening sunshine through the window.

"I'd try back about Monday if I were you. Or maybe Tuesday. Because you see, once the temperature comes up – "

"Yes, I know," you sigh, turning your hat around and around by the brim. "Then he'll have to bury those other folks first. I just hope nobody else dies before Monday."

As you are walking down the hall, you hear her nervous giggle behind you.

The sun glare off all the snow is blinding, and you squint against it, wish you could hold your breath against the smell of automobile exhaust. Cars are parked at the curb, motors running, but no sign of the drivers. You expect the cars are left running because it's so cold that some of them might not start again if the motors were switched off, but it looks like everyone in town is preparing for a fast getaway, like they've just robbed the bank. You wonder that no one steals those cars, just hops into one and drives off, but then, everyone knows everyone, so everyone would know who had stolen their car the second that someone did it. Even you. In town for days only, and everyone knows who you are and what your business is. They think. They didn't exactly know Elsie's business, now did they?

You're walking along by The Steak House, just at that corner where the alley goes along the side of the building, when a red pickup pulls into the alley in front of you, blasting the horn, and you just about drop over. For a minute, just a minute you forgot about Jack Mason, and that was probably your undoing, you think. Any minute now, you're expecting that bullet to hit right in the middle of your chest and exit through that icy spot in the middle of your back. You're going to be another bump on Elsie's story, and one that won't get rubbed off no matter how long they talk about it.

15

January 23, 1970, Noon

Friendship

The driver leans across and rolls down the window, and then you see that it's a woman, a woman wearing a knitted cap, hot orange with navy blue stripes.

"Hey, you look like you've seen a ghost," she says.

You clutch your hand to your chest and take a deep, steadying breath.

"For a minute, I thought I had. My own."

"Never mind. Well, get in and sit down before you tip over," the woman says.

"Ma'am?"

"Come on, don't look so damned scared. I weigh ninety pounds soaking wet. Get in. You know who I am."

"Ma'am?"

"I'm Nancy Marks," she says in an exasperated tone. "Now, will you get in?"

She's an angel, you think, an angel with sun wrinkles around her eyes and gray-streaked brown bangs showing beneath that bright cap. You get in, glance out the dirty back window to see if anyone else might have been following you, even though you wonder how the hell you'd know if it was Jack Mason since you never saw the man. That's something else you should have asked Irene: what does he look like? You imagine a big man, over six feet, threatening as an angry bear.

"You look like you could use a cup of coffee," she says as she puts the truck in reverse, backs out, and drives down the street.

"Something stronger, I think."

"Sorry, I don't drink," she says with her lips tightened over her teeth and her hands tightened on the steering wheel.

"Steak House is right back there." You motion behind you.

"Yeah, but the co-op café has better specials, and I'm starved."

Some kids in an old brown Chevy Bel Air going too fast are unable to stop at the intersection, run on out into the middle of Main, turning a complete circle on the snow-packed street.

Nancy pumps the brake and steers around them.

"Little brats," she mutters.

"They're just kids having a good time, maybe playing hooky," you say mildly.

She gives you a quick glance.

"The Mason brothers and their friend were just having a good time, too," she says.

You don't know what to say, so you don't say anything.

You're sitting at a table for two in the middle of the café where anyone can see you, conspicuous as hell, but all the booths are full, and most of the tables, too, even though it's only eleven-thirty in the morning.

"Sure you don't want something to eat?" she asks as she shovels a bite of fish and then a bigger bite of macaroni and cheese into her mouth.

"No, thank you," you say, blowing on your coffee to cool it. The pancakes are still firmly stuck to the inside of your stomach, but it's entertaining to watch Nancy put away the food. Finally, she pauses long enough to notice you watching.

"What? Don't look like what you expected, do I?" She points to her messed up salt and pepper hair, visible now that she's pulled off the stocking cap. "The last year or so has just about turned me all gray."

"No," you say. "I was just wondering where a little woman like you puts all that food."

She laughs then, unselfconsciously, her mouth wide open displaying a number of silver fillings.

"No," you say, "you're not at all what I expected."

She keeps her eyes on you while she drinks from her coffee cup, puts it down, and then she says, "What I want to know is why you didn't come look me up."

115

You set down your coffee cup, take your hands off the table and put them in your lap, lean forward a little, but you can't look her in the eye. You should have made an effort to go see her days ago, you think.

"Well, lots of reasons," you say. "I didn't know you existed until after I got here, and then what I did hear made me think you might not be too happy to meet me. Then, I didn't have a car to get out to your place in the country. Came in on the bus as far as that little town across the state line in Nebraska and hitched a ride the fifteen miles into Jackson with a guy who says he picks up freight down there at the bus station and brings it on up here."

"Yeah," Nancy says. "Jackson is so far out in the sticks you can't even take the bus directly here, but you could have called once you got here. Once you knew about me."

"I know," you say.

"Never mind," she says, "I can understand." Her voice is soft and low like she's just been rejected by a lover.

"It's just that I didn't know how you'd feel about me, being who I am and all," you repeat, and this time you do look at her. "You could have called *me*."

"I did try finally, you know, when it became obvious that you weren't going to get in touch with me. The people at the Dakota Hotel said you'd checked out. I was surprised to see you on the street. I thought you'd given up and left."

"No. I'm staying with Oscar DuCharme."

She laughs.

"Ah, that old fox. I might have figured."

"What's that supposed to mean?" you ask.

She waves her hand.

"Oh, nothing, nothing. I like Oscar. He's a pretty good old guy. It's just that I think he's carrying a load of guilt around, that's all. I think all the Indians in this town are, and one or two of us white folks are, too."

"You mean because of Elsie – "

"Shh! Keep your voice down."

116

You glance around the room, but everyone seems engaged in eating their own food, sharing their blizzard stories. The coat rack in the front is invisible except for the steel legs sticking out from under the pile of coats and hats and scarves. A single brown glove lies on the floor beneath, palm up, fingers bent and beckoning, a dismembered hand with secrets to keep. The floor is a sloppy mess of melted snow, mud and dried dirt.

"Here, let me pay the check, then we'll go somewhere else and talk," you say.

You reach for your wallet and the meal check, but she grabs a fork and pretends to threaten you, so you get up and go wait by the front door. The waitress is the same one from the other night. You think she must have gotten her shift changed or be pulling a double. She looks exhausted as she blows away a strand of hair that's falling into her face. It may be cold outside, but the waitress is sweating as if it were August and middle of the harvest season.

Inside the pickup cab again, you shiver, marveling at how fast it has cooled off in just the short time you were in the restaurant.

"Where shall we go?" you ask.

"Not many places to go, really, not public places, that is. There's no privacy in Jackson in public places. Everything in a small town is public except for private houses and even then . . ." She lets her voice trail off.

"So," she says brightly. "Your place or mine?"

"Mine. Oscar won't mind."

She shifts the pickup into gear.

"Good. I was hoping you'd say that. It's a long drive over slick roads to my place."

Oscar's living room is warm, the frost accumulation on the south windows melting and running down onto the sill. Unsure of the proper manners for a guest, you knock on the door and then open it hollering, "You home, Oscar?"

He sits in his usual place, a cigarette almost burned down in the ash tray at his elbow, both television sets tuned to a game show, and the slack, dazed expression on his face tells you that he has been napping. You think that someday he'll burn his house down if he doesn't quit smoking and napping at the same time.

Then he notices Nancy's presence, heaves himself out of the chair, takes her hand and bends over it a little, a courtly gesture.

"You doing all right, Oscar?" she asks.

"Can't complain much," he says. "I'm awfully good for the shape I'm in. How about some coffee? Been on the back burner for a while, but enough sugar will fix that."

"Sure," she answers, and you help her off with her coat.

"You can turn the televisions off. It was just something to keep me company during my nap," he yells back at her from the kitchen.

Nancy switches off the television set, then reaches over and stubs out the last fire from Oscar's cigarette, fans the air, and sits down on the end of the sofa. You sit down on the other end.

"Where's Lowan?" you ask.

"Outside," he calls back. "Neighbor's bitch terrier is in heat, so he's waiting outside the shed where she's locked up."

He comes back carrying three cups of coffee on a plate he's using for a tray, goes back for cream and sugar.

"It's strange," he continues. "Wrong season of the year a bitch to come in heat. I don't know. Maybe they got their own version of the deer woman. Maybe Lowan will come home crazy."

"Oh, Oscar," Nancy says. "You don't believe in all those old folk stories do you?"

He sets the can of condensed milk and sugar in a cracked blue bowl down on the end table.

"Why not? You believe in all those old folk stories wrote up in the Bible, don't you?"

Nancy's shoulders stiffen momentarily, but then she relaxes, reaches for the sugar bowl.

"Yeah, yeah, yeah," she says. "Well, to each his own, I guess."

He settles in the orange chair that gives off a creak from the exhausted springs.

"You just say, 'I guess'? Don't sound too sure of your faith," he comments.

118

"Oscar, I did not come here to spar with you over religious convictions," Nancy says. "I didn't come here for coffee either, but since you're providing it, could I have a spoon to dip this sugar with and another one to stir my coffee with?"

Oscar starts to get up, but you wave him back down, go to the kitchen and collect two spoons from the drawer beside the sink, the one that sticks so you have to jerk it open.

"I'm glad you came to visit, whatever the reason," Oscar says. Then he changes the subject. "You know, I saw you uptown, maybe five or six times last year, and you didn't stop to talk. So, why are you here? Woman like you, active in the church, big farm to take care of. You're a busy woman."

"I came to talk about Elsie," Nancy says. "I think it's about time."

Oscar points at you with his chin.

"Well, you have to get in line. He was first."

"I kind of had in mind a three-way conversation," she says.

"A three-way. I don't know, Nancy, if it was two women and me, then maybe." Oscar has a sly expression and a little half smile.

"Why, you randy old goat!"

You smother a smile with the back of your hand, notice that it smells like the wet wool of your gloves.

Oscar puts up both hands in self-defense and leans away chuckling. "Just kidding! Just kidding!"

"Well, on second thought, if I was a few years older and a few years bolder, I might consider a two-way," Nancy says with a straight face.

"Would you two stop flirting!" you blurt it out, and then you realize that it's the most forceful thing you've said since you got here, maybe since you got the word about Elsie, who was never alive to you in your life, but a revelation of what should have been. You remember that moment of sudden knowledge and the way your heart shriveled in your chest.

Both of them stare at you, and you mumble some apology about being tired and bored from all the courthouse waiting, days of waiting, waiting.

Nancy waves her hand, that so-characteristic gesture she has, and you notice again her suntanned hand, wrinkled and calloused from too much hard work, finger joints twisting a little with the beginnings of arthritis.

"It's all right," she says. "You've been through a lot."

"Well, Oscar says, clearing his throat. "How about this. You tell me your stories, and I'll tell you mine. Since he's already heard most of mine, how about you go first?"

Nancy leans back on the sofa, crosses her legs at the knee, and nods.

"All right."

16

Taking the Measurements

So Elsie made up more of her beaded leatherwork – handbags with drawstring tops and rosettes beaded around the sides, starbursts of color in red, blue, and yellow with a narrow band of beading above. The dolls were a better selling item, and she made several of those, and belts, but those were mostly a tourist item, or so the locals seemed to think, so she only sold a few of those. She used every tiny scrap of leather, making tubes that that she then beaded around and attached to a thong for use as a key chain. Then, there were the moccasins, but she only made two pair.

One morning Father Horst sat on his worn tweed ottoman, his stocking feet on butcher paper, while Elsie kneeled in front of him drawing around each foot with a fat black pencil like the ones that children use in kindergarten. The good Father was more than a little embarrassed, as if the removal of his shoes might violate his vow of chastity, and to tell the truth, he really didn't want a pair of moccasins anyway. The idea had never occurred to him. He knew that after Elsie made them, he would have to wear them, at least around the house. Or so he thought.

"Is that all," he asked when she was done with the drawing.

"No, not yet," she said as she took a yellow tape measure out of her faded apron pocket and began wrapping it around his feet in various places. Her touch was gentle, but it was a woman's touch. Elsie did not look up to see him, staring at the wall just below the ceiling and silently saying a Hail Mary. She was innocent and despoiled and violated and sensuous all at the same time. He thought of Mary Magdalene washing our Savior's feet with her tears and drying them with her hair. He looked down at the top of her head, at her hair, thick braids folded neatly across her head like a crown, and he could tell that when it was unbraided, it would fall in shimmering waves below her waist, remembered seeing it that way when he had gone to talk to her about not tanning hides anymore. He imagined that every night before she went to bed she unbraided her hair, and he saw her standing naked with her small breasts half covered with the long hair while she brushed it, russet nipples peeking out from beneath the strands, static electricity shooting blue sparks from the brush. He jerked his eyes up to the wall again, started an Our Father.

While she carefully wrote the measurements down on the back of an old envelope, he hastily pulled on his black oxfords and tied them, stood up.

"Well, then," he said. "That must be all."

He made a pretend gesture of looking at his watch.

"I have to be going out to the hospital to see Mrs. Anderson and her new baby."

Elsie looked up at him, smiled sweetly.

"No, you don't. Mrs. Anderson and her little boy were let out yesterday."

"Oh, oh," he said. "Yes. Of course. You're right. What was I thinking?"

Elsie rolled up the length of butcher paper, put the envelope and the pencil and the measuring tape in her pocket.

"I'm sorry," she said. "But I can't talk to you all day, you know. Today is one of my cleaning days."

Donald Marks planned to stop at Elsie's for the fitting before he went on over to the Knights of Columbus meeting in the church basement, but the weather had warmed up, thinning the ice on the farm pond. A white-faced heifer had wandered onto the edge of the ice and fallen through, and although that point in the pond wasn't deep enough for her to drown, she couldn't get out either. She struggled to get back up on the ice, frantically pin wheeling her front legs, but the ice only broke up, slipped beneath her hoofs as she struggled for purchase. Donald had come out of the house to leave for town, heard the heifer bawling, saw that she was tiring and would drown eventually. He went back to the house for the hip waders that he wore when he went fishing, to the barn for a block and tackle, drove his pickup down to the pond edge. It was hurry, hurry because the heifer was weakening fast. She was big with calf, due to deliver in a month, and clumsier even than cows usually are. He hooked the block and tackle to the front frame of the truck, shoving the other curious heifers aside. They assumed that the pickup meant hay or cottonseed cake and crowded around, alternately looking for a handout and staring in bewilderment at the entertainment provided by the thrashing heifer in the pond.

Donald pulled on the hip waders, grabbed the end of the rope and waded into the chunky ice and water, but the heifer was just beyond his reach. He made a loop in the rope, aimed it for her tossing horns, missed. Her eyes rolled and snot came from her nose. He aimed and threw, aimed and threw, but each time the loop fell short or she thrashed at the last minute and the rope slipped off.

"Sooo, bossy, sooo," he crooned like he would to a milk cow.

He would have to get closer. He stepped forward into the oozy mud of the pond bottom and the water rose to an inch below the top of his waders. Giant chunks of ice, broken then stirred by the frantic movements of the heifer bumped against his legs, sloshing icy water over the top of the waders. He gasped as it ran down inside. The cow's legs slowed and she gave a long sigh, whooshing out her breath in a snotty stream, and closed her eyes.

"Don't give up on me now, old girl," he muttered. "Come on, hang in there."

He flung the rope again, past her head a little and thought it was another miss, but at the last moment the heifer jerked her head sideways and the loop fell over one horn. The rope tightened abruptly, and Donald, unprepared, was jerked off his feet belly first. A giant floe of ice slid out from under him and dumped him into the water. He gasped, sucking in water, scrambled for purchase on the slippery pond bottom, came up choking and coughing but still grasping the rope.

"Hey, you all right?"

Nancy had heard the commotion and come to help.

"Well, hell, no, I'm not all right," he coughed out. "Do I look all right? Christ, this heifer is going to suicide and take me with her."

Nancy didn't answer, but got into the pickup, put it in reverse, hollered out the open door, "Tell me when!"

Donald backed up, found a more solid place on the pond bottom to brace his feet, tugged the rope. The cow was relaxing, her head dropping lower into the water.

"Take up the slack!"

Nancy released the clutch, and the truck started backwards, but then the motor died, and it lurched forward, dangerously close to the edge of the pond.

"Jesus Christ!" he yelled. "Give it some fucking gas!"

The truck cranked again, whining and turning over, groaning and complaining, and then the motor caught again. Nancy revved the engine, let out the clutch slowly, and the rope between the bumper and the cow tightened perceptibly. She backed another foot, two feet, and the heifer's head came up level with ice chunks, her neck turned slightly from the pull on one horn, neck stretched like a chicken's on a chopping block.

"All right, now," Donald yelled. "Take it back slow."

The truck moved back; the cow's neck stretched farther, but her body, like a water soaked sponge didn't move, and the rope slid up her horn an inch, another inch, until it gave way. The rope end came off, flew forward and the knot caught Donald on the side of the head like a fist, right on his ear. He saw stars, staggered backwards struggling not to pass out, to keep his footing. Tipping slightly, he flung his hand sideways and caught himself on an ice floe, which, jammed against another chunk, miraculously held steady. He levered himself slowly upright, unable to speak through the pain.

Nancy was hollering from the edge of the pond, but it barely registered in his consciousness. He heard the shhhh of the rope dragged past him over the ice chunks, and he obeyed and went quiet inside, felt himself falling forwards onto the ice floe. The heifer came around and gave another lunch, a frantic, desperate move that shoved another ice cake at him, wedging him upright between two solid cold props, his upper body lopped over in a curl like that of a happy cat's tail.

Nancy reeled in the rope hand over hand, shakily formed another loop, muttered to herself, "come on, come on, come on." She flung it, but it passed low over the heifer's head passing right between the horns. Again and again she threw the rope in determined desperation, all the time glancing out of the corner of her eye at Donald turning into a popsicle as the sun went down in a lavender and pink glow and the temperature started to drop, forming a crinkly scum of thin ice on the pond between the big ice chunks. Her arms were exhausted, but still she pitched and pulled the failed loops back.

She was crying by then, her face wet with tears and snot like the heifer's and starting to freeze on her cheeks, and at last the rope fell exactly right, and she gave a cry of joy, rushed to the pickup. She put it in gear, backed it up. It occurred to her only after the cow had slid out on the bank and she had roped Donald and pulled him out that she should have pulled Donald out first. But then, she knew, if she had saved him and the cow died, he would not have been grateful. As he staggered, groggy, to the house leaning on her shoulder, she looked back and saw the heifer struggle to her feet.

An hour later after a hot bath, Donald claimed that he felt fine and irritably insisted on going on to the Knights of Columbus meeting, even though it would be half over by the time he got there.

Nancy pauses in her story.

"That's not the end of what happened. I don't know exactly, but after all that happened later, I can guess."

17

March 15, 1968, Evening

Another Kind of Measuring

The parking lot was full, and the street in front of the church still held half-melted drifts, so Donald parked on the street over behind the church and walked through the vacant lot to the basement entrance. The other men kidded him about why he was late, but not much. Most of them had been in similar situations and understood the importance of saving even one stupid heifer. The profit margin for ranching was so slim, one cow dead or alive – yes, just one cow – made a difference.

The business part of the meeting was over almost as soon as he got there, and the men put together smaller groups to play penny ante poker. He was about to beg off and go home, when Father Horst reminded him that he was supposed to have stopped at Elsie's before the meeting to be fitted for moccasins. As he climbed the basement stairs and went out the back door he hoped that Elsie had already gone to bed, but light from her windows shone on the half melted and refrozen snow. He sighed, walked over, and tapped gently on her door.

She opened it immediately, and he knew that she had been waiting.

"I'm sorry I didn't come earlier," he offered. "Had an incident at home that had to be taken care of."

She didn't answer, just smiled.

He entered the kitchen, standing uncertainly by the table with his hand on the back of a chair.

"What shall I do?" he asked.

She pulled out a chair from the table and motioned to him.

"Sit."

He turned as he sat down so that light from the sixty watt light bulb in the overhead fixture fell on the side of his face where the rope had smacked him. Just below his left temple there was a gouged out streak on top of a big purple knot, his ear was swollen big and red, and his left eye was swollen partially shut.

Elsie's hands went to her mouth.

"Oh!" she said.

Donald grinned.

"That bad, huh? Well, I tell you, it feels as bad as it looks. But you should see the other guy."

Elsie giggled nervously.

"We – we – could do this some other time," she said.

"Nah. I'm here now."

Reluctantly, Elsie picked up the pencil and butcher paper from the table, hesitated a moment, and then knelt to pull off Donald's boots. He started to push her away to do it himself, but almost tumbled sideways off the chair. She stood and helped him back upright.

"I'll do it," she said. "Relax."

He put his elbow on the table, leaned his head on his hand and closed his eyes.

Quietly, Elsie pulled off his boots and set them aside, gently lifted each foot an inch or so and worked the paper beneath his feet.

The kitchen was warm and smelled of baked bread and something else, something musky, moldy, like the stock pond smelled in summer. He turned his eyes without moving his head and saw the blue graniteware roasting pan on the floor by the old gas kitchen range. An inch of water and two big flat rocks were inside, the turtles – one red, one yellow – perched on the rocks, necks outstretched staring at him. He was sure of it, though he couldn't see their tiny little eyes, only that their heads were pointed right at him. He had heard somewhere that the Indians considered turtles to be fertility symbols, and he wondered which of the turtles was female, or if they both were, or if neither one was, and then he though they might be gay turtles. His mind floated off into a dream of happy turtles, one red and one yellow, dancing and laughing.

Elsie nudged him. Gentle as the nudge was, his chin slipped off his cupping hand. He caught himself and sat bolt upright again.

"I just need to measure some, and then it's done," she said.

He nodded dreamily and watched as she looped, held briefly, unlooped the yellow tape measure from several places on first one foot and then the other. She was gentle, her long fingers with short white nails touching lightly, moving the tape around to read the numbers, writing them down on the flip side of the envelope she had used to record Father Horst's measurements.

She stood slowly, and his eyes followed her up, up, until she stood in front of him, head tilted slightly, a wrinkle of concern between her eyes.

He nodded.

"Just tired and worn out," he said.

"You should drink some coffee before you drive home," she said.

"Okay."

He watched her swish the coffee pot in a circle checking to see if there was any left, set it back on the burner, strike a match, and light the flame, turn it down on low.

"I have oranges," she said. "Maybe you need some food."

"No. Not hungry. Not much."

She reached for the bowl of huge round orange moons on the counter top.

"Let me peel one for you."

"No. No, really. I'm fine."

The turtles stared at him. Time stopped frozen, jumped forward rapidly to catch up. Elsie moved across the kitchen like a character in an old time movie, too fast with jerky movements. He felt himself falling, felt her catch and lower him carefully to the floor.

He dreamed. He was sitting by the pond, tossing rocks into the water. Two of them didn't sink, but floated on the surface, rose higher and moved towards him, rippling the water, and then two turtles crawled out on the bank beside him, settled at his feet and watched. He felt a moist snuffling on the back of his neck, not a frightening feeling but easy, like when his mother had gently swabbed the back of his neck with a washcloth when he was little. He closed his eyes, and the touches became slower and distinct like little soundless kisses.

He came awake staring at a blue surface with white freckles, then realized that his nose was just inches from the side of the graniteware pan that held the turtles. The room was indistinct in early morning light, but he smelled coffee and suddenly, he was ravenous. He started to sit up, but lay back when a pain struck him in the side of his head like a hammer. He groaned and laid his head back on something soft. A pillow. Elsie must have stuck it under his head. He was covered with a quilt, too, but his bones ached from the hours spent lying on the floor, and the time spent fighting the heifer and the ice floes in the pond the day before. His spine felt bruised, as if someone had rolled him over on his stomach and then jumped on him.

He managed to sit up, head in hands, when Elsie came softly into the kitchen dressed in the same dark flower printed dress she had worn night before.

"You look really bad," she said. "Should I get Father Horst?"

"What?"

"Should I get – ?"

"No, no. I'm fine." He rubbed his hands down his face, feeling the scratchy morning whiskers. He started to get up, groaned and sat back down.

"You need a doctor," Elsie said. "I'm going to get Father Horst."

"No! No, I'm okay. Just a little stiff and sore. Here, help me up."

Elsie gave him her hand and helped him stand, the quilt puddling around his feet.

"But you have to drink some coffee before you go."

"All right," he said, and then he asked, "you got a couple of pieces of bread or something?"

She scrambled two eggs, browned two pieces of bread in the oven, while he sat at the table looking out the window.

"Nancy will be worried," he said, as she put the plate of food in front of him.

"No, she won't."

Then he knew that she knew about him. That he often didn't come home, often went off to run some town errands or something and didn't come home for a while.

"Well, maybe a little this time." He gestured towards his face, the skin around his eye black as a summer storm, the eye barely open.

She ducked her head, smiled a little, lips just turning up at the corners.

When he had eaten the food and drunk a cup of strong, black coffee, the energy surged back into his bones. He felt strong, virile, and the throbbing in his head had receded.

He reached for his boots, pulled them on, and stood up. Elsie stood, too, kissed her fingertips, and touched them to his bruised face.

He walked around behind Elsie's house, across the lot with the big cottonwood where she had dangled her hide stretchers just months before and climbed the old fence to the street. The pickup, contrarily, started easily, and he drove away in the quiet of an early gray morning before the town had begun to stir.

18

January 23, 1970, Afternoon

John Caulfield

"Well," Nancy was saying, "I was more than a little put out when Elsie showed me the moccasins she had made for Donald." She's being a little too mysterious, you think, and you just wish she'd spit it out, but she keeps silent, swirling the coffee grounds in her cup.

"All right, I'll bite," you say. "What was the matter with them? Did she do a bad job?"

"No, they were beautifully done, all laced up tight and the bead design sharp as a focused picture. That's hard to do, you know, 'cause leather stretches so much, but it was the wrong design."

"I heard that," Oscar says. "Supposed to be wheat sheaves or something like that and she did turtles."

Nancy sets the cup down on the end table with a sharp rap.

"Yes! And not just any old turtles, either. There was Tom on one toe and Dick on the other. One red and one yellow, beautiful, but I mean, it wasn't what I'd asked for and they didn't even match. If they'd both been red, or both yellow . . ." She trails off, shaking her head.

"I could tell she was nervous about it," Nancy goes on. "She kind of hung her head and wouldn't look at me. I asked her why she had done that, but she never really answered me. She just stood there. Finally she tried to snatch the moccasins out of my hand, said she was sorry. Said she couldn't redo them, pulling out the stitches on the beadwork would make the leather all funny, and she didn't have another piece of leather big enough to cut out another pair. Said she'd already used the last of it to make Father Horst's moccasins, and sure enough, those moccasins were there on her table for me to see. But the design on those was perfect for him – a white cross surrounded by dark blue beads. She just looked so, so – pitiful and sorry,

I guess you'd say. So I got out my wallet and tried to hand her the money, but she wouldn't take it. I put it on the table, took the moccasins and left."

It's getting on into late afternoon, the sun slanting around to the southwest and getting redder as it sinks lower. The pancakes that Oscar made for your breakfast have finally moved out of your gut, probably the acid in all the coffee you drank has dissolved whatever tarry glue it was that stuck them to your insides. Your stomach growls loudly. Oscar looks at you and chuckles.

"Maybe I should start calling *you* Lowan," he says. "Your stomach sings."

"Not very well, either," Nancy laughs.

"I got some cheese in the kitchen. Good old commodity cheese, none of that Velveeta stuff," Oscar says. "How about if I make some sandwiches? And some more coffee."

"So how did Donald like the moccasins?" you ask around a big bite of cheese and mayonnaise and bread gone a little too dry.

"He laughed," Nancy says. "Just laughed. And then he took the moccasins and put them away. I never saw him wear them. And I got over my mad at Elsie pretty quick. I mean, she was so quiet and unassuming and never said anything mean or unkind about anybody, even about what happened to her up in Mobridge. How you stay mad at somebody like that?"

"That must've been – what?" Oscar puts in. "Not quite a year ago?"

Nancy squints at Oscar's yellow plastic electric wall clock, as if it could give her the answer. There are brown runnels down the face of it, where Oscar's smoking residue had clung to it and then been assaulted by the steam in the kitchen.

"Yeah, that would be about right."

"Hmm." He leans back in his chair. There's a dob of mayonnaise on the end of his nose, but neither you nor Nancy say anything.

"That's about the time that John Caulfield got all happy. Remember?"

"I sure do," Nancy says. "He even stopped drinking, not that anybody noticed right away. He got hired on full time out at the livestock auction barn, where he worked part time when he was sober, and when they needed extra help. Winter times there isn't any yard work do to, and most people shovel their own snow, except for the old folks, but they can't afford to pay someone to do it. Winter is a pretty lean time around here for a drunken handy man."

"Jim Walker died, that's why John got on," Oscar says.

"I take it Walker worked at the auction barn?" you ask.

"Yeah." Oscar shakes his head. "Some people die young, you know? That old saying that only the good die young, well, it ain't always true, but for Walker, I think it was."

"See," Nancy says. "He was a good family type man. Did his job, and believe me, working at the auction barns is a *job*. It's hot in the summer and the flies – and in the winter, you freeze your butt off out there chasing cows and pigs around the pens with no shelter and that wind coming out of the north."

"Didn't drink," Oscar says. He rubs his face and accidentally takes off the mayonnaise blob. "Wasn't a churchgoer or a joiner, but he was always friendly and smiling. His kids were decent; his wife seemed happy. And then one day, old Jim just dropped over in the sales ring. Just standing there prodding some old cow around, and when the auctioneer hit the gavel and knocked her off to the highest bidder, Jim just dropped like a tree falling. Didn't make a sound. They say he was dead before he hit the sawdust."

Nancy shakes her head.

"Really a sad deal," she says. "He was only forty-two years old. Heart attack and didn't even know there was a thing wrong with him."

They observe a moment of silence for Jim Walker, and then Oscar picks up the conversation, and you feel like it's okay to take a sip of your coffee, blessedly fresh with no grounds floating on top.

"His dying left a big hole in the workforce out there, you know," Oscar says. "They had to have someone. John knew the job and was already working part time, so they moved him right in. Old man Hausman talked about it down in the Legion club bar. Bragged on

John. Said he had his doubts, but John just sort of grew into the job. That's when people took notice that John wasn't spending his money in the bar anymore, wasn't harassing people for handouts when he ran out of money. He even bought himself some clothes that didn't come from the basement rummage at St. Mary's Episcopal. Remember that one light blue shirt he wore with that gray Pendleton coat?"

"Not exactly," Nancy says. "I just noticed he was looking pretty sharp for a town drunk – well, ex–town drunk."

"I remember that shirt," Oscar says. "It had a little knobbly weave in it. I'd've liked one like that for myself. Don't know where he bought it, though. Guess it's a bit late to ask."

"Seems pretty odd to me that a job would make that much change in a man like that," you say.

"Well," Nancy laughs, "the job had something to do with it, but there was this other little thing."

Oscar is tilting his chair back, balancing it on the two hind legs.

"Can't find shirts like that around here. Maybe he got it down in Valentine or over in Winner, except I don't know how he'd get there. Didn't have a car."

"Probably hitched," Nancy says.

19

April 9, 1968

Cats in the Bushes

John Caulfield stared into the blurry mirror in his bathroom. The tub was an old-timey claw-footed one, but the sink was a 1950s update – a squarish affair with chrome legs that looked too spindly to be stable. He worried about that himself, so he was careful never to lean on it when he looked in the mirror. The bathroom adjoined his tiny bedroom and together the bedroom and bathroom were one of the ten cabins at Jackson Lodges, a run-down tourist place on the far west side of Jackson next to Highway 18. His was number 8A, the third from the right in the row of ten. It took him a few years, but he eventually figured out what the *A* meant. There weren't any with a *B* or *C* suffix, but the fact was that the ten cabins were the first part of three proposed phases of building. The tourist business had never been good enough to add the B and C units.

For the first time since he couldn't remember when, he didn't mind looking into the mirror. He really wasn't that old, he thought, but over the past several years he'd come to think of himself that way, especially on the mornings when he awakened from a one- or two- or three-day toot, eyes bloodshot with bags underneath, forehead and cheeks wrinkled from the dehydrating effects of alcohol.

He turned his head as far to one side as he could, examining the haircut he'd gotten the day before. Not bad, really. It wasn't white-walled up the sides, and it wasn't too long on top either. He turned his face straight on and looked into his own green-blue eyes. Clear, perfectly clear. Then he opened his mouth in a broad grimace and examined his teeth. Miraculously, after all the fights he'd been in and all the times he'd fallen down hard, he still had them all. Well, the ones that counted anyway, the ones people could see when he smiled. He held his hand over his mouth and nose and blew hard.

Thought he detected a sour taint. He opened the medicine cabinet and took out his toothbrush and toothpaste.

When he finished, he gave another swipe at his hair with a comb, stuck it in his back pocket and plucked the shirt off the door knob where he had hung it. It was blue with a shadow stripe of a slightly lighter blue with a dobby weave on every other stripe. Not a western shirt with snaps, something he regretted, but the buttons were nice pearlized plastic ones, not bad.

In his tiny bedroom he shrugged on the gray jacket that dressed up his jeans just right, pulled on his boots – black cowboy boots. He probably would have hocked them a long time ago, but they'd gotten pushed under his bed where he had forgotten about them until he'd been sober for a while and cleaned his room. He debated about wearing his winter topcoat over the jacket. He only owned the one, a green army style parka that he wore to work in, cleaned but permanently stained with grass stains, mud, and cow shit. He opened his door, sucked in the crisp evening air. He could do without the overcoat. It would be cold walking home later, but he'd survived many colder nights when he had passed out drunk in the alley behind the Legion club.

He checked his battered Big Ben wind-up clock. Seven o'clock. Too early. He should've planned his time better, but it had been so long since he'd been invited to someone's place that he'd forgotten how to time the getting ready and the getting there. He stacked his two thin pillows at the iron headboard of his bead, sat on the edge and swung his legs up, boots hanging off the edge, carefully so as not to muss his clothes up, cautiously leaned back against the pillows. He was very nervous. He'd never had a date before, even in high school.

Finally he couldn't stand it anymore and decided he could leave but just walk slow, but when he was halfway down the hill into town, he had to speed up just to keep warm. At the first street to the left he turned and walked past St. Mary's Episcopal Church, which was all alight, cars parked on both sides up and down the street. He turned back onto a side street to avoid being seen, walked over two blocks and then north for two more, crossed the vacant lot, around the corner of the little house and knocked on the door. He was worried that he might have worked up a sweat, maybe he stank, and was about to sniff his armpit to check when the door opened.

He reached to pull off a cap he wasn't wearing, turned the gesture into a sort of half salute.

"Hi. I guess I'm early. I can just stay out here for a while if I'm too early," he said, and then felt like a fool for saying such a stupid thing.

"Come in," Elsie said with a smile.

Father Horst had his window open and he smelled the heavy scent of the lilac bushes blooming just outside. It was spring, but a cold night. He had been awakened by the sound of a horrendous cat fight beneath those same bushes. He lay there a minute thinking about Cat and how he'd came limping in a few days earlier with his ear chewed up and an eye puffed. He yelled out the window to no effect, and finally sighed, gave in and got up. He pulled on his pants and the moccasins that Elsie had made for him – he found them very useful, after all – and padded softly outside to look for Cat.

There was no moon and no street lights, so the night was blacker than the inside of a black billy goat at midnight. He kept one hand on the side of the building as he walked slowly around, listening to the persistent cat yowlings, and calling softly for Cat. Not that it would do any good, he knew. A queen in heat in the spring attracted a following of mindless suitors who never heard anything beyond the rush of hormone filled blood in their veins.

Halfway around the house, his hand knocked into something that bumped and bounced on the ground in front of him. Cautiously, he leaned over and felt around until he grasped the handle of the rake that he had propped against the house yesterday. He'd been hopefully spading and raking the little garden plot and praying that the winter was over. Now, he picked up the rake and, balancing it in one hand with the other hand touching the wall, he continued around to the lilac bushes, where he proceeded to chastise the fighting toms with the rake handle. The light from his bedroom window just above showed two streaks of cats – one white and black spotted, and one that looked gray – dash from beneath the bushes and off into the darkness. Not Cat.

Well. Cat wasn't involved, but at least he might be able to sleep now, he thought, and then from less than twenty feet away, he heard the fight resume. He threw the rake down in disgust and started feeling his way back around the house.

At the corner, where the old cracked sidewalk passed the back of the rectory and wandered the short distance over to Elsie's little bungalow, he was stopped by a light, suddenly switched on in Elsie's kitchen. Assuming the caterwauling had awakened her, too, he was about to go tell her he'd tried to put a stop to it but it was hopeless, when the front door opened and a man stepped out.

Father Horst was stunned and stood silently, confused and blank for long moments as the man on Elsie's front step quietly chatted with Elsie, who was still standing inside the house. He thought that Elsie might be sick again, and someone had come to help, but there was no urgency in the man's voice. What could be wrong then? He started to step forward, make his presence known, but just then, Elsie stepped outside the house completely naked. She leaned over and kissed the man on the cheek, and his hand reached up and tweaked her nipple. Then the man turned, the light fell on his face, and Father Horst recognized John Caulfield.

He was afraid for a moment that Elsie might have seen him, or John, but then he realized that Elsie's feeble kitchen light did not penetrate the sixty or more feet to the dark side of the rectory. John stood a moment after the door shut, straightened his shoulders as if he were a rooster that had just topped a hen and walked away, not across the back lot, but right up the sidewalk towards Father Horst. He ducked back around the corner, waiting silently and feeling like a voyeur, a snoop, feeling outraged and embarrassed, too.

He waited until he was sure John had gone, then he sneaked back inside the rectory. Yes, *sneaked*, he told himself. Like a common, grubby eavesdropper, *sneaked* back inside his own damned house! He thought about his moccasin-fitting with Elsie and his own im-

138

pure thoughts, and in his confusion, sought the only solace he knew. He knelt at the side of his bed and began to pray the rosary.

He had reached the fourth Hail Mary of the first decan when he heard a soft scrabbling under the bed, heard purring, and felt Cat winding around his knees, stepping on his calves with sharp claws. He dropped his forehead onto the knobbly chenille bedspread and moaned. Outside, the cat fight in the lilac bushes picked up exactly where he had interrupted it.

He didn't sleep the rest of the night and was preoccupied with his thoughts the next day, when he should have been concentrating on the preparations for Easter. When he met with the Ladies' Altar Society to discuss the decorations for the church, he found himself drifting in and out of the conversation and when it was concluded, discovered to his dismay that he had agreed to Mrs. Huffman's totally inappropriate proposal to have orange tiger lilies on the altar. Then he had to undo it, and insist on the traditional pure white lilies. She was understandably confused, more than a little upset at his flip-flopping decisions, and left in a huff when he answered her sharply.

Nancy lingered after the meeting, brewed tea for the two of them, and sat down across from him at the kitchen table.

"Want to talk about it?" she asked.

"Yes and no," he answered. He scrubbed his hand vigorously through his thick mop of blond hair.

"Take your time," she said.

He thumped his hand down on the table.

"It's not like I'd be betraying the seal of the confessional, but it still feels uncomfortable to mention it to anyone."

"All right."

They sipped their tea in silence for a few minutes. Outside a meadowlark cheerily called out that spring had indeed arrived, and Nancy was distracted into thinking about her garden. She had the seeds already, ordered by mail from Gurney's Nursery over in Yankton. In another couple of weeks she would order this year's batch of chicks from the hatchery down in Norfolk. It was coming on the busy season of year, a time she both dreaded and looked forward to. Dreaded because of the work load, looked forward to because it kept her mind occupied, but more important because Donald, too, was so busy and tired that he didn't roam. As much.

She had about decided that Father Horst wasn't going to talk about whatever was bothering him when he spoke.

"I need to confess something," he said with a slight lift of his lips.

She smiled in response.

"I'm not a priest. I can't absolve you."

"I'm not sure if it's absolution I need, but I certainly need advice."

He pressed his lips together as if he was trying at the last minute to keep the story to himself.

"Last night, a cat fight under the lilac bushes woke me up, so I went outside to break it up."

He paused, fiddled with the sugar spoon.

"Yes? Cat fights happen a lot this time of year," she said.

"When I was coming back inside, I saw Elsie's kitchen light go on. And then the door opened and a man stepped out."

Nancy's eyes went wide.

She was terribly afraid of what she would hear next. The warm, sweet tea soured in her stomach; she wanted to run to the bathroom, out the back door, to the church and kneel in front of the statue of the Holy Virgin. She slid her chair back, but Father Horst wasn't paying attention to her. He held his hands in front of him, picking at a hangnail on his middle finger.

Get hold of yourself, woman, Nancy told herself.

"Maybe it was just someone come to buy some of her crafts stuff, or maybe one of the people she cleans for," Nancy said.

"In the middle of the night? Then Elsie stepped out and kissed the man. Elsie was – " here he had to stop and clear his throat. "Elsie was naked." He went on staring at his hands.

"What? She was *naked*?"

She pressed a hand to her forehead.

"Wait a minute. Who was the man?"

"He had his back to me at first, so I couldn't see his face, but when he turned around it was John Caulfield, plain as day."

Nancy had a difficult time disguising her relief that the man was not Donald. She got up, carried her cup to the sink, and pretended to rinse it out, looking out the window where she couldn't see Elsie's house, but only the tangle of weeds from last year along the half-fallen-down fence between the church property and the big cotton-wood in the vacant lot.

Immersed in his own distress, Father Horst did not recognize Nancy's except to connect it with his own concerns.

"I know," he said. "What can I do about it, really? They're both adults and even though the church is adamant against sex outside of marriage, what authority do I really have? That such behavior is taking place on church property is outrageous, but it's *Elsie*. It's not as if she were hanging out on the street corner with a sign advertising her services. I have to speak to her about it, though. This can't continue."

"Have you thought about it from the other side?" Nancy asked, still staring out the window. The meadowlark circled, perched on the fence, a sprig of dried grass in his beak. Nesting time, spring.

"What other side? What do you mean?"

Nancy's distress had turned to anger. She turned to face him.

"What do you mean, 'what do I mean?' It isn't like Elsie was the only party to this, you know. What about John?"

He still didn't understand.

"What about John?"

"You're so determined that this is all Elsie's fault! Well, she didn't go out and spit spider silk on John and drag him into her web. Who do you think started this whole affair? Surely you can't believe after all trouble with men that Elsie has been through that *she* would initiate this?"

Father Horst frowned and bit his lower lip, that lip that half the women in the parish had dreamed about kissing. Nancy was part of the other fifty percent, the half who saw him as a priest, untouchable.

"Well, I don't really think – " he started, but Nancy didn't let him finish.

Her apprehension before the revelation, her relief had all turned into anger at her own complacency in the face of Donald's infidelities, at her religion for keeping her trapped in a bad marriage, at her own lack of courage to step outside what Catholicism taught and what the family and the town would think if she left Donald. But most of all, at her fear of what she would do, how she would earn a living if she ended her marriage. She thought about Mary and Margaret, the sisters whose lives she must live as well as her own, of the chicks she would order soon, naming some of them Mary and some of them Margaret, and some of them Joy for the child she would never bear.

"That's the trouble, you aren't thinking! At least not in any rational way. It's all that old Catholic Christian shit, isn't it? It's the sin of Eve holding out that goddamned apple, and how do we know some man didn't make up that story just to cover his own ass? Blame it on Eve, blame on it women, and when does it ever *stop*? For the love of God, Horst, it's been almost two thousand years! How long is the church going to go on perpetrating that lie, or if it isn't a lie, how long do women have to pay for it? Even God forgives. Why can't the church?"

She was yelling now, and she knew she was, but she couldn't lower her voice.

Father Horst sat in his chair with his mouth open.

"Nancy, it's not like that," he said, his own voice, against his will, rising.

"Yes, it is! The first thing you thought of was that Elsie is a whore!" The word, whore, came out a top volume, and then Nancy realized that Elsie might hear. She swallowed hard against the rising bile.

"It never even occurred to you that John carries at least half the guilt."

He had no answer, because it was true.

"Well, I can't really go speak to John," he offered. "He isn't even Catholic."

Nancy's eyes narrowed, her mouth pulled in air. She seemed to swell to twice her size.

"You hypocritical son of a bitch!" she yelled, louder than before, and she didn't care who heard her. "*Elsie* isn't Catholic, either, but you're going to 'speak to her' about it."

He stood up.

"Now, wait just a minute here, Nancy. Elsie is living on church property. Technically, she is an employee of the Holy Roman Catholic Church, of Our Sacred Heart parish, even if she isn't Catholic, and her actions reflect on the local parish and the church as a whole. I have to speak to her, it's my duty."

"Your duty! Your duty!" Her words came out in a fine spray of spittle. "Your duty is to the care and protection of your flock, and any other stray sheep that happen to need help. Elsie is a refugee, an abused and troubled person who may not even be quite right in the head after what happened to her. She's still an innocent, I don't give a *shit* what you saw! If anything, she needs protection from John, and you're going to attack her and let him go on his merry way. Tempted by the sin of the apple, he is. Poor innocent man."

He just stared at her, without a thing to say.

She snatched her handbag from the countertop, stomped across the kitchen and out the door, a ninety pound lightning rod of ire.

He stood a moment before he thought of something to say, dashed after her.

"Nancy, Nancy, listen to me!"

She was halfway down the walk and going away fast.

He ran and caught her arm, dragging her to a halt.

She jerked away and glared at him.

He put up his hands in a conciliatory gesture.

"All right, all right. Maybe, I've been coming at this from the wrong point of view – "

"Maybe! Maybe!"

She started to turn away. He grabbed her arm again, dropped it quickly.

"I'm sorry," he apologized. "I won't detain you forcibly, but just listen for a minute, will you? Can't we compromise, meet somewhere in the middle?"

143

She took a deep breath and set her face.

"Say what you need to."

"What about this? I'll talk to John, and you talk to Elsie?"

She thought a moment. Suppose Donald had offered to talk to her, Nancy, a long time ago? Suppose he hadn't just sat there at the table those first times not saying a word while she heaped her anger on him, and then during the last few years, when she didn't even try to talk to him. Suppose, just maybe, she could have talked it out with him, came to a compromise that left her some dignity and gained his fidelity.

She nodded slowly.

"Okay."

Father Horst stepped forward to hug her, but she placed her hand in the middle of his black shirted chest.

"But not today. I'm too pissed."

He dropped his arms at his sides.

"Yes, yes. I perfectly understand."

She turned to walk away, but just as she reached the street where she had parked her pickup, he called after her.

"So, you'll pick up the lilies from the florist down in Valentine?"

The pickup door opened with a *creak*, sprung from the time a bull bounced his head off it last fall.

"Go get them yourself."

20

April 11, 1968

Friends or Lovers

John Caulfield was nowhere to be found. Father Horst drove out to his cabin three times, but no one answered the door, morning, afternoon, or night. He drove up and down the streets expecting to see John walking along them somewhere. He drove out to the auction barn and asked after John from the owner, Dick Hausman, who said that since the work was a little slow, he hadn't minded it when John asked for a few days off. He said that John has been such a lifesaver after the crisis over Jim Walker's death. Except Hausman didn't use the word "death." He said, "after we lost Jim," which sounded strange to Father Horst's ears, like Jim was still alive and just wandering around somewhere back in the pens chasing pigs. And maybe, so was John.

But three days after he disappeared, John was back in town, and although Father Horst expected he would return, he also expected John to have the wasted appearance of a three day drunk, and it was so.

But before John came back, Nancy talked to Elsie.

It was the Holy Thursday, and Nancy had prayed the Stations of the Cross, prayed for faith and understanding, ashamed of her outburst at Father Horst. Afterwards, she walked over to Elsie's house and had already knocked on the door before she remembered that it was Elsie's cleaning afternoon at the Packwoods' house, so she was surprised when Elsie opened the door and just stood there.

"Can I come in?" she asked.

Elsie hesitated a moment and then stood aside without saying a word.

Nancy entered, sat her handbag down on the table and removed the black lace mantilla that she had worn over her head while she was in the church.

"What's wrong, Elsie? Isn't this your cleaning day at the Pack-woods?"

Elsie didn't answer, stood a moment awkwardly chafing her hands together.

"Elsie?"

Elsie walked to the sink, started rinsing the cup and plate there, scouring out a black cast-iron skillet.

"Elsie, come sit down here and tell me what's wrong."

Elsie didn't answer.

"You know, I might be able to help if you tell me what's wrong. We're friends aren't we?" Nancy was folding the mantilla to put into her handbag.

Something broke in Elsie then. Her feet covered the floor in two bounds of her long, muscular legs, lunged at the smaller woman and flung her arms around her neck.

Nancy staggered, but her arms came up to clasp Elsie around the middle just above the waist.

Elsie sobbed, her face muffled against the scratchy wool of Nancy's spring green suit.

"Elsie, Elsie," Nancy crooned at her like she was a baby, a very big baby to be sure, but innocent as one smelling like the powdered cleanser she'd just used on the skillet instead of sour milk.

"Come on, honey, sit down, and we'll get it sorted out."

Nancy fumbled behind her for a chair, pulled it out and tried to get Elsie to sit, but Elsie clung to her as if Nancy were a life raft slowly deflating. Nancy sank into the chair slowly, and Elsie eased down to the floor, her head in Nancy's lap.

"We've been through a lot together, you and me," Nancy said, smoothing the braids of Elsie's hair. "Whatever it is, we'll get through this, too." A thought occurred to her.

"Elsie," she asked, "has Jack Mason come to bother you?"

Elsie went still, and then she said, in a sort of surprised tone through a full nose, "NOoo." And Nancy decided that Elsie didn't know about Jack Mason's threats. Anything less than Mason, she could handle. She thought.

"Mr. Packwood," Elsie said.

"Packwood? What about him?"

Elsie told her story, her voice muffled in the folds of Nancy's skirt.

Packwood, it seemed, had over the past few months become more and more bold, but by small increments – a too close conversation begun over a perfectly valid subject such as the shower curtain needing the soap scum scrubbed off or the top of the refrigerator needing a good wipe-down, subjects that the usual man in Jackson would never notice, subjects that Mrs. Packwood might rarely notice. Then there were the early comings home from the restaurant at times when he knew his wife had errands to run before going to the restaurant herself. There were half-compliments that were just a little too intimate, about Elsie's beautiful calves, and did the thighs match as well, and finally a gesture at lifting her shirt an inch or two, ostensibly to check out her fine muscle tone. She pretended not to notice, tried to stay away from him. Yes, he made her very nervous, he scared her, but just when she was ready to run, he would stop, distance himself, and she would tell herself that there wasn't anything there at all. But, after weeks of his seeming indifference, last week he had cornered her in the bathroom.

She was leaning over scrubbing out the tub, the water gushing noisily so she didn't hear him approach, didn't know anyone was around. She was grasped and held from behind, felt something push up against her bottom, a big object with an iron bar in the middle, felt hands on her hip bones holding her.

She had gasped, jerked and almost fell into the tub, caught herself on the edge with one hand and looking back, saw his pants, khaki ones that she had ironed so many times, saw his shoes – black, spattered with grease from frying hamburgers at the restaurant grill, a little dried bit of something stuck to one of the laces.

"Oh my God, Elsie, how did you get away?" Because obviously, she had gotten away, but had she gotten away before anything happened?

Having told the main part of the story, having done with the crying, Elsie did not want to talk further. Nancy pushed her.

147

"Elsie, how did you get away?"

A long silence, and then Elsie said. "I just kind of turned fast and he fell into the tub."

"Okay. And then?"

More silence.

"I ran away from that place."

"Oh, Elsie, I'm so glad you're safe."

Nancy leaned over, her head resting by Elsie's, her arms around Elsie's shoulders, feeling the strong panel of muscle across Elsie's upper back.

And not a goddamned thing more to be done about it, Nancy thought. No one saw it; no one heard it, and no one would want to hear about it. She knew how it went. Any woman's word, but particularly an Indian woman's word, an Indian woman who was known to have been raped, considered to be not quite bright – no way would talking to Packwood or the sheriff or anyone else do anything but bring Elsie unwanted attention and sympathy for Packwood, even though everyone knew how he was. Nancy was angry, but resigned. What could she do? Well, she could comfort, and so she did.

She eased Elsie up and into the chair, went to the sink and ran water into the coffee pot, a hospitality that Elsie had never ignored before now. It seemed so odd, this role reversal, but she measured grounds into the pot, set it on the stove and lit the burner.

Nancy glanced at Elsie sitting quietly at the table. No way did this picture, this new information, seem to fit with Father Horst's tale of a willing Elsie standing at the back door naked in the middle of the night, kissing John Caulfield, but Father Horst was a priest, a man Nancy had known for several years, a man of God, not a liar. It was like there were two Elsies.

She went over and sat down in the chair next to Elsie, took her hand.

"You are safe, Elsie," she said. "It isn't like before. Packwood can't hurt you, I don't think he would go that far. What did he do when you left?"

Elsie shuddered.

"He laughed," she said. "I heard him laughing. There in the tub. It echoes, you know."

And Nancy thought of the sound box that was her own tub and shower stall at home, and how Donald, whose singing voice was weak and thready, came out of that place in the mornings, rich and loud, when he sang in the shower. Packwood must have sounded like the devil himself to Elsie.

It was dark the night Father Horst saw Elsie and John. Horst had said so himself. What did he really see? Maybe it wasn't an obvious love tryst. Maybe Caulfield had forced himself on Elsie. Jesus, was there a conspiracy among all the men in the world against Elsie?

She couldn't accuse Elsie now of willingly carrying on with John, in spite of Father Horst's request. How could she even ask such a thing?

She spoke tentatively.

"Elsie, you know John Caulfield. Has he ever tried anything with you?"

Elsie's head came up and her eyes blazed.

"I hate him!"

"Oh, no, Elsie! John tried to rape you, too? *Did* rape you?"

The fire went out and Elsie's eyes dropped.

"No. No. I just don't like him anymore."

"Why not Elsie?" Nancy probed, but there would be no more answers from Elsie, and she didn't mind that now. She had spoken with Elsie, as Father Horst asked, and there was no more to be said. The matter, whatever it was, seemed ended. He could talk to John or not, as he pleased, and maybe he would get more information out of John, and maybe it just didn't matter anymore.

She got up and poured herself and Elsie a cup of coffee.

"I need another job," Elsie said.

"What?"

"To take the place of the Packwoods."

"Oh," Nancy said, "Don't worry about that. I'll put a notice up on the church bulletin board and you'll have another one like that." She snapped her fingers.

149

She tried once again to find out what had happened between John and Elsie, but Elsie wouldn't talk further, so Nancy left it. Father Horst would be happy about it, she thought, even if it meant Elsie had lost a friend as well as a lover.

21

Summer, Fall and Winter, 1968

Replay

Father Horst never did speak with John Caulfield, who had gone to hell in a hand basket again. He started showing up for work at the auction barns on his way to getting drunk, completely drunk, or recovering from a drunk. Then he showed up late or failed to show up at all. Hausman was exasperated, but also disappointed because he truly had wanted John to turn his life around, had even spoken to John's parents about him hoping for an easing of tension there, if not an actual family reunion. John's parents had listened and smiled at the first reports, but when things went downhill, and Hausman stopped promoting John to them, they retreated to their original position: they had no son. When the high school let out in May, Hausman hired a kid, Paul Fogel, who had just graduated as John's replacement. The kid was a little slow upstairs but dependable and not going anywhere but Jackson. He had no other prospects and a seventeen-year-old wife who was pregnant.

Elsie did get another job cleaning for Dr. Hunter and his wife. Hunter was the local dentist, a man who had come to Jackson planning to stay a few years and move on, but gotten stuck, and now in his early forties, he was frayed and tired from overwork and resigned. His ditsy blonde wife, Cindy, was the receptionist who didn't make his life easier because she always messed up the appointment schedule, so that some days he had three or four people with toothaches fuming in his waiting room while he hurried as fast as he could doing a routine cleaning, and some days there were no patients at all. The wife had one talent though, and that was having children. There were four Hunter boys and a fifth child bouncing in Cindy's belly. Cindy couldn't cook either and couldn't discipline the boys, so the house was always in a mess. Elsie was needed and appreciated.

Events in Jackson that spring and summer seemed very like a replay of the previous summer, when Elsie had just arrived, had two houses and the rectory to clean, except that Elsie and John Caulfield no longer had lunch in the park or spoke to each other on the streets. She avoided him, and he, her. John had receded two years, to the time before Elsie came. He was sober often enough to earn his rent and food money, but little extra for his booze, so that he was often in trouble for panhandling and annoying customers outside the Legion club and the town package liquor store.

The crops were good that summer, wheat and oats, rye and barley lush and green with just the right amount of rainfall. Alfalfa fields bloomed lavender, and pretty red Hereford calves with clean white faces bounced and ran beside mama cows. Farmers bragged to each other about the state of their fields, inflating the estimates of bushels per acre they would harvest in late July. The town merchants observed gleefully, knowing that they would get a good share of those profits, while the banker tilted back in his chair, hands folded across his round belly and thought about all the crop loans the farmers would clear off the books instead of just paying the interest and renewing the loan. Everyone prayed that the weather would hold. It did.

To Nancy's chagrin, Donald's chasing didn't slow down as it usually did when the work load increased. Twice a week or more he was gone to town for a variety of reasons – the mower broke down and he needed a part, he ran out of wire for the baler, needed salt or mineral block for the cattle – and he would come home bleary eyed and tired the next morning, get a shower and go right to work. Nancy thought about asking him if the parts store and the feed store were that busy that he had to stand in line until dawn to get what he needed, but she didn't. She threw herself into her gardening, canning dozens of quarts of green beans, bread-and-butter and beet pickles. She cooked elaborate, hearty meals, which Donald devoured like a starving hobo, but he grew thinner, and dark circles appeared beneath his eyes. Nancy thought that if he was this bad in the summer, what would he be like when fall and winter, his regular chasing season, began?

A week after the Fourth of July, the custom harvesters began trailing into town, mobile businesses with the owner and his family in a nice travel trailer, the battered buses for the hands who drove the trucks towing combine harvest machines. The town experienced that population doubling with the harvesters all parked on the empty field on the south side of town and expanding onto the parking lot of the grain elevator. Seen from a crop-duster plane above, Jackson proper was a regular shape with the welter of buses and travel trailers, trucks, and combines, forming a temporary tumor on the side.

The town overflowed with harvest workers, crowding the two restaurants, drinking at the bars, occasionally joining the Indians in the town's tiny jail. The bolder ones whistled at the women on the street, and the parents of teenaged girls refused to allow them uptown unaccompanied. Elsie stayed in at night, walked to her jobs and back quickly, head down, and when she wasn't working, she was at the library reading many books there but checking out few. The weather held, hot and dry, and two weeks after the harvesters came, the tumor was excised and they moved on, following the ripening grain north.

Donald grew thin, but Elsie gained up to her previous, pre-illness weight, and then more bloating up like a brown dirigible. She couldn't get enough to eat. Elsie was at the grocery store more often, bantering with the children, showing them her turtles, but mostly buying more food, her beloved oranges and other fruit, but also cake mixes and pre-baked goods. She craved all the sweetness of life, but not the salt. She never bought potato chips.

The county fair came and went, school started, the summer waned into fall with the usual turning leaves, cool mornings, pheasant hunting season and the accompanying American Legion pheasant supper. Signs around town read:

All You Can Eat Pheasant Supper
Three Dollars a Plate
Birds Donated by Local Hunters
Proceeds to Charity.

153

Then it was November and people were thinking ahead to Thanksgiving and Christmas. Except for a few unlucky farmers whose crops had been hailed out, most had money in their pocket to spend for Christmas. Crops might fail for the next four years, probably would, but this year, they would celebrate and pretend that all good things went on forever.

Deer season came, and the locals competed for the antlers with the most points, for the first deer to be taken, for the biggest deer, each one draped over the hunter's pickup and driven through the streets. An early cold snap brought the deer out into the fields early in the morning where they grazed on the dropped grain from the summer harvest, easy targets for hunters. By the third week of the season, most of the hunters had bagged their deer, and the lights at the locker plant burned far into the night while Kolcek and his daughters and their husbands worked to process them all. By the end of November, the ranchers' fall round-ups had ended, and except for replacement heifers, all the spring calves had been sold and shipped, but the pace didn't slow much at the locker plant. Now, all the ranchers and some locals who bought beef on the hoof were sending a few animals that had been saved back from the fall sale to be slaughtered, cut up, and packaged for their own dinner tables. Colder weather was good for the Kolceks. When there was no more room in the huge cooler, the carcasses could be hung in the big slaughter room without fear of the meat going off, but towards the second week of December they had to scramble to clear out the cooler. The weather turned unseasonably warm, a repeat of the previous year.

Father Horst loved the people of his parish, was firmly committed to his calling, and obediently served where he was sent, but though he was still relatively young, he dreaded the Dakota winters, remembered his growing-up years in Pennsylvania where the winters were cold, but couldn't compare with those in Jackson for pure viciousness. He had requested a transfer to a parish near his sister in central Pennsylvania, but he hadn't told his parishioners yet, not even Nancy. The church administration was erratic – they might transfer him within months, might not transfer him for years, might not even acknowledge his letter at all. No use noising around his desire to move on until it was a fact. That knowledge, become common, might make his parishioners doubt his commitment to them, and then if the transfer never came through, he would be dealing with suspicious people for the rest of his working life – maybe until he died.

But just lately, even though he was not yet forty, it seemed the cold seeped into his bones and crystallized there. So, when the temperature made that rare climb above fifty and stayed there for three days, on the third afternoon, he carried a cup of tea outside to take a turn around his little garden spot. The seed catalogs would come in soon, junk mail to some folks, but a welcome peek into the warm near future for him as he pored over the bright colored pages of flowers, the new (and sometimes odd) offerings of vegetables. Blue potatoes, giant squash, burpless cucumbers.

Outside, he sat the teacup down on the ground, took the pitchfork and began turning the compost pile, not that it really needed it. The cold weather kept it from rotting as fast as the warmer weather, but it was a formality, a confidence that spring would come, that the compost would have turned into a black, rich loam ready for spreading on the surface and turning in with the spade. As he dug the fork into the pile, among the not-quite-dried-out potato peelings and coffee grinds, he saw a small grayish brown bit of fur, a mouse he assumed, but then he wondered why Cat would have put a dead mouse on the compost pile instead of eating it. Strangely, it appeared to have no head or legs or tail. He stopped, flicked it over with his fingertip. It wasn't a mouse, but a piece of deer skin, and not just a dried up bit from Elsie's hide tanning project of the previous year, oh, no. This shred still had a bit of red flesh clinging to the raw side. Fresh. New. This piece of hide had been part of a live deer, walking around less than a month earlier; he was sure of it.

He dropped the pitchfork, and his eyes went to the tree behind him in the vacant lot. The lot was lower than the churchyard by some feet, tall winter dead sunflowers and brush and weeds and the

155

overgrown lilac bushes intervening. He squinted his eyes at the tree branches, walked to the squashed down half-fallen fence and stared, but there were no incongruously large squares, Elsie's tanning frames, dangling from the branches.

Maybe, he thought, one of the neighbors had gotten a deer and dressed it out themselves in their back yard and the scrap was just a remnant of that process dragged home by Cat, a remnant that she could chew, but too tough for her to swallow whole. He looked at the ground around the garden patch and the surrounding yard, and found two more bits, then three, then half a dozen as if the yard had suddenly decided to grow it's own hairy hide, but was just getting started.

He *knew*, he just knew that Elsie had done it again, but he couldn't figure out where and how. The scraps must be the trimmings that she removed from the hides before lacing them into the frames, but surely she hadn't been bold enough to just toss the scraps out in the yard. He went to check out the garbage can and then he remembered. For the past two weeks Elsie had insisted on taking the can out to the street on the days the collection truck came by and bringing it back when it had been emptied. The garbage would have been collected this morning, but Elsie was still on one of her cleaning jobs, so she wouldn't have brought the can back in yet.

He walked out to the street, to the can, which seemed to take on a suspicious collaboration of its own. It had been emptied, the dented lid carelessly flung on the ground beside the can. He turned it so the light fell inside, and there clinging to the side was another chunk of deer hide. He was instantly furious, angrier than he had ever been in his life.

He didn't bother to pick up the can and lid, but marched with long strides straight back to Elsie's cottage, tried the door, and it was unlocked. But when he turned the knob and opened it, the stench nearly knocked him backwards. He jumped back, yelled, "oh my God," turned his face to gulp up clean air. She must have the stretchers of hides in her house! He pinched his nose and peered into the house, but there was nothing in the kitchen. Somewhere in the back of his mind, he wondered how Elsie could eliminate the stench from her own clothes and person when she went to her cleaning jobs. Against his own compunctions about invading other's privacy, he entered her kitchen, glanced down the short hall and there, lining the wall, were three stretchers of hides, and in her bedroom he saw another leaning against the far wall behind the bed.

How can she live in this stink? He wondered. Keeping his nose pinched one handed, he dragged the frames out one by one with his other arm, heedless that the heavy wooden two by four frames made deep scratches in the linoleum, heaved them into the yard. Then he opened all the windows, left the door open and went back to the rectory where he turned the shower on full, pulled off his clothes and cleaned himself in water so hot he could barely stand it but not as hot as his temper.

How could she *do* this! And why? These were the questions revolving in his mind, questions for which he had no answers other than the ones his anger created: She was deliberately undermining him. She was ungrateful. She was too stupid to remember last year's experience, but he knew this last was not true, but the alternative, that she had done it to defy his authority, to make him look foolish, was not something he wanted to accept, either. She was always cooperative, unassuming, did her work without complaint, and really annoyed him at times with her insistence on keeping the ashtrays constantly free of his pipe cleanings, his newspapers neatly stacked, when sometimes he had them laid out in seeming disarray because there were articles he wanted to follow up on, sources of inspiration for sermons, or for dealing with parishioners or parish affairs. But how could she be so insistent on neatness and still do what she had done, when it meant living in unbearable stench? Getting deer skins to make up her bead and leatherwork projects couldn't be that important, could it? She didn't make that much money from it, did she? And doing that kind of traditional crafts work wasn't a cultural imperative, a religious conviction, not like keeping the holy days of the church. He knew that the other Indians in town didn't insist on tanning hides in their backyards and houses, or at least he was pretty

157

sure they didn't. Did she really need those tanned deer skins? Then he remembered that he had promised to find another source for tanned deer skins, and he hadn't bothered to follow up on it. A tinge of guilt lowered the temperature of his anger. But, she could have asked! But, you didn't do what you promised, an inner voice told him. And he knew he couldn't confront Elsie as he had planned. She would be home in an hour or so. She would see the hides, still laced in their frames tossed out in the yard. She would know that he knew. He was afraid of his own temper, afraid of how far he might go if Elsie defied him, or worse, had no response at all for what she had done. But those hides couldn't stay out there in the yard, the smell would attract stray dogs and cats, and disgruntled neighbors.

He pulled on his clothes and went to find John Caulfield.

Two hours later, John, miraculously sober but hung over, was two feet down in a trench he was digging in the church yard, and not happy about this job. He was not only to bury the hides, but to chop up the stretchers and bury them, too. It wasn't that he minded work, any work, but destroying the frames he had made seemed like he would be negating a kindness he had done for Elsie, and he did so few of those for anyone. No more for Elsie, either. But the ax lay beside the pile of framed hides and when the trench was deep enough, John crawled out, took up the ax and began tearing up his kindness. He had done a good job in the making of the frames; he would do a better job of destroying them. He chopped with a vengeance.

Father Horst did not speak to Elsie, but he told Nancy about it, berating himself for not finding a leather source for her.

"Don't you think you're enjoying your new found sin of omission a little too comfortable?" Nancy asked.

He was indignant. "What are you talking about? Of course, not! What I did – or didn't do – wasn't a sin! Just a slip, an absent-minded mistake, but it wasn't right."

"Oh, stop it. So what? You forgot something, all right, well, so did I. You know I usually visit Elsie a couple of times a week, and what with getting the cattle rounded up and shipped and feeding the neighbors who come to help and Thanksgiving and starting Christmas shopping and all that, well, I haven't been over to Elsie's in three weeks. If I had been doing what I usually do – " She stopped a moment. "Well, come to think of it, I told Elsie I wouldn't be stopping by for a while. You don't suppose – "

No, it couldn't be that Elsie deliberately planned to do this while she knew Nancy wouldn't catch her. Elsie was ingenuous, but not sly.

"Suppose what?" He stopped pacing and took the unlit pipe out of his mouth.

"Nothing, nothing. But you don't see me, pretending to be a martyr because our sweet but naïve friend repeated something she knew better than to do, do you?"

He didn't have an answer. Neither did Elsie, although she wasn't asked.

Elsie went into an isolated sulk for two weeks, but it was a planned sulk. She stocked up on groceries before she locked herself in her house, responded to knocks on her door with a peek out the front window and a shake of her head, but refused to open the door, even when her cleaning customers showed up to demand why she hadn't been coming to work.

January 23, 1970, Afternoon

Lowan

Lowan clawed vigorously at the back door. Oscar got up stiffly and let the dog in.

"You little whore monger," he said, but the dog just gave him a knowing look and trotted over to noisily lap at his water bowl, a battered metal pan with the handle missing but the screws still attached to the side.

Nancy glanced up above the dog at the clock and yelped.

"It's past four o'clock! I've got to get home. I've got chores to be done before dark," she said.

"No need to rush off," Oscar said. "Chores will still be there tomorrow."

Nancy ignored him and went to put on her coat, talking to you over her shoulder.

"Look, there's not much more to the story if you can get that slow-thinking old fart to tell you," she said, nodding at Oscar.

"Some stories take time," Oscar protested mildly.

"Yeah, well, you'd better tell it to him faster. He needs to know the whole thing before he gets old and dies." Then she was out the door and gone.

You look at Oscar and raise your eyebrows.

He sighs.

"All right. But this is going to take another pot of coffee. And neither one of us is going to be able to sleep when it's all told."

You don't know if he means the story will be that disturbing or if the caffeine will keep you awake.

Winter: December 1968 and January 1969

Elsie's Business

"This is what happened," Oscar said. "Or so they say."

Just about the time that deer season started, some of the men of the Roberts family and few others went a little crazy, Oscar said. Little Mack, a distant cousin of the man Elsie's mother was married to, was the worst. He didn't want to leave the house; he screamed in the night, and when awakened would not, or could not, tell his family what had frightened him. And then, when he did get out of the house, he would be gone for days and no amount of searching by his worried family would turn him up. They took to tying him to his bed, a process he allowed willingly, like a young woman of old times whose legs were tied together at night and then tethered to a female relative to prevent her from roaming or being stolen in the night by an overly amorous suitor.

Then one day, Little Mack happened to glance out the window when one of the hunters drove down the street parading his newly shot deer on the hood of his truck. Little Mack screamed like a girl, ran and hid under the bed, pushing himself trembling back against the farthest wall. His mother tried prodding him out with the broom handle but, she finally determined, she could have poked him as full of holes as a sieve and he wouldn't have budged.

And there were others, like Georgie Dubois and Porky the Pine, who exhibited similar symptoms. The women were at their wits end, and then Georgie claimed he saw a deer walking down Main Street in broad daylight, looking in the windows of the package liquor store where he had went to buy a little courage. He trembled and pointed, yelling something unintelligible. The clerk saw nothing to remark, and finally decided that Georgie must have the DT's and really needed the liquor, so when he was a few pennies short for his pint of whiskey, she made up the difference herself.

The men who were ambulatory and able went to Oscar for ceremonies, advice, and the women walked uneasy, while the white people in town went on about their holiday business cheerfully unaware of the crisis brewing in the alternate dimension that was the Indian part of Jackson. Christmas came and went and the tension still hung over the Indian community, a dark anticipation that spoke to the people in dreams, stalked the men in nightmares, and would eventually enable Mary Crow Bird to become the best bead worker of them all because she saw the deer woman, twenty years later her work displayed in the museum of the American Indian Art Institute in Santa Fe, selling for high prices in Taos and Phoenix and Tucson. But that was the woman gift, the opposite of what the men endured, the men who had no will to speak out, who couldn't say no to the deer woman.

Elsie resumed cleaning the rectory and went back to her regular customers, who took her back gratefully, but not without severe lectures. Two years of no cleaning woman during the Christmas holidays right when they needed it the most did not make them happy, but, they told themselves, she was an Indian, and what did they expect. For her part, Elsie assumed her usual bland expression, taking the lectures without comment and going on about her business when they were finished. Father Horst found himself missing Elsie's household fussiness, as the newspaper pile grew untidy and the ashtrays overflowed, and his anger was buried beneath the ashes and paper and hauled out to the trash when Elsie got down to work again.

She was thinner from her self-enforced isolation, probably her groceries had run out before her determination had. She still avoided John Caulfield, though; she never mentioned him to Nancy again.

Just after Christmas, Father Horst's notice of transfer came through. It was not what he had really wanted – he was being reassigned to a parish on the Salt River Pima Reservation in southern Arizona. His anguish came close to overwhelming him when he read the letter; he really had his heart set on being closer to his own family again. He had nieces and nephews he had never seen, and as he got older, nostalgic memories of a happy youth spent there. But after a few hours of reflection, he supposed that the church authorities assumed he now had experience working with Indians, although he had few Indians in his congregation. Mostly, they attended Holy Cross on the reservation or didn't attend at all. He recalled his vow of obedience, and he thought about the warmer winters in Arizona. That would be something to be thankful for. He thought he had read that there were orange groves under irrigation there.

The Saturday night after New Year's Eve was quiet, and Sheriff Ed Parker was on duty alone. The deputy had come down with a bad case of the flu, but it was the turn of the county sheriff's department to stand the night watch to let the city police have the night off, so Ed was it. The weather report had predicted a slow moving storm to come in bringing several inches of snow, and about nine o'clock, right on schedule, Parker looked up from his *Field and Stream* magazine, glanced out the window, and saw snow falling, heavy big flakes that seemed to keep falling forever as if the bottom of heaven had collapsed and all the angels were molting.

He made the rounds of the town in his patrol car a couple of hours after that, leaving dark tire marks in the quickly accumulating snow as he followed the grid of streets, from the north side of town back to Main Street, from Main Street to the south and back again. Back at the little police station, he parked the car on the side street facing south in the hopes that doing so would keep the cold wind from freezing the heater-melted snow into ice by morning when he had to make one more round before turning over the office to his deputy – if the deputy was able to get himself out of bed.

The phone was silent, the furnace kept the little office too warm while the prisoner's cells were like ice boxes. He drowsed in the warmth, pulled off his shirt around two in the morning and lay down on the sagging sofa. He slept.

Hours later, he awoke, his back complaining, eased himself upright, and glanced at his watch. Five a.m. He stood up and stretched, poured himself the last cup of thick coffee from the percolator and walked back to the cells to check the prisoners. There were only two of them, regulars, who had been in jail for two weeks, and would be there for another, or until more Indians were arrested who could work out their fine as pickup men on the garbage truck. These two sat upright on one of the only two bunks, tipped over against each other for warmth, snoring gently.

Parker went back to his office and pulled on his shirt, coat, hat, and gloves. He would make one more round of the streets before the deputy came on duty at six. He thought he'd skip church today. The snow had stopped coming down, but more might be on the way. It was a good day to sleep.

He swept the snow from the windshield with his arm, noticed the ice crust on the windshield, started the motor and flicked the defroster on high and went back inside to wait. He was not in the ice scraping mood. Fifteen minutes later he climbed behind the wheel, put the patrol car in gear and listened to the crunch of snow and ice as he backed up, turned and drove west. Past the silent Presbyterian church on the corner, down the steep hill, past the Dakota Hotel. Past the square white prairie style frame house where the superintendent of schools lived, and across from that house and farther along the similar but smaller clapboard houses where other middle class folks lived. His own house was at the end of the street, the last house but one, and on the corner lived the retired home economics teacher. Her kitchen light was on.

She was always an early riser, and the thought occurred to him that all old people got up early. Maybe they needed the extra time to worry about their bowels. He grinned at his own little joke.

At the end of the block, he turned to the right and started back east up the hill, tires slipping a little on the snow. When he got back to the office, he'd call Walt, the street maintenance man, to get his butt out of bed and sand the steeper areas of the streets. Walt would whine about it, say it wasn't necessary on a Sunday with so few people about anyway, but he would insist. Walt was just plain lazy. He wished the city council would fire the man and get someone else, but Walt had a crippled kid and a wife in poor health. Parker knew he'd be putting up with Walt for a long time yet.

The car crested the hill, passed the rectory of the Presbyterian church, through the intersection. No one about, no one at all, except a dog belonging to somebody or nobody, trotting across the road, winter fur thick, heading for the trash dumpster behind The Steak House, stopping briefly to sniff at some round orange object, something barely visible in the growing light, something orange half buried in the snow. The dog only paused, then went on to another orange something, and then Parker noticed there were a series of orange somethings, a crooked dotted line in the snow, going up the slight incline leading around behind the dumpster. He pulled the patrol car over to the curb and got out. Two steps off the curb he leaned over the orange something and discovered it wasn't an orange something, but an orange. He followed the dotted line – one, two, three – here two of them dropped together, then another and another. From behind the dumpster he heard the dog worrying at something, looked up and took another step forward. There was a bundle of something there and the dog had hold of it, shaking it back and forth. A body, oh shit, another Indian drunk and froze to death.

"Hey, hey," he yelled and clapped his gloved hands together with a muffled sound. "Get away from there!"

The dog ignored him. He ran at it, fist upraised. The dog let go, and stepped back. He picked up a frozen orange and flung it striking the dog in the flank. It yelped and ran off a few yards, turned, and stood defiantly.

He bent over and turned the body over.

Elsie's yellow and red printed headscarf was more red than yellow, and stuck deep into a groove in the top of her head, blood, darkest red in the half light, covering her face like some macabre raspberry sundae. He groaned and quickly averted his eyes, away to the right at the dumpster, and there was a spray of frozen blood on the side of the dumpster, the new white dumpster that the city had bought to replace the old rusted out ones. He was outraged. He was sick. He forced his eyes back to Elsie. Beside her lay a torn grocery bag, another orange inside and a couple of cans of stewed tomatoes.

A little way away from it, a five pound bag of red potatoes and a jar of Skippy peanut butter, the kind with a blue label. Chunky style.

Jesus, he couldn't think. What was the matter with him? He hastily felt for a pulse in Elsie's neck. Jesus, he couldn't *think*. Of course, she was dead; it was damned obvious she was dead. Jesus, he had to go to church today, now, no way out of it, but yes, there was. He'd be up to his ass investigating what the hell happened here. He wished he could go to church. He could go back to the jail and pretend he hadn't saw this, let somebody else report it, go home and sleep until someone rousted him out to tell him the news. No, he wouldn't be able to sleep.

He stood on shaky legs, looking around. From the looks of the wound on her head, the weapon had been a long, narrow object. He walked around slowly, kicking at the snow, and turned up an iron bar about four feet long, and he knew what it was – the bar used to prop open the lid of the dumpster when several bags of garbage had to be pitched in at the same time. It was crusty with frozen blood on one end, but he knew there would be no fingerprints. No one in his right mind would have been wandering around last night without heavy gloves on.

The dog still crouched in the snow, waiting, whining a little. He ran at it, yelling, and the dog jumped and ran, looking back occasionally, but he yelled again and ran after it, and the dog loped away down the street, into a yard and around behind a house.

Shit. Shit, shit, shit. He looked down at Elsie again, looked at the thick layer of snow on her coat, brushed off in the place where he'd caught on to turn her body over. Laying beneath her was her cloth bag, the one she'd carried everywhere. He remembered then, and reached inside. The dying warmth of her body had melted some snow on it that had then rapidly refrozen sticking the sides of the bag together, closing the top. Inside was a worn pink wallet with seven one dollar bills in it, a wadded up stiff handkerchief printed with violets, a grocery ad torn out of the newspaper, Tom and Dick.

Turtles hibernated in the winter, didn't they? He turned Tom in his hands, pulled off one glove and felt the coldness of him, a frozen

166

rock. He thought that if he pitched against the side of the dumpster it would shatter into a million turtle pieces. But turtles survived frozen in the ice all winter, didn't they? He didn't know. He didn't know anything about turtles. He knew about politics, about making small town people compromise even when they didn't want to, about keeping people from getting so angry that that they did foolish things, about soothing feelings and getting reelected. He didn't know anything.

He put Tom in one pocket and Dick in the other and walked back to the patrol car to use the radio.

Father Horst did not remember saying mass at seven o'clock. He had been on autopilot because there was no one else to say mass, and because he couldn't not do it, and because in the winter there was only one mass at seven o'clock and people couldn't be expected to wait, could they, or not to have a Sunday mass at all? They couldn't wait while he made sense of what Parker had told him at ten minutes to seven, not time enough to ask for details or to wonder what happened or to think what he could have done to prevent it, him, the keeper of the flock who was supposed to protect them from the wolves, except Elsie didn't really belong to his flock, not technically, but she was a human being, part of the larger flock of humanity. He did not see the faces before him in the church, except for one, except for Nancy, and he knew he had to tell her when the mass was ended, and how could he say that last line, "the mass is ended go in peace," and extend his hand, make the sign of the cross, when there was no peace, but no, he could not think like that. So he said the mass and read the announcements, and he gave his planned sermon, and he wondered if the wolf that got one of his sheep was sitting there looking up at him, but he couldn't believe that, didn't want to believe that. There had to be some terrible mistake; it had to be an accident. While he went through the motions of the mass, another part his mind prayed over and over for guidance, for solace, for understanding, for acceptance of God's will, but he couldn't get past the first line of the Hail Mary. Hail Mary, full of grace; Hail Mary, full of grace; Hail Mary, full of grace; Hail Mary, full of grace.

Father Horst asks Nancy if she doesn't want to call Donald to come to town. Donald had missed mass again. Nancy's face is set and white with shock, but she isn't crying yet. She is making sandwiches in the rectory kitchen.

"You shouldn't be alone," he tells her.

She looks back at him sourly, mayonnaises another piece of bread, slaps a piece of cheese on it.

"Donald didn't come home last night," she says. "It's the winter rut season, don't you know? And if he doesn't get his ass home this afternoon, I suppose I'll have to get the hay sled out and buck some bales and some cotton cake onto it and go feed. Maybe. Right now, I just don't care about Donald or the damned cows."

They sit in the living room of the rectory, Father Horst and Nancy, Sheriff Ed Parker and the county coroner, Frank Staley, the sandwiches drying out, untouched, on a plate on the coffee table. But the coffee goes down.

Parker has already told the story of finding Elsie in more detail, but the details don't reveal anything, least of all what they all want to know: who did it. Frank Staley has given his best guess for preliminary cause of death, and not a difficult guess to make: a hard blow to the head delivered from the iron bar. Death instantaneous.

"It was quick, so at least she didn't suffer," Staley adds.

"Didn't *suffer*! She didn't *suffer*! So you think that makes it okay? And what do you mean, she *didn't suffer*! Her whole life was about suffering," Nancy says, and not quietly, either.

"Nancy, come on, you know I didn't mean it like that," he pleads.

She clenches her teeth, looks at her coffee cup clenched equally hard in both her hands.

Father Horst strikes a match to light his pipe, sits back, lets it burn down, and drops it into the ash tray, his pipe still unlit.

"We can't undo what's been done," he says. "God knows, I wish we could. I don't know if we could have prevented this or not. Seems to me that we did all we could do, the best we knew how for her, and now she's in God's hands."

No one offers a reply.

168

"Any idea who did it?" she asks Parker, although she's already asked that before.

"Nothing yet, but, like I said, it's early. Far as I know, nobody in town had any reason to kill her," Parker says. There are dark circles under his eyes, and his back still hurts from sleeping on the lumpy office sofa. He eases back in the chair he sits in now, slopping a little of his coffee on his shirt front.

Nancy looks up at him, her eyes narrowed.

"Well, what about your good old buddy, Jack Mason?"

Parker sighs.

"He isn't my 'good old buddy,' he's just an acquaintance. And I've already called Earl Petersen up in Mobridge. He called me back and says that Mason acts shocked, but says he was home all night and his wife will swear to it."

"Oh, really? Any other reliable witnesses?"

Parker shrugs.

"Dunno. Peterson up there is checking it out further."

Nancy turns to Frank Staley.

"What time was Elsie killed?"

Staley thinks a minute.

"Hard to say. Usually you can tell by the temperature of the body, when rigor sets in, all that. But she was out in the cold, so her body would have cooled faster, and then partially frozen. Masks things, you know. My best guess is sometime around ten o'clock last night because the stores close then, and she was coming home from the store with her groceries," he says.

Parker nods agreement. He's thinking that was just about an hour after he made his rounds in the patrol car. If only he had waited another hour, things might have been different.

"That makes sense," is all he says, though.

"All right," Nancy said. "It takes about four to five hours to drive from here to Mobridge. He could have been here, done it, and been back up there by three this morning."

"You're forgetting that snow storm last night," Parker says. "Would take at least a couple of hours longer to drive back in that."

169

"All right. So, say it would have taken seven hours instead of five. That would put him home at five o'clock this morning. When did you call up there?"

Parker hesitates.

"I'd have to check the log, but it was about ten o'clock."

"See?" Nancy says and leaned back on the sofa.

Father Horst strikes another match, puts it to his pipe, and then puts it down again, dropping the blackened match in the standing ash tray by his chair. His pipe stays in his hand, cold.

"Nancy, it doesn't make any sense for Mason to do it," Father Horst says. "At least, not now. Things had all quieted down about Elsie and those boys. Why would Jack Mason want to stir it all up again?"

"That's just the reason he would do it now!" Nancy says. "'Cause it has all quieted down, so people would think he *wouldn't* be involved now. Don't you see?"

"Well, supposing that he did want to do her in, but he'd bided his time. There wasn't any urgency about it was there? So why on earth would he risk life and limb to drive down here in a snowstorm? Seems to me that if he waited this long, he'd just wait a little longer for a more convenient time," Parker says.

"I'll wait until we hear if his alibi checks out up in Mobridge," Nancy says. She puts her hand to her eyes suddenly. "I can't believe we're just sitting around here discussing Elsie's murder like it's some damned puzzle to solve. Like she was just an object that we don't care about anymore. What's wrong with us? What's wrong with me? I should be crying. A good woman that I considered my friend is dead, murdered, and here I sit just discussing it."

Father Horst puts his pipe down in the ash tray, reaches out and touches her shoulder.

"There's no prescription for grief," he says. "There's no right way or wrong way to go about it. You're doing what you need to do now, the most loving way to grieve for her. You're trying to help figure out who and why. You'll cry when you're ready."

Nancy does give a little sob then, stifles it, reaches in her pocket for a tissue and blows her nose.

Father Horst lights another match.

Nancy snaps at him.

"If you are going to smoke that stinking pipe, then light up and smoke it, but stop just lighting matches like a little kid!"

Father Horst stares at the lit match, shakes it out, gets up, and puts his ashtray with the pipe in it on a shelf of his bookcase. There is a pile of newspapers on the floor in front of it. The *Sioux Falls Argosy*, the *Omaha World Herald*. The latest issue of the weekly *Jackson Messenger*. He'd have to get used to cleaning up his own messes again, just when he'd gotten comfortable with someone else doing it. Not just someone else, comfortable with *Elsie* doing it.

Parker clears his throat.

"Well, there is another reason we came over here," he says, "other than just to discuss what happened. I want to take a look around her house."

Nancy groans.

"Does that have to be done now? Can't it wait? I mean, she's not even cold yet." Then she thinks about that – Elsie was certainly cold – and she starts to laugh, and then she catches herself, starts to cry again, her hand over her mouth.

Father Horst comes back to her side.

"It's okay to laugh," he says. "Sometimes that's all we have. Elsie would understand."

But Nancy pushes him away, blows her nose again.

"Nancy," Parker continues, "I'm not just being a ghoul here. There might be something in her house that would give us some idea of who did this ugly thing. A threatening letter maybe, I don't know."

"He's right," Staley said. "It's not a question of waiting a decent interval to go through her things."

"Dragnet," Nancy says. "Looking for clues, like some damned TV show."

They put on their coats then, and Parker reaches into his pockets, finds Tom and Dick, and brings them out without thinking.

"Oh, God," Nancy says.

"Here, give them to me," Father Horst says. Taking the turtles, he walks back to the kitchen, opens the refrigerator and puts them inside. They should go into the coffin with Elsie, he thinks.

The four of them walk through the unmarked snow to Elsie's door, wait while Father Horst fumbles with the second set of keys, unlocks the door.

It is cold inside; Elsie must've turned the heat down before she went out to the store. In spite of the cold, the place smells slightly of decay, from the last tanning operation, Father Horst thinks, and feels guilty that he has been so hard on Elsie over it.

There are a few pieces of mail on the table, but nothing of significance, just box holders from her postal box – one, an outdated flyer from the Jackson Merchant's Association that had printed in big red letters on white paper: SHOP LOCAL FOR CHRISTMAS, and a list of stores with the items offered on sale. The kitchen is clean, dishes in the drainer with a worn red checked dish towel draped over them to keep out nonexistent dust. The trash can is empty except for some orange peels. She must've eaten the last one and went out to the store for more.

A picture calendar from the Jackson Feed Mill hangs above the table opened up to November. She hasn't turned the page yet. Parker looks at it, flips back a few months, forward to December, but Elsie has written nothing on it at all.

They stand and stare at each other.

"Might as well check out the bedroom," Frank Staley says.

He hesitates a moment, then squares his shoulders and walks down the short hall, pausing a moment to glance into the bathroom. Nothing out of order there. It smells faintly of chlorine cleanser from the clean sink and tub. The turtles' blue graniteware pan sits on the floor by the toilet. A towel so old and faded it is colorless hangs on the rack, folded neatly in thirds, a faded red washcloth, now dry, is draped over the lavatory faucet.

Frank enters the bedroom with Ed Parker, Nancy, and Father Horst crowding behind him. The room is spare and just as neat as the rest of the house. The bed is neatly made up with the old pink chenille bedspread tucked under the pillows, nothing on the stand by the bed, and the only other furniture is the bureau. Five library books are stacked neatly on top, all photo travel books like you see on peoples' coffee tables. The old yellowing window shade is half drawn, and the small closet contains Elsie's few dresses, her pair of good shoes, which are just newer versions of the brown oxfords she wore every day.

Parker opens one of the bureau drawers, realizes it contains Elsie's underwear, and backs away.

"Umm, Nancy, I think maybe you ought to go through this," he says.

Nancy finds nothing of note there or in the next two drawers down either. The fourth one holds various jars containing beads – tiny Czech seed beads in white and black, red heart beads, blue and that kind of yellow that looks like butter so the Indians called it greasy yellow. The bottom drawer holds leather, just scraps, with no piece bigger than the palm of her hand, and a small box with needles and thread. She is just closing the drawer, when Parker speaks up.

"Hello, what's this?" Parker is kneeling and pulling a box out from under the bed. It is wide and shallow and comes out from under the bed in a slithering motion on the cold slick linoleum.

Elsie must have waxed the floor recently, Nancy thinks.

Parker carefully lifts off the lid. On top are a couple of cedar branches and below that, an object wrapped in leather formed in the shape of a turtle with beading on it.

"What the hell is this?" he asks.

They crowd around him, curious, expectant, wary of what might be inside, maybe expecting some Indian ritual object.

Parker turns the turtle bundle over and begins to undo the lacings on the back. His cold hands fumble with the stiff leather strands, but slowly he unlaces them and lifts the leather flaps open. Inside is the mummified remains of a baby, from the size, just a newborn or maybe a fetus of eight months or so.

He lets out an "ahhhggghh" and drops it back in the box. He leans away, gagging. The others stand in silent shock.

173

"Holy sweet Jesus," Father Horst says. He crosses himself and begins to pray, leaning against the wall.

Nancy just stands there, hands at her mouth.

Parker stands up, notices Nancy's horrified expression, puts aside his own nausea. He leads her back into the kitchen, pulls out two chairs from the table. He pushes her into one of them where she sits, moaning a little and rocking back and forth. He falls heavily into the other. From the bedroom comes the sound of Father Horst's loud prayers.

Staley loosely wraps the leather back around the mummy, looks through the cedar boughs, and turns up another piece of leather, shaped like a turtle and beaded, but this one is flat and empty with nothing inside, to his relief. Some things bother even a coroner. He puts the lid back on the box and pushes it aside. He leans over and looks under the bed, in case there is another box. There isn't, but back a little farther is something else. He lies down flat, stretches with his arm and snags it--or two of its. A pair of moccasins that mean nothing to him, but might to Nancy. He leaves Father Horst still praying and goes back to the kitchen, handing the moccasins to Nancy.

"What's this?" he says. "Ever see Elsie wear these? They look way too big for her."

Nancy takes the moccasins and looks the imprint of feet that had been scuffed into the soles. She turns them over and stares at the two turtles beaded one on each toe, one red and one yellow.

24

January, 1969

Funerals

Big events happened next over those three days from Saturday night until Tuesday night, three events that set Jackson reeling. First, of course, was the discovery of Elsie's body, but then on Sunday night John Caulfield showed up at the sheriff's office, stinking from a drunk, not that the latter was unusual, but his hysteria was something he had never displayed before, something different from his belligerent drunken state or his sullen, hung over state.

After the deputy had calmed John down enough to understand what he was saying, the deputy put in a shaky phone call to an exhausted Parker to come back to work, while John sat in the cracked leather side chair, shivering and exuding alcohol from every pore. The deputy left him sitting there, marched back to the cells and kicked out the two Indians, told them just to beat it. They stared at him in disbelief and confusion and then walked out, into the gray cloudy cold. The deputy led John, now calm and passive, back to the cell, slammed it and locked it. After pacing the grimy little office for half an hour, the deputy was about to call the sheriff again when Parker walked in.

"All right, what the hell is going on that you couldn't tell me on the fucking phone?" Parker demanded. "I haven't had more than two hours sleep out of the last twenty-four, so this better be good."

"Shit, boss, I've got John Caulfield back there in the cells," he motioned with his thumb back down the hall. "He just confessed to the murder of Elsie Roberts."

"What! What! What the hell did he say?"

The deputy's eyes were huge. He never expected anything like this to happen to him. He thought it only happened in big cities and on television programs. His head felt big as a watermelon, and he wasn't sure if it was still the flu hanging on, or this other thing.

"He said he'd been pissed at Elsie for months, mad enough to kill her," the deputy went on. "He said that he got drunk last night, or started yesterday afternoon I guess, he wasn't clear on that. I guess he must have bought his first bottle around ten o'clock in the morning. He said – "

Parker interrupted.

"Well, get to it, what the hell did he say about the killing?"

"He says he doesn't remember doing it, but he knows he did it. He says it must have been him."

"That all? That's not a real confession. What the hell does he mean – " Parker stopped himself. "What the hell am I asking YOU for when you got Caulfield himself back there locked up!"

He turned and strode swiftly down the short hall with the deputy right behind him. He opened the door to the cells, and stopped so suddenly that the deputy crashed into his back.

"Christ."

In the cold breeze stirred by the opening door, John Caulfield swung slowly to and fro, his body suspended by his belt from the overhead pipe that carried water to the deputy's little apartment above the jail.

Parker, so exhausted he felt even his ears must be asleep, ransacked Caulfield's cabin and found nothing. No bloody clothes, no nothing. What in the hell made John so sure he had done it, he wondered. The waitress at The Steak House said John had come in for his usual hangover meal – tea and dry toast – and when he heard about Elsie he let out a cry like a dying animal and ran out without his coat, without paying. From the time, Parker figured that John had went straight to the sheriff's office and told his story to the deputy.

Could've been John, he told himself. But he wasn't completely sure.

Elsie's murder came first, and then John Caulfield's confession and suicide. They say things come in threes, good things and bad things. The third bad thing came on Tuesday around noon when Steve Laveaux walked into the sheriff's office. Parker was back on duty after finally getting in eight hours of sleep in a row, but he didn't feel rested or relieved, and the dark circles beneath his eyes had sunk lower down onto his cheeks, like the bottom half of an archery target with his own black pupils as the bull's eyes.

Laveaux was a big man, fat to tell the truth, and how he stayed that way on the meager diet of government commodities was a mystery. Laveaux himself said it wasn't the amount of food he ate, but the kind. He said Indians were meant to eat buffalo and wild fruits and vegetables, not the heavy starchy diet of government handouts.

He stood nervously, moving from foot to foot in the doorway of the sheriff's office. He was bundled up in layers of clothing that, over his naturally big body, made him look like a blanket-wrapped badger, the flaps on his cap sticking out at right angles like mule ears.

"I got some bad news I got to tell you," Laveaux said solemnly.

Parker thought it couldn't be any worse than the things that had happened over the last few days.

"And that is?" he asked.

"You know," Laveaux said. "That long hill going down into Rosebud town from the north?"

"Yeah."

"Well, it's got those deep ditches on either side, you know, and the road is kind of cut into the hill."

"Yeah, yeah. What about it?"

"People get stuck in there when a big snow storm comes through, or they run off the road and get stuck in those ditches. I live right down there at the bottom of that hill, so in the winter I sometimes get people walking into my place."

"So, who walked into your place on Saturday night? Or was it Sunday morning?"

Laveaux suddenly snatched off his cap, as if he'd just remembered it was on his head. His hair stuck out all over his head.

"Nobody. I walked up there to see how deep the snow was on Sunday. I was thinking it might be easier to get out to town for groceries by going that way. The road going out of Rosebud south had a big drift acrost it. The hill road going north was snowed full, bank to bank. But the wind had been blowing and I saw a shiny blue patch sticking up out of the ditch, and I knew it was somebody's car or something. I went over there and dug down to the driver's side window, and there was a person in there, frozen solid." He stopped there as if he still saw that face, that body frozen bolt upright, hands on the steering wheel, head tilted back a little with the eyes closed and the cheeks slightly rimed with frost like a three day growth of white beard.

"Oh, God," Parker said, pressing his hand to his forehead. "And who might this victim be?"

Laveaux pressed his lips together as if to keep the name inside.

Parker stared at him.

"There wasn't anyway to get through up Rosebud Hill. It's gonna take a snowplow or spring thaw to clear that out. Took me and my neighbors all day Sunday and Monday and half of this morning to dig through that snowbank on the road coming south out of Rosebud. I came as soon as I could. It's Donald Marks," Laveaux said.

Parker swallowed hard, thought of Nancy. He knew it was going to be a long time before he got another eight hours of sleep in a row.

Nancy was double numbed, walking through her days in a dream, one part of her mind continuing all the busy work chores that she always did – cooking, cleaning, knitting – but not much knitting, because she had gotten so adept at it that her fingers held the needles and made the stitches of their own accord, leaving her mind too free to think. She got a neighbor boy to help her, and the two of them took on the daily task of feeding the two hundred plus head of pregnant cows, replacement heifers, and herd bulls – Donald's work, but she didn't think of that, wouldn't think of that. It was just physical labor that tired out her thin body and allowed her fall asleep faster at night, when the house was dark and empty as it had been so many times before when Donald had taken off, but this time, not to return. She tried not to dwell on the obvious connection between Elsie and Donald, not the why or the where or the when. She refused to see the face of the mummified baby, but she dreamed, and in her dream the baby was both of her dead sisters, Mary and Margaret combined into one. The baby should have been her own, the one she had at last given up on having and holding, warm, soft, and smelling slightly of milk and baby powder, sleeping gently in her arms.

She hated Donald. She loved Donald. She thought about all the times when he left her alone on his prowling nights, all the times when she worried that he might have been in a car accident or something, about all the times she wished he was dead. And now he truly was dead.

She made the funeral arrangements, went through the embarrassment of the service feeling the waves of pity that came from the people in attendance, felt the genuine sympathy and support of Father Horst, who appeared to need more sympathy than he gave, as if his store of human kindness was close to exhaustion and only his faith kept him on his feet, saying prayers, patting her shoulder.

The coroner's inquest into the death of Elsie Roberts and that of the mummified baby or fetus found at her house was held on Thursday, the day after Donald's frozen body had been brought back to Jackson, propped like some bizarre mannequin on the seat beside the snow plow driver, who had dug Donald's pickup out of the snow with the help of all the Indian neighbors, Coroner Frank Staley, and Sheriff Ed Parker.

The inquest was a public hearing, after all, and every curiosity seeker in town was there, overflowing the room in the courthouse, out into the halls, waiting for information to be whispered down the standing line like that old game called telephone, or gossip. The information that the people on the end of the line got was as garbled as the results in the game, as multiple shocking bits of information came down the line, but the inquest conclusions came out on the front page of the *Jackson Messenger* on Friday: death at the hands of person or persons unknown for Elsie, and for the fetus or baby, which could not be exactly determined, death by unknown causes. That decision on Elsie's death had been pushed through by Sheriff Parker, in spite of John Caulfield's confession. The deputy testified that John was in a bad emotional state, and he had only said he *must* have done it. Besides, John was a crazy drunk, who might say anything, had a belligerent attitude, but he had never ever really hurt

179

anyone. He might have just snapped and killed her, Parker testified, but personally, he didn't believe it.

If Elsie's murder shocked the town and gave them a titillating topic of conversation, the revelation about the mummified baby found under her bed sent them into an ecstatic state of hyper gossip. Of course, everyone assumed that the baby had been the result of the rape back in Mobridge, but Frank Staley's testimony at the inquest threw doubt on that idea, and then the gossip went to an even higher level.

Staley testified that he couldn't pinpoint time of death or the age of the mummy, but that it was *at least* a year old. Dr. Weston from Mobridge, who had cared for Elsie after the rape, was embarrassed. He admitted that he had not given Elsie a pregnancy test after the rape, as he should have done, he said, but now he couldn't say whether or not she had become pregnant as a result of the rapes; however, he thought that with all the trauma she had endured it was unlikely that she had become pregnant. His testimony was discounted by the local physician in Jackson, Dr. Horgan, who testified that in his own practice, he had treated women who had become pregnant as a result of violent rape. And Dr. Horgan dropped yet another tantalizing piece of information: Elsie had recently given birth, within the last six weeks, but no one had turned up a second fetus. Had it been only an early term fetus, naturally aborted? A full term baby dead at birth, or worse yet, murdered by Elsie? If the second baby had been a full term birth, where was the child? Nothing had turned up in a further search of Elsie's cottage.

Neither Sheriff Ed Parker, nor Dr. Horgan, nor any of the other witnesses had answers to those questions. That very absence fueled the rumor mill. The second child was buried somewhere on the property, and would turn up with spring thaw. The second child has been given to one of the women in the Indian community, and everyone eyed the newborns in town speculatively. The mothers took to leaving their children at home. There was even speculation that Elsie had killed the child in some bizarre rite and consumed the body.

On Friday, the coroner released Elsie's body to the county for burial. The funeral was on Saturday, and was as well attended as the inquest had been. Parker stood in the back, in his gray dress uniform, Stetson in hand, and watched the crowd carefully. No one acted suspiciously; there were no dramatic outbursts of emotion, no hymns sung, no shouted confessions, only the dry words of the standard service read out by Frank Staley, coroner and undertaker. Elsie was not a Catholic, not even a Christian to anyone's knowledge, and so Father Horst could not bury her from the church. He felt very badly about that, as he sat in one of the brown metal folding chairs in the front row close to the cheap coffin purchased by the county. But he could have masses said for her soul, and he would do that.

When the service was over, everyone filed by the coffin to stare at Elsie one more time, to comment later about what a good job Staley had done on making her crushed skull look as normal as possible, about the two turtles, one red and one yellow placed on either side of her head, as if they had just crawled up on the white satin pillow out of some dark pool of water.

Nancy attended. It was not a hard decision for her, even knowing what might have happened between Donald and Elsie. Nancy saw Elsie as a victim, a wounded young woman, a child really, who had never recovered from that first situation at Mobridge, who had been drawn slowly and inexorably to this moment. No, she did not blame Elsie, she blamed Donald, and she was terribly afraid of what Donald might have done. She did not so much feel the need to pay her respects to Elsie, as to put in an appearance before the people of the town. They didn't know about the moccasins under Elsie's bed yet, but they would soon, and they would talk. Inevitably, with Caulfield's guilt in question, Donald's would come up next. Nancy wanted to listen at the funeral for any talk that might already be starting, but she heard none, not about Donald anyway.

Nancy recalled the day of Elsie's murder when Donald had fed the cattle around ten o'clock in the morning as he usually did, then went to the barn as he usually did during the winters, when he had the

181

time to repair any machinery that he hadn't had time to do more than patch together during the busy summer season. He came in and ate a late lunch, took a short nap, and around three o'clock said that he was going to town for some machinery parts and to play a few rounds of cribbage down in the Legion Club.

Nancy had reminded him of the weather service warning about a storm coming in, but Donald said he probably be back long before it hit, and if it got bad, he'd just stay in town the night. Nancy doubted it all, expected there was a woman somewhere that he was going to see, but she let him have his lie, as usual.

Then Parker had told her that he had found out from his inquiries that Donald had left the Legion Club around nine-thirty or so on Saturday night and hadn't been seen in town after that. Why would he do that, why would he head out across the rez with a storm coming in? Parker didn't have to spell out the possibilities to her. And Donald's truck had slid off into the ditch going north, *up* the hill and away from Jackson. Where had he been going and why? He had been born in this winter hard country, and he knew not to take off across country with a storm coming in. What was he running from? She told herself that maybe he wasn't, maybe there was some woman he was going to see up there north of Rosebud, maybe down in Ghost Hawk Canyon just beyond. That woman certainly wouldn't be coming forward with any information.

Nancy expected there would be gossip about what Donald was doing on Rosebud hill heading away from Jackson in the middle of a storm, but she hoped people would assume it had to do with Donald's philandering, and nothing to do with Elsie's murder. She hoped, not that she cared what people would think of Donald. He was too dead to care about it, and hadn't much minded his reputation when he was alive, but she didn't want to face the whispers behind her back about her husband. But she had loved him. Yes, she believed that. And she had loved Elsie too, and she wanted to keep their deaths separated in her own mind as long as she could.

She was spared an inquest into Donald's death thanks to Staley and Parker, who justified it by saying that someone froze to death under similar circumstances every winter, that this was just another of those tragic events. Let the town speculate all they wanted to later about whether or not Donald should be considered a suspect in Elsie's murder.

The town seemed to believe Caulfield was guilty. He had confessed, hadn't he, even though it was an odd confession. Some certainly considered Donald as an alternative suspect later on, but John Caulfield or Donald Marks, either one was a more comfortable suspect than the third alternative: that some murderer still walked in their midst. The white folks told themselves that if it wasn't Marks or Caulfield than it had to be an Indian affair, that it had to be some conflict or some problem within the Indian community that they knew nothing about, didn't want to know about, except they were afraid that some evil might cross that line from the dark side of town, the Indian side, and attack their own security, their own white lives.

The Indians kept their mouths shut, even among themselves mostly. They worried about Georgie and Porky Pine, whose whereabouts at the time of Elsie's murder couldn't be pinned down exactly. And the others, the men who had seen the deer woman – well, there could be one that they hadn't known about, whose craziness had been hidden. But they didn't really believe that one of their own had killed Elsie. They remembered the deer woman stories, remembered that in the stories, none of the men afflicted had ever attacked the deer woman herself head on. She was too powerful, but they were afraid it *might* have been one of their own, that some new story with a far different twist had come into being in Jackson, and they feared that the end had not been told yet. Elsie was dead, but the Indian community feared the spirit of Elsie as much as they feared her murderer. They smudged their houses with cedar and sage to repel bad spirits.

Then the final funeral was held, the one for Donald, who had not been in a state of grace, but was a Catholic and buried from the church with all the ceremony and dignity that Father Horst could muster under the circumstances. But, like many winter funerals in

183

Jackson, the curtain did not descend on the final act for a few days longer. The ground was too frozen for the actual burial, so the bodies were stored in the morgue at the undertaking parlor for another week. When the weather broke, five final interment services and burials were performed on the same day, one right after the other, before another hard freeze would mean further delay. Frank Staley presided over the burials of Elsie Roberts, John Caulfield, and the mummified baby; then Donald's final interment presided over by Father Horst, and last of all, the burial for an old man who had died of a heart attack was conducted by the rector of St. Mary's Episcopal Church.

Father Horst decided in late February that he should leave the entire premises in an clean and orderly condition for his successor, so when he had done cleaning the rectory, he went out to Elsie's former cottage and started cleaning there. He imagined he smelled decay inside, but of course, it was only his imagination, he told himself, and indeed, he found no more bodies, but he found something else that had fallen down behind the drawers of the bureau. He found Elsie's birth certificate, and when he had read it carefully, he took it over to Sheriff Parker's office. Phone calls were made.

25

January 24, 1970

Insomnia

It's four o'clock in the morning; your head is buzzing from too little sleep and too much coffee, but now, you think you might have most of the story. Lowan, who had been sleeping on the floor beneath the table, has long since given up and gone to a night nest on the sofa.

"So that's where it got left, huh? Before I came up here, I mean," you say.

Oscar looks as bright as if he's just slept for hours. Must be all those naps he takes during the day, you think.

"Pretty much," Oscar says. "Elsie's story kind of quietened down. Other stories happened. Lots more goes on in small towns than you'd think."

You don't say so, but you know that's true, coming from a small town yourself.

Oscar rubs his chin.

"Let's see. That spring there was that smart ass Blaeger kid drinking and driving in the middle of the day, hit a carload of Indian women and kids broadside. Tore their car right in two and killed about half of them. He got up on manslaughter charges, but it was dropped cause he agreed to go in the Army. Stirred up of us Indi'ns from Standing Rock to Pine Ridge to Rosebud, cause an Indi'n doing the same to a carload of white women and kids – well." He just shakes his head. "Course, it ain't over yet, what with Viet Nam and all. The spirits take care of justice, you know. Then harvest season one of the farmers cutting his own wheat got his arm ran into the guts of the combine. Probably would have made it out of that okay if the hired man had of just shut off the thing or reversed the traction gears, but instead he got panicked and tried to pull his boss out. They both got sucked in, and came out in the grain bin all minced up like sausage and those cracked beef bones like I buy for Lowan. The wife came out to see why they hadn't come in to dinner. She ended up in a hospital her own self. Let's see, what happened to her? Oh, yeah, I think she sold up the place and moved to some family of hers in – where was it? I think it might have been California."

He's quiet for a minute, and you hope he isn't thinking of any more minced-up farmer stories to tell you.

"Course," he says, "there's always the usual number of pregnant teenagers having to drop out of high school and get married. One of them was Ed Parker's oldest daughter. Like to broke his heart and tore up his own marriage, 'cause he blamed himself, and his wife blamed him for not being home more." He pauses. "You know, I've been thinking. There just ain't enough entertainment for kids around here," he says. "Not enough toys, either. They end up with nothing to play with but themselves."

He slaps the table and announces that it's time for bed.

You hear the sounds of tooth brushing in the bathroom, spitting in the cracked porcelain sink, the toilet flushing, and when he comes out, Lowan jumps up off the sofa and follows into Oscar's little bedroom behind the living room.

You lie in the bed in your own room, surrounded by the dark rounded shapes of Mrs. Oscar's clothes piled on the floor, comforting in their presence. Your eyes are permanently opened by the stories and the coffee, and you wonder if you can ever sleep again. Oscar was right. Elsie's story was too big to be told all at once. This last chunk has almost done you in.

You spend the next few days just lounging around the house with Oscar and Lowan, mostly, except for a couple of trips uptown to the grocery store. You buy some food to contribute to Oscar's menu – bacon, eggs, dried pinto beans instead of the navy beans that Oscar usually cooks, hamburger, bread, milk, and fruit – apples that you picked out while avoiding looking at the pyramid of oranges right next. You'd like to cook some ribs for Oscar with some Texas hot barbecue sauce, but to do it right you need a barbecue pit where they

186

can be smoked. Oscar doesn't own such a thing. Ribs aren't right if they are cooked in an oven. At the checkout counter you remember you were going to buy some grits, and you ask the clerk for the whereabouts, but the aisle she sends you to is lined with canned goods, and when you ask the clerk idly flicking the cans with a green feather duster, he points at the cans of hominy. You give up, pay for what you got and go back to Oscar's house.

In between watching Oscar's game shows, you ask a few more questions.

"Where you figure that mummy baby came from?" you ask.

Oscar shakes his head.

"Don't know. Could be Elsie's, but could be something she carried down here from Mobridge. She did get to collect some things of her mother's house that she brought with her. Could've been Mary's baby. Elsie's little sister or brother."

"You think?"

"Naa. I think it was Elsie's. I think she had it that first winter after she came down here."

"Think she aborted it?"

"Naa. If she was going to do that, why wait until it was full term? Frank Staley said it could have been full term baby, just small cause it had been dried up like that."

"The second baby. The one she had just before she died. Is there more to that story? They ever find it?"

"Never did. Tore up the ground all around that house, too. There wasn't so much as mouse bones buried. Plenty of mouse shit, though." His shoulders shake.

You wonder about that. You wonder if there is a child growing up somewhere around Jackson that will have Elsie's full lips, long legs and healthy musculature, a boy maybe, whose Elsie-inherited features might not be noticed or remarked upon. But what about the father's features?

"What did Donald look like?" you ask.

Oscar looks at you speculatively.

"Blond. Big blond guy, burned red as a beet in the summer. His mother was a Swede. And before you ask, Caulfield was just a plain old white guy – nice looking, but just regular. You know regular brown hair, regular eyes. Just regular."

"Seems to me he was pretty irregular for a regular guy," you say.

Oscar's shoulders shake again.

26

January 27, 1970

Ceremonies and Arrangements

You're back at Coroner Staley's office again, but this time the red-headed secretary is already there, digging through papers on the desk top, again. You wonder if that's her official job designation: digger. Or maybe desk diver. She barely glances up at you.

"He's not here," she says unnecessarily.

"Well, ma'am, will he be in today?"

"Doubt it. Had a couple of deaths over the weekend." She finishes rifling one stack of papers, shuffles them back together, starts on another.

"Anyone I know?"

She doesn't get your humor.

"A stillborn baby and old man Seivers. The old man died in his house with the heat on high, and the neighbors didn't find him for two days. It's a hurry-up deal."

Halfway through the second stack of papers, she finds a yellow form, pulls it out with an "aha!"

"Now, what can I do for you?" she asks.

"Never mind," you say.

You walk half a block up the street, jaywalk across to Staley's funeral parlor, and you don't even wonder if one of the few cars and trucks parked on the street belongs to Jack Mason. Or you wonder only a little. When a threat is constant, after a while, you get used to it, kinda. You think about it, but you just can't live in a constant state of high alert, but your blood pressure probably stays higher than it ought to be. Maybe the man doesn't really exist, you think, because everybody talks about him, but he never seems to put in a personal appearance to you. He's the bogey man in the dark.

The funeral parlor is by far the best decorated place in town, with thick carpets, pale green painted walls hung with tastefully blurry landscape paintings and a lighted picture of Jesus. A gray sofa and pair of chairs sit against the far wall with a Bible on an end table. There's an announcement board on an easel that lists upcoming funerals, a couple of memorial books to sign on a tall table, and off to one side, a mahogany desk in an alcove. A corridor leads off the reception area to the viewing rooms. Staley's wife, you assume she's his wife, comes out of the back somewhere, a chunky woman with graying hair wearing a tasteful navy blue suit and dark pumps.

"Hello," she says, "Frank has been wanting a word with you. He's indisposed at the moment, but can you wait for a half hour or so?"

Staley wants to see you? This is ominous, you think. You thank his wife when she brings you a cup of coffee from someplace in the back, fresh brewed and hot. You sip it and you think that Oscar's mud has spoiled you for the taste of good coffee.

Staley comes up the corridor from the back in his shirt sleeves, hurrying. He greets you and invites you to follow him to his office just off the main corridor, where you perch on the edge of a chair, a comfortable overstuffed chair, with two boxes of tissues on the table beside it, and brochures of coffins.

"Sorry, I haven't been available much lately," he says. "I'm the only undertaker in the county so my time isn't really my own."

Even from six feet away across the desk you can smell him, not the smell of embalming chemicals, but the smell of whiskey on his breath. Probably needs it with his kind of life. He probably knows personally almost everyone he has to embalm and bury. Must get to a guy after a while.

"I understand," you say. "You've got your priorities."

"That's right, that's right. But we need to talk about this exhumation. Everyone concerned has agreed to it, I mean, the sheriff and all officials of the county including me. Of course, you understand the weather delay." He stops there, looking intently at you, and you know there is something more here, some other reason for the delay.

"There are laws that have to be followed, you understand."

You nod your head. You suspect you know where this conversation is leading – right around to the wallet in your back pocket.

"I have to obey the laws. I can't afford to get my license suspended, and it isn't just my livelihood, it's that I owe a duty to the people of this county. There aren't many people willing to practice this far out in the middle of nowhere. If I'm gone there isn't anyone willing to take my place."

You see the gold signet ring on his pinkie finger, the pricey furniture in his office, and you have your doubts about what he says. People will live most anywhere if the money is there. Plainly, Staley isn't starving to death. You suppress a sick grin because you've just had a thought. Who undertakes a dead undertaker?

"The exhumation order is approved," Staley is saying, "but there are laws about transporting bodies, especially across state lines. Then some states have their own laws and they're all a little different, but generally, it's this. The body has to be embalmed and enclosed in a coffin that is of a certain minimum standard quality, and it has to be sealed for transport. The original intent is to preserve public health, of course."

It is going to be about money, just like you thought.

"Now, the coffin the Elsie was buried in wasn't the best we have to offer. Not that we didn't do right by the young woman," he hastens to add. "But this county doesn't have a lot of money. The deceased has been buried for just about a year now, so that coffin has bound to have deteriorated to some extent, which means it can't be sealed properly for transport."

"It's my understanding," you say, "that the coffin doesn't go directly into the ground. That the coffin is placed in a vault sort of thing. Like a box to hold the box."

Staley tilts his chair back and steeples his fingers over his chest.

"That's true," he says, "but there are several quality levels of vaults, just like there are coffins, and like I said before, the county isn't rich. So the vault for Elsie Roberts is only guaranteed waterproof for one year."

You wonder how anyone would know if the vault failed before the year was up. It's not like a family would dig up a deceased loved one to check on the deterioration – or nondeterioration – of the vault. But you ask the question that is the only one that matters now.

"How much?"

He tilts his chair forward, opens a drawer and pulls out a form with handwritten figures on it, slides it across the desk to you.

You run down the list of charges for a new vault, new coffin, mileage fees to transport the body, extra money for the driver – down to the triple underlined figure at the bottom. You're glad you're sitting on your wallet in your back pants pocket. You feel the magnetic pull of the paper form, tugging those dollars right out your wallet and beckoning them into Staley's hand with that gold signet ring, see his fingers closing around them and the bills crumpling in the middle like a fat green paper bow tie. The figure is four hundred dollars more than you have.

You push the paper back across the desk to him.

"Any chance of the city or county helping out on this?"

Staley assumes a sad expression, the one you imagine he wears for every funeral he conducts. He shakes his head slowly.

"No, sorry. The county fund is bone dry. We've already had to bury more indigents than we could afford, mostly Indians. Been a bad flu season up here."

You stand up and put your hat on.

"I'll have to get back to you," you say.

"Well, you do that. I'm sure that if you try, you'll come to the right decision," he says and offers his hand.

You shake hands, as briefly as you can make it.

You walk back to Oscar's house, going through the list of your relatives in your head, but none of them have a penny to spare. You think of your own little piece of property and how many years you struggled to pay it off before you retired, and know that you couldn't pay even the smallest mortgage payment out of your little retirement check. It's not just four hundred dollars that you need. There's also the money to pay for getting yourself back home. You've thinking that maybe you spent your savings on a wild goose chase, all because you had some idea that common decency mattered. It does, but most poor people can't afford it.

When you get back to Oscar's, Irene is there, and you guess that today the boys are in school. You hear Oscar and Irene in excited conversation as you approach the front door, your boots crunching on the frozen snow, but they stop abruptly when you walk in. They can tell by your face that everything has gone wrong.

"What?" Oscar growls. Lowan senses the tense mood and barks out the door as you close it, as if to keep at bay whatever evil spirits have followed you. You sink yourself down on the sofa, tired of it all, tired to the bone, but you tell. You expect an outburst of anger from them, but it doesn't come. Irene and Oscar still sit in their same positions; they just aren't smiling anymore. You know how it is. You've been here before, not in Jackson, but in bad situations, and you know the old saying about the golden rule, that the man with the gold makes the rules.

"*Ho eyes*," Oscar says. "Long time ago, the government divided up our land and gave pieces of it out to the people, because there were few of us. The *wasicu* knew if they made the pieces they gave out to us small enough, there would be lots of big pieces left over for them. They gave those old Indians deeds to it, you know, my ancestors, too, but sometimes there were disputes over the best pieces."

You're not in any mood for another one of Oscar's stories, especially not one that starts out with what sounds like it's going to be a boring history, but Irene catches your eye and wiggles her fingers and wrist at you, motioning you to be still and listen. So, you do.

"There was this one man named Two Boys because he was a twin and the other one died. Anyway, he didn't have no family or nothing, but he had been kind of raised by this other Indi'n family, so he wanted his piece of land near their place, but someone else, some *takasi* of the wife wanted that land, too, so the old man gave up his claim and let the wife's cousin have it. He accepted another piece of land quite a ways from them, but he didn't want to live on it. He lived up there around Red Shirt Table with this other one family. So, turns out, the piece of land he got was down near here, and it turned out to be good farmland, flat you know, good dirt. Somehow the *wasicun* overlooked it, and Two Boys got this piece. So then, different *wasicun* tried to get him drunk, you know, get him to sell it, but Two Boys didn't drink. Not much anyway, not enough to loose his sense. So, finally they gave up, and Two Boys leased it to a *wasicu* farmer down here. Every year he had to come to town to get the lease renewed. Him and this farmer would meet up at The Steak House and the farmer would try to get the lease for less money, but Two Boys never gave in. It was good land, you know, make seventy-five bushels of wheat to the acre, for real, not just some farmer bragging. Some years Two Boys could make that farmer pay a little more for that lease, but he always let that *wasicu* think he got the better of the deal. Two Boys played dumb Indi'n, you know. He wore his hair old style in braids, kept the blanket, pretended not to speak much English.

"So this one time, Two Boys comes to town to get his lease signed again and collect his money from the *wasicu*. Well, the guy thinks he's going to intimidate Two Boys, make him feel stupid and little, see, so he brings a bunch of his white friends with him, and they're sitting there around a table drinking coffee when Two Boys comes along. This *wasicu*, he says to Two Boys, '*Hau, kola,*' just like they're old friends.

"Then the *wasicu*, he picks up his water glass and drinks it all, and he says to Two Boys, 'Go get me a glass of water.'

"Two Boys takes the glass and disappears to the back of the restaurant. Comes back with a glass of water. The *wasicu* drinks it and says to Two Boys, 'I'm still thirsty. Get me another glass of water.' Two Boys takes the glass and goes off again.

"All this guy's friends, they're laughing, cause they think it's funny to see this ignorant old Indi'n jump to wait on their friend.

"Two Boys comes back with a second glass of water, and the *wasicu* farmer says, 'I'm still thirsty. More water.' Two Boys takes the glass and disappears again to the back of the restaurant, but he comes back holding the empty glass."

Irene has already started to laugh, so you know she's heard this story before, probably dozens of times.

"The *wasicu* farmer says, 'Where's my water? I'm still thirsty!'"

"Two Boys says, 'Can't get you more water. There's another *wasicu* sitting on the well.'"

"So, after that they changed Two Boys name. After that they called him Makes Water."

Irene is busting up now, tears running down her face, and Oscar sits there, solemn as if he were in church, shoulders not moving an inch.

You can't help it, you smile, and then you start to laugh, too. And then you spoil it all. You ask, "Well, did he get more money on his lease?"

Irene slaps her forehead, and Oscar just looks at you.

"If I couldn't tell better by looking at you, I'd say you're part *wasicu* yourself," he says.

"You got to *listen* to the stories," Irene says. "They'll give you the answers."

"What answers?" you ask, and you feel like a dumb little kid for asking.

"The answers to everything," she says.

"I got my answer from Staley," you say. "I've done what I can, and it wasn't enough. I thank you for your hospitality, but I have to go home tomorrow. You know anyone can take me to the bus station?"

Oscar shifts in his orange chair.

"Listen," he says. "The Roberts family are going to hold a ghost feast, a wiping of the tears ceremony for Elsie up in the canyon. It's been just a little over a year since she died, so it's time to put away mourning now and let her go from us. We should have done it back in December, but you know, people kind of wanted to forget about Elsie. Until you showed up. You need to go. Kind of put her to rest for you."

"I don't understand," you say. "I thought she wasn't part of – you know – part of everybody else. The Roberts, I mean. Or any of the rest of you folks."

"Well, she wasn't really, but she was everybody's relative, you know. Besides, some of the people are kind of thinking that if they

195

do this ceremony, they're won't be any more young men seeing the deer woman. So it's kind of double useful."

"That's what I come here to tell both of you," Irene says. "It's going to be Saturday. At some cousins of the Roberts' up in Ghost Hawk Canyon. My husband and I will come get you both early Saturday morning."

27

January 31, 1970

Wiping the Tears

The sun isn't up yet on Saturday when Oscar calls you for coffee and breakfast. While you're eating as few of his pancakes as good manners will allow, you ask him if there is anything you should know about this ghost feast ceremony, anything that will be expected of you.

"Just stick beside me," he says. "I'll tell you what to do when."

You're still nervous when Irene and her husband, Roger, and the boys show up. Roger is a big man, his bulk filling half the front seat, his head almost touching the head liner of the car. He gives you a quiet greeting. You and Oscar get in the backseat and the boys curl up under blankets and go back to sleep as you make the drive west out of Jackson, up the long hill past the tourist cabins where John Caulfield used to live in Number 8A. The car is filled with the smell of cooked meat coming from a lidded big pan on the floor between Irene's feet so it won't tip over.

You look at Oscar, and he explains, "For the feast," points his lips at a bag of groceries on the floor of the back seat. A can of coffee is on top.

A few miles west of town, Roger turns off the highway onto a narrower paved road to a little town he tells you is Greasy Water. There's a little store and a gas station there, a few houses scattered nearby, but soon the pavement ends and Roger drives slowly through tracks worn into the snow, over roads that wind here and there like a line of string carelessly flung out on the ground.

The sun is full up when the car suddenly drops down a steep hill into a canyon in the prairie, totally unexpected from the flat perspective, until you are there and going down through a one lane cut in the snow. The hill is so steep that your ears pop, and at the bottom the road widens a bit, the tail end of the car slithers on a slick spot. The boys, wide awake now, yell, "Do it again, Dad, do it again!"

Through the pines and winter bare cottonwoods, you glimpse a frozen creek yards off the road, and you think of catfish jumping in hot summer weather, cut up catfish dipped in cornmeal batter, frying up golden brown in big black skillets.

A couple of miles farther on, Roger turns the car sharply to the left between berry thickets onto a road that you wouldn't even have noticed was there except someone has shoveled a way through the snow for cars. Back into the thickets and the trees sits a log house, small, with smoke rising from a tin chimney, and in the yard, half a dozen cars and men standing around several fires that have been lit in a circle. There's a big shed with double doors opened and a table inside with stuff piled on it.

"That's for the giveaway," Oscar says, and then seeing you don't understand, he says, "It's customary. Most ceremonies include a giveaway from whoever is sponsoring it. The Roberts this time, except since this wasn't really planned far enough in advance, so other people have contributed stuff."

You look at the goods piled up and see there are cases of soda pop, a couple of blankets, cans of coffee, bags of sugar, other stuff, too. Somebody better take that soda inside pretty quick, you think, before it freezes and busts the cans.

Roger stops the car and everyone gets out, the boys yelling and rushing towards half a dozen other kids piling out of the cabin. Irene carefully carries the big pan of meat in front of her into the house.

"*Hau, kola,*" Roger hollers at the men. One of them comes over to him and they clasp shoulders.

"*Ho eyes, tokeske oyaunyanpi huo?*" the man says.

"*Hena, waste yelo.*"

You and Oscar are looking over the selection of goods.

"Who's it for?" you ask.

"Everyone," he says. "Everyone takes something. Doesn't look like much yet. There'll be a lot more by tonight."

By tonight. Looks like a pretty big pile already to you. You look at the small cabin, at the cars and people already here and know that they won't all fit into that house. It's going to get damned cold before this is over, you think, understanding now the reason for those bonfires in the yard.

The cars and the trucks keep coming, the giveaway pile grows, and you and Oscar are asked to help others build what looks to you like an igloo made of bent-over tree limbs with the ends secured it the middle. It's a small structure, with a hole dug out in the middle, and when you're done, some tarps are thrown over it, the edges weighted down with rocks.

"What's this for?" you whisper to Oscar.

He grunts as one of the tree limbs comes undone, whips back and slaps him in the gut.

"Sweat lodge," he says.

"What's that?"

"To sweat, what else?" Then he explains more. "It's a purification rite for the *wicasa wakan* before he performs the ghost ceremony."

The *wicasa wakan*, as Oscar points him out to you, doesn't look like anybody special, just an old man, older-looking than Oscar even, with a red wool scarf tied on his head under a battered cowboy hat, and layers of clothes covering his skinny body.

Late in the afternoon, as if a silent gong had rang that everyone except you had heard, women pour out of the little house like columns of ants, the men gather and the crowd becomes silent. The *wicasa wakan* steps out of the sweat lodge, his body, naked from the waist up glistening with sweat, reflecting the dying sun and the red flames of the bonfires. A big drum sits in the middle of the crowd on top of an upended old car hood, put there, you suppose, to keep the bottom of the drum dry. Five men crouch around it, each with a single drumstick. They strike the drum in unison, the sound continuing and echoing and behind you in the crowd a voice begins to sing. The *wicasa wakan* takes up his redstone pipe.

Some children are scuffling in the back and one of the women says to them, "Shhh, *anagoptanye! Wastepe!*"

It begins.

Twenty-eight years you swept the floors, mopped them, waxed them, buffed them. You picked up the pieces of broken chalk from the classrooms, you scrubbed out the toilets and unclogged them when the kids dropped stuff down there that shouldn't be dropped down there. You knew that Mrs. Clayton in fourth grade room 27 was a stickler for having the blackboards washed every week, that Miss Ingersol in second grade room 11 didn't much care about the blackboards, but her trash cans, by God, better be emptied every day. You learned about that look on Principal Adams's face, that look that meant you better stay down in the basement repairing broken desks or anywhere out of his way. You watched kids come into kindergarten and go up the scale of grades and out the other side, and some of them you remembered because they were good kids and some of them you remembered because they weren't. You looked forward to the summers when you could to stay home and tend your garden and go fishing. You accepted the summers when you had to find some other work to make ends meet, the summers when you had to go places you didn't want to go and never wanted to see again.

And then the last years came, when your knees hurt so from arthritis that it was hard to bend them, when the floor polisher kick as it hit spots with too much wax made your spine felt like a whip being cracked, and you loaded up on pain pills to sleep at night, so you could get up in the morning and do it all over again. The last graduation. The speeches and congratulations and thank yous and the piddly retirement pay that was all right because you'd saved your money for years. Money that you'd mostly spent now for Elsie. The gold watch on your arm, the traditional retirement gift that you didn't think would mean a stinking thing to you but did.

The ceremony is ended. The people are lining up for the giveaway. Oscar pushes you into line, and you move forward shuffling in the snow. The woman ahead of you says to her companion something about that red blanket on the end and she hopes it's still there when it's her turn. The line moves forward, pauses, moves forward, and the pile dwindles some and it's your turn, but you stand there and wonder what on earth you would do with any of this stuff. You could always use the groceries, but it feels silly to carry it back on the bus.

Oscar nudges you.

"Take something," he says.

You step forward. You reach up your coat sleeve, pull off your gold watch, and place it carefully on top of a ten pound bag of sugar. Step away. For Elsie.

When the gifts are all gone, the women bring out the food from the house and put it on the emptied table where all the giveaway stuff had been. The people line up again, filling their plates, standing or squatting around the bonfires and eating. They go back for seconds, and then they bring out their *wateca* buckets to fill up with the leftovers. As the women are cleaning up the tables, the drums begin again. You're tired and exhausted and cold, and you can't believe there is more to this ghost ceremony.

The *wicasa wakan* spreads a blanket on the cleanest patch of snow he can find and begins to speak in Lakota. The people line up yet a third time, dance in a slow dipping, one-two rhythm past the spread blanket dropping coins and bills as they pass. There are at least a hundred people, and the dance is slow. When it is done the drums give a final thump. The *wicasa wakan* gathers the corners of the blanket together bagging the money in the middle, walks through the snow and hands it to you. Your arms are frozen at your sides.

The *wicasa wakan* bounces the blanket up and down, making it jingle and rustle. Oscar nudges you so hard you almost fall over.

"Take it," he says.

You take the blanket and the *wicasa wakan* steps back.

"Say 'thank you,'" Oscar whispers, but the heavy blanket has weighted your tongue.

"*Pilamaya*," he says for you, turns and shouts to the crowd, "*Pilamaya!*"

There are nods of assent, smiles, here and there a muttered *waste yelo*, *waste k'sto*. The people head towards the cars carrying their *wateca* buckets and tired kids.

Waste yelo.

28

February 1, 1970

The Kindness of Strangers

The money is spread out on Oscar's table in neat stacks of change and paper bills – quarters, nickels, dimes, a few tens, one twenty, and a whole lot of ones. You've counted it three times, and it keeps coming up the same. $316.25. Oscar reaches for the Big Chief tablet and the stubby yellow pencil to check the figures again, but you stop his hand.

"Don't," you say. "It's the same answer."

He puts down the pencil and pushes the tablet aside.

"Sometimes there's a different answer if you look long enough," he says.

"Not this time," you say. "I have to leave tomorrow. So I'm back to the same question. Know anyone that can take me to the bus station?"

Oscar doesn't speak for a minute.

Then he sighs and says, "Yeah. Roger's cousin isn't working. He'll take you. I'll walk over to his house in a little while and ask him."

You wave your hand at the money on the table.

"I got to give this back."

Oscar crosses his arms.

"Can't. That would be an insult," he says.

"All right. Then use it to buy stuff for the next giveaway."

Oscar doesn't say anything. He just picks the money up, a pile at a time and dumps it into a brown paper bag.

A little later, after Oscar has walked over to see Roger's cousin, you hear footsteps in the yard. Someone bangs on the door, and the first thing that you think is that Jack Mason has found you. There's a moment of panic and then a voice hollers, "Oscar! You home?" You think that Jack Mason wouldn't know Oscar's name, probably.

You open the door to Frank Staley. He's standing there in the cold, his breath streaming whiskey scent. He covers his mouth with a brown leather gloved hand, coughs.

"Oscar isn't home right now, Mister Staley."

"Doesn't matter, I really come to see you," he says.

"Me?"

"Yes."

You motion for him to come in. He stomps the snow off his overshoes and steps inside, looking around curiously.

"So, what do you need to talk about? The price gone up?"

"Come on, now, that's not fair. I have to make a living, and there are laws to follow. I can't just – "

"Never mind, never mind. I understand." But you don't.

"It's good news. A third party has agreed to pay for the expenses of transporting the body."

"What? Who?" you ask.

"I'm not at liberty to divulge that. It was a charitable donation, shall we say."

Nancy Marks, you think. Or maybe she got the Catholics to do it, even though Elsie wasn't. But maybe you're not hearing right.

"They're paying for transport, right? What about the vault and the coffin?"

He waves a hand.

"Oh, that, too, that too. And the exhumation order is all signed. If the weather holds, we can exhume the body day after tomorrow. This is Sunday, so you can be on your way by, say, Wednesday afternoon."

You're thinking that there's some good people in this town and some bad ones, too, and all in all, you'll be glad to be gone, long gone. And you're thinking, too, that this town will be glad to have you gone.

"Wednesday? Why not Tuesday afternoon?"

"Goddamn it man, the body had to be removed from the old vault and coffin and placed in a new one, you know. And who knows who might die in the meantime, give me a break. I run the place pretty much by myself."

"Sure, sure," you say. "Okay, Wednesday afternoon."

You're wondering if Roger's cousin can take you to the bus stop on Wednesday instead of tomorrow, but then, Staley says, "You can ride shotgun with the driver. That's a customary courtesy."

You wonder why he didn't have the manners to mention that "customary courtesy" before, but you think about the dollars that are going to stay in your wallet for a little while longer, so you just say, "Thank you."

Staley takes hold of the door knob, and he voices what you've been thinking just a minute ago.

"I don't mind telling you that this town will be glad to put an end to this whole Elsie business. It's been a bad deal from start to finish. Looks like it's about finished."

You want to say that it isn't finished, and will never be as long as whoever killed her isn't known. All that you can hope for is an uneasy peace for yourself and a better resting place for Elsie.

"I figure the crew should have the grave opened around noon on Tuesday if you want to be there," he says as he goes out the door.

29

February 3, 1970

Digging Up the Past

The yellow machine steadily chews away at the muddy ground, growling like a beast digging out prey from a hiding place. The kerosene ground heater has been moved aside, two men who work part time for Staley stand ready for the final digging, waiting until a third man on the backhoe has cleared away most of the soil. There's a chain coiled loosely to hook onto the vault when the dirt has been removed.

You and Oscar and Nancy sit in her pickup with the heater running. There's a little knot of curious people standing off among the gravestones, watching.

"What I'd like to know is why *he's* here," Nancy says, pointing at the crowd.

"Who?" you ask.

"Packwood," Nancy says. "I suppose he's just come along with those other town nosies hoping that the coffin falls apart and the body fall out so they'll have some disgusting story to tell around their supper tables."

"You didn't have to be here," Oscar tells Nancy.

"Yes, I did," Nancy says. "Whatever happened, she was my friend."

"I don't know as how she was much of a friend," Oscar says. "Considering."

"Well, you know that old saying. A friend in need is a friend indeed," Nancy quotes.

"Not always," Oscar says. "Sometimes a friend in need is a pain in the ass. Or worse."

Nancy's not said a word about the money paid for the body transportation, the new vault, and coffin, but you feel like somebody ought to say something.

"I appreciate what you've done," you say.

"What? Being here? Like I said, in spite of everything, she was my friend."

"I mean," you say, "the money."

Nancy frowns and looks at you.

"What money?"

You can tell that she isn't pretending. She doesn't know what you're talking about.

"Staley is charging a nice chunk of change for transporting the body. I expected that, but I didn't expect to have to pay for a new vault and coffin, too. It was more money than I could get hold of." You don't mention the ghost ceremony or the money collected there to help pay Staley.

"Staley is *charging you* – why that son of a bitch! I'm giving him a piece of my mind!"

She starts to open the pickup door, but you stop her.

"No. No, it's all legal as far as I can tell, although I think he bent the law to put some money in his own pocket. Let it go. Somebody else paid for it. I don't know who. He wouldn't tell me."

Nancy closes the pickup door and puts her mittened hands – pink knitted mittens – in her lap.

"Truth is I couldn't have paid if I had wanted to. Donald didn't have any life insurance, but you can bet that didn't stop Staley from charging me top dollar. In spite of Donald's – well, I couldn't just bury him in a pine box. People would talk. And the ranch has lost money this past year. Most everybody did pretty well, and so did I, but with Donald gone, I had to hire a lot of outside help for work that he used to do."

The three of you are silent for a minute, thinking.

"So, who do you think came up with the cash?" Oscar asks.

Nancy shakes her head.

"I don't know. The good people of this town don't have any money, and the bad ones that have it aren't parting with it, even to get rid of a bad memory."

Oscar nods toward the knot of spectators.

"Maybe Packwood?"

Nancy narrows her eyes.

"Well, he's got the money. But I can't think why he would pay out a dime of it."

The backhoe takes too big of a bite, hits the top of the vault with a crunch.

Nancy winces. The three of you get out and stand as close to the grave as you can while still staying out of the workers' way. It seems appropriate; it seems strange. A funeral in reverse.

Staley waves the backhoe off, and the gravediggers squish through the melted snow and mud, jump down into the hole with their shovels. In a moment they've cleared the rest of the dirt out and attached the chain. The backhoe moves back in and lifts the box. It tilts a little, but the gravediggers rush over, steady it as the backhoe lifts it out, deposits it on a gurney. There are no accidents, no surprises, but the vault has a slightly smashed in top from where the backhoe dug too deep.

Well, doesn't matter, you think. Had to buy a new vault anyway. Coffin, vault and all are loaded into the back of Staley's hearse, which has been lined with a tarp to protect the interior from the mud. The backhoe operator starts pushing the mud and dirt back into the hole. You watch Staley drive the hearse down the slight grade, turn onto the highway, just as a new black Chevrolet Impala turns off the highway and onto the cemetery road.

"Somebody's late for the party," Oscar says.

The car moves slowly up to the edge of the little crowd. Nancy clutches your arm.

"That car has Mobridge license tags! I bet that's Jack Mason! What the hell is he doing here?"

The driver of the Impala cracks open his car door, gets out and walks towards the three of you, and you're shocked. He's a little man, barely five foot, five inches tall and skinny. He's wearing a silver belly Stetson, starched jeans, and black top coat. His shiny black boots slip a little in the mud. The top of that fancy Stetson *might* come up to your nose. And you were scared of him! But then, you think again. Little men are often underrated, and little men often carry an equalizer, and Jack Mason has his right hand buried in the pocket of that black top coat.

He walks slowly up to the three of you, but he looks right at you. His eyes are that sun-faded blue that's almost white, crinkled around the edges from too much squinting into the wind. He has a nose like a hawk, too big for his small face, and his thin lips are pinched. He may be a small man, but his face says that he gets his way.

"Need to talk to you," he says. "Alone." He starts walking up the incline to a group of tall tombstones.

"I'll come," Oscar says.

Mason turns abruptly, and points at you.

"I just want to talk to him!"

Well, it's broad daylight in front of witnesses. It isn't likely that he's going to kill you. Isn't likely, you tell yourself, as you follow him.

He stops at a pink granite tombstone that's almost as tall as he is.

MARIE ELIZABETH ESTESEN, it reads. And below that a floral wreath encircling the dates: June 10, 1891–October 17, 1959. It's a double tombstone and another name is etched next to hers: PETER JAMES ESTESEN. But there are no dates below his name.

"Someone you know?" you ask.

Mason looks puzzled, then gets it.

"No, no." He glances at the tombstone as if to make sure, turns back drilling you with those white eyes.

"Look," he says. "I'm just tired of this whole mess. I'm tired of it, you hear? I'm worn completely out with it, and my wife – well," he turns a bit and looks down the hill. "Well, my wife hasn't been the same. She's had a stroke, now. First the boys dying and all."

"I hear that 'the boys' weren't exactly innocents. There are exceptions to that old saying about the good dying young." You're shocked at your own nerve, saying that right out like that, but you're tired, too. You half expect Mason to pull a gun out of that right hand coat pocket and blast you, but he doesn't. He bristles only a little.

"Raising a pair of boys ain't easy! It's this country, it's the times, it's – hell, I don't know – " he waves at the sky. "It's in the weather for all I know! Yeah, I admit, I never had any use for an Indian, and I still don't, but I never taught my boys to be killers or rapists, either. I swear to Christ, I never did that." He subsides for a minute, turns and leans his hand against the tombstone, turns back to face you.

"Christ, you try raising two boys up here," he goes on. "YOU try it! What about your kids? Did you do such a fine job with yours?"

You don't answer. You can't answer. He knows the answer, and you can't look at him. You drop your head.

"Look, man, I know people said I might have done it, that I did it, that my wife was lying to cover for me, but *I swear on my boys' heads, I DID NOT KILL THAT GIRL*. Elsie. I didn't do it. Yeah, I checked it out a few months after my boys died when I started hearing rumors. But I was satisfied that the girl wasn't talking. So I let it alone. I *wanted* to let it alone. Why the hell would I stir it all up again by coming down here and killing that girl?"

You turn back and look at him.

"I don't know. Why would you? Why are you here now?"

He takes a deep breath.

"Do you know what you've done? Do you know? When my wife heard that you were stirring up this whole mess again – well, it just set her off. She's had a stroke, I said. She can't even talk. She just cries, sits in the rest home and cries. I want this *over* with, that's why I'm here. *I want that dead girl and you to hell and gone out of our lives.* You understand? I want an end to this."

"You know, I got a right to be in this, too," you say, "you know it."

"All right," he says, "all right. But is this the end of it? Can I tell my wife it's over? It ain't never going to come up again?"

"As far as I'm concerned," you say. "I'll be taking Elsie out of here tomorrow. But I can't promise what else or who else might bring this up again. You never know what bones someone might dig up."

"And I'll do everything in my power to keep those bones buried," he says.

"You'd do that? Cover up a murder? Cover for a murderer? How do I know you aren't covering for a murderer right now?"

He pulls his hand out of his pocket and the hand is empty, but you think he may actually make a fist and reach up to hit you on the nose with it, but he drops his hand to his side.

"Let it go," he says, and he turns his back to you. "There's been enough dying."

"Yes. There's been too much dying. Too much violence altogether, and it didn't start with Elsie. It began a long time before that."

He doesn't answer for a few minutes, and then he sniffs as if he has a bad cold, reaches into his pocket and pulls out a handkerchief to blow his nose. His voice is thick when he speaks.

"Just take the girl's body and go. Hear me?"

"Gladly," you say, and you walk back to where Oscar and Nancy are waiting beside her pickup.

30

February 4, 1970

Going Home

It's two o'clock on Wednesday afternoon and you're at the curb in front of Staley's funeral parlor, standing beside the hearse, the driver inside with the motor running. Oscar and Nancy are standing there saying their goodbyes.

"I remember the day I brought her to town," Nancy says. "I think sometimes that I shouldn't have done it, but then where else would she have gone?"

"You did good for her," you say. "Thank you."

Nancy reaches up and hugs you.

"It wasn't enough."

"You did the best you could," you tell her, "can't any human being do more than their best."

You reach out to shake Oscar's hand and he takes your hand in both of his.

"I can't thank you enough," you say.

"Same as I do for any relative," he says. "Same's they would do for me. *You'd* do it for me."

"Yes," you say, "I would. But I still thank you."

"Come back," he says, looking up at the thin veil of snow beginning to fall. "Weather is a lot more pleasant in the summertime."

"I been here in the summertime," you say, "And it ain't."

Oscar's lips lift in a little smile.

"Can't blame a guy for trying."

"You come visit me," you say. "Anytime."

"I don't know as how I'd get along with them civilized Indi'ns."

The hearse driver honks his horn and hollers out the window.

"Storm coming in! If we're going to get out of town, we'd better go now."

You climb into the passenger seat in front, and wave as the driver backs out and starts down the street.

"You mind if I play the radio?" he asks.

"Nope," you say, and you really don't, even when he turns to some rock and roll station playing Elvis Presley. It's alive.

You turn around and glance back at Elsie's coffin in the back, remembering that word that Oscar said to Irene.

Cunksi. Cunksi. We're going home, daughter.

He ha'yela owi'hake.

UNIVERSITY OF NEBRASKA PRESS

Also of Interest in the *Native Storiers* series:

Mending Skins
By Eric Gansworth

Shirley Mounter, a Tuscarora woman and chief storyteller among the acerbic and often hilarious speakers who overflow the pages of *Mending Skins*, defies anyone to protect, let alone reclaim, her image. Shirley's land is now, after a long fight, forever lost to her in the construction of a water reservoir that feeds the government's hydroelectric plant. The story of this battle is the story of Shirley's generation and the faltering generation that follows.
ISBN: 0-8032-7118-2; 978-0-8032-7118-0 (paper)

Bleed into Me
A Book of Stories
By Stephen Graham Jones

As Stephen Graham Jones tells it in one remarkable story after another, the life of an Indian in modern America is as rich in irony as it is in tradition. Rife with arresting and poignant images, fleeting and daring in presentation, weighty and provocative in their messages, the stories of *Bleed into Me* demonstrate the power of one of the most compelling writers in Native North America today.
ISBN: 0-8032-2605-5; 978-0-8032-2605-0 (cloth)

Hiroshima Bugi
Atomu 57
By Gerald Vizenor

Ronin Browne is the hafu orphan son of Okichi, a Japanese boogie-woogie dancer, and Nightbreaker, an Anishinaabe from the White Earth Reservation who served as an interpreter for General Douglas MacArthur during the first year of the American occupation in Japan. To confront the moral burdens and passive notions of nuclear peace, Ronin draws on samurai and native traditions, and the result is a dynamic meditation on nuclear devastation and our inability to grasp its presence or its legacy.

ISBN: 0-8032-4673-0; 978-0-8032-4673-7 (cloth)

Order online at www.nebraskapress.unl.edu or call 1-800-755-1105.

Mention the code "BOFOX" to receive a 20% discount.

Moonwind

Other books by Louise Lawrence

Moon

wind

Louise
Lawrence

1 8  1 7

——————————— HARPER & ROW, PUBLISHERS ———————————

Cambridge, Philadelphia, San Francisco, London, Mexico City, São Paolo, Singapore, Sydney

——————————— NEW YORK ———————————

Library of Congress Cataloging-in-Publication Data
Lawrence, Louise, 1943–
  Moonwind.

  Summary: One of two teenage winners of a trip to
earth's first lunar base falls in love with an astral
extraterrestrial who has been stranded on the moon for
thousands of years and who needs his help to repair her
spaceship so that she can return home.
  [1. Science fiction]   I. Title.
PZ7.L4367Mo 1986   [Fic]   85-45507
ISBN 0-06-023733-3
ISBN 0-06-023734-1 (lib. bdg.)

179437

For Margaret Clark,
who provided a new beginning

Moonwind

1

She dreamed.

And the ship voice called her.

"Wake up, Bethkahn!"

She opened her eyes. Light in the cryogenic chamber was dim blue, and when she turned her head she could see through the transparent dome that covered her . . . curved silver walls and empty sleeping berths, a doorway leading into loneliness. She was the only one alive on a dead uncharted world, and she could not bear it. The ship knew that and should not have woken her.

"What do you want?" she asked angrily.

The ship voice hesitated before replying.

Then it told her.

"We are no longer alone here, mistress."

Bethkahn lay unmoving, not daring to believe, yet

believing anyway in spite of herself. The ship would not lie to her. Rondahl had returned . . . Mahna had returned . . . the whole crew had returned. Elation filled her, and all she had suffered seemed silly now that it was over. She wanted to leap from her berth, laugh and sing, rush wild through the blue-silver spaces to greet them. But she had been trained at the Galactic Academy and was no longer a child. She was a junior technician aboard an explorer-class starship, and Rondahl would expect her to behave as one. But joy and relief spilled over as tears, and she grinned stupidly, cried stupidly, not caring that the ship was watching her.

The ship had seen emotion before. At first she had had to tell it how she felt and why. But then it had learned to recognize cause and effect, and although it could never share her feelings it seemed to understand. Through her fear and panic, desperation and despair, it had done its best to comfort her. Now, seeing tears and smiles, its voice stayed silent, allowed her some moments to herself.

"How long have I been sleeping?" she asked it.

"Ten thousand orbital years," it replied.

She could not take it in. Ten thousand years was too long to imagine. Time in the cryogenic chamber had been suspended with her life, centuries compressed into seconds. It was as if she had slept and woken a moment later exactly as she was, untouched by age or experience. She laughed with the sheer joy of it, and her thoughts turned back to the beginning.

*   *   *

4

A faulty stabilizer, Rondahl had said, as the ship spun sickeningly through pulsing dimensions of time and space. And spinning still, it had slowed to sublight speed, emerged among unknown suns in a remote arm of a spiral galaxy. They had landed on the attendant moon of an unknown planet to make repairs. To Rondahl it had seemed a bonus, that turquoise blue world turning in the black sky over them. Jewel-bright and beautiful, it was waiting to be explored. The whole crew had gone there, and Bethkahn had watched them leave—a fleet of tiny survey craft, their wings catching the light, speeding over the crater rim to vanish among the stars. And she, being the junior technician, remained behind. She had to mend the stabilizer, Rondahl had said.

At first she had not really minded. Perhaps she had even been glad. Fresh from the Academy, an inexperienced girl on her initiation flight, it had not been easy. Mahna had been kind to her, but Rondahl had seen her as a nuisance, and the senior technicians had given her all the boring routine jobs to do. Adjusting the stabilizer was just one more. She had to remove the wall panel and crawl on her stomach through the flight control conduits.

The ship voice had guided her. Usually it spoke only to Rondahl and Mahna, who were in charge of it, but with Bethkahn alone on board she became its mistress. It had been a wonderful, awesome experience having the whole vast starship working for her and responding to her presence. It had given her a feeling of freedom and power, and she had reveled in her solitude. She

5

could command it to speak or be silent. She could draw on the knowledge contained in its computer mind. There was a fault, it said, in number three stabilizer. Bethkahn found it blown, two metal blades sheared off under pressure and the whole stabilizing unit needing to be replaced. But when she checked the storeroom she discovered they had run out of spares. She could have made a laser weld, but the power packs were all on empty. It was then Bethkahn realized they were in trouble.

"What shall I do?" she had asked the ship. "We can't take off without a stabilizer!"

"That's Rondahl's problem," it informed her. "You must leave it for him. He took the risk, and I told him repeatedly I was due for an overhaul, advised him to return to base. But he paid me no heed. There's nothing you can do, Bethkahn."

So Bethkahn had learned that Rondahl the ship master was not perfect, and she waited nervously for his return. Suddenly time had assumed a meaning. She grew aware of its passing and needed to measure it. But the ship had nothing to go by. Parsecs and megaparsecs could not apply. They had to work it out by planetary motion, the moon and its world revolving around the nearby star. They had counted in moondays—one . . . two . . . three . . . eye blinks in eternity. But Bethkahn, trapped in one space-time dimension, experienced its slowness. Solitude changed to loneliness, and although the ship voice kept her company it was not the same as having the crew around.

Rooms and corridors oppressed her with their silences. She missed Mahna's laughter and Rondahl's frown. But down on the planet's surface they were absorbed in their survey and did not notice time. Bethkahn waited and waited. Half of one orbital year was nothing, the ship voice had said.

Eventually she tried the transmitter, but no one answered her. Lost on that blue, bright world beneath its swirling atmosphere, she supposed, they did not hear. She dispatched the last long-range scanner. But the survey craft were hidden by drifts of white cloud, and the life traces of the crew were indistinguishable among millions of other life traces. The planet teemed with primordial existences, and neither Bethkahn nor the ship could identify the ones they knew. And when the probe burned up during a volcanic eruption, her anxiety turned to panic.

The planet was geologically unstable, and Rondahl might never return. Bethkahn might be trapped forever in a crippled starship far from the main flight paths. She would not listen to the ship voice trying to calm her. She transmitted a general distress call across the galaxy, transmitted and transmitted until the delicate circuitry fused and was useless. Then she could do nothing else but wait . . . through moondays blinding white and long airless nights, years turning to decades. How long her messages would take to reach the starbases only the ship could compute, but it would be thousands of years, it had said, before help would arrive. And then

7

who would hear her? Her voice crying through a dead transmitter? Or see the starship buried in moondust under a millennium of time?

For her mistake Bethkahn had blamed the ship. She had screamed in her isolation and despair, beat with clenched fists on its cold curved walls, hating everything it was—an unfeeling machine, a jail of white light, a useless metal artifact that could do nothing to help.

Through years of madness she had gone outside and searched the moon's barren surface, looking for someone who would love her, arms that would hold her, another living being to comfort her and care. But nothing lived on its pock-marked surface. Nothing moved among its mountains and craters and oceans of dust.

The ship was all that remained for Bethkahn, her only sanctuary, her only friend. Again and again she returned to it, sobbed out her heart in its silver-white halls, told it how she felt. She had said she would rather die than live through an eternity of loneliness and asked it to destroy her. But the ship was programmed to preserve the lives of its crew. One day Rondahl would return, it said, and instead of death it offered her sleep and forgetfulness, an escape route of dreams in the cryogenic chamber. But now it had woken her. It said she was not alone anymore, that Rondahl and Mahna were back. Or maybe it had not said that?

Her senses sharpened. The last traces of sleep fled from her head, and she pressed the button. The transparent dome of her sleeping berth raised automatically, and automatically the blue light brightened to white.

8

Curved silver walls glowed with reflected radiance. Bethkahn sat up. She could hear the silence and sense the almighty emptiness stretching away.

"What do you mean?" she screamed. "There's no one here! Where are they?"

"Outside," said the ship. "They are outside, Bethkahn. And they are not who you think. They are not Rondahl or Mahna or anyone else we know."

"You mean we are being rescued?"

The ship sighed deeply.

"Not exactly," it said.

2

Bethkahn pulled on a shimmering suit, waistcoat and trousers that flared and folded and clung to her shape, insubstantial as light. Gold and vermilion the fire colors flickered, moved as she moved through silver curving corridors toward the main console room. A thousand questions flittered mothlike through her head. The ship was agitated, adding to her confusion, hinting at things that did not make sense, and evading the facts.

"So what exactly are you telling me?" Bethkahn asked. "If they have not come from the star worlds to rescue us, then where have they come from? Who are they?"

"They have come from the planet," the ship voice said.

"But they have nothing to do with Rondahl?"

"They have everything to do with Rondahl, mistress. That is what I am trying to tell you. The life-trace comparisons are unmistakable. Each one is individually different, but each one shows a degree of similarity to various members of our crew that is too great to be coincidence. These beings who have come to this moon are familial, Bethkahn. They are related."

"That's ridiculous!" Bethkahn told it. "How can they be? You must be mistaken."

A door slid open before her, revealing the great dark astrodome dotted with electronic stars, quadrants of the galaxy charted and explored, and the multicolored tracks of the main flight paths. Home world was a speck of green light, Khio Three distant and unreachable, disturbing a longing that was instantly suppressed. Bethkahn mounted the central dais, seated herself in the silver chair where once Rondahl had sat. She was unqualified and had no right to it, but the ship called her "mistress" and functioned for her benefit—every wire and circuit in its mechanized body, every thought in its computer brain. Now her slim fingers threw the switches, bringing its dozen blank vision screens to life.

She ran a life-trace comparison for herself, trying to match the psychic energy patterns of the original crew to those who had recently come here, overlaying peaks and troughs, noting the incidence of identity. The ship voice was right. The similarities were undeniable. They were kindred souls, and Bethkahn could offer no dispute. This one was related to Rondahl. This one to Keirharah. This one to Dahn . . . Dahn, with his blue eyes, who had once gazed at her in love. Bethkahn bit her lip and looked away, feeling the anguish inside her,

11

not knowing how to bear the implications. She could see the ghost of her own face mirrored in the blank vision screen beside her, a girl with coal-black hair and garments of fire.

"They have bred," she said dully.

"That is the logical conclusion," said the ship.

"But why?" wailed Bethkahn. "I don't understand! How could they stay there, and breed, and leave me here? How could they abandon this mission? How could they? Why should they? It doesn't make sense!"

The great ship sighed, sound echoing through its halls, imitating emotion. For ten thousand years it had protected Bethkahn from the knowledge, keeping it from her, not wanting to destroy the only hope she had. But now it had no choice. Its safety was threatened and it had to tell her the truth.

"Ten thousand years is a long time," the ship voice murmured. "And there is something I have not told you, mistress. Before Rondahl departed for the planet he sent out a probe scanner. It landed on an oceanic island and relayed the surface conditions. Believing it safe, the survey ships followed. I monitored them, of course. I monitored the seismic tremors and saw them destroyed. The island continent sank beneath the sea a few planetary days after touchdown."

In the long silence Bethkahn neither moved nor spoke.

"Rondahl was stranded," the ship voice said sadly.

"And you let me go on believing . . ."

"I let you hope," the ship voice corrected.

"You lied to me!" Bethkahn said harshly.

12

"No," said the ship. "I merely concealed the facts. Having worked with Rondahl through eons of light years it was worth saying nothing. There was always a chance he would find a way."

"What chance?" Bethkahn said angrily. "There was no way he, or any of them, could escape from a primitive world without building some kind of replacement craft. And that's not like replacing a blown stabilizer! Physical tasks need physical bodies! And we don't have physical bodies! We have astral bodies! The only power we have is the power of our minds, and there are limits as to how much minds can influence matter. It takes a body of flesh to refine raw metal, forge component parts, assemble a ship! There was never any hope for them!"

"Not unless they entered flesh," agreed the ship.

Bethkahn considered it. It was a common enough practice—a way of exploring, experiencing, and gleaning information from the various worlds they surveyed. She had been in flesh herself, briefly, during a landfall on the fifth planet of Bahtoomi's star. Stepping from the landing craft she had seen lake water lapping on a pebbly shore, rose-gold, reflecting the light of a red giant sun in a pure pink sky. Dark birds wheeled and screamed above crimson reed beds, and a faint musty fungoid scent drifted on the wind from the forest of red-leaved trees behind her. They had moved among mulberry shadows and come to the lakeside to drink, Bahtoomi's deer with their mottled plum-colored pelts, spiraling horns, and velvet black eyes. Bethkahn would have been content merely to watch them, content with her own sense perceptions, but Mahna had told her to enter one and become enfleshed.

Often, as a child on Khio Three, she had been one with trees and flowers, her spirit absorbed by the natural forms around her. But Bahtoomi's deer were alien and wild, sentient creatures with souls of their own, and Bethkahn had been reluctant, almost afraid. Then she felt warmth and heartbeats, the power of muscle and sinew, heard lake water ripple and leaf rustle and bird cry, smelled a thousand separate scents. Ears pricked and nostrils flared. One scent, one sound triggered a sweet sharp thrill of alarm, and the body responded, bounded away, leaped through fern brake into forest and sped through the red crimson flickering of shadows and light.

What Bahtoomi's deer had feared was instantly forgotten. It had neither memory nor imagination, and Bethkahn, sharing its sensations, sharing its skin, could not even guess. Its motivation had changed to hunger, and it browsed with the herd on mushrooms that tasted of bonemeal . . . until death fell on it from above. Bethkahn felt claws tearing flesh, felt pain and terror, smelled blood, saw cat eyes glitter, and heard an animal snarl. And the cry was hers when its fanged teeth ripped the deer's throat. She had fled, sobbing, back to the survey craft and never wanted to be enfleshed again.

But Mahna had found her, made her become a bird to overcome her fear . . . a sky hawk riding the windy air, to hover, plunge groundward, and kill. Talons curled and clutched, and a small life ended. Bethkahn ripped and fed, knowing the hunger of the hunter, its joy in the hot taste of her prey. In flesh she had killed and been killed, experiences alien to her nature, not easy to understand. Flesh was never easy, Mahna had said. It was cruel always, a mixture of violence and beauty, bittersweet feelings that were difficult to bear. Their kind seldom stayed enfleshed for long. They experienced it briefly and were glad to be free.

But the ship voice suggested . . .

"It was a primitive world," Bethkahn repeated. "It showed no signs of civilization, no indication of life forms advanced enough to understand intricate instructions or build complicated machinery. Even if the crew had entered flesh, even if they had found a suitable species, they would have needed to establish an evolutionary program, and that would have taken them thousands of years. . . ."

Bethkahn stopped talking.

Suddenly she understood.

"Are you saying this is what they have done?"

"It seems a logical hypothesis," said the ship.

There had been evolutionary programs before in other parts of the galaxy. Bethkahn had learned of them at the Academy—transcendent worlds where flesh was made beautiful by the spirit that inhabited it. Some volunteered for it, saw it as a challenge, a way of gaining individual understanding. And flesh had its advantages. It was a mind-body combination that had built this ship, set Bethkahn and others of her kind free to travel the universe.

She knew the theory. It was spiritual possession. Not the temporary sharing of a host creature's body, as she had done with Bahtoomi's deer, but permanent, throughout its lifetime, the controversial eviction of its soul. Those from the stars, encased in flesh, mated with those of the chosen planet, engendering hybrid children. And when the body died, they entered another, were born again, reincarnating over and over and repeating the process of interbreeding, their spirits mingling and strengthening and reinforcing the original strain. Each new generation of children became increasingly accomplished, increasingly advanced—apes evolving to angels in a few thousand years.

But for those involved there were risks attached. If the spirit was not strong enough, flesh could become dominant, the mind obsessed with the body it inhabited. Souls could degenerate, turn hedonistic, renegade, or bad. Trapped within flesh a soul could lose sight of its origin and purpose, even lose sight of itself. Those involved needed guidance and monitoring, galactic counseling and spiritual help in times of trouble. It was madness to think of initiating an evolutionary program on an unknown planet without off-world supervision.

"Rondahl wouldn't do it," Bethkahn said.

"I think he has already done it," said the ship.

"He would never risk it. None of them would!"

"But those outside are their descendents," said the ship. "We cannot deny it, Bethkahn. They have come from the same planet. Their life traces show too many exact matches to be explained in any other way. These souls bound in flesh are Rondahl's solution, and I do not like them. They must not discover us, mistress. They must never discover us here."

3

Bethkahn stared at the vision screen, at the pale life-trace flicker of an unknown being. It was flesh bound and fleeting, having no memory of Khio Three, its link with the stars, inheriting only some vague indefinable sensing, an ancestral instinct that was driving it toward them. It had come to this moon as a step on the way and was unaware of her, not knowing her plight. And the joy of Bethkahn's waking was gone to despair as the long-ago loneliness reached out toward her, disturbing a terror and longing from which she could not escape. Rondahl's descendents were not to be trusted, the ship voice had said.

"I want to see them," Bethkahn said fearfully.

Time flickered on the vision screen, sequential events that the ship had recorded and of which Bethkahn had been unaware. Her long-ago distress signal brought a response. Rescue ships came and continued to come—freight carriers, star cruisers, exploration vessels from every corner of the universe. But each one headed for the planet, lured by the bright blue shimmer of sunlight on water, its swirling atmosphere, its myriad indications of life. They paid no heed to a dead moon where Bethkahn had been sleeping, although the ship had done its best to attract attention. Again and again it had sent out the short-range scanners, their small power jets whirling up the dust of dry lunar seas, trailing gray walls of mist across the desert landscape. A dozen tiny transmitters bleeped messages that were never heard, radiophonic voices feeble as gnat whines dissolving among the stars. At other times the ship had activated its main drive units, blown itself free of dust and debris until the crater smoked like a great volcano. But no one noticed and no ship landed . . . until the Earth beings came.

"Earth?" said Bethkahn.

"Their name for the planet," said the ship.

"They do not use the galactic tongue?"

"Either they have not been taught it or it has degenerated and become unrecognizable," the ship voice replied. "I have compiled vocabularies of two principal languages."

"So they are two different species?"

"They are all one species," said the ship. "But there are many tribes, many subdivisions, many cultures, rituals, and languages. There are superficial variations among the main ethnic groups, but the biological infrastructure . . ."

"Just show me," Bethkahn interrupted.

It was Earth year 1969, and there was the flesh of which the ship voice had spoken, the first tentative arrivals—two grotesque humanoid shapes, helmeted and faceless, emerging from an equally grotesque lunar module. A voice gabbled words which the ship voice translated. "This is a giant leap forward for mankind." Through the eyes of a scanner Bethkahn stared at them— space-suited bipeds lumbering around on the Moon's barren surface, leaving their footprints in the dust and planting their flag. She had wanted to love Rondahl's descendents. She had wanted to rush outside and welcome them. But she could not feel kinship for those alien primate things. Her whole being shrank from them, and tears prickled her eyes.

"He has failed," she whispered. "Rondahl has failed. Those are not advanced evolutionary beings. They are subhuman! Cavorting imbecilic monsters!"

"They have reached their moon," the ship reminded her.

Bethkahn shuddered.

"I'm going back to the cryogenic chamber," she said.

"You can't do that!" the ship said urgently. "I need you, Bethkahn. Those earth creatures are dangerous, mistress! They threaten us!"

Bethkahn stayed, watched in alarm as the ship continued to replay the last long century of time—a succession of lunar landings and bloated humanoid forms who remained for a few hours and then departed. Red, white, and blue, their starred-and-striped banners hung motionless through succeeding decades of silence.

But then, fifty years later, the Earth beings returned. From the rim of the crater high in the mountains, a single scanner watched their spaceships arrive, a fleet of sleek transporters bringing in people and supplies. Unseen in the distance it recorded the building of their moonbase, an underground complex and prefabricated buildings rising from the dust. Technologically they had advanced beyond belief. Gone were the cumbersome space suits they had worn before. Bethkahn saw slim limbs clad in silver fabric, saw grace in their movements, a familiarity of form that no longer repelled. Their domed helmets showed no facial features but only reflections, yet she relaxed as she watched them and smiled in her relief.

They were not monsters. They were lithe as Bahtoomi's hunting cats and surefooted as the dancers on Aravis Nine. And how many times had Mahna told her not to judge life by appearances alone? But the ship voice had said they were dangerous. Bethkahn studied them warily, their sleek ships landing and departing, their wheeled machines fanning out across the Moon's surface. There were close to a thousand flesh-and-blood beings living and working within the sealed environment of the American base, the ship voice informed her. More manned the remote outposts, and far to the north the Russians had established a similar base. Russian and American—one species, two tribes. Bright points of light on the video display map showed their whereabouts.

"Sinus Iridum . . . Mare Vaporum," the ship voice said.

Haltingly Bethkahn repeated the names, meaningless syllables of an unfamiliar language, words sounding strange on her tongue. Bay of Rainbows, Sea of Mists, the ship voice translated. Strange misnomers, but they made the bleak moon seem suddenly beautiful, an alien dreamlike world. What kind of minds culled mists and rainbows from barren deserts of dust? What kind of beings had Rondahl's descendents become? And why were they dangerous?

"Give me an infrastructure scan," Bethkahn said quietly.

"Screen three," said the ship.

Bethkahn pressed the button, and the form appeared—bone structure fleshed in white light. It was not some grotesque parody of herself. It was a physical replica, a flesh-and-blood body molding to the spirit that inhabited it, a being bred in Rondahl's own image. Delight shone from her eyes. Such knowledge changed everything. She was no longer alone on a dead, uncharted world. She had only to walk to the moonbase and hold out her hand.

"These beings are beautiful!" she said.

"They are flesh," said the ship.

"I can talk with them . . . laugh with them . . ."

"Predators," said the ship. "They prey on other life forms and kill one another."

Bethkahn shrugged.

"Flesh has to eat," she said.

"But they commit murder," said the ship.

"Murder?" said Bethkahn. "What do you mean?"

The ship seemed to pause before replying, its presence hovering in the white light on the edges of her vision, an impression of entity that was gone when she turned her head. Many times in the past Bethkahn had been deceived into believing the ship was alive. It was an illusion born out of loneliness, for it simply existed mechanically and was all around her—in the curved walls of the main console room, in the astrodome stars and the navigational computers, in the manufactured circuits of its mind. It was a thing of logic, not capable of making moral judgments, but it came very close to judging the Earth beings now.

"What do you mean?" Bethkahn repeated.

"Flesh can corrupt," the ship voice said. "It can subordinate the spirit within it. They are not beautiful, Bethkahn, nor is their world. Their communications tell me . . . terrible things take place on it—war and famine, cruelty and monstrous acts of destruction. I fear what will happen if they should discover us. I am afraid, Bethkahn."

Bethkahn stared unseeingly at the shape on the vision screen—bones fleshed in light, a living being, beautiful, dangerous. Flesh was never easy, Mahna had said. It was cruel always, and Bethkahn could not forgive. She could forgive a predator that killed to live, but not an intelligence that murdered life, a spirit that did not care.

"I am afraid!" the ship voice repeated.

"You are a machine!" Bethkahn said harshly. "You

cannot feel fear. And I am immaterial, so they can do nothing to me. I'm going back to the cryogenic chamber, and whatever else happens I don't want to know!"

"Mistress!" squawked the ship. "You have to help me, mistress! They could break into me, take me to pieces, or blow me up! If I am destroyed who then will care for you? Think of it, Bethkahn! Think of it! You can't let that happen! You cannot ignore them and hide away. You have to mend my stabilizer as soon as possible and let me take you home!"

4

He dreamed.

And Karen called him.

"Hey Gary! Wake up!"

She switched on the light, and Gareth squinted into the sudden brightness. She was wearing a lurid green jump suit, and the room was painted white, spartanly furnished, and small as a clothes closet, with a wash-basin and a single chair. Window blinds sealed out the view, and in the alcove opposite his bed a blank computer screen reflected his face. He had a headache from last night's reception, and Karen had no right to come barging into his room.

"What do you want?" he asked irritably.

"Drew's waiting to see you in his office."

"Who the hell's Drew?"

"Drew Steadman, the base medic. You met him last

night, remember? The tall guy with red hair? He and Commander Bradbury will be showing us around after breakfast, but first you have to have a medical check."

"I had one before we left," Gareth muttered.

"It's only routine," said Karen. "Pulse rate and blood pressure, that kind of thing. I guess he just wants to make sure we've survived the journey okay. This place is fantastic, Gary, it really is. I can't wait to see it."

The room reminded Gareth of a cheap motel, stark and impersonal except for his travel bag lying unpacked on the floor. It offered no clue as to where he was. And Karen's loud American drawl and the green of her jump suit made his headache worse. Pain thumped with the light behind his eyes. He rolled over and pulled the bedspread up around his ears.

"Don't go back to sleep!" said Karen. "You'll miss the sunrise, and Drew says it only happens once every twenty-eight days. If you turn left at the end of the corridor his office is the third door on the right. Shall I open your window blinds?"

"Let 'em alone!" growled Gareth.

"Are you always so grouchy first thing in the morning?"

"You never heard of a hangover, girlie?"

Karen laughed.

"There's ham and eggs and waffles for breakfast," she informed him. "And they stop serving at nine. Better ask Drew to give you some Alka-Seltzer. I'll be waiting for you in the cafeteria in half an hour."

"Make it forty minutes," Gareth said.

"I don't know how you can lie there anyway. We're on the Moon, for Christ's sake, and you're wasting time! How can you lie in bed, Gary?"

"Because you're in my flaming room and I've got nothing on!" Gareth told her.

She left, finally, returned to her own room to put a new roll of film in her camera, her presence lingering in the smell of her perfume and chewing gum. Gareth dressed in jeans and a sweatshirt and weighted canvas shoes, ran a hand through his hair, and made his way to the base medic's office. A man in a white coat opened the door to him.

"Doctor Steadman?"

"Drew," said the base medic. "You feel okay?"

"I've a headache," said Gareth.

"You also have your sweatshirt on backward."

Gareth had no recollection of having met Drew Steadman during last night's reception, but he liked him immediately—a tall, red-haired, friendly American. Unlike Karen, Drew was quiet and soft-spoken, easy to talk to and willing to listen. He had graduated in space psychology and had been on the Moon for almost three years. He gave Gareth a glass of fizzing liquid that made him belch, a pill for his headache, and a quick physical checkup.

"Welsh?" he said.

"That's right," said Gareth. "The first Welshman on the Moon. Put my shirt on, can I?"

"You can," said Drew. "And don't forget the dragon goes in front."

Gareth waited, soothed by the room's stillness as Drew filled in details in his file. It was dark outside, the moonbase a sprawl of lighted buildings nestling near the foot of the Lunar Apennines in the Mare Vaporum, Sea of Mists. Solar panels gleamed silver in the starlight, and great telescopic dishes marched away over the sharply curving horizon. The roadway and launch pads were smooth scars in the dust. Inside, the air-conditioning hummed softly and a pot of geraniums bloomed coral pink on the filing cabinet.

"So how does it feel?" Drew asked at last.

"Unreal," said Gareth. "As if any moment now I'm going to wake up and find myself back on Earth. I can't believe I'm here!"

Drew smiled.

"Some prize, a trip to the Moon. You're here all right—where science and religion finally meet."

"You read my essay?"

" 'The Lunacy Syndrome,' " Drew quoted. "We have all read it. Karen's too. What gave you the idea?"

"Uncle Llewellyn preaches in the local chapel when anyone turns up," said Gareth. "It's the same all over, dwindling congregations in all the churches. But go to the Moon and you come back converted, see? A well-known phenomenon it is. All I did was speculate why."

"Where did you do your research?" Drew asked him.

Gareth grinned.

"What research? I made the whole thing up, straight off the top of my head. It's a talent, see? The only thing I'm good at—telling stories. A born liar, according to my mom. I always knew that one day it would come in useful. Never mind Canterbury Cathedral, here's where the big religious experience really happens. God is alive and well and living on the Moon. Never dreamed I'd actually come here though."

"That's quite astonishing," said Drew. "Your Lunacy Syndrome is uncannily accurate for a work of the imagination, and you are not at all what I expected. What do you think of Karen's essay?"

"That was something else," said Gareth. "Sheer magic, I thought, until I clapped eyes on her."

Drew nodded in understanding.

"She's even more surprising," he said.

Karen Angers was not at all what Gareth had imagined the writer of "Phoebe Unveiled" to be. He had imagined someone pale and quiet and poetic, a delicate, thoughtful girl he had been half in love with before he left Wales. But Karen was loudmouthed and gawky, an extrovert, and batty as an English cricket pitch. From the moment he had met her in the departure lounge at the Kennedy Space Center, everything about her seemed to grate on his nerves—her inane prattle, her constant gum chewing, her gee-whiz enthusiasm, her embarrassing familiarity. She had seemed to take possession of him, her touch on his arm demanding his attention. She called him Gary and was inescapable. And the ten tons of photographic equipment she had brought with her had made the trip to the Moon seem like a package tour. Now, looking at Drew Steadman with his keen gray eyes, white medic's coat, and dangling stethoscope, Gareth sensed a certain sympathy.

"I suppose you found nothing wrong with her?" he asked hopefully.

"I'm afraid not," said Drew.

"Did you try shining a light in her ear?"

"Meaning she doesn't hear too well?"

"Meaning you can probably see right through to the opposite wall. That girl's got a brain the size of a pea!"

Drew Steadman laughed.

"That's not nice, Gareth. Karen can't be that bad."

"She can't even get my name right!" Gareth said.

"It's only for one month," Drew said consolingly.

Four weeks on the Moon—that had been the prize offered in the international essay competition organized by the World Educational Council—one boy and one girl, under the age of eighteen, to be guests at the American base. And so they had arrived—Gareth Ewart Johns from Aberdare, Wales, and Karen Jane Angers from California, U.S.A.—on the regular freight shuttle at the end of an eighteen-hour flight.

Gareth's memory remained hazy . . . harsh light shining on the polished floor of the reception area . . . the click-flash of Karen's camera when he shook hands with Commander Bradbury . . . peculiar feelings of semiweightlessness and flight fatigue . . . roast-turkey dinner and champagne corks popping. His mind was a muddle of names and faces and voices and no person clear in it, except Karen—Karen with her shocking-pink travel suit, her photographic apparatus, and her overloud mouth, dominating the whole show. Gareth could have been in a hotel restaurant or a McDonald's. Karen had killed the Moon and destroyed whatever first impression he might have had.

And soon she would destroy the sunrise too, turning black to white as it swept across the dusty landscape. With her yak-yak, click-flash, hey-Gary drivel, he would gain nothing from it. She would turn it into a tourist spectacle, like Buckingham Palace on the King's birthday. Gareth needed to be alone, feel the Moon's almighty desolation, and catch the wonder when the sunrise happened.

"Is there anywhere I can go to be alone?" he asked.

"Evasion tactics?" asked Drew.

"If you like."

Drew frowned.

"I'm not sure I do like. Up here on the Moon we have to learn to get along, and you can hardly avoid Karen for twenty-eight days."

"How about half an hour, just to watch the sunrise?"

"The observatory should be empty at this time of day."

"Thanks," said Gareth. "How do I get there?"

Drew gave him directions.

"And don't stay too long," he warned. "Solitude can be dangerous on the Moon. Your Lunacy Syndrome has its dark side, Gareth, and human sanity is a fragile thing. Any funny effects I want to know about, right?"

"If I see any little green men, you mean?"

"I mean anything at all," said Drew.

5

The Moon was lonely. Gareth had sensed it even with Karen around. But now, having escaped her, he felt the impact. It was not the loneliness of Wales, mountains and bog and the curlews calling. Out on Pen-y-van was a kind of peace and grandeur. But here on the Moon was a loneliness that terrified, a monstrous isolation. Solitude was dangerous, Drew Steadman had said, and Gareth knew what he meant. No place on Earth could produce feelings such as these.

High on the catwalk of the domed observatory there was nothing to separate him from the stars. The immensity awed him—darkness and distance, a gold-black balance of time and space—infinite space, eternal time. Those stars had been there since before the forming of the world, before life evolved and apes became men. They would be there when the world ended and people ceased to be—fabulous shining suns, small as dust motes in the cosmic eye of God.

Gareth clung to the railing. Such thoughts brought everything down to size. All the achievements of the human race amounted to nothing, and individuality was swept away. His whole life would be less than a billionth of a second in the time scale of the stars. He was born and then gone, instantly snuffed out, a microscopic particle that momentarily flashed into existence before dying into oblivion. The realization of his own insignificance appalled him, and the terror grew. Mindless and insensate, the universe destroyed him, reduced him to a fragment of being, a tiny spark of life about to go out.

"God!" said Gareth. "You're supposed to be up here! Don't do this to me!"

Documented evidence suggested that few people returned to Earth unchanged by the lunar experience. Astronauts became evangelists, and hardened space technicians turned into religious gurus. Gareth had dubbed it the Lunacy Syndrome and tried to imagine it—some almighty mystical moment, an awareness of the sublime. But the Lunacy Syndrome had its dark side, Drew had said, and this was it—everything meaningless, including himself.

"Autosuggestion," said Gareth. "Damn you, Drew! And you can't stand it, can you? No," he said. "Best get out of here!"

He turned away, sensing the floor space far below him, seeing the great dome sweeping above his head, a shift in perspective.

Since the dawn of time men had looked up at the stars and called them heaven, generation after generation striving to reach them. Why? What was up there? Out there? Suddenly Gareth knew. It was a peculiar feeling, as if the fragment of being he had become detached itself from his body, swelled and soared, recognizing and knowing—the universe was not meaningless and empty, mere space and substance moving without purpose. It was deliberate and designed, charged with energy and power, a gold-black enormity in the mind of God of which all things were a part. And Gareth did not belong to the Earth. The stars were calling him toward them. The Moon tugging his heart. Terror changed to ecstasy. But then the lights snapped on and everything fled. He was back in his body, back in his own head.

Flaming Karen!

"Hey, Gary! Are you in here?"

Her voice echoed hollowly through the acoustic spaces, and the stars were gone among reflections of yellow light on the dome of transparent plastic. She put an end to Gareth's astral affinities, his intimations of immortality. Fifty feet below, in the well of the observatory, metallic glints showed on the mass of computers and radiographic equipment, and the sensation of height made him feel giddy. Instinctively he stepped backward, his weighted training shoes clattering on the metal gantry and betraying his presence. Karen looked up— a girl with long brown hair and a too-wide mouth standing in the doorway.

"Gary? Is that you?"

"Put the lights out!" he said.

"I'm coming to join you!" she shouted.

The observatory snapped back into darkness. Gareth heard the hum of machinery below and the rattle of her steps on the stairs, the clomp of her moon shoes along the catwalk. Then she was beside him, starshine in her eyes and the white gash of her smile, the inevitable camera hung around her neck.

"Hi," said Karen. "How's your headache?"

Gareth turned and leaned on the windowsill.

And she leaned beside him.

"Hi, Karen," she said. "I'm fine now, thank you for asking. And I'm sure glad you could join me up here. Gee, Gary, it's real sweet of you to say so. And you don't have to apologize—I only waited twenty minutes in the cafeteria for you to show!"

"How did you find me anyway?" Gareth asked.

"Drew told me where you were. He said the view is better from up here." She pressed her face against the glass. Her breath made mist on the plastic surface as she surveyed the barren landscape outside, the floodlit buildings, the black velvet sky, and the stars. "I don't see the Earth," she announced.

"It's below the horizon," Gareth informed her.

"Were you trying to avoid me?" she asked.

"Whatever gave you that idea?"

She touched his hand.

"I think it's real nice to have someone my own age," she said.

"The verb 'to have' implies ownership," Gareth said stiffly. "I'm not a consumer item."

"Okay," said Karen. "Then it's nice to *be with* someone my own age. It puts us together, I guess. All I want is for us to be friends, Gary. Instead of sneaking off, tell me what I'm doing wrong."

Gareth glanced at her.

Her chewing-gum breath was peppermint sweet.

And her touch went on.

"You really want me to tell you, girlie?"

"Well, I don't understand," she said. "I've tried my damnedest to be friendly with you, Gary. I know you English are apt to be reserved . . ."

"Right!" shouted Gareth. "Let's get a few things straight, shall we? You Gary me just once more and I'll jump on your bunions, girlie! The name's Gareth— G A R E T H! And I'm not English, I'm Welsh! I come from Wales, see? And I'm not used to being crowded. I like a bit of space between me and the next person. When I want to be touched up I'll let you know, but until then you keep your hands off me! You got all that, have you?"

Karen moved a respectable three paces away from him.

"Sure," she said. "I get it."

"Good," said Gareth. "Just stop chewing gum by my earhole and maybe we can be friends."

"You're not very nice, are you?"

"You did ask for it, girlie."

Karen fiddled with her light meter.

"Which direction does the sun come up?" she asked.

"Behind us," said Gareth.

"Drew says there are mountains nearby."

"The Lunar Apennines," said Gareth.

"I did some climbing at summer camp."

"Is that significant?"

"We could borrow some space suits and a buggy."

Gareth stared at her.

He could not believe she was being serious.

"It'll be fun," she said.

"You've got no more idea than the man in the Moon!"

"Woman," said Karen.

"Pardon?"

"She's feminine," said Karen. "Phoebe . . . Diana . . . the white Goddess. Every poet who's ever written has seen her as female. Haven't you read my essay?"

"Yes," said Gareth. "And it's got nothing to do with scientific fact. The Moon's not a flipping holiday camp!"

They might have argued, but then the sunrise happened. Karen stayed silent, and he did too, seeing the sun strike the distant mountains, stark white peaks floating in utter blackness, unsupported islands beyond the Mare Vaporum, Sea of Mists. They were sharp and spectacular, etched against the sky—Mount Bradley, Mount Huygens, Mount Conon, Mount Ampere—white as bleached bone.

"Snow tops!" breathed Karen. "Oh boy! That's really

something. Out of this world. Mind getting out of the way, Gary-eth? I want to get a shot."

"I don't know why you bother," Gareth said. "You can buy perfectly good postcards at the souvenir shop."

Click-flash, click-flash went Karen's camera.

"I didn't know they had a souvenir store here," she said.

"Every self-respecting moonbase has a souvenir shop, girlie. Moondust egg timers, moon-rock paperweights, ashtray craters, that kind of thing. You can hire skis too, if you haven't brought your own."

Karen looked at him suspiciously.

"Skis?" she said.

"They've got ski slopes on Mount Hadley," said Gareth. "Didn't you know? They run excursions twice a week."

Karen frowned and stared at the sun line creeping down the mountains. Soon a blast of daylight would hit the ocean floor, and already the plastic dome was darkening, reactolite blue, tingeing rocks and ridges with cerulean hue, filling clefts and valleys with indigo shadows. The harsh landscape was softened, its bleak beauty become a gentler thing.

"You're making fun of her," said Karen.

"Making fun of who?"

"Loneliness makes her cruel, you know."

"Who are you talking about?"

"The Goddess," said Karen. "The one the poets write about. She's ruthless and has no mercy. Don't laugh at her."

For some reason Gareth did not laugh. Poetic image or scientific fact, he caught the truth contained in Karen's words. The Moon *was* cruel. One careless moment and it would kill.

6

The base commander was waiting with Drew in the reception area, a burly middle-aged man in a navy-blue overall. Last night, in his United States Air Force uniform, Jefferson Bradbury had looked the part. Now, given a vacuum cleaner, he would pass for a moonbase cleaner, Gareth thought, everybody's favorite uncle, affectionately called J.B. But there was a hard glint in his eyes when he glanced at his watch, and an edge to his voice as he asked why they were late. Strict time-keeping was essential, he informed them, and Karen explained they had gone to the observatory to watch the sunrise. Breakfast smells drifted from the cafeteria, and Gareth's stomach felt hollow with hunger, but J.B. was taking them on a tour of inspection, so he fell into line.

"Can we go to the souvenir store?" Karen asked.

"What souvenir store?" J.B. asked.

"Gary says every moonbase has one."

One bushy eyebrow raised quizzically, and the steel gray eyes of the base commander fastened on Gareth. He saw humor in their depths and something else.

"The lad's a comedian," J.B. said to Drew.

"I'll make a note of it," Drew replied.

"There are no souvenir shops here, young lady," J.B. told Karen. "Maybe in fifty years' time . . ."

Doors to the main communications room opened and closed automatically, and the quiet corridor gave way to a barrage of noise. Low sunlight filtering through the reactolite windows turned Drew's red hair to a peculiar shade of puce. Faces looked gray and ill. Later, in the glass houses, plants bloomed with untrue colors in blue-green jungles of thick heat. Purple tomatoes fruited in Gareth's brain as they toured the swimming pool and recreation area, and went down in the elevator.

Like an iceberg city, most of the moonbase was below the surface—for insulation purposes, J.B. said. Normally Gareth would have been impressed. But the underground ways troubled him. The lights were too bright, and geometrical dimensions of walls and corridors and floor tiles played tricks with his eyes. He saw curving uprights and strange vanishing infinities. Distances telescoped, and, like Alice in Wonderland, Gareth felt himself either too big or too small. He even saw white rabbits breeding in the bio lab, and J.B.'s face was hatched with lines, a Tenniel illustration come to life, smile creased and heavy jowled. A thousand Karens, wearing caterpillar-green jump suits, reflected in the chrome fitments of the chemistry laboratory and blew pink bubbles of gum. Hunger, thought Gareth, was making him light-headed.

"What time's lunch?" he asked Drew.

They had hot dogs and doughnuts in an underground snack bar, but he still felt weird. Wherever they went—through all the kitchens and living quarters, computer rooms and research laboratories, workshops and power plants—Gareth was prey to the same bizarre impressions. Things assumed a nightmare quality, and his mind was woolly as a Welsh sheep's. He could hear his own voice asking questions, but the answers had no meaning. He could hear Karen yakking and failed to follow what she said. Absurdly Gareth wished that she would touch him, her hand on his arm confirming he was actually there. But he had drawn circles in the air around himself, and Karen touched Drew instead.

"Gee, this is fantastic!" she said.

It seemed to grow more fantastic with Gareth's every step. Walls keeled and floors sloped at idiotic angles—down or up, he could not tell which. His head floated and was unconnected with his legs. He swayed drunkenly, clutched a vending machine to save himself from falling, and its gargoyle mouth spewed coffee at his feet. Gareth stared at it, a pool of brown liquid shining stupidly in the light, contradicting all physical laws. And the floor dived downward like a playground chute.

"Are you all right, son?" J.B. asked him.

"You're supposed to put a cup underneath," said Karen.

"That was deliberate!" Gareth said wildly. "Waiting to get me, it was! I only touched the side of it! And who designed this place? Max flaming Ernst? Everywhere's wrong! I mean . . . look at it!"

"Look at what?" Drew asked quietly.

"Water flows downhill," said Gareth. "So why isn't it? And look at them angles! They're supposed to be ninety degrees! You ever been in the crazy house at Barry Island funfair? Makes you feel queer in the head, it does, but this place is worse. I can't stand it!"

J.B. pressed the intercom button.

And talked to the wall.

"Val? This is J.B. I'm in corridor D-seven. Have someone check this vending machine, will you? I also want a twelve-hour delayed countdown on that return shuttle. And get through to Medical. Tell them to send . . . ?"

"Fifty mils of B-thirty-six and a hypodermic," said Drew.

"You can't send Gary back to Earth!" shrilled Karen.

"He's severely disorientated," said Drew.

Lying on the bed in his own room, the funny effects stopped and reality stabilized. Horizontals and verticals remained true. His mind grew calm, soothed by the blue-gray daylight, the tranquilizing drug, and Drew's presence. He even accepted the color changes—puce hair, gray skin, forget-me-not walls. It was no worse than the orange streetlights in Aberdare.

"You won't really send me back to Earth, will you?"

"That's up to the base commander," said Drew.

"But there's nothing wrong with me now!" Gareth left the bed. "Look you—one leg, no hands—steady as a rock, see?"

He swayed wildly.

And Drew gripped his arm.

"I just need some practice," said Gareth.

"You need to lie down," said Drew. "I'll look in later."

Gareth lay still, listening to the soporific hum of the air-conditioning and refusing to sleep. He was annoyed with himself, annoyed with Karen. She stayed unaffected, her brain functions normal, but he was space drunk and incapable of controlling his body and about to be shipped out. He would never walk on the surface of the Moon beyond his window, or set his foot upon the Sea of Mists.

"Can't let that happen, can you?" Gareth asked himself. "No," he replied. "I got to practice. Mind over matter, that's what it is."

By the time Gareth reached the gymnasium, his coordination had improved. There were white lines marked on the floor for basketball games, and soon he could walk them all without falling over. Then he tried running. After that he did pushups, body bends, and balancing acts. And in the end he could stand on one leg even with his eyes closed. His confidence was restored. There was nothing wrong with him; now all he had to do was convince Drew and J.B.

At the sound of the meal buzzer Gareth headed for the cafeteria, but J.B. was not impressed to see him recovered. He was angry. Drew, apparently, had gone to check on him and found him missing, and the whole moonbase had been alerted. While Gareth had been holding a floor show in the empty gymnasium, they had been searching, fearing his space sickness might lead him to do something stupid, endangering his own life. Louder than the canteen clatter from the serving hatches were the base commander's whiplash words.

"I never thought," Gareth muttered.

"Then you'd better start thinking!" J.B. snapped. "Carelessness can cost lives up here! From now on you don't do anything or go anywhere without permission, right? And what's this garbage you've been telling Karen about ski runs on the Lunar Apennines?"

Gareth glared at her. She was seated in the window bay at the base commander's table, watching him anxiously, a hint of fear in her eyes. And outside on the launch pad the freight shuttle waited to take him home. Gareth was on probation in more ways than one.

"Permission to eat?" he asked Drew.

They dined on steak, served with sweet corn and reconstituted mashed potatoes, blue tinted and tasteless as straw. Gareth did not speak to Karen, nor did he speak to her afterward in the moonbase bar. He played darts with the freight-shuttle pilot instead, but all the while he could feel her watching him among the sounds of canned music and J.B.'s guffaws of laughter in the sapphire light. Later they went swimming. In the turquoise pool warm with sunlight, Gareth felt fully revived, and Drew's office in the morning no longer seemed a threat. But the enjoyment was gone out of

Karen, her chatter subdued, and going back to their rooms she trailed miserably behind him. Go to bed, Drew had told them, but Karen stood in his doorway. Flowers of indescribable colors wreathed her bathrobe, and water dripped from her hair.

"You got something on your mind?" Gareth asked her.

"Don't go," she said.

"You're the one who's going," Gareth said curtly. "It's ten to midnight, and I've got a medical checkup in the morning."

"Don't let them send you back to Earth!" said Karen. "I couldn't bear it here without you."

"Tough," said Gareth. "You should have thought of that before you opened your trap to J.B. Ski runs on the Moon! For crying out loud . . . you must have known I was joking!"

"Please Gary, you're the only one there is!"

"Gareth!" said Gareth. "So what's wrong with Drew?"

"He's twenty-eight, for Christ's sake! I need *you!*"

"I told you this morning . . ."

Karen shook her head.

Blue drops scattered, and there was fear in her eyes.

"You don't understand! It's not like that! You're the only reason I'm not scared out of my mind!"

"Scared?" said Gareth. "There's nothing to be scared of, girlie."

"Nothing," said Karen. "And that's what frightens me. I'd rather die than face that kind of emptiness. If you go back to Earth I'm coming too. I'm not staying here by myself."

46

Beyond her, in the corridor, the bright light darkened. Heavy shutters activated automatically and closed out the sunlight. Duplicating Earth time the moonbase simulated night. Daylight streaming through Gareth's window seemed incongruous now. Yet Karen waited, scared of it—the outside vacuum and the Moon's loneliness where no one was.

"I won't be going back to Earth," Gareth assured her. "I'll get up early in the morning and go for a workout. So you can go back to bed and stop worrying, girlie. The Moon's not seen the last of me. *Nos da, cariad.*"

"What?" said Karen.

"Good night, darling . . . in Welsh," said Gareth.

7

Bethkahn paced the ship's shining floor. Her red clothes rustled in the silences, made scarlet flutterings in the crystal pillars that arched and towered above her head. A thousand images moved and danced as she passed among clear glass tables and headed for the pool where rainbow fish swam—biological specimens taken from Athos Four, surviving as she had for ten thousand years. Their fins made spectrums of the light passing through them that flashed between dark reflections of lily leaves and ferns. A jungle of plants glistened with damp drops, roots feeding on a mulch of slime and fish bones and their own decay. A small mechanized work unit with robotic arms sprayed and cleaned and tended. Bethkahn surprised it. Menial and voiceless it stared at her with green unwinking eyes, then scuttled away. Work units were programmed to be unobtrusive.

She sat on a padded bench seat among the rank scents of vegetation. She had come here to think, but the movements of the fish distracted her and she remembered how things used to be—curved windows open to a sweep of stars and the hall behind her alive with music and laughter. It had been a gathering place for off-duty crew—an intermingling of all the various departments, a kaleidoscope of uniformed colors, diaphanous, drifting—and robotic waiters served amber wine in tall glasses. Now the windows were smothered with dust, and the great room was silent, empty save for herself. But the memories stirred and ghosts teemed in her head—Rondahl and Mahna, Elveron planet finder, Dahn from Biology, and Keirharah who had taught Bethkahn to mind-sing.

Keirharah the enchantress, Rondahl had called her. On Athos Four, their second landfall, she had called its creatures to her—birds to her hands, horned sheep and wild cats walking beside her, day moths fluttering their wings in her hair. She had charmed the rainbow fish from sweet-water pools into Dahn's collecting jar, charmed away Bethkahn's initial shyness, and sung a softness into Rondahl's eyes. Keirharah would have mothered magic in her flesh-bred children, fostered a love of all that lived, a sense of worship and wonder. Perhaps she had taught them how to sing, her music in their language, in their minds—echoes of mists and rainbows, showers and shadows, of a landfall planet Bethkahn had never seen.

Words that were beautiful named the lunar seas. But

their Earth was not beautiful, the ship voice had said. Terrible things took place on it—motivations of greed and hatred and fear. Flesh had corrupted the souls of Rondahl's descendents, and the ship feared discovery. It was fear based on logic, it had said. Chances were it would be damaged beyond repair, Bethkahn captured and imprisoned, and home world become unreachable forever. Bethkahn thought of it longingly—Khio Three with its myriad milk-white towers, its blue-grass hills and gardens of flowers. The ship was the only hope she had of ever returning there, and she was bound to protect it, bound to do as it asked. She had to think of her future and disregard the past. But the ghosts remained—Keirharah singing in her memory . . . Mahna mind-hunting sand dragons on Chinnah Five . . . Dahn going white and golden among hanging vines. He was not forgettable—the flash of his smile and the searing blue of his eyes and the sunlight on his hair, honey colored . . .

"Go away!" she said.

"Bethkahn?" said the ship.

"You too!" she told it.

"I can't," it said.

Sometimes its logic made her angry—a computerized mind in a metal carapace hatching its plans. They could not wait any longer for Rondahl to return, the ship had decided. They had to escape from this moon as quickly as possible. Bethkahn must restore it to full functioning order—approach the American base, slip inside, and weld together the broken bits of stabilizer unit. It was all very simple and straightforward, except that somewhere, in order to avoid discovery, she would have to enter flesh, take possession of a human body. And that was not like catching a ride with Bahtoomi's deer, resting briefly within it, quiescent and experiencing, not interfering in its life or death. Bethkahn would be dealing with a being capable of conscious thought, an intelligence that might well become aware of her intrusion, that might refuse to share its body and decide to fight.

"I don't like it!" Bethkahn said definitely.

"Mistress?" said the ship.

"I've never done it before."

"It's standard procedure," said the ship.

"It's against the rules!" Bethkahn retorted. "We are forbidden to influence the physical, mental, or emotional functioning of any host creature we may enter. Even animals have a right to know and experience their own lives! That's why the Galactic Council was talking of outlawing evolutionary programs. They may even have done so, in which case you're asking me to commit an unlawful act. And if it isn't unlawful it's certainly unethical. It's unethical to force my way into another's body and override its will!"

The ship stayed silent, considering Bethkahn's objections. It was programmed humanely, to care for its crew and all life forms within it, to cater to their basic needs and harm nothing. It was for Bethkahn's sake it had planned their escape, but she talked of ethics, al-

51

truistic and often illogical, and questioned its morality. In the white light the great ship pondered and very carefully selected its words.

"I never suggested you use force, Bethkahn. I merely suggested you should share a body, hide within it, utilize its hands."

"And if it objects, what then?" Bethkahn inquired.

"How else can I solicit assistance without taking possession? If the American beings are as dangerous as you say they are, they are hardly likely to cooperate, are they? Otherwise I could simply go to them and ask to borrow their welding equipment."

"There must be a way," the ship voice murmured.

"So tell me it," Bethkahn instructed.

"Keirharah would mind-sing."

"Not even Keirharah could mind-sing a whole moonbase," Bethkahn pointed out. "And we are not dealing with animals. These are intelligent beings, probably deaf to enchantments. And I am not Keirharah. I could maybe persuade a fish to feed from my hand but not a man to surrender his body and open his mind."

"It's your choice," the ship voice said stiffly. "You can either do as I suggest or not do as I suggest. But if you choose not to, I have already calculated the likely consequences."

Bethkahn bit her lip. Into human hands could fall a power undreamed of—a galactic spaceship and a girl who had come from the stars. Whether through fear, or desire, or curiosity, once discovered they would not be let go. And no harm would be done to the body she borrowed. She would simply be requisitioning it for a few hours of use, just a few hours to enter the moon-base, weld the stabilizer, and allow the ship to take off. However unwilling she or the Earth being might be, it was not much to ask. And maybe the ship's suspicions of human nature were unfounded? Maybe Bethkahn would find one who would agree to lend itself and co-exist?

"All right, I'll do it," she agreed.

"I bow to your decision, mistress."

"I shall need to know more about them."

"Details can be analyzed from my recordings," said the ship.

"And I may need to communicate with them."

"I have prepared hypnotapes of their language."

"I shall need a floor plan of their moonbase as well."

"That information will be stored in the cerebral memory banks of the host," the ship voice informed her. "You can extract . . ."

"Not if I'm denied access," Bethkahn interrupted. "If I take control of its mind then whatever he or she knows may be unavailable. I could end up inside what is virtually a walking corpse, in which case I shall need to know where I'm going. Why don't you tap their computer system?"

"I have already done so," the ship said loftily. "I took my knowledge of their language from their computers and almost betrayed my presence. They are alarm coded to deter infiltration by any outside agency. They assumed I was Russian, but I would hesitate to try again."

"You have to risk it," Bethkahn decided.

"If you insist," the ship voice muttered.

"And send down a scanner. We have to get closer. We have to observe these Earth beings. Once within flesh I need to know how to conduct myself. I need to know their routine, their relationships, their human habits."

"A scanner might be spotted," the ship voice objected.

"So might I," Bethkahn replied.

"I don't like it!" said the ship.

Bethkahn half smiled. Often in the ship's tones she had heard an echo of Rondahl, but now she heard an echo of herself. It was learning from her, adjusting its personality, subtly changing its role. She was a junior technician, and once it had been totally responsible for her. Now, if it was to fly again, it was dependent on her. And she sensed in its manner the true beginnings of a partnership.

8

In the shadows of the loading bay Gareth waited through the last few seconds of countdown. Inside his helmet, he could hear Karen chewing gum, the slow inhalation of Drew's breath, and the hiss of oxygen. Radiosensitive cells picked up every small sound. But the takeoff was silent. Silver in the sunlight, in a blast of dust and fire, the ship lifted slowly from the launch pad. Karen filmed it with her video camera, flames reflecting deep inside her head. And Drew was beside him, headless and burning, silver miniatures mirrored in his eyes. It might have been frightening, but Gareth focused his attention on the real thing—one Earthbound shuttle arching upward into the night-black sky, its flight path curving toward the stars where he belonged and being lost among them. Drew's voice sounded ultraloud across the suit's transmitter.

"There goes your escape route, Gareth!"

"Assuming I wanted to," Gareth said.

"That was fantastic!" said Karen. "Really fantastic! I never dreamed I'd get to film a spaceship taking off."

"If not for you I would have been on it," said Drew.

"Did you mind giving up six weeks of your leave?" Karen asked him.

"I volunteered," said Drew.

"Why?" Gareth asked suspiciously.

"Professional interest," Drew replied. "For those who come to the Moon there's usually a three-month training schedule, but you two have come here psychologically unprepared."

"You mean the first one to see a fairy sitting on a toadstool gets a prize?" Gareth asked. "Is that why you and Doctor Chalmers let me stay? To provide Karen with a bit of competition? A medical guinea pig, am I?"

"Not exactly," said Drew. "We let you stay because both Doctor Chalmers and I thought you could handle it, because you yourself wanted to stay, because Commander Bradbury agreed, and because you seem to be coming to terms with your symptoms."

"He's been up since five-thirty practicing," said Karen.

"Oh *has* he?" said Drew.

"Sure," said Karen. "He'd not have passed the physical exam otherwise. He was falling about all over the place, like someone drunk. We had to invent some coordination tests."

"You could park a moonbuggy in your gob!" Gareth said furiously.

"The ship's gone, so what does it matter?" Karen asked.

"It matters," said Drew, "because I don't like being hoodwinked! Because space sickness can be dangerous, and if anything happens to Gareth I shall be held responsible! I told you at the beginning—if you feel anything out of the ordinary I want to know! There's a Russian freighter due in at nightfall, so if you two are not very careful you're going to be on it!"

"See what you've flaming done!" said Gareth.

"How was I to know?" Karen muttered. "We're sorry, Drew."

"If Gareth so much as coughs you're to report it!" Drew said sternly.

"I will," Karen promised.

Gareth did not speak what he thought. It was all her fault—Karen with her big mouth yakking. She would be watching him now, waiting to squeal. And for the next thirteen days he would have to live with the uncertainty, knowing he was vulnerable, symptoms of space sickness waiting to take him over. He had only to give in to them, let go of his concentration. Grimly Gareth fixed his eyes on the stark sharp dividing line between shadow and light, followed it with his gaze. Visual distortions could be conquered by common sense. Whatever he saw, the angle between floors and walls was always ninety degrees, and the floors were always level. He refused to be fooled by any bizarre impressions. That was not a gigantic wheeled beetle squatting in the loading bay behind him, it was a common moon-buggy with black windshield eyes.

"Can we go for a ride?" asked Karen.

"Tomorrow," said Drew. "Today we walk."

Karen left her video camera in the air lock, and they headed out across the Sea of Mists. They had oxygen enough for three hours, heavy cylinders strapped to their backs made almost weightless under the Moon's low gravity. A clock dial on Gareth's wrist ticked away the minutes, its hand moving toward the red danger zone, which would trigger an alarm and give him twenty minutes to live. Such knowledge made life seem suddenly significant, but Drew said they would be back in the moonbase by then.

Brown-gray dust spread in all directions, featureless terrain except for the buildings behind them and the distant ridges toward which they were heading. Three elongated shadows moved blackly beside them. Balled yellow in the Moon's early morning, the sun hung low above the eastern horizon, detracting nothing from the inky spaces around it, but dimming the stars. Inside his suit Gareth could feel no heat from it. But in a few more hours, Drew said, they would be able to fry eggs on the rocks.

"So you can't grow daffodils on the Moon?" asked Karen.

"You can't grow anything," said Drew.

"And there are no pumpkin fields in Copernicus? Nor a pickle factory?"

"Who said there was?"

"Gary told me that by using bodily waste—"

"Gary?" said Gareth. "Who does she mean? Who's this Gary person she keeps talking about?"

"Karen," said Drew. "His name is *Gareth*. And you should know by now not to believe everything he says. Didn't you hear what J.B. told you yesterday? There's no climate on the Moon. There's no snow on the mountains, no rain, no wind, no air, nothing to support life."

"I was just making sure," said Karen.

"Pickle factory!" said Drew. "That's crazy!"

"Why does he tell such outrageous lies?" asked Karen.

"It's probably pathological," said Drew.

"I heard that!" said Gareth. "It's slander! And I come from a long line of Welsh bards!"

"In that case it's hereditary," said Drew.

The ridges were jagged against the sky. Gareth could see them from the window of his room. They seemed higher now, after half an hour of walking, but no closer. It was an effect of the foreshortened horizon, Drew said, which was something Karen failed to understand. Gareth could hear the mastication of her jaws, gum bubbles popping, her dumb questions as Drew tried to explain. An assault on his privacy it was, as if she was there inside his helmet, and Drew had forbidden him to switch off. But suit-to-suit transmission was limited to visual distances. If Gareth put the horizon between himself and them he would be out of range.

He quickened his pace, his shadow striding beside him, and the ridges ahead, mountains beyond and to the west of him. In full daylight the Lunar Apennines were not so spectacular—just humped hillocks or a series of molehills. High as the Swiss Alps, Drew said they were, but you needed to be among them to gain any impression of magnitude, for the curve of the Mare Vaporum lopped them off at the roots.

"If there's no weather on the Moon how come they called it the Sea of Mists?" asked Karen.

Once upon a time, said Drew, back in the sixteenth and seventeenth centuries, when the Moon was first charted and named, it was believed to have an atmosphere. Astronomers claimed to see mist or clouds in the Mare Vaporum, fog patches rolling out from the deep valleys of the Apennines. They even claimed to see live volcanoes.

"That one does look like a volcano," said Karen.

"Mount Conon," said Drew. "It's just a mountain with a crater on top of it, made by the impact of a meteor, just like all the others, or so we believe. It's possible we're wrong, of course. Our geological survey team has yet to go up there and check it. Could be Conon is a genuine volcano."

"So the old astronomers might have been right?" said Karen. "They might really have witnessed an eruption?"

"Hardly," said Drew. "Even if Conon *is* a volcano, it's been extinct for millions of years."

"But they must have seen something to make them believe," Karen persisted.

60

"Or else they believed first and then saw?" suggested Drew.

Gareth saw.

Something flashed high among the ridges . . . sunlight on glass . . . and flashed again, a blink of metallic brightness. "What's that then?" His voice, loud and intrusive, broke in on Drew and Karen's conversation. He turned to look for them—two small space-suited figures half a mile behind. They were no bigger than the plastic toys he had played with as a child. The impression terrified him—toy people and the vast loneliness around him, the moonbase gone beyond the curve of the horizon and something watching him. Gareth panicked, went running toward them, giant strides reducing the distance until they became life-size and human.

"Are you trying to take off?" Drew asked him.

"There's something up there!" Gareth said.

"Where?"

"Up there!" Gareth waved his hand toward the ridges. "Winking," he said. "A person with binoculars or a telescopic rifle. We're being watched!"

"I don't see anything," Drew said.

"Maybe it's someone from the Russian base?" Karen suggested.

"Or a bird-watcher looking for cuckoos?" said Drew.

"I'm being serious!" said Gareth. "We're being watched, I tell you!"

"Gareth!" Drew said warningly.

"I mean it," said Gareth.

"Okay," said Drew. "Try not to let it worry you. Keep a hold on yourself. I'll give you another shot of B-thirty-six as soon as we get back to base."

Gareth stared at him. He was Drew inside the dark glass helmet where the hills reflected, thinking Gareth was either clowning or sick. Based on an association of twenty-four hours, a history of pickle factories, white rabbits, and jackknifing walls, it was inconceivable that he could be balanced and rational and, for once, telling the truth. And, staring at the moonscape in Drew's helmet, he saw nothing moving or flashing among the high rocks in his face filled with boulders and dust . . . only a pint-sized silver figure that was Gareth's own self.

"Can I?" asked Drew.

9

The next morning they were scheduled to visit the Geological Research Station at Manilius, all day in a moonbuggy traveling there and back. But Karen refused to help load supplies. She complained of stomach cramps, and Drew believed her, so Gareth went out alone, testing his nerve as the air lock closed behind him. With a full three hours of oxygen he could have headed for the ridges behind the moonbase, but he did not trust himself to cope with the isolation. What had flashed up there among the high rocks would have to wait. His behavior was monitored, and a man by the name of Jake Kelly was expecting him to report to the loading bay. Gareth rounded the corner and crossed the concrete floor to where the moonbuggy waited. A space-suited figure humping boxes from the supply chute to the trailer paused to watch him approach.

"Are you Jake Kelly?" Gareth asked.

"You must be Taffy," said the man.

"Doctor Steadman told me to give you a hand."

Inside the trailer Gareth stacked the boxes that Jake unloaded from the chute. He was an immense man, tall and powerfully built and inclined to fat. His biceps bulged beneath the sleek fabric of his suit. He had been born in the Rockies and had worked as a lumberjack before coming to the Moon. Each box, which Gareth struggled to lift, Jake tossed toward him as if it contained nothing more than straw. Unstacked cartons piled up around him, and the thud of each one landing produced no sound, only an echo on the bed of the trailer that traveled upward through his feet.

"Will you slow down!" Gareth yelled.

The trailer creaked as Jake clambered on board.

"Put some backbone into it, Taffy."

Gareth heaved and sweated.

"What the hell's in these things? Lead, is it?"

"Pickled pumpkin," said Jake.

Gareth shot him a look. The shadows were deep inside the trailer, cutting down on the reflections. He could see Jake's face, bearded and grinning, the twinkle of his eyes behind dark glass. Now Gareth knew why the straight-faced scientists at the next table had smiled at him during breakfast, and why J.B. had said he was buying up shares in Heinz. Drew must have told the whole moonbase about the pumpkin fields of Copernicus.

"Daffodils and pickle factories," chuckled Jake.

"Damned good that. And the girl actually believed you? What else have you got lined up for us in the way of light entertainment?"

Gareth shook his head. "Nothing," he said. "I've got to watch myself, see? Any more funny business and I'll be shipped out on that Russian freighter that's due in at nightfall."

Jake laughed.

"Don't you believe it, Taffy. Our base commander knows what's good for us. You and the girl are a breath of fresh air as far as we're concerned, a genuine break in the monotony. He won't ship you out, and you'll soon find your moonlegs."

There was something reassuring about Jake Kelly. Hired for his brawn rather than his brains, he was blessed with a practical down-to-earth understanding of things. Space sickness was nothing to worry about, he said. He had suffered from it himself when he had first come to the Moon ten years ago. It wore off after a while. And it was nothing compared to some of the other psychological effects he had experienced. Driving alone over the Moon's barren surface Jake reckoned he had experienced most things.

"You drive alone?" Gareth asked him.

"Now and then," said Jake. "Now and then it happens I do. And all it takes is a mechanical breakdown and you're staring death in the face. That's when you start praying. That's when you find out whether or not Jesus loves you. Grown men weep out there, and scream. It's the silence, I reckon, the godawful loneliness of it. Sets you thinking, it does. Then you begin brooding. That way you're heading for trouble. So you hang on to your pickle factory, Taffy. Laugh and the fear won't get you. We've all got our methods, and Drew Steadman knows it. Mine is to sing."

Jake's fine baritone voice filled Gareth's helmet with the Anvil Chorus as he stacked the boxes. Somehow it was hard to imagine the big man being afraid, yet he claimed to be—out there, where the sun smacked on the deserts of gray-brown dust, and the ridges rose, and nothing lived or moved, and the light flashed on a fragment of glass or metal, small and far away . . . once, twice . . . three times.

"Gotcha!"

Gareth straightened his back, fixed his eyes on a pinnacle of rock. Something shone among the shadows to the left of it.

"See that?" he asked Jake.

It took a while for Jake to locate the spot, and he could see nothing unusual. But unlike Drew he did not dismiss it as a figment of Gareth's imagination or a symptom of something wrong. It was probably a piece of broken satellite, he said. The Moon was littered with scrap metal—ancient orbiters that had crashed to the surface and broken up, defunct landing craft and unmanned survey machines, both American and Russian. It was a likely explanation and might have been acceptable, except that Gareth could have sworn he saw it move.

Click-flash.

"Smile please, Gary!"

Flaming Karen! Her taking photographs! And something reflecting her flash unit out on the ridges.

"Gareth!" he yelled. "My name's Gareth! Will you never learn?"

He leaped from the trailer, expecting the ground to strike but finding nothing until a few split seconds later, when he was already off balance. Click-flash. Karen snapped him as he crash landed on concrete and dust, and he did not see the answering flash from the ridges . . . he saw stars.

"I've come to see if we're ready to go," said Karen.

"*I* am," said Jake.

Gareth picked himself up. A sharp pain shot through his ankle, and his eyes watered. Space sickness was one thing, but Gareth felt like a walking accident. Jake half carried him back inside the moonbase. An X ray confirmed that his ankle was not broken, but it was badly sprained. Dr. Chalmers applied the strapping and advised him to keep his weight off it for the next few days. Wincing with every step and barely able to hobble, Gareth was hardly likely to do much else, and Drew considered leaving him behind. But Karen refused to go on the Manilius trip without him, so finally, with Jake's help, Gareth made it to the buggy, and the air lock doors sealed him inside. He watched the pressure gauge rising to normal.

"You can take off your helmets," said Drew.

Gareth switched off his oxygen, released the seals, and stowed his helmet in the space under the seat. The air was cool in the cab. He could hear the hum of the motor, and Karen's voice came suddenly loud as she too removed her helmet. She said the moonbuggy reminded her of an RV. It could seat eight and sleep four, Drew told her. There were emergency food and medical supplies, a portable-gas stove, and the toilet was in the closet at the back.

"If we get stranded," said Drew, "we can survive for days in one of these."

Jake flicked the radio switch.

"Echo to moonbase . . . time, eleven fifty-three. . . . We are signing out."

"Moonbase to Echo," replied a woman's voice. "You are an hour and twenty-three minutes behind schedule. We'll inform Manilius to expect a delayed arrival. Have a good run."

"We're not *likely* to get stranded, are we?" Karen asked worriedly.

"With Gareth on board anything's likely," said Drew.

Jake drove eastward into the morning. A crescent Earth hung blue through the side window, and Earth time made it almost noon, but the moonday had hardly begun. A low sun dazzled their eyes, and the landscape was dimmed by the dark glass windshield, barren deserts with nothing to see except tire tracks imprinted in the dust and an occasional route marker. It grew rougher later—the buggy lurching over stones where the ridges ended, and the trailer jolting behind. But mostly it was flat, visually boring, an unchanging horizon curving beneath a jet-black, starless sky. They talked some, ate canned-meat sandwiches and doughnuts, drank Coke from cans. Jake sang operatic arias, and the pain in Gareth's ankle eased to a throb. But outside nothing changed.

Manilius happened gradually after three hours of traveling—a line of low cliffs in the distance, rising higher and higher as they drew nearer, until finally the crater walls towered nine thousand feet above their heads. Jake stopped the buggy on the edge of its shadow for Karen to go outside and take photographs, but all Gareth could do was stare at it.

It was magnificent, awesome! Rising dark and sheer, a towering cliff over a mile in height . . . and Drew and Karen, absurdly small in their silver suits walking toward it. Her voice came across the buggy radio. It made the Grand Canyon look pretty stupid, she said. And Pen-y-van dwindled to a pimple in Gareth's head. He had traveled two hundred and fifty thousand miles to reach this place, but, sitting in the moonbuggy next to Jake, he was as far away as if he had stayed in Wales.

The Moon was unreachable and always would be. Men could no more experience it directly than goldfish could experience dry land. Not in a body of flesh and blood could Gareth walk barefoot through the dust, touch the hot rocks, and breathe in the airless spaces. He was trapped inside a mobile environment, inside a space suit, inside his skull.

But then he was not.

The moment that had happened high on the gantry of the observatory happened again. Some part of him came free. Detached from his body he knew no confines, no possibility of death. He knew he could go outside and live and he felt no pain in his ankle as he made for the door. Far far away, in another reality, he heard Jake whistling *The Pirates of Penzance*. Then, as his hand reached toward the button, something hit him. Hard fingers gripped and hauled him back and the voice of the big man from Wyoming blasted his mind.

"Are you out of your head, Taffy? What the hell are you trying to do? Kill both of us? The outer doors are supposed to be closed before you enter the air lock! And next time you want to go outside put your helmet on!"

10

Gareth might have killed himself on the trip to Manilius had Jake not taken action. He would never forget the shock of his own fear, Drew's alarm when he returned to the buggy, and Karen's face turned white with fright. What Jake had said was true—space sickness was nothing. Other psychological effects were far more dangerous. "Give way to unreality and you're dead!" said Drew. Gareth had to be alert at all times, awake to his own mind trying to deceive him, to the dreamlike feelings that now and then came stealing over him. Twice, on the return journey, Karen prodded him, and he thought she would never get his name right.

The next three days were spent at the moonbase, and Gareth was given a thorough medical check. He was even wired to the encephalograph machine, but his brain patterns proved normal, and his symptoms of space sickness were almost gone. Physically, Gareth was fit, except for the game ankle, which limited his ability to get around. But being at the moonbase was different from being in a buggy. There was room to move, solid ground under his feet, twice-daily video shows, pool tables and the swimming pool, and a computer library. There were people to talk to, things to do, and little chance to be bored. Outside, said Drew, it was boredom as much as anything that gave rise to peculiar mental states, and J.B. loaned him a pocket chess set.

"The moment you feel yourself slipping, concentrate on that," the base commander advised him. "Get some real difficult moves going. If you sharpen up your logic you're less likely to be taken in by anything that's illogical."

What had happened to Gareth was not so unusual, and everyone had their methods of dealing with the Moon's effects. Drew composed poetry. J.B. played chess, and Jake sang. But faced with the next trip Gareth felt nervous. It was only a hundred miles across the Sea of Mists to the outpost in Marco Polo, but almost immediately he began to feel strange. The moonbuggy bothered him—the soft hum of its motor, the vibrations, the feeling of confinement, and the monotony of the landscape outside. It was all too easy to let go of his concentration, sink into reverie, and cease to pay attention to the conversation around him. The chess set was meaningless. He wanted to get out.

Karen tapped him on the shoulder.

"Hey Gary! Are you still with us?"

Gareth rounded on her.

"My name's . . . oh forget it. Yes, I'm still with you. What do you want?"

"I was just checking," she said sweetly.

Her accuracy was uncanny, but after a while it became irritating. Again and again Gareth was forced to notice her—the peppermint scent of her chewing gum, her bilious yellow sun top, her jangling earrings, and her nonstop chatter. He did not want to know about the American way of life, her Mom's fashion boutique, her Pop's business enterprises, her kid brother's gerbils, the backyard swimming pool, and the beach house. For some reason the things Karen talked about made him angry. And just because he seemed unusually quiet did not mean there was something wrong with him.

"Will you quit poking me!" Gareth said savagely.

"So why don't you say something?" Karen asked.

"Because you never stop talking, that's why! And most of what you say is stupid! You want to try living in Aberdare for a few years. Never mind the private swimming pool and summer cottage—the only vacation we ever get is a cheap day excursion to Barry Island and a paddle in the sea! Uncle Llewellyn has lived all his life on Social Security payments, and Mom's been out of work for the last five years. All right for some, it is, but what about the rest of us?"

"I've heard things were bad in England," Drew murmured.

"Taffy's from Wales," Jake reminded him.

"And we've got it worse," said Gareth.

"You don't have to take it lying down," said Karen.

It was a discussion that lasted all the way to Marco Polo, ranging from Gareth's mother's fancy man and the upsurge of vandalism in Aberdare, to the Middle East war and the famine in Africa, and how Gareth did not have sufficient brains to gain a place in the university. What went on in the Welsh valleys was hardly Karen's fault, but it was one way of getting to know each other and plumbing the depths of each other's characters. They were four people putting the world to rights, and they paid no heed to the Moon. Gareth was unaware of the journey until they arrived.

Marco Polo was just another crater, and the outpost just another blue plastic bubble similar to the one in Manilius. It was home to three men and a woman—a metallurgist, a geologist, a cartographer—and Captain Slim Peters, who was a mountaineer from the U.S. Marines. They had corned-beef hash for lunch, and afterward Captain Peters escorted them up to the crater rim while Jake and the others unloaded supplies. Three space-suited figures climbed the narrow path, with Gareth limping behind. Inside his helmet voices of those below cheered him as he reached the top and were suddenly gone as he crossed the horizon and emerged onto the heights.

A scene of gaunt grandeur met his eyes. The rugged slopes of the Apennines were all around. The sun crept toward noon. Shadows were smaller, and the stark harsh contrast between darkness and light was even more intense. Valleys looked black and bottomless. Ridges, bone white, curved northward and southward like a monstrous spine. From the sheer edge Karen came walking toward him.

"Would you like to borrow my camera?" she asked.

"What for?" asked Gareth.

"Well, I never realized you couldn't afford to buy one and I've got others. So you can have this one. Keep it if you like."

"No thanks," Gareth said gruffly. "A memory is cheaper to run."

"I can let you have film," said Karen. "And you can get it developed in the moonbase darkroom."

"I think that's a very nice gesture," said Drew.

"But I wasn't looking for charity," Gareth objected.

"It's a gift," said Karen. "Happy birthday."

Her generosity embarrassed him. A camera was too much to give and too much for Gareth to accept. Finally, at her insistence, he agreed to borrow it. He took shots of Drew and Captain Peters with the mountains behind them, and Karen posed for him with a lump of moonrock in her hand. She said it had an odd shape and reminded her of something. It reminded Gareth of something too— the shape of a vertebra with a hole where the spinal column had once passed through. And Karen was gullible enough to believe.

"That's no stone!" Gareth said excitedly. "It's a fossil, see? A bit of fossilized backbone, look!"

"Hey Drew!" shouted Karen. "Look what I've found!"

"I heard," said Drew. "And it's just not possible."

"Well it sure looks like one!" shouted Karen.

"*Bovis lunaris*," said Gareth. "Part of the coccyx, I reckon."

Drew and Captain Peters took turns in studying it, their faces inscrutable inside their helmets, twin darknesses filled with stars. It was a stone that resembled a bone. Probably basalt, Captain Peters said. But Gareth was adamant. He could recognize a fossil when he saw one, and he had a talent for making the impossible sound plausible. It was proof, he said, of a prehistoric Moon where herds of *Bovii lunarii* grazed on the lichen that had once covered the rocks before the atmosphere seeped away into space. It hardly mattered whether Drew or Captain Peters believed him or not, they were willing to join in the search. Stones turned into carpi and metacarpi, and Karen found a fragment of rib. For her, *Bovis lunaris* became a reality, and its bones traveled back with them across the Mare Vaporum, an inexhaustible talking point.

"So what the hell *is Bovis lunaris*?" Jake asked.

"*Was*," said Karen. "They're extinct, you see."

"The literal translation is mooncalf," said Drew.

"Ah," said Jake. "I've heard of them."

"A close relation to *Assinus maximus*," said Drew.

"Herbivorous," said Gareth. "Monsters, they were. No natural enemies, see? The whole Moon got overrun. And once they'd eaten all the ground cover, stripped the place of oxygenating plants, they couldn't survive. It was quite a few million years ago—the equivalent of the early Jurassic."

"What I'd really like to find is a skull," Karen said wistfully. "Or a jawbone perhaps."

"Their last browsing ground was the mountains," said Gareth. "High rocky places where the dwindling vegetation still remained. We could try searching the ridges behind the moonbase."

"We could go there now," Karen said enthusiastically. "It's only a small detour and we've plenty of time before dinner. Can we, Drew?"

"Haven't you had enough for one day?" Drew asked.

He wanted a swim before dinner. He wanted an hour in which to relax. But Karen had made up her mind. He did not have to wait, she said. She and Gareth could *walk* back to the moonbase if Jake would drop them off. But not for one moment would Drew allow Gareth to go unaccompanied. He came with them, searching with Jake and Karen across the lower slopes of the ridge for the bones of a mythical creature he knew did not exist, while Gareth seized the opportunity. Fixing his eyes on the high pinnacle of rock, he headed upward, and not until Drew discovered a lump of fossilized dung did he notice Gareth was gone.

11

It was dark and soundproof inside the language booth, allowing no distractions. Bethkahn lay still. She had to empty her mind of all thought and become receptive, her only function to absorb. Preset, the hypnotape began to play, the voice of the alien computer reproducing its original learning program and teaching her to speak. No words to begin with, just the basic sounds of consonants and vowels and the corresponding symbols that appeared on the wall screen before her—the same sequence being repeated and repeated until Bethkahn had committed it to memory.

She pressed the PROGRAM ADVANCE switch and graduated to words, sounds, and syllables being strung together to form nouns and verbs, adjectives and adverbs. Pictures bestowed meanings—blue flower . . . laughing woman . . . run quickly. Slowly the hypnotape wound on. Sentences, which were infantile at first, grew in complexity as her understanding increased. Then the dull chant of the computer gave way to a human voice, and speech became music in her head. She no longer needed the vision screen. If she closed her eyes the words themselves invoked images, meanings that subtly altered with every change of emphasis, tones, and undertones sweet as Keirharah's song.

Through hours and days Bethkahn listened, and it seemed to her that some of them knew who they were— souls within flesh, aware of the immortal part of their being. From the man's voice reading she gleaned a thousand intimations, and intimations of other things too. Their human song could change within a single breath. Words told of blood and violence, of men who killed and were heralded as heroes, who committed murder and called it an act of love. She heard of mass slaughter made glorious in battle, hymns praising monstrous acts of cruelty and war. Both beautiful and terrible were the beings portrayed in the language Bethkahn learned, creatures of conflict whom she thought she would never understand.

How much of their speech and literature the starship had filched from the moonbase computers Bethkahn did not know, for she had no chance to reach the end of it. The ship's presence intruded. White light split the darkness, beat on her closed eyelids, flashed off and on, insistently, demanding her attention. The Earth beings fled from her head as she switched off the hypnotape and opened the language booth.

Shadowy and silent the great laboratory stretched away. Here were stored hypnotapes of every known galactic language and holograms of every planet they had visited—flora and fauna, climate and topography, culture if any. Once a dozen technicians had worked in this laboratory processing and programming the information gathered by the survey teams. Now it was dimly lit and eerie, long ago abandoned, and the ship voice echoed urgently among the filing stacks.

"You must come to the control room at once, mistress."

"Why?" said Bethkahn. "What's happened?"

"We are in trouble, I think."

Bethkahn moved swiftly. The lab shadows released her into a lighted corridor where her red clothes flickered like fire on the curved walls. There was a fear inside her worse than she had ever known. Something had happened that threatened the safety of her ship. Her ship . . . she had never thought of it in that way before. It had always belonged to Rondahl. But now, just recently, it had become a part of herself—a fifth limb, or a protective shell, an extension of her mind—and she would be helpless without it.

In Rondahl's chair Bethkahn took her place, brushed away the black strands of hair from her eyes. Waist long, it needed cutting, and her clothes were creased from a week in the language booth. Above her head the dark astrodome gleamed with stars, and around her the vision screens flickered into life.

"What's happened?" she repeated.

It was one more replay, seen through the eye of the scanner they had recently deployed. A telescopic lens showed her the blue domes of the American base, so close she felt she might almost touch them. Quite clearly in the loading bay she could see a water truck being filled, a gloved hand connecting the hose to the main tank. But suddenly the focus altered. A moonbuggy headed toward the ridge where the scanner was stationed, parked in the desert where the rocks began. Four space-suited figures disembarked and disappeared below the ledge. For several minutes the scanner waited motionless, then inched forward. Its lens angled downward, and Bethkahn gave a startled cry. A pair of blue human eyes were staring at her from behind the dark glass of a visor, and a moment later the scanner went blank.

"He found it?" she whispered.

"Yes," said the ship. "I did warn you of the risk."

"What shall we do?"

"You tell me," the ship said dismally. "They will take it to pieces, I expect. They will see it as alien, proof of our existence, and begin a search."

"I'll go to the moonbase and retrieve it," Bethkahn said.

"It's not in the moonbase," the ship voice muttered.

"Then where is it?"

"Right now," said the ship voice, "it is traveling in a southwesterly direction across the Sea of Mists. There is a time lag, you see, and I didn't want to disturb you."

Fifteen hours ago the ship had deactivated the scanner. Nothing functioned in it except the automatic tracking device, a small bleep of light on a grid map of the area. It had never entered the moonbase, the ship voice said. It had remained outside it, stationary aboard the moonbuggy.

"For fifteen hours?" Bethkahn said. "And you never informed me?"

"What good would it have done?" the ship voice asked. "I didn't know what to make of the situation. I can draw no conclusions and cannot advise you. I cannot fathom the workings of their alien minds. I don't understand what they're doing, Bethkahn. I'm afraid, and I don't understand!"

"Rerun the video sequence," Bethkahn said.

"How will that help?"

"There might be some clue."

The film flickered.

Blue eyes stared at her, just as before.

"Freeze it," she said.

Bethkahn studied his face among a host of reflections. He was young, she thought, younger than she was, an inexperienced youth. Maybe he had not realized the significance of what he had found? Maybe he had kept it to himself, not shared the knowledge of the scanner's existence? His blue eyes reminded her of Dahn and showed no hint of cruelty. Forgotten feelings fluttered inside her, butterfly wings of love and longing. It was not enough that the starship cared for her. She needed a person—a voice, a smile, another living being beside herself. And the boy had taken her scanner. She needed that too.

"There might still be time," she said.

"Time?" said the ship.

"The boy has our scanner, but I think he doesn't know what he has. He has shown no one and told no one, perhaps. They're not searching for us. They're out on a routine run, which means they will be returning. Track them. Tell me when you know where they're going. I can intercept them on their way back."

"Mistress!" the ship voice said in horror.

"Do you have a better idea?" Bethkahn asked it.

Protesting, the ship voice followed her along the labyrinth of corridors and into the wash unit. To act on impulse was a mistake, the ship voice said. Action needed to be planned. Silver drops showered from Bethkahn's hair. Warm air blowers dried her, and robotic work units sucked the moisture from the floor. Naked, in a hall of mirrors and wardrobes, she chose her clothes— gray misty trousers with a cowled overgown to hide her hair. Outside on the moon's surface she would be indistinguishable from the desert and the rocks. Blown dust would hide her movements from their eyes.

"And give us away!" snapped the ship.

"Until I enter the buggy," said Bethkahn. "Until I take him, enter the Earth boy's flesh. He can drive me back to the moonbase, and mend your stabilizer. One journey, one risk, and he may not fight me. I have to try it, don't you see?"

12

It was a silvery metal sphere the size of a soccer ball. At first Gareth had thought it was a bomb and was afraid to touch it. But who would plant a bomb on a moon ridge miles from anywhere? Common sense caused him to dismiss the theory, and he picked it up. There were several circles carved on its surface and five small holes bored into its underside. Held in his gloved hand it seemed weightless and hollow, a fragile mysterious thing. But he had no chance to examine it further. Drew blew his top.

It was understandable. Gareth had risked life and limb to climb the ridge and ignored all orders to come down. But he could not ignore the anger that simmered across the transmitter. Drew's message came loud and clear. He did not care what Gareth had found—a moon cuckoo's egg or a giant ball bearing from an alien spacecraft—if he was not back in the buggy within a quarter of an hour he would be answerable to the base commander, propelled back to Earth on the end of J.B.'s boot and never mind the Russian ship. With his fists full of bones from *Bovis lunaris*, and Karen beside him, Drew returned to the buggy to wait.

Having found the sphere there was no way Gareth would leave it behind, nor could he hurry. Slowly and carefully, mindful of the weakness in his ankle and its tendency to pain, he started to climb down, the sphere clutched to his chest. He was afraid it would drop, its eggshell-thin walls smash among the rocks. It took him thirty-five minutes to reach the buggy, and Jake drove away the moment he entered the air lock. Inner doors opened automatically when the air pressure rose to normal, and Drew was too mad to notice what Gareth smuggled inside—a silver sphere nestling in his upturned helmet and slyly transferred to the space under his seat.

The next morning, when they left for the satellite tracking station on Mount Serao, Gareth transferred it again—into a plastic bag saying WILLIAM'S GOOD FOOD STORES, ABERDARE LIMITED, along with his paisley pajamas and a spare pair of socks. And there it remained for the duration of the journey, like an itch that he could not scratch. He longed to take it out and look at it, but after all he had gone through to possess it he would not risk having it taken from him. Whatever the object was, it would have to wait until he returned to base.

Gareth had already decided it was some kind of robotic spying device. Russian perhaps? But he could not think why. High on the ridge it had been strategically placed to watch the moonbase, yet the Russians had satellites in orbit so why would they need a ground-based unit as well? Its purpose troubled him, nagged at the back of his mind, just as Karen nagged him to pay attention. She gave him no chance to ponder things out, and Drew was still angry. He banged Gareth's next fantasy squarely on the head. Those were *not* the infrastructures of gorgonzola mines, Drew said. They were the remains of Surveyors six and four, which had landed in the Sinus Medii over a hundred years ago. And not even Karen was prepared to believe the Moon was made of green cheese formed from the milk of the mooncalves' mummies.

"Better luck with the next one," Jake said.

"They wising up, or am I slipping?" Gareth asked.

"We're just getting to know you," Drew said darkly.

"Yes," agreed Karen. "And we're not *that* moronic!"

They stopped to take photographs and fragments of metal for souvenirs before driving on. Jake had taken the long route past Hyginus Rille and Chladni Crater, and now he turned north into the desert of the Sinus Aestuum. Earth time made it midevening when they drove up Serao's hairpin trail to the satellite base. The other moonbuggy, which had hauled the water tank, had arrived long before them and already unloaded. Gareth joined Jake in the trailer unstacking food supplies, and later Charlie Kunik, who was the driver of the Juliet buggy, played his guitar at an impromptu party.

Serao was a permanent base—three blue plastic domes on the mountain's summit, underground living quarters, and a staff of twenty. Solar panels gleamed silver in the sunlight of the Moon's high noon, and telescopic dishes were radio linked to those in the Mare Vaporum. On Earth it was long past midnight when Gareth went to bed—a sleeping bag on the backseat of the buggy and Jake on the front seat, snoring, while he lay awake. Sunlight filtering through the dark glass roof was impossibly bright, and the beer and barbecued beans he had had for supper gave him indigestion. He sweated in the heat of his sleeping bag and could smell the stench of his socks.

On the return journey the two moonbuggies traveled in convoy, heading south through the Sinus Aestuum. They would cut through the ridges, said Jake, and be back at the moonbase in time for the evening meal. A full Earth hung as a blue bead in a black-gloved sky. Sunlight faded it, said Drew. It was best seen at night, jeweled turquoise, shedding its light on the deserts of darkened dust. But still Karen insisted they stop to take photographs. Gareth yawned and waited. Deprived of sleep his eyelids felt heavy, and the air in the buggy was stifling and stale.

Jake nudged him.

"Either sleep or stay awake, Taffy. Do one or the other, but don't get caught between the two."

"Why not?" asked Gareth.

"Pink elephants," said Jake. "You're liable to start seeing things that aren't really there. Hypnogogic images, Drew calls it."

"Thanks," said Gareth. "I'll remember that."

He opened J.B.'s chess set and arranged the pieces, and Charlie Kunik driving the Juliet buggy had gone over the horizon before Drew and Karen returned to their seats and Echo was on the move again. Desert to the right of them and sun-baked ridges to the left. The lunar scenery was not conducive to alertness. It moved and swayed as the buggy moved and swayed, and was almost hypnotic. Gareth was hardly aware of the dozy sleepy feelings creeping over him until Karen poked him in the ribs.

"I was talking to you!" she drawled.

"Pawn," said Gareth, "to queen's bishop three."

"You don't fool me," said Karen. "You were miles away."

It was true. Gareth *was* miles away, being driven through a gaunt landscape of tumbled rocks and heading upward into the ridges. Half an hour of time had disappeared without trace. It was as if the moonbuggy and all its contents had suddenly been transported from the Sinus Aestuum to here. And the Earth beyond the window had changed its position. It shone in a blue halo around Jake's head, made him a bearded angel, the patron saint of the Moon's mobile grocery service ascending into heaven. Ahead the roadway ended in a sheer edge of sky. Gareth yelped and clutched the seat.

"For Christ's sake stop!" screamed Gareth. "We're going over the flaming edge! You've got to stop!"

"What's he talking about?" asked Karen in alarm.

"I don't want to die yet!" yelled Gareth.

A hand touched his shoulder, firm and strong.

"It's okay," said Drew. "Okay Gareth, just calm down. There's no edge, nowhere to fall. The trail goes up the ridge and down the other side. Look at it again . . . think about what you're seeing . . . concentrate your mind."

"Do you want me to stop?" asked Jake.

"Keep going," said Drew.

Quietly and calmly Drew kept talking, and back in his right mind Gareth realized he had seen an optical illusion. The Moon had fooled him with one more dangerous deception. He fixed his gaze determinedly upon the trail ahead, the high edge where the land ended and the sky began, waited as the buggy drove toward it and topped the rise. It was solid ground all the way to the moonbase—the trail winding down through a landscape of canyons and rock stacks and deep pools of shadow. Down and down and around the wall of a mesa. A few eddies of gray-brown sand swirled among the stones.

"It's a bit like Arizona," Karen said.

"The last stagecoach from Serao," said Jake.

"The wind's getting up," said Gareth.

"Is that the best you can do?" asked Drew. "Has your imagination finally failed you?"

"It's nothing to do with imagination," said Gareth.

89

"It's happening, see? Look you out there."

"God almighty!" cried Jake.

They rounded an outcrop of rock and he slammed on the brakes. Karen fell forward, cracked her head against the front seat, and the chess set fell to the floor, scattering its pieces. Saved by the safety harness, Gareth saw what Jake saw—the Juliet buggy crashed at the foot of a nearby cliff, its air lock door open, the driver slumped at the wheel. Without his helmet, Charlie Kunik was dead. And something moved at the mouth of the canyon, coming fast—a moonwind rising and a whirling tornado of dust.

Blood poured from a cut in Karen's forehead, but Jake did not wait for the living or the dead. Echo edged past the wreckage and sped as the moonwind moved toward them. Dust swirled past the windshield, obscuring Jake's vision, but Gareth saw to the heart of it. Someone was running—a shape without substance yet definitely there—a shadow girl, lithe as an Arabian dancer, her clothes gray and gauzy, her dark hair blown by the wind. Just for a moment Gareth glimpsed her, her face pale and beautiful and the dust whirling behind her eyes. Then she was gone, and the storm was gone, and Jake drove at full throttle down the empty trail.

"What the devil was that?" asked Drew.

"God only knows," Jake said shakily.

Gareth knew.

"Did you see her?" he asked. "Did you see what she was? Scheherazade, see-through as gauze. A flaming ghost!"

Karen dripped blood on her bilious yellow sun top. "That's not damned well funny!" she screamed. "We might have been killed!"

"But I *saw* her," said Gareth.

And there at his feet, escaped from the confines of the carrier bag, rolled a strange silver sphere. Gareth stared at it in a moment of understanding. Hers, was it? The shadow girl who might have killed them? Looking for it, was she? Wanting it back? And had she killed Charlie Kunik instead? Slyly with his foot he kicked it back where it came from.

"I *did* see her," he said.

"Just shut up!" said Drew.

13

Bethkahn returned to the ship. Its hatches were buried, but the doors to the hangar bay remained open, blocked by a great dune of dust that had fallen inward. Bethkahn skidded down the slope. A bevy of robotic work units with vacuum-cleaner arms who had been set to clear it fled as she entered, retreating into the darkness. Their green eyes peered at her from behind the pillars, stupid mechanical things whose minds had only one purpose.

"You can get back to work!" Bethkahn said harshly.

Hearing her voice the ship switched on its lights. She saw the empty hangar bay stretching away, vast as a galactic conference hall. Her gray robes were mirrored in its shining floor, and from all around she could feel the starship watching her, its electronic sensors summing her up. She needed it, desperately. Maybe she even cared for it. But sometimes it was too much there, inescapable, witnessing everything, and she could not face the questions it was bound to ask. Tears shimmered in her eyes, and broken pieces of stabilizer rattled as she shed her backpack.

"You failed?" asked the ship voice.

"Isn't it obvious?"

"I told you not to go."

"All right! So you were right! There's no need to gloat!"

"What happened?" the ship voice asked her. "What went wrong?"

"I don't want to talk about it," Bethkahn replied.

"I've a right to know," the ship voice argued. "I'm the one who will be disemboweled if we should be discovered. I need to analyze the information—"

"I said I don't want to talk about it!" Bethkahn screamed. "Please!" she sobbed. "Please leave me alone!"

She wanted to run from it, hide from it, but there was nowhere to go. The ship was around her, everywhere, and she could not make such terrible confessions. She fled up the wide ramp to the basement corridor. Heavy metal doors barred the entrance to the ship's powerhouse, and a spiral stairway wound around the central column. Bethkahn took the steps two at a time, then paused on the first-floor landing. There was a circular lounge with alcove seats and picture windows showing a dozen different worlds—hologram landscapes that were deceptively real. She saw the golden cities of Cheoth One, whirru-birds flying above the purple plains of Korberon, and blue moonlight shining on the snow-capped mountains of Grath. And in between the corridors led away like spokes of a wheel.

It had been ten thousand years since last Bethkahn had visited these lower regions, the maze of passages and sleeping quarters that had once been assigned to the crew. But now she remembered her own room nearby, a second class cabin for junior staff with a door that closed to keep people out. Maybe the ship voice would not follow her there? Maybe it would respect her privacy and not intrude? Bethkahn sped down the corridor and shut herself inside.

The room was as she had left it—her sleep robe discarded among the pink crumpled covers of her couch. Music tapes were scattered on the floor where they had fallen, and a hologram image of her mother smiled from the wall niche among a garden of flowers. Kesha would have been informed of her disappearance, yet she smiled. She would smile forever under the sun of Khio Three, her blue dress blowing in the wind, among day moths that never died and everlasting flowers.

Her mother smiled as Bethkahn cried, wept for an ending she did not understand, the death of a man and her ignorance of his flesh. She wept for an Earth-born boy she had wanted and lost, and the mess she had made of things. She wept in despair, knowing what she had always suspected—that she and the ship would never escape from this moon. It was just a hope they had built up between them and tried to act out. Now it was over. A man had died, and Bethkahn could not try again.

Omnipotent within itself, the great ship watched her and wondered why she cried. It referred to all her past emotions, compared old causes, and saw no reason. It concluded this to be a new distress, a reaction to something that had happened outside and which the ship could not guess. Insufficient data, its computer banks said, and it did not know what to say to her or how to extract the information. It had to remain silent, waiting patiently, waiting until her tears subsided, and all it could hear was an occasional sob. It must be careful how it questioned her, and all it knew of compassion Bethkahn must hear in its voice.

"Mistress," it murmured. "I know I am only an unfeeling machine, and what you feel I cannot understand. I know I am not Mahna or Keirharah, but I am here and I do care. To the best of my ability I have always cared. I want to help you, Bethkahn, but I need you to tell me . . ."

Bethkahn raised her head. Strands of her dark disheveled hair clung to the tears on her face, and the silver shine of the ship's walls were all around her. It had a right to know, it had said. Its future depended as much on her as hers depended on it.

"He died," she said brokenly.

"The Earth boy?" it asked.

"The driver of the buggy," she said.

"You must tell me everything," said the ship.

Bethkahn stared unseeingly at the opposite wall. "He died when I opened the door," she said dully. "Before I could even reach him. Instantaneously, without a cry, his flesh frozen and dead. And his soul stayed inside him, staring at me through his eyes, refusing to come free, refusing to forgive, silently screaming that I had murdered him. He didn't understand. He didn't know how to live without bones and blood. He just screamed and screamed, and I couldn't bear it, knowing I'd killed. You said the moonbuggies carried their own environment. But he was *dead!* And when the second buggy came around the corner I didn't know what to do. I was afraid I would destroy *him* too, the boy with blue eyes and those who were with him. I was afraid and held back and he *saw* me. He knows I exist! And if I open the doors of the moonbase I will kill them all! We're stuck here now, and there's no hope, not anymore."

The ship voice stayed silent, absorbing the things she had said and searching for an explanation. It had rifled the moonbase computers while Bethkahn had been away. It had taken floor plans, work schedules, blueprints, details of outposts and personnel files, anything it considered might contain useful information. Blueprints of a moonbuggy confirmed that each vehicle possessed an air-lock system. There should have been no escape of atmosphere when Bethkahn opened the outer door, not unless the inner door had foolishly been left open. Depressurization would kill instantly, but it was not her fault.

"It was an accident, Bethkahn," the ship voice declared. "It wasn't your fault. If the driver had followed the safety regulations he would not have died. You cannot blame yourself for the death of his flesh, mistress. You cannot give up hope."

"It is crime against life," Bethkahn said bleakly. "And I committed it."

The ship voice sighed.

She was not thinking logically, her mind clouded by emotion. And when dealing with emotion the ship was generally incompetent.

"Listen to me!" it said sternly. "That man's death was a mistake, and it was his mistake—not yours! If you come to the console room I can prove it. Now you must put it from your mind, Bethkahn, and next time we must allow for their carelessness."

"Next time?" Bethkahn said fearfully.

"There will have to be a next time," the ship said firmly. "And if the Earth boy saw you, it will have to be soon."

"I can't!" she cried. "I dare not risk it! I could not bear to murder him too!!"

There was no question of murder, the ship voice said. The moonbase was protected by a triple air-lock system. What had happened to the buggy driver could not happen again. It would be perfectly safe. They would work out her every move exactly, every small detail. They would study the work schedules, study the personnel files, choose the flesh.

"It must be a logical operation," said the ship.

"And that's easy for you," Bethkahn said sourly.

"One of us has to be," said the ship.

"I'm not leaving yet!"

"When you leave depends on what Gareth does," said the ship.

"Gareth?" said Bethkahn.

"His name," said the ship. "I have deduced it from the personnel files by a process of elimination—his age, weight, height, and the color of his eyes. Room A-forty-one. If he takes the scanner there we can afford to wait. But if he takes it to the laboratories you must leave immediately."

Bethkahn stared at the wall. His name was Gareth. Through a dark glass window his blue living eyes had stared into hers, and she could not forget. More than the dead man screaming murder, she remembered him.

"What else do you know of him?" she asked.

14

When Gareth claimed to have seen a girl near to the place where Charlie Kunik's buggy had crashed, no one believed him. It was a figment of his imagination, said Drew, a shadow perhaps, or a rock shape seen through the dust. The Moon had fooled him before, and not ten minutes previously he had suffered an optical illusion. If he used his common sense he would know it was impossible. There had been no girl out there, and there were no such things as ghosts — at least not on the Moon.

But despite what Drew said, Gareth was convinced he had seen her. Her pale face haunted him, delicate and beautiful, framed with drifts of dark hair. She was as real as the metal sphere he had smuggled into the moonbase in the plastic shopping bag. That night in his room he was able to examine it—two hemispheres fitted together, offering access to its innards if only he knew how to open it. Later he would produce it in evidence, proof of the ghost girl's existence and as unearthly as she was. But first he needed a screwdriver, something fine and sharp to pry it apart. A nail file maybe? Karen was sure to have a nail file. But the corridor was dark and shuttered, the moonbase sleeping, and no line of light showed under Karen's door.

Gareth had to wait until morning, but with Drew at the breakfast table he had no chance to ask, and then J.B. came to join them. The base commander's eyes were hard as rivets, and coffee slopped from the cups when he banged down the file. He had just finished reading the preliminary reports, he said. Jake's account of what appeared to be an accident, and Drew's corroboration. It was all quite straightforward except for the ghost of Fatima dancing through veils of dust. "Hallucination—question mark," Drew had written. But J.B. suspected it was one of Gareth's stories, as ridiculous as pumpkin fields and pickle factories and, under the circumstances, in very poor taste.

"A man has died!" the base commander snapped. "And you'd better come clean, Sinbad! Is this one of your yarns?"

"No," said Gareth. "I *saw* her."

"Hell," said J.B.

"It's psychovisual," said Drew. "Remember the guy who thought he saw a mermaid in the Sea of Tranquility?"

Breakfast cereal crackled in Gareth's dish.

And the base commander sighed.

"Let's try looking at it rationally," he said.

Conversation was muted in the cafeteria around them, the atmosphere saddened by the news of Charlie Kunik's death. Gareth knew what the base commander was after, an admission, based on logic, that he had been seeing things. Across the table Karen watched him, a Band-Aid covering the cut on her left temple. She had been too busy bleeding to notice what had happened, and all Jake had seen was the dust. A storm of dust on a world without weather, whipped up by a moonwind that should not exist: that in itself was disturbing enough. Probably it had been caused by a moonquake that the seismographs had failed to register. Or possibly it was a new phenomenon, something never before encountered on the Moon's surface, inexplicable and dangerous. It was that possibility J.B. wished to rule out, along with Gareth's tale of a ghostly girl in gauzy Arabian costume.

"It was an illusion, son," J.B. said in exasperation. "You must *know* that?"

Gareth shook his head.

"I know what you want me to say. I'm not dumb, see? All right, she might not have been real. She might have been a mental projection or a dream image. But I can't swear to it, can I? I don't know if she was real or not. I only know I saw her."

Not for one moment did J.B. believe Gareth's account of things, but as base commander he could not take the risk. He had to allow for the possible existence of an alien life form. The whole moonbase was placed on standby, in a state of yellow alert. The fleet of buggies that were sent to recover the wreckage and Charlie Kunik's body were ordered to maintain constant radio contact, and the trip to Copernicus was temporarily postponed. Confined to base, Gareth and Karen spent the morning in the swimming pool with Drew giving them lessons in life-saving techniques. And J.B. at lunchtime said the dust storm had been confirmed by satellite recordings, but still no cause could be found. Through the blue window a single buggy was returning home, and Drew crammed the last of his sandwich into his mouth. He had to assist with the postmortem, he said, and for one afternoon Gareth and Karen would be left to their own devices.

"Try not to do anything stupid," he begged.

"Who? Me?" said Gareth.

"If there's anything you can't handle . . ." Drew said to Karen.

"I'll use the intercom," she promised.

"See you this evening," said Drew, and headed for the door.

"What's he mean, 'If there's anything you can't handle'?" asked Gareth.

"He means you," said Karen. "Who else would he be worried about? Funny things happen to you, or hadn't you noticed? Did she have a ruby in her navel?"

"You're dafter than I am," Gareth said.

"But not dumb enough to believe a story like that," said Karen.

"No?" Gareth looked at her. "Still got the bones of

Bovis lunaris, have you? Ever thought of getting them authenticated?"

Karen frowned at him—a girl with long brown hair damp from the swimming pool, her white flying suit made turquoise by the light. Seen in the high street of Aberdare, Gareth might have thought her attractive, but now ketchup dripped from her hamburger and suspicion showed in her eyes.

"What are you hinting at?" she asked.

"Nothing," Gareth said innocently. "But if you took them to the Geology Department you could have them carbon dated. Find out how old they are."

"I'll do that," Karen assured him. "And if they're not genuine . . ."

Gareth pushed back his chair.

"I'll leave you to it then."

"Aren't you coming with me?"

"They're your bones, girlie."

"Drew said we had to stay together! And I don't know the way!"

"I'll tell you the way," said Gareth.

Karen followed him back to his room. It smelled of sleep and staleness, and he had not made his bed. Dirty socks and last week's jeans and sweatshirt were strewn on the floor. More clothes spilled from his travel bag. A broken strut from Surveyor Four occupied the single chair, and his parka was slung over the back. A plastic shopping bag, saying WILLIAM'S GOOD FOOD STORES, ABERDARE LIMITED hung on the handle of the closet door, and two empty Coke cans rattled when he knocked against them. Gareth switched on the computer. Floor plans of the moonbase flickered on the screen, and Karen wrinkled her nose in disgust.

"Just look at your room!"

"The Photography Department is on Level B," said Gareth.

"It's worse than my kid brother's!"

"Geology is on Level C. Turn left at the elevator, and it's the second door."

"You haven't even unpacked!" said Karen.

"Level D is refuse and recycling," said Gareth.

"How can you live in a mess like this?" Karen grumbled.

"What's this?" said Gareth. "It's a blasted nuclear arsenal!"

"It's a blasted pigsty, you mean!"

"An underground silo!" Gareth said. "It's loaded, I tell you! I thought nuclear weapons in space were banned by international treaty?"

Karen unhooked the plastic shopping bag.

And threw it at his head.

"Put your dirty clothes in that," she told him. "We'll take them to the laundry rooms. No wonder Aberdare is a slum with you living in it!" She took the parka from his chair. "This is supposed to be hung up!" she said.

She had not been listening to Gareth, nor had he been listening to her, and before he could stop her Karen opened the closet door. A coat hanger rattled as Gareth crossed the room, slammed shut the door to the corridor, and stood with his back against it. And Karen could not fail to see the silvery metal sphere sitting on the shelf.

"What *is* it?" she asked.

"What's it look like?" he said. "It's a moonbuggy's egg."

"It's that giant ball-bearing thing!" said Karen. "You really did find it! Why didn't you tell us? Why didn't you show us? Drew mightn't have gotten so mad if you'd said you really had found it."

"I did say," Gareth reminded her. "And he didn't want to know. So now it's mine. And if you want to get out of this room intact you can keep your mouth shut about it, see?"

"Sure," said Karen. "If it means that much to you I won't say anything. Can I look at it?"

"Providing you swear not to tell."

"I swear."

Karen took it from the shelf, an orb shining with light, exquisitely fashioned and almost weightless in her hands. Gareth could see her face mirrored in its curve. She turned it carefully, noting the holes underneath it and the five curious circles carved in the smoothness of its surface. Its clear metal misted with the closeness of her breath.

"It's beautiful," she said. "I see why you want to keep it. But what is it?"

"Lend me your nail file," said Gareth, "and maybe we'll find out."

15

"Give! Damn you!"

All afternoon Gareth had been struggling to open the sphere, and Karen had got bored long ago and left him. Now, with it wedged between his knees, he once again applied the pressure, trying to lever the two halves apart. Nothing happened except that the nail file snapped and the sphere shot away from him, rolled hollowly across the floor. He was about to retrieve it when Karen returned from the Geology Department. There were tears in her eyes, fury in her voice, as she flung the bones of *Bovis lunaris* on his bed.

"Basalt!" she shrieked.

Gareth grinned at her.

"And basalt to you too, girlie."

"I'd like to kick your stupid teeth in!" Karen said bitterly.

"What have *I* done?"

"You made me look a complete idiot!"

"You shouldn't have believed . . ."

"I'll never speak to you again!"

"Have that in writing, can I?"

"And give me back my nail file!" Karen said.

It was broken in two. She threw the pieces back at him, told him to screw himself, and left, slamming the door. She did not speak to him at the dinner table and she spent the evening with Valerie Doyle from Communications, laughing and talking in the moonbase bar, while Drew stayed in his office writing the postmortem report. Gareth played darts with Jake and went to bed early, tried yet again to open the sphere and finally gave up. He needed something finer and sharper—a medical lancet, or a pocketknife perhaps.

The next morning Karen had still not forgiven him, and J.B. at breakfast was fuming about a falling-off of safety standards and people who were too damned lazy to lean over and press a button. Charlie Kunik had died from rapid decompression, Drew said, which would not have happened had he been driving with the inner door closed. It was assumed the impact of the crash had somehow caused the air lock to open, but what had caused the dust storm remained a mystery. They were running a full computer check in the hope of finding a clue.

Gareth was in the swimming pool when the base commander sent for him. He thought maybe they had found some proof of the ghost girl's existence and wanted to question him. But what they had found, J.B. said grimly, was a major security leak that was partly traceable to terminal A41 in Gareth's bedroom. Gareth tried to explain. He had searched through the floor plans in order to locate the Geology Department, but he knew nothing about any blueprints or work schedules or anyone's personal file. He was threatened with a full-scale investigation by the FBI, and life imprisonment for espionage. Alcatraz, J.B. said, was about to be reopened especially for him.

"But I never did it!" Gareth insisted. "I never touched them blueprints or anything else!"

He was blamed anyway, even by Drew.

In the lunchtime cafeteria Drew blasted him.

"I told you not to do anything stupid! I turn my back on you for one afternoon and straightaway you head for trouble!"

"All I did was look at the floor plans!" Gareth retorted.

"*And* the nuclear silo," Karen said slyly.

"That was an accident!"

"Don't give me that!" snapped Drew.

"I'm innocent, I tell you!"

"Innocent?" Drew said bitterly. "You only need to open your mouth and you're guilty of some gross misrepresentation of the truth! And I'm the one who is held responsible! I don't want to hear any more from you, Gareth! Not one word for the rest of the day! Or it won't be Alcatraz, it'll be instant lobotomy! Is that clear?"

Karen smirked and squirted mustard on her hot dog, and Gareth understood. For the rest of the day he had to pretend not to exist. It was not difficult. Karen would not speak to him. Drew would not speak to him. Jake was busy loading the supply trailer for the Copernicus run, and, with the moonbase on yellow alert, no one else had time. Alone among almost a thousand people Gareth watched Drew and Karen walk away. They were going to play pool. And he could either go and watch the afternoon video show or sit in the library and read a book, Drew had said. He was not even allowed in his own bedroom.

Gareth watched a film on flamingos, read the opening chapters of the *Zen Buddhist Handbook*, and practiced meditation—controlled breathing and his mind emptied of thought. He forgot his anger and resentment and entered a state of dark drifting calm. Images welled up from the depths of his subconscious . . . a transcendental being, beautiful and alluring, calling to him from the heart of dust. He floated toward her, leaving his body behind . . . imagined Drew finding it, sitting cross-legged in the moonbase library minus its occupant. It was one way of passing the time.

The dinner buzzer sounded, and back inside his body of flesh and blood Gareth found that nothing had changed. Drew and Karen and the base commander talked among themselves, and he was excluded from the conversation. Their laughter hurt, and the steak and french fries stuck in his throat, threatening to choke him. He did try. When he asked for the salt Karen passed it, but when he asked who had won the pool game he was ignored. It was unjust punishment! Every expression of his personality was being denied, and he might as well not be there. And if there were no more dust storms in the next twenty-four hours, J.B. told Karen, she could go to Copernicus.

"What about me?" Gareth asked loudly.

J.B.'s flint-gray eyes fixed on his face.

"You," said the base commander, "are a pain in the fundamental orifice, son. And where you're going I have yet to decide."

"Apologize, can I?" Gareth asked.

"Who to?" asked Drew.

"As far as I'm concerned you needn't bother!" Karen said sourly.

Gareth stood up.

"In that case I'll go to bed!"

"And keep your hands off that computer!" said J.B.

There was laughter behind him, but Gareth did not look back. He made his way to the table where Jake was sitting and asked if he had a pocketknife. Graham Sanderson, who was sitting next to Jake and worked in the Vehicle Maintenance Department, searched his navy-blue overalls. The knife had a naked woman on its hasp and several blades. It was a present from his girl friend in Pasadena, and Gareth promised to return it.

Late-afternoon sunlight was bright on the desert beyond the window of his room, the ridges sleepy with heat. He wanted to go out there, but the blue glass trapped him and the walls caged him in, and he did not like what had happened between himself and Karen, himself and Drew. He tidied his room as an act of atonement, found J.B.'s chess set and Karen's camera. She had wanted to give it as a gift. A nice gesture, Drew had said, but Gareth had made her a laughingstock. Fragments of basalt rattled in the wastebasket, and the Geology Department snickered. She had really believed they were bones.

"How would you like it?" Gareth asked himself. "A nice girl, Karen. Generous. You should have gone for her, shouldn't you? At least she's real."

He sighed, smoothed the bedspread, and picked up the silver sphere. He was obsessed with a fantasy, a face in his head, dark haired and haunting him. Feelings, sharp as knives, shot through his guts when he thought of her. He had dreamed or imagined her, according to Drew, but the sphere was real enough. He could feel the grooves of circles beneath his fingertips, flush with the surface and varying in size. It belonged to her. He knew it belonged to her. But what *was* it? Gareth took the knife from his pocket and opened the smallest blade.

"Just one more go," he promised. "And if that doesn't work you're to hand it over, see?"

He pried at the center seam and failed to shift it. He pried at the circles one by one. Nothing happened. Then something did. A radio antenna shot upward, and the sphere came to life, sprouted arms or legs and jets of white light. Gareth yelped, dropped it in fright, but it did not fall. It floated on air, hovered and sank and slowly settled, its tripod legs finding the floor. And there it squatted, like a grotesque silver insect bent at

111

the knees, its abdomen swiveling, its camera-lens eye panning the room until it fixed finally on him. Gareth cowered against the wall, expecting it to attack, send out a death ray aimed at his brain. His mouth was dry, and his heart hammered.

"Drew?" Gareth whispered. "J.B.? Karen? Somebody help me!"

The thing made no move. It simply watched him, positioned between him and the door. He reached blindly, feeling for something to throw at it, knock it off balance and make his escape. He found the camera and J.B.'s chess set. "Just stay where you are!" he breathed. Click-flash. One shot was all Gareth had time for before he hurled the chess set. It struck hard. Plastic split and pieces scattered as he dropped the camera and leaped for the door. He turned as he opened it, saw the robot thing swerve and recover, and slammed it inside. Gareth took one step and banged into Karen who was coming to look for him.

"Drew says if you want to join us—"

Gareth gripped her arm.

His face was colorless and she stared at him in alarm. "What's wrong?"

"It's got legs!" Gareth said wildly.

"What has?"

"In my room! It's got legs and an eye!"

"What are you talking about?"

"That giant ball bearing thing! It's a blasted robot!"

"Ha ha!" said Karen.

"Go take a look!"

Karen opened the door. There was nothing there—
only a silver sphere among the chess pieces lying on
the floor. It had withdrawn its appendages and become
as it was before, lifeless and inert. Karen did not believe
him, but Gareth believed. He was white and shaking
and she could sense his fear. Give way to unreality and
the Moon would kill. However infuriating Gareth was,
Karen really did care for him. And at that particular
moment he cared for her, needed her as he had never
needed a person before—her warm flesh and her dumb
conversation, her human sanity. A chewing-gum kiss
brought them together.

"Tell me I'm not going mad," he said.

"You," Karen said softly, "are the maddest person I
have ever met. Bananas Gary."

"Yes," said Gareth, "that's what I thought."

16

Bethkahn sat in the silver chair. The grief for the man's death was behind her now, her gray clothes changed for a midnight-blue tunic suit spangled with stars, anticipating nightfall. She had nothing to do except wait. Her flight path was charted. The navigational computer set to begin the countdown. And the scanner trace on the vision screen still remained stationary. Room A41, the ship voice had said, among the apartments assigned to temporary guests. With the next lunar dawn, Gareth would return to Earth, and it seemed to Bethkahn that he had no intention of handing the scanner to the moonbase authorities. As with the flower she had picked on Cheoth One and preserved in resin, he intended to keep it as a souvenir. Or maybe he kept it for another reason? Hiding the fact of her existence? Covering her traces?

Whatever his reasons, she had come to believe he would never give her away.

"We cannot trust any of them!" the ship voice had said. But staring at the bleep of white light Bethkahn smiled fondly. Gareth was giving her the time she needed—time to prepare herself, to be sure of her plan and eliminate the possibility of error. She needed to wait until nightfall and approach the moonbase directly under cover of darkness. Work schedules showed that the Earth beings kept only a minimum security watch during each sleep period, and the base plan layout showed there was a blind spot. If she approached from the ridges, due east beyond the furthermost dome, she would not be seen. The three main air locks faced south and north, but she would use the air lock in the loading bay— double doors for vehicle access to the Maintenance and Supplies departments, and single doors for personnel. A security checkpoint directly beyond noted the identity of all who passed out or in, but during the sleep period there was only one man on duty. That one man would become Bethkahn's flesh for the few hours she needed him—long enough to weld the starship's stabilizer, to make her way to Gareth's room and take back the scanner. She could abandon the body and leave before the moonbase awakened. No one would know she had been and gone. If the security guard had any memory he would think he had dreamed it, and only Gareth might guess.

"Seventy-two hours," Bethkahn said softly.

"Mistress?" said the ship.

"In seventy-two hours it will all be over. I shall be on my way back here and we can be gone from this moon."

"I wish it were sooner," the ship voice muttered.

"We agreed it's safer to wait until nightfall," Bethkahn replied. "Had Gareth been going to betray us he would have done it already."

With one last glance at the moonbase floor plans, the air lock blueprints, and the Earth beings' duty roster, Bethkahn cleared the vision screens and checked the internal scanners. Down in the hold the army of robotic work units were still clearing away the encroaching dust. It was nothing to worry about, the ship had assured her. If worse came to worst, it could blast itself free. Nothing could stop it taking off. But mixed with Bethkahn's joy was an underlying fear—that the ship was not space-worthy, that it was mechanically unsound and incapable of reaching Khio Three. If it should malfunction again she could be stranded on another empty world throughout another ten thousand years of loneliness. The thought filled her with dread. She needed someone—someone to talk with, to travel with her, to share.

"Have you checked your circuits?" Bethkahn asked loudly.

"All systems are functioning," said the ship.

"If you should break down on me . . ."

"I shall make it," the ship said confidently.

"Can you give me a guarantee?"

The ship stayed silent.

"Can you?" Bethkahn repeated.

"I am old," the ship voice finally admitted. "I am not the latest model, Bethkahn, and I should have had an overhaul a long time ago. I shall do my best, of course, but I cannot give you a guarantee."

Bethkahn understood. Something had changed between herself and the ship. Not long ago it would probably have lied to her or covered up the truth, but now it spoke openly as it would have done with Rondahl. Ten thousand years of immobility had done it no good, it said. It had been suffering from metal fatigue before it came here, and its innards were clogged with cosmic dust. Now, with the moondust and prolonged disuse, its condition had deteriorated. There was dust around its main vents, in its power housing and cable housing. There was a frayed wire in its hypodrive circuitry, and one of its conductor coils showed evidence of warping. It did not anticipate trouble during take-off, but it was worried about the vibrations during light-speed velocities.

"So how do you rate our chances?" Bethkahn asked.

"Fifty-fifty," said the ship.

"I'll replace the frayed wire," she told it. "And we can send in the microdroids to remove some of the dust. Maybe I can replace the conductor coil too."

"Not without assistance," the ship voice said.

Bethkahn bit her lip. It always came back to that. She needed someone . . . not just for her own sake but for the sake of the ship. Her psychokinetic powers were not sufficient to maneuver the conductor coil into place, hold it in position while she secured the connection. She needed another pair of hands, another mind. Bright stars on the astrodome blazed above her, and the scanner trace bleeped on its screen of white static. But the vision screen changed, even as she watched it, flashed into form and color. The stolen scanner had been suddenly reactivated, and her cry was involuntary. She was seeing into a room with blue-white walls, a view of distant ridges through a tinted glass window, and a blank computer screen. Then, as the lens panned slowly through one hundred and eighty degrees, she saw Gareth crouched in the corner—his blue eyes, his dark hair, his fear.

Bethkahn stared at him. Even in flesh his beauty made a pain in her, revealed the soul that swelled inside him, vital with life. She perceived the warmth of him, the depth of his being, his thoughtfulness, his humor. She wondered if he thought of her, after the man had died and their eyes met, if she for him was unforgettable. She watched him reach for the camera, saw the flash and saw him hurl the plastic box. Then, in one fluid movement, Gareth leaped and was gone, and Bethkahn was alone again, staring at a closed door, at white static.

The ship had deactivated the scanner, but the pain remained, cruel and terrible, a longing she could no longer ignore. She wanted Gareth, needed him, desperately, urgently. She needed him with her to have and to hold, enough to drag him from his body, his soul from his flesh—take him, make him come with her in a starship across the galaxy on a journey that might never end. She wanted to scream for the things she felt. She was afraid of her own love, her own desperation. Her fists clenched, and her fingernails bit into the palms of her hands. But the ship had a different fear.

"That's it!" said the ship. "There's an end to us! It was ignorance holding him back! Now that he knows what he has, he is bound to tell. We cannot wait for nightfall, Bethkahn. You must get to the moonbase as soon as possible—before they come looking. Do you hear me, mistress?"

Bethkahn raised her head.

She loved an Earth boy and could not go near him.

"I'll go," she said harshly. "I'll go there tomorrow, be there when their next sleep period begins. But I won't take back the scanner."

"You'll let our technology fall into alien hands? That's illegal, Bethkahn!"

"Not so illegal as murder," Bethkahn replied.

"Murder?" said the ship. "Who's talking about murder? I told you before—it was accidental death! And it won't happen again."

"Won't it?" Bethkahn said quietly. "We need him, don't we? We *need* the Earth boy. You need him to help replace your conductor coil, and I need him too. But more than that—I happen to love him."

The starship went into shock. She could feel it, dumbstruck in the white light around her. Somewhere in its data banks it would have the basic information about

119

love, and eons of time with Rondahl must have taught it something. But trying to relate what it knew to Beth-kahn and Gareth, and work out the implications, scrambled its computer circuits and left it temporarily stunned. Its light grew darker, and spluttering noises came from its voice box, and if Bethkahn had not felt like crying she might have laughed.

"Love?" squawked the ship. "You cannot love flesh!"

"I can love the spirit within it," she replied.

"His?" said the ship. "Predatory? Corrupted? His whole breed is bent on cruelty and destruction! He's not spiritually evolved, Bethkahn! He's not like you!"

"How do you know?" Bethkahn asked harshly. "How can you ever know? You're nothing more than a festering heap of scrap metal! But I know the rules, and you don't need to worry. I won't go near him, won't touch him, and you'll never learn how wrong you are! I'll just mend your stabilizer and leave!"

"And what about the scanner?" the ship voice asked stiffly.

"Gareth can keep it, do what he likes with it. They can all do as they like with it. I don't care! Why should I care? I'm not answerable for the actions of Rondahl's descendents—for a lousy planet in this far-flung arm of the galaxy! I'm just a junior technician . . ."

"And I could be dismissed from the service!" said the ship.

17

High on the walkway of the domed observatory Gareth and Karen stood together. A moonbuggy with its water trailer headed away across the desert—Jake, taking Charlie Kunik's place, making an emergency run to Marco Polo, where a broken valve had drained their supplies. Computers rattled down in the well of the floor space, and voices echoed as the men exchanged their duty shifts. Just for once Earth time and Lunar time coincided. It was late evening, ten past ten by Gareth's wristwatch, and at any minute the Russian ship was due to fly past. Something worth watching, Drew had said. And taking Gareth's hand Karen had dragged him from the moonbase bar. Now with her arm linked through his, she snuggled close to him.

"This is nice," she said.

"Mmm," said Gareth.

"We could have been like this from the beginning instead of wasting a whole two weeks."

"Just don't get any ideas," Gareth warned her.

"I won't," she promised. "But I bet Drew suspects."

"Suspects what?" Gareth asked in alarm.

"I bet he suspects what's happened between us," said Karen. "We haven't fought for one whole day. But I haven't told him anything, if that's what you're worried about."

He relaxed again, seeing the buggy grow small in the distance and the sun, dim blue, through the reactolite glass hanging low above the Lunar Apennines. Tomorrow they would leave for Copernicus, but now the shadows were creeping toward him, and nightfall was only thirty-six hours away. And somewhere outside, on the Moon's barren surface, was an alien girl in whose reality only Gareth believed.

"She knows I have it," he murmured. "So what's she waiting for?"

"Who?" said Karen.

"That girl," said Gareth. "And that robot thing. It must contain some kind of tracking device. She wanted it back but she chose the wrong buggy, see? And when she opened the air lock Charlie Kunik died. Maybe that's why she didn't try it with us. But in the first place the sphere was on the moon ridge watching this base, so it must be something here she's after."

Karen stared at him.

"Are you being serious?"

"You ever known me to be anything else?"

"And you really believe . . . ? She's not *real*, Gary!"

"If she's not real then I'm nuts," Gareth said quietly. "But I know I'm not nuts so she *has* to be real. And there's nothing unreal about that ball-bearing thing, is there?"

"So what are you saying?" Karen asked.

"That somewhere outside is an alien life form," Gareth stated. "And you know her too, girlie. She's female, you said, and loneliness makes her cruel."

"I was talking about the *Moon*," said Karen. "Phoebe . . . the white Goddess . . . an abstract embodiment . . . the way men see her. Gee, Gary, you're not saying she's the one you saw? That's crazy! She's just a poetic myth!"

Gareth stared thoughtfully at the blue lunar landscape, the ink-black sky beyond the mountains where the sun dimmed the stars. It was here in the observatory that the Moon had really begun for him, thirteen days ago, in the first moments before morning. Since then it had changed everything, his whole way of thinking, his whole way of life. The Lunacy Syndrome—and he was caught up in it, no longer caring very much about his physical existence, caring more about his mind and soul, convinced he was more than simple flesh and blood. And the girl was a proof of it, an ephemeral being, discarnate and existing beyond death.

"Myths are rooted in fact," he said stubbornly. "And why, since the dawn of human thought, has the Moon been female? Race memory, is it? Maybe once upon a time we knew she was here. Maybe in the dim and

123

distant past our ancestors visited here . . ."

"Space travel has only been around for a hundred years," Karen reminded him.

"How do you know?" Gareth asked her. "It might have been around for billions of years. It's conceit to think we're the only intelligent life forms in the universe! And the sons of God looked upon the daughters of the Earth and saw they were fair. Originally our ancestors might have come from the stars. Why else are we so obsessed with reaching them? And I'm not the first to put forward that particular theory. The whole of the was-God-an-astronaut brigade would back me up."

"All right," said Karen. "Suppose it's true. If the girl is real she must have lived here for thousands of years, so how has she survived?"

Gareth grinned.

"Gin," he said. "One hundred percent pure spirit. Like the Arabians used to keep in bottles and magic lamps."

"Oh very funny!" said Karen.

"Seriously," said Gareth. "I was reading about it yesterday in the *Zen Buddhist Handbook*. Everybody has an astral body. She's noncorporeal, see? A ghost, stranded here, wandering. My God, there's loneliness for you. She's probably desperate enough to try anything. And where's her ship?"

"Ship?" said Karen.

"She's bound to have a ship. How else could she have got here?"

"Flying carpet?" suggested Karen.

"You don't believe me, do you?"

Just then the Russian ship passed overhead. It was larger than the American transports—white with red fins and a hammer and sickle emblazoned on its side. It streaked low over the mountains, arched gracefully upward, and slowly sank, tail down in a blast of fire, toward the landing site in the Sinus Iridum. Nothing remained but the mountains, dark shapes edged with light, the cone of Mount Conon that the ancient astronomers had claimed to be a live volcano. They must have seen something to make them believe. Flames of a spacecraft landing perhaps? A belching of smoke or dust?

"Mare Vaporum," Gareth said softly. "Sea of Mists. But suppose it was dust? A dust storm witnessed from Earth that the ancient astronomers thought was cloud? A dust storm, Karen, blown by a moonwind. You saw it. I saw it. Even Drew saw it. And she's at the heart of it. Been here for centuries, she has. Bound to make a move soon, isn't she? Kill two birds with one stone, see? Take back her spying device and whatever else she's wanting. She can't trust me to keep quiet much longer."

"I think you should tell this to Drew," said Karen.

"Getting the wind up, are you?"

"If that girl comes here . . ."

"Not real, you said."

"But if she is . . . ?"

"Who's going to believe me? I've told Drew already. I've told J.B."

"You haven't told them everything!" Karen said urgently. "If you hand over that blasted ball-bearing thing they'd know you were telling the truth! They'd know it wasn't made anywhere on Earth! For crying out loud, Gary! You can't keep something like this to yourself! We could be in danger here! J.B. *has* to know! And if you won't tell him, I will!"

"Think he'll buy it coming from you?"

"Why shouldn't he?"

Gareth grinned and kissed her on the forehead.

"Remember *Bovis lunaris*?" he said.

"What?" Karen stared at him. "You mean it's another one of your little jokes?"

Gareth ducked as she swung at him, laughed and ran, his footsteps thudding along the metal passageway and down the stairs. Men in white coats watched with amusement or alarm as he charged between the computer banks, Karen screaming behind him as to how she would ram his blasted ball bearing down his neck, along with six jars of pickled pumpkin and a bunch of daffodils. Her rage, his laughter, drifted away along the corridor toward the guest bedrooms. They were young and lively—a breath of fresh air, most people said. But Karen did not think it funny. Her fists beat on the closed door as Gareth leaned against it, and her voice came muffled from the other side.

"I'm going to kill you!" Karen yelled. "You rotten lying swine!"

"Who says I was lying?" Gareth yelled back.

"What's that supposed to mean?"

"Work it out!"

"I'm going to tell Drew anyway!"

"You do that, girlie. He'll laugh his head off!"

"You'll pay for this, you Welsh oaf!"

"Nos da, cariad!"

"Don't 'darling' me!"

With one last kick at the door Karen went away, and, still leaning against it, Gareth smiled. He should not have told her, should not have involved her, but he had needed to test his theory, share the responsibility of knowing. She could either believe him or not believe him, tell or not tell. It was just one more of Gareth's fantastic stories. But whatever happened no one could say he had kept it to himself. Karen knew too—there was an alien girl intent on entering the moonbase. All Gareth had done was give her a few hours of time, another day or maybe two, bluff and double bluff until someone realized that he always had been telling the truth.

18

Gareth slept with her face in his mind, her dark hair and the shadows of her eyes. Then suddenly he awoke. Noise blasted his ears, a siren sounding the red alert. He sat bolt upright, thinking he was dreaming. It was twenty past two by his wristwatch, and he had forgotten to close the window blinds. The distant ridges were blue and still in the sunlight, but the siren went on and there were voices in the corridor and people running. Gareth leaped out of bed and pulled on his jeans. It was some kind of emergency, the start of a mass evacuation perhaps, and he did not have time to hunt for his sweatshirt. Naked to the waist Gareth opened the door, collided with Karen in her candy-pink dressing gown. He saw fear in her eyes, her face white as paste, and her voice screamed louder than the siren.

"Dust!" shrieked Karen. "She's coming, just like you said!"

"Who's coming?" Gareth asked in alarm.

"The girl!" shrilled Karen. "And Jake's out in the buggy. He'll be killed if she catches up with him! We'll all be killed!"

The corridor was dark. Blue light shone from their rooms and shone yellow from the elevator nearby when the doors opened. Security guards with laser guns came running past them, the base commander following behind, bawling instructions and buttoning his shirt.

"Never mind the oxygen loss! Just get that air lock open! Tell Kelly to drive straight in and we'll close it behind him! And turn off the siren!" With his shirt sleeves dangling J.B. turned his attention to Gareth and Karen. "You two can stay in your rooms!" he barked.

"What did I tell you?" Karen said wildly. "Jake's out there and she's after him!"

Gareth gripped her arm, propelled her across the corridor and into her room. She too had not closed the blinds, and the window faced across the open desert. He saw then why Karen was afraid—saw the moon-buggy heading home, and behind it, blotting out the horizon, was a great wall of dust. As a child Gareth had had nightmares about tidal waves, but now he was seeing one—a gigantic dust wave sweeping toward the moon-base, threatening to engulf Jake's buggy, engulf them all, as the siren wailed and Karen screamed beside him.

"Don't let it get me! I don't want to die! I want to

get out of here! Let go of my arm! Please, Gary! Let me go! Let me go! We're going to be killed!"

She screamed and struggled.

And he slapped her face.

"Don't talk crap!" he said harshly.

Karen backed away from him as the siren suddenly ceased, sat on the bed in the silence and touched her face. His finger marks showed an angry red, and he stared at her helplessly, then stared through the window at the buggy racing toward the loading bay and the desert rising behind it in the seconds before it struck. The sunlight dimmed. Dust blasted the window, hurled by a moonwind, savage and silent in one almighty demonstration of power. Gareth expected the moonbase to buckle and crack under the force of it, expected his own instantaneous death. But the storm passed over them and was gone as swiftly as it came. A few small eddies whirled across the landing pad and lay still. Human voices took over, and Karen sobbed softly in the aftermath of shock.

"The driver made it!" someone shouted.

"What the hell was it?" asked another.

And the intercom crackled.

"Maintain red alert. Top-level personnel report to their posts. We have an unidentified phenomenon. Repeat . . . we have an unidentified phenomenon."

"Inside or out?" Gareth said softly.

"It was true," wept Karen. "Everything you said was true! And we could have been killed!"

"It's not her intention to kill," said Gareth.

130

"How do you know?"

"I just do."

Karen took a handkerchief from her pocket and wiped her eyes.

"We've got to tell Drew," she said. "This time we've *got* to tell him."

"Tell me what?" Drew asked from the doorway.

"She's hysterical," Gareth said quickly.

"That's right!" Karen said angrily. "I'm hysterical! And you sure enjoyed slapping my face, didn't you?" She looked at Drew. "Do you know what Gareth's got in his room?" she asked. "A robotic spying device! He found it that day on the ridges. Someone's been watching this moonbase. He figures there's an alien spaceship nearby and that ghost girl he saw was real. She's the cause of the dust storm and now she's come *here*."

"See what I mean?" said Gareth. "Believe that and you'll believe anything."

"Out!" said Drew. "I'll deal with this."

Gareth returned to his room. He had maybe five minutes before Drew was convinced and came looking. Somehow or other he had to get rid of the sphere. Silver and shining he took it from the shelf in the wardrobe and stuffed it in the shopping bag, then put on his moonshoes and sweatshirt. Maybe he could dump it among the foam-rubber mattresses in the gymnasium? In the food supplies or linen supplies? Or bury it in the glass houses among the tomato plants? Why he should take such a risk he hardly knew. It was just something he had to do . . . for the sake of the girl.

Cautiously Gareth opened the bedroom door. The corridor was dim-lit and empty, the panic over and no one about. He headed away toward the recreation area, but he had not taken more than a dozen steps when the intercom crackled. "Doctor Steadman . . . your assistance is required at number three air lock," a woman's voice said. "Will Doctor Steadman please report to number three air lock immediately." Karen's door opened in response and there was nowhere Gareth could hide.

"Where are you off to?" Drew asked.

"The lavatory," said Gareth. "What's going on in number three air lock?"

"Search me," said Drew. "In the morning I want a word with you. Officially. In my office. Nine-thirty sharp."

"Karen tell you everything, did she?"

"She told me enough," said Drew. "And Karen's impressionable enough without you filling her head with rubbish, especially at a time like this! We've got enough to contend with as it is, and we don't need aliens!"

"I won't tell her no more," Gareth said solemnly.

He opened the bathroom door. Harsh light shone on Drew's red hair, showed the mock severity on his face, and the shopping bag rustled as Gareth sidled past him. A fast hand caught his arm.

"I'll just have a look at it," said Drew.

"A look at what?" asked Gareth.

"Whatever you have in the bag that's causing all the fuss."

It might have been the end of everything, but away in the distance, toward the Vehicle Maintenance Department, someone screamed. It was a terrible inhuman sound that seemed to go on and on—a man screaming in agony or anguish, or the maddened howling of an animal in pain. Broken metal smashed against the walls, and someone came running, a pale shape at the dark end of the corridor heading toward them, footsteps pounding. Seeing them Dr. Chalmers skidded to a halt. His white coat was ripped to tatters. There was blood on his face and he was breathing heavily.

"Steadman . . . thank God it's you!"

"What's happened?" Drew asked in alarm.

"The buggy driver," Dr. Chalmers gasped. "Something's radically wrong with him. He's fighting like a madman. Homicidal. A danger to himself and everyone else. A full-blown psychosis, it looks like. A voice in his head, someone taking over his body. He's broken one guy's wrist. The base commander got a fist in the face, and no one can get near him. I'll go get help and the hypodermic. You get down there. He's in the main storeroom."

Dr. Chalmers went running on toward Medical.

And Drew turned to Gareth.

"Do what you have to, and go back to your room," he said quietly.

"Was it Jake?" Gareth asked sickly. "Was it Jake he was talking about?"

"Just do as I ask," said Drew. "And don't say anything to Karen. I'll talk to you in the morning."

He was gone then, walking away. Darkness dissolved him and Gareth entered the bathroom. Light shone on white-tiled walls, and thoughts whirled in his head. Human sanity was a fragile thing, and Jake, who had known the Moon as no one else, who had sung in its solitude, had gone insane. Something terrible had happened to the big man from Wyoming. What had he seen in the heart of the dust storm? What had pursued him across the deserts of the Sea of Mists? The alien girl? The one Gareth was protecting? Some kind of devil wanting to possess him, was she? Taking over Jake's body? Her voice heard in his head?

Mirrors on the wall above the sinks reflected Gareth's face—pasty pale from lack of fresh air, his dark curls tousled from sleep. It was his fault, what had happened to Jake. He had known all along the girl was real, and he should have reported her. He should have shown Drew the sphere and made him believe. Loneliness made her cruel, Karen had said. She had killed Charlie Kunik and it might have been deliberate. Now she had taken Jake's mind, and that might be deliberate too.

"Know what you've got to do, don't you?" Gareth asked himself. "Yes," he said grimly. "You've been had for a sucker, boy, and never mind her looks. First thing in the morning, one alien ball bearing for the base commander, definitely and without fail."

He nodded and entered the stall.

And a few minutes later he left with the shopping bag.

19

When Gareth left the bathroom a man's voice shouted.

"Hey! You!"

He turned in alarm. Two security guards were coming toward him, black shapes in the semidarkness with a shine of light on their hard hats. A white gauntleted hand pointed a laser gun in his direction, and a flashlight shone on his face, dipped as he was recognized.

"Gareth!"

He eyed them warily.

"Going to arrest me, are you? Unlawful urination during off-peak hours?"

"This is the smart aleck who broke into our computer banks," one guard told the other. "Been late-night shopping, son?"

"Not exactly," said Gareth. "It's something I picked up, see? A robotic spying device from an alien spaceship. Going to give it to the base commander, I was. Available, is he?"

The first security guard gripped Gareth's arm.

"Okay, funny guy, let's have you back in your room. With a full-scale search going on we've no time for games."

"This is important!" Gareth protested.

"You're darned right," said the guard. He frog-marched Gareth down the corridor. "Room A-forty-one. In you go, fruit cake. And stay out of the way."

Gareth paused with his hand on the door handle. Way up ahead there was daylight and voices in the main reception area, and back along the corridor the other guard was shining his flashlight in all the unoccupied rooms. In the gloom and silence Gareth could sense it— the night full of disturbance, the atmosphere bristling with unease. They were looking for someone, and Gareth knew who. She was alien and dangerous, and she was inside the moonbase, and sooner or later she would come looking for him.

Room A41—the luminous number was painted on Gareth's door. He had only to go inside and lock it, but his skin prickled as he opened it, and he almost cried out. The room was in darkness, blackness so absolute it made a wall against his eyes. Someone had lowered the window blind in his absence, and when he felt for the light switch the electricity failed to work. His heart missed a beat. Someone or something was inside his room, hidden and waiting in the unrelieved dark. He could actually feel a presence. Fear paralyzed his muscles and dried his throat. And the security guard watched him, the beam of the flashlight sweeping toward him. He had one split second to make up his mind.

"Gareth?" someone whispered.

Flaming Karen!

Gareth entered the room, closed the door, and leaned against it. She had scared him stupid, but now he wanted to laugh at his own fear. He waited for the security guards to clear the immediate area, listened to the pitch-black humming of the air-conditioning and his own breathing, their footsteps moving away along the corridor.

"What the hell are you playing at?" he said.

Magically the strip light in the ceiling began to brighten, a dim illumination slowly gathering strength. Gareth saw the room whitening around him, the outline of the bed and someone standing beside it. He caught his breath. She was not Karen. She was insubstantial as a mirage in the desert, yet he could see her exact in every detail—the blue shimmer of her clothes, the pallor of her face, amber eyes and drifts of dark hair. He could see the computer screen through her midriff and the shadows of the alcove behind her. Nervously biting her lower lip the alien girl regarded him, waiting as Gareth stared at her through the first few seconds of shock.

"You!" he said.

"Don't give me away," she begged.

"How did you find me?"

"Room A-forty-one—my ship took the information

from your computer. I didn't mean to come here but I didn't know what else to do, who else to turn to. Help me, Gareth. Please help me."

She was not like Karen. She had his name right and her voice was quiet, strangely accented, yet perfectly distinct. Her pale hands were held toward him in a gesture of appeal. Gareth clenched his fists. Only five minutes ago he had decided to hate her, but her amber eyes held him, beautiful and deep, and there were feelings inside him he did not know how to cope with. But he was not about to trust her. Her ship thieved knowledge, and he got the blame. Charlie Kunik had died from her actions, and Jake had been driven insane. Hesitantly the ghost girl moved toward him.

"Don't come any closer!" Gareth said harshly.

"My name's Bethkahn," she said.

"Stay away from me!"

"I won't harm you," she said.

"So what happened to Jake?"

"Who's Jake?"

"The buggy driver you came in with. No harm, you say, but what did you do to him? Raving, isn't he? And you're responsible for that."

Her expression crumpled. He saw a look of anguish in her eyes that was replaced by weariness. Her whole body sagged in defeat as she slumped on the chair and ran her fingers through her waist-long hair. She had so much power, but whatever had happened between her and Jake had left her beaten. She stared at the floor, shuddered as she remembered, and he wanted to pity her. But his voice was ruthless and he needed to know.

"What did you *do* to him?" Gareth repeated.

"Nothing," she said brokenly. "I did nothing. He was too strong for me, and I couldn't control him. He wanted to kill me, tried to destroy me . . . destroy himself and everyone else. All that rage, and hatred, and horror . . . those terrible feelings. I couldn't stay in him, couldn't bear it. I tried to talk to him, but he wouldn't listen, wouldn't understand. I only needed his body for a few hours of time—the use of his flesh, the use of his hands. I wouldn't have harmed him, no more than I would harm you. It's against our laws to damage life. I left him in the storeroom. They said he was mad, but it wasn't my fault. It wasn't!"

She raised her amber eyes to look at Gareth.

Her eyes watered in the light.

"What about the other buggy driver?" he asked. "Charlie Kunik, the one who died?"

"I never meant to kill him," she said. "I never intended . . . But I'll live with it now—his death on my conscience—my ignorance, my mistake. Those feelings just now—I'll live with them too, and the damage I've done to the mind of a man. I wish the ship had never woken me. I wish I'd slept forever, never come here, never learned of you."

"So how can I help you?" Gareth asked.

"I wish there was another way . . ."

"Just tell me what you want."

"I dare not risk another mind . . ."

Gareth stared at her.

Suddenly he sensed Jake's horror.

"You want to borrow *my* body? Come inside and take possession? Hell's flaming bells! You really expect me to . . . No way, girlie! Help's one thing, but not that!"

"I'm not asking for that!" Bethkahn said vehemently. "Not from you, Gareth! Just mend my stabilizer, that's all. And give me back my scanner."

Gareth smiled in relief and held it toward her, a shopping bag saying WILLIAM'S GOOD FOOD STORES, ABERDARE LIMITED, then looked where she pointed. There was a bag on his bed, not transparent as she was, but bulky and substantial and made of some toughened gray material. Scrap metal clattered when he opened it and tipped out the contents. It was some kind of rotor blade with two of its arms sheared off. It needed welding, she said. Without it her ship could not take off, and she had been stranded on the Moon for ten thousand years.

"Alone?" he asked. "For ten thousand years!"

"Except for the ship," she replied.

"What happened?"

It was a strange tale Bethkahn told. She was a junior technician aboard an interstellar spaceship. It was her first voyage, she said, and something had gone wrong with the ship. They had landed here, on this moon, to make repairs. It was just a broken stabilizer, a routine replacement. The rest of the crew had left her to it, taken the survey craft and gone to explore the nearby Earth. They had never returned, she said. Their survey craft were destroyed in a volcanic eruption when the island continent sank beneath the sea.

"Atlantis?" gasped Gareth.

"I don't know," she said. "I only know it happened, that I was stranded here. And the laser packs were empty and there were no spare stabilizers on board. I thought I would be here forever, alone forever. I couldn't stand the loneliness of that. So my ship let me use the cryogenic chamber. Sleep was the only way I could forget. And then it woke me, told me you were here, and finally I came."

"I'm glad about that," Gareth said softly.

"I didn't want to come," Bethkahn confessed. "But I had no choice. One day your kind would have found me, held me captive for the knowledge I possess, and taken my ship apart."

"You make us sound like ogres!"

"Not you," Bethkahn said quickly.

"I'm no different," said Gareth.

She stared at him.

Her amber eyes softened and his insides lurched.

"Aren't you?" she murmured. "I think you must be. Why haven't you betrayed me, Gareth? Why did you keep my scanner and give it to no one else? Why, after the buggy driver died and you saw me, didn't you tell? And why are you sitting here now, talking to me, instead of raising the alarm? Will they help me, Gareth? The ones who are searching? Will they mend my stabilizer and let me go free? Will they?"

"No," he said.

"Then why are you?"

20

The storeroom was dark, a concrete cavern full of stacked boxes, with narrow windows set high in the apex of the roof, where dim blue sunlight filtered through. Somewhere in here was Bethkahn's escape route—a service air lock that led directly to the loading bay outside. She stared about her, trying to get her bearings, her amber eyes raking the shadows between mountains of supplies. The air was pungent with unfamiliar scents of dried fruit and spices, and the cold storage units made a soft humming of sound. Gareth's breath was white mist beside her.

"Over there," he said softly.

Bethkahn followed him. A forklift was parked by the wall, and beside it a ramp dived down into the darkness of the air lock. She regarded it nervously, reluctant to commit herself and reluctant to leave the boy from Earth whom she would never see again. She wondered if he felt as she did, but just for the moment Gareth paid her no heed. Instead he studied the control panel. Dual control buttons opened and closed the hatch, and a square of green light showed when he flicked the switch.

"Do you know how to operate it?" Bethkahn asked anxiously.

"No," he said. "But I'm about to learn."

"Maybe there's another way out?" she suggested.

"The main air locks will all be guarded."

"The corridor wasn't."

"That was my good judgment and your good luck," said Gareth. He slung the shopping bag containing the scanner down the well of the service chute. "Now you," he said.

"It's so dark," she said nervously.

Gareth looked at her.

Shrewd blue eyes fixed on her face.

"Don't want to go, do you, girlie?"

She shook her head and her lower lip trembled. Maybe he saw and understood why, for he suddenly reached out his hand. He was trying to touch her—a lock of her hair, the curve of her neck, the blue soft fabric of her tunic top and the nebulous warmth of her being beneath it. He touched and his hand passed through her, and she was not tangible, not to him, no more than light or air. He sighed, knowing it impossible, sharing her sadness in a moment of finality.

"It's been nice," he said thickly. "Nice meeting you, girlie. You've taught me a lot. Same underneath, we are, but you've got to get out of here. Your ship told you right. If anyone should find you, they won't let you go free. You've got to go while the going is good, see, and leave it to me."

Bethkahn wanted to cling to him.

But she made herself smile.

And her voice stayed calm.

"Good-bye Gareth," she said.

It was hard to leave him, hard to turn away from him, but Bethkahn had promised the ship. She entered the black gap of the air lock and slid down the ramp. The hatch door closed behind her, shutting her inside a claustrophobic space as dark as a tomb. There was no chink of light, no movement, no sound but the rustle of the plastic bag, until the mechanism wheezed into life. An unseen door opened before her and sent her catapulting through. This time she was in a depressurization chamber. She could hear the suction pumps working, feel the vacuum around her, and the last hatch opened onto a blaze of natural light. An emerald blindness temporarily deprived her of vision as she slid down the supply chute to fall among dust and shadows on the concrete floor of the loading bay.

For a few moments Bethkahn lay still, stunned by the emptiness and silence that flesh could not survive. Noises heard inside the moonbase echoed in her head. She felt giddy from the change of pressure. Then she picked herself up, picked up the bag with the scanner, ran for the nearest buggy, and crouched between its wheels, its bulk hiding her from anyone who might approach. She could see beyond the shadow line the sunlight of the open desert and the distant ridges stark against the blackness of the sky. Just a few meters of concrete between herself and freedom. But she had to wait awhile before she made her final escape. She had to allow Gareth sufficient time to return to his room. For her sake, as well as his own, he could not be caught in the corridor when the alarm siren sounded the next red alert.

Slow minutes slipped by, time imagined in her mind like the tick of his wristwatch or the beat of his heart. In thirty-six hours she would leave this moon, but all she could feel was a kind of grief. She had lived through the loss of the whole ship's crew, but it seemed as nothing compared to the loss of Gareth. Almost, she thought, she would be leaving behind her own soul, and knowing him made the loneliness a thousand times harder to bear.

"Stop it!" she whispered. "Stop it, Bethkahn!"

She pushed the thought of him from her, preparing to run. It was mind over matter, and she needed to concentrate. Dust particles shifted, swirled across the concrete, and were drawn toward her. The moonwind rose, and the dust grew thicker, whirling around her, veiling the sunlight beyond. She was the eye of the hurricane, the vortex of the storm that moved as she moved, a towering tornado bursting from the loading bay and sweeping away toward the ridges. She knew what she was to those who watched from behind the blue glass windows of the moonbase—a thing of terror they would never understand.

With the dust gone behind her Bethkahn climbed the ridge, searching for shelter among the high shadows of the rocks. The sun was poised above the rim of the mountain crater where the starship was. Mount Conon, Gareth had called it, named after a barbarian hero in a comic-strip book. The ship would not be too happy knowing she had told of its whereabouts, but right now Bethkahn did not want to think about the ship. She looked back at the moonbase, a sprawl of buildings on the distant horizon, glowing blue and golden in the last long hours before sunset. She tried to pick out Gareth's room—somewhere between the domed observatory and the arch of the loading bay—wondering if he too was standing at the window looking out for her.

And in the sky beyond the moonbase was the Earth from where he had come, turquoise blue and three parts full. A madhouse, Gareth had said, all right for those who had money but not much joy for the rest. It had been beautiful once, he had said, but now it was spoiled by idiot men, and he did not rate its future prospects very high. Almost Bethkahn had offered to show him the gardens of Khio, the golden cities of Cheoth and the rose-pink worlds that revolved around Bahtoomi's star. It would have been easy to tempt him, but she had held her tongue.

"Tell me where you come from?" he had asked.

"It's just an ordinary planet," she had replied.

146

"In another dimension?"

"Only in distance."

"You mean I could go there, just as I am?"

"It's nine thousand light-years," she said.

He understood. He would be dead before he reached it, his flesh turned to dust. Bethkahn did not tell him he would also be alive, his spirit traveling beside her, enduring through time. She could have persuaded him that his flesh did not mean very much, but one man's soul had screamed to her of murder, and she was afraid that those who were born into bodies could not live free of them. Emotionally Gareth was bound to his flesh, and Bethkahn gave him no hint of hope or possibility. Underneath they were the same, he had said, but she would not take him from the people he knew, from the man named Drew and the girl named Karen, and the planet of his birth.

Bethkahn's eyes watered in the Moon's sunset light. She moved to sit in the lee of a boulder, sighed and settled, the bag at her feet. WILLIAM'S GOOD FOOD STORES, ABERDARE LIMITED, it said, in green and red lettering. It was all she had to remind her of Gareth— a shopping bag and the memory of a meeting that should never have happened.

It should never have happened, but it had, and Bethkahn could not forget. Ridiculous . . . serious . . . he could change in a moment, and she had met no one else like him. Impossible to reach to the depths of him, distinguish the difference between truth and lies. He had told her of Earth, and she had listened, appalled to hear of the evolution for which her kind was responsible, the extent of injustice and cruelty. Yet that same evolutionary program had produced Gareth—his intelligence, his awareness, his quality of caring. No, he was not forgettable—his smile, his laughter, the glorious strangeness of it after all these centuries of time.

She sighed and tipped out the scanner. By this time in the Earth's tomorrow she would owe Gareth a debt of gratitude that she could never repay. Leave it to him, he had said, and she knew she could trust him. One mended stabilizer would be sent down the supply chute for collection during the next sleep period, and all she had to do was wait . . . wait, as the starship was waiting—an unfeeling machine, its tireless computers fearing what had happened to her, wondering and worrying and programmed to care. Fear was logical, it had said. Bethkahn activated the scanner, waited for the lens eye to find her, and started to signal.

"I shall be twenty-four hours late in returning. . . ."

21

Sleep was his alibi. Gareth ignored the wail of the siren, raised voices, and footsteps running. He ignored Karen when she came to his room. "Can I come in?" she asked plaintively. His eyes stayed shut and she went away, and a few minutes later the siren sound ceased. The next thing he knew was Karen shouting him awake, the scarlet glare of her blouse seen through the squint of his eyes and her gold necklace glinting in the light.

"Who let *you* in here?" Gareth said sourly.

"It's twenty to nine," she told him.

"And I'm tired."

"Tired?" scoffed Karen. "What have you got to be tired about? Most of us have been up all night, but you slept right through it. You never even heard!"

"Heard what?" growled Gareth.

"At twenty to five this morning there was another

149

red alert," Karen informed him. "I came here needing company, scared out of my skull, and you never even woke up! Four hours I've been sitting in my room waiting for morning, and who cares? I've never been so lonely in all my life. And all you've done is lie in bed and snore!"

"Can I help it if I'm a heavy sleeper?" Gareth muttered.

"You must have cloth ears!" Karen concluded. "And if you want breakfast you can't lie there any longer. Gee, Gary, please get up. I've got no one to talk to and I'm scared all on my own. Please get up."

"You want to try it for ten thousand years, girlie."

"Try what?"

"Nothing," said Gareth. "Just get out of my room and let me dress."

When Gareth entered the cafeteria Karen was sitting alone at the table in the window bay, crumbling a cracker and sipping orange juice, staring bleakly around the almost empty room. Canned music played in the background, but the room contained a mood and a silence. A few morning faces were grim and haggard from lack of sleep, and no one smiled. He collected ham and eggs from the serving hatch and went to join her.

"Where is everyone?"

Karen shrugged.

"I guess they're busy. That's what I was telling you. No one bothers with us anymore, not even Drew."

"We're on our own then?"

"It sure seems like it."

Gareth almost smiled. The less people bothered about him the better. It suited him fine—no Drew, no base commander, no organized itinerary. Everyone was preoccupied with last night's happenings, and he could do as he liked. He could go to the Vehicle Maintenance Department, use the welding equipment with no one peering over his shoulder and asking what he was doing, or why. He only needed to be rid of Karen.

"We were supposed to be leaving for Copernicus this morning," Karen said gloomily.

"You can forget about that," Gareth told her.

"So what shall we do instead?"

Gareth looked at her, swallowed a mouthful of ham.

"You mean what will *you* do? I've got something on for the rest of the morning."

Karen stared at him.

Blue feelings flickered in her eyes.

"Are you saying you don't want me around?"

"I never meant it like that," Gareth said quickly.

"So how *did* you mean it?"

"I've just got a few things to do, that's all."

"Like what?"

"Socks," said Gareth. "I've got to wash some socks, for one thing."

"That should take you at least ten minutes," Karen said sarcastically.

"Plus half an hour to write some notes, an hour looking for the pawn I've lost from J.B.'s chess set, and two hours explaining to Drew about that load of bullshit you sold him last night. And why should I be accountable to you for my time? Not bound to stay together, are we? And have you never wanted to be by yourself? There's quietness out on Pen-y-van, girlie, and I need it, see? I told you that right at the beginning."

But the fact remained—Gareth wanted to be rid of her and she knew it. The hurt actually showed in her face. But there was nothing he could do about it, no way he could explain. The disk of the sun hung low above the rim of Mount Conon, where a crippled starship lay, and all he had was this one day. Tonight Bethkahn would return to the moonbase, and her need was greater than Karen's. She would be trapped here forever if Gareth did not help her.

"I'm sorry, girlie, but that's how it is."

"Screw you!" Karen said viciously.

"Meet you for lunch, I will."

"Don't put yourself out!"

"Ellen!" J.B. shouted. "Bring me a coffee!"

Karen turned her head at the sound of the base commander's voice, smiled as he came toward them. He was smartly dressed in his Air Force uniform, but last night's happenings had taken a toll. Dark circles ringed his eyes. He needed a shave, and a purple bruise showed on one cheek, where Jake had hit him. He heaved a sigh as he sat beside them, waited for the serving woman to bring him coffee, then turned his attention to Karen.

"Well, young lady, how are you this morning?"

"I never slept a wink," said Karen.

"That makes two of us," J.B. said.

"What happened to your face?"

152

"I . . . er . . . walked into a door."

J.B. stirred sugar into his coffee.

And glanced at Gareth.

"Are you all right, son?"

"As well as can be expected under the circumstances," Gareth replied.

J.B. nodded.

"Yes," he said. "And under the circumstances I think it best if the two of you return to Earth. There's an investigative team arriving this evening from the Russian Base, and Bronski has agreed to a delayed takeoff of the Soviet ship. We're waiting for a U.S. Government clearance for it to land at Kennedy, plus confirmation from the Kremlin, but you leave on the Russian hopper for the Sinus Iridum tomorrow morning. They've had no disturbances over there, and as we don't know the dangers involved I'd rather you were both gone from here. I'm sorry to cut short your stay. It's been nice having you. . . ."

"I'd rather leave anyway," Karen said.

"It's the only thing to do," said J.B. "Under the circumstances. We'll contact your parents, and Drew will be traveling with you. Okay with you, son?"

"No," said Gareth.

"Well, I can't stop to discuss it now," said J.B. "I'll see you this evening, but I won't be changing my mind."

The base commander swilled his coffee and left. Gareth stared at the egg yolk congealing on his plate. It was all settled. Come tomorrow he would be going home, back to Earth, to the gray hills of Wales, Mom and her lover, and the housing project in Aberdare where vandals ruled and dog muck fouled the pavements. He would be going home to a life in a decaying industrial nation, closed-down coal mines and acid rain and small chance of getting employment. He would be selling his soul to the Department of Social Security for a weekly handout, and nothing to look forward to except premature balding and senile decay. It was not life Gareth would be returning to, but a kind of dying.

Desperate feelings churned in his stomach. He had come too far, and the Moon had changed him. Before, Pen-y-van had meant something to him. The gray mountains and the land of his fathers was the only place he knew. But now it meant nothing, offered nothing, and he did not want to go back there. There was no future for him on Earth and nothing he wanted. It was a world run by lunatics, and he would be trapped on it forever, like Bethkahn on the Moon, and unable to escape.

Suddenly Gareth knew how she felt, her screams echoing in his mind through ten thousand years of isolation. And he, with the mad world waiting, felt his own scream rising inside him. Go back to Earth and he would never be free again. There was agony inside him, despair black and destroying. He was sick with it, cold with it, and there was no way out.

"Is something the matter?" Karen asked him.

He looked at her, wildness in his eyes.

"I don't want to go!" he said. "There's nothing there! Nothing on Earth! Nowhere, not for me!"

"You can come to Santa Barbara," Karen said generously.

"What's the point?"

"Pop will find you a job."

"You don't understand!" wailed Gareth. "There's nothing *anywhere*! No reason! No purpose! Worth it for you, it is, but not for me! There's no meaning on Earth! Here's where the meaning began. Here! I want to go on, not back! For crying out loud—there's not even any hope!"

Karen stared at him. She wanted to help him, but she did not know how and she never would, nor did she begin to understand. Life was different for her. She still cared about having and getting, but he only cared about being. He did not belong on that teeming, struggling planet. He did not belong in Karen's world of backyard swimming pools and beach houses. She reached out to touch him, but Gareth pushed back his chair and walked away.

22

Karen was packing her bags and had no need of his company, so Gareth left the camera on the bed for her to find, picked up the bag containing the broken stabilizer, pocketed Graham Sanderson's knife, and headed away down the long corridor. He ignored the arrow that pointed the way to Medical. Accidentally and on purpose he had decided to forget the interview with Drew. This was his last day on the Moon, and he intended to use it. He would see Bethkahn's stabilizer mended and returned to her if it was the last thing he ever did.

His lips set in an obdurate line, and determination drove him. He passed a group of scientists by the elevator, but no one stopped or questioned him, and security guards in the nearby checkpoint paid him no heed. Gareth's expression was enough to tell them he knew exactly where he was going and for what purpose.

Double doors to the Vehicle Maintenance Department opened automatically and allowed him inside. The room was vast, filled with noise and bustle and pop music playing. Naked light bulbs hung from steel girders, and overhead skylights let in a little natural light. But shadows were predominant, areas of gloom and darkness, and coldness exuded from the concrete walls and floor. Garage smells assailed him—the reek of oil and sweat, greased machinery and dirty overalls. He heard the clatter of wrenches and the scream of a saw cutting through metal. A buggy stripped of its side panels showed a maze of multicolored wires, and another was suspended over a pit with a team of mechanics working under it. Unnoticeable among the noise and chaos, Gareth watched in bewilderment, his mind gone blank. But then among the sounds he heard the hiss of a welder and saw in the dark distance of the room a shower of sparks, and made his way toward it.

"Excuse me!" Gareth shouted.

A man in navy overalls turned toward him, his face lost among the reflections in his protective headgear. Lifting his visor, Graham Sanderson smiled.

"Hi Gareth. What can I do for you?"

"Your knife," said Gareth, and held it toward him.

He could hardly believe his luck! He had known Graham Sanderson worked here but he had not known he was actually a welder. He stayed to watch, shielding his eyes from the glaring point of laser light, seeing the blue sparks flying. He said he had always wanted to try his hand at welding, that he might even like to take it up professionally, and soon he was dressed in a greasy white boiler suit and extra headgear, listening and learning, attempting to grasp the basics. Under Graham Sanderson's guidance Gareth reinforced a fuel injection pipe without much trouble.

"Try something of my own, can I?" he asked. "Use that spare welder over there? I won't get in your way."

It was a souvenir from Surveyor Four that Gareth produced from the bag. He had picked it up in the Sinus Medii, he said, and he wanted to weld together the broken pieces and take it back to Earth. Graham Sanderson examined it curiously. It appeared to be some kind of rotor with two of its blades sheared off. Its function puzzled him, nor did he recognize the metal. It was an alloy he had never come across before. Other men gathered around, and Gareth started to sweat.

"Where did you say it came from?" one of them asked.

"Surveyor Four," said Gareth.

"It's damned odd," said another.

"But can it be mended?" Gareth asked anxiously.

Initially, to the men of the Vehicle Maintenance Department, it was regarded as a curio, a temporary distraction that challenged their powers of deduction during the official coffee break. They discovered that the metal was heat resistant, unaffected except by the hottest temperature. White heat melted it, but theoretically it was capable of withstanding reentry into the Earth's atmosphere, and they could not understand why it had been taken out of production. They could only assume it was discarded for its brittle qualities, its proneness to fracturing.

"But can it be mended?" Gareth repeated.

"It's a three-hour job," said one of the men.

"I've got nothing else to do," Gareth assured them.

"It would take an expert, son."

"If you'll just show me how to start . . ."

Gareth was surrounded by experts. Among the blast of a rivet gun, the fine whine of a drill, and machine tools singing all around him, he watched as the pieces of stabilizer were clamped in a vise and saw the laser light spark. Gobbets of hot metal fell to the floor, liquefied like mercury. It was not easy. When Gareth took over he was awkward and incompetent. The men had to take it in turns, leaving their own work to spend time with him, instructing him, advising him, showing him how. And Gareth was always willing to stand aside and admire their expertise.

To the men of the Vehicle Maintenance Department he was grateful in more ways than one—glad of their company and lunch in the snack bar, the noise and music and shouted conversations that gave him no chance to brood. It was time being utilized for a purpose, and it was midafternoon when Gareth left. The stabilizer hung heavy and solid in the gray bag over his shoulder. It was as strong as it had ever been, Graham Sanderson said. Strong enough to withstand the takeoff of Bethkahn's starship, Gareth thought, and there was a kind of joy in knowing that. She would have a future now, freedom to travel and something to hope for. But depression gripped him when he thought of himself.

He did not have any hope. He would be returning to Earth. Trapped in a prison of flesh he would serve out his sentence, his life continuing as it had before . . . inescapable . . . unless . . . ? A huge fear touched him, and he cut off the thought, and there were voices drifting through the open rectangle of a nearby doorway— his doorway. Drew and Karen were inside his room! Gareth stopped walking, thought to hide in the bathroom, but they saw him and so he walked on. They were blue-gray shapes in the gloomy light of the Moon's sunset, distant beings in another reality. He was remote from them and unrelated. And something had ended hours ago between himself and Karen.

"Been poking in my room, have you?"

"I was looking for my camera," Karen said.

"And where have *you* been?" Drew asked him.

"Vehicle Maintenance," Gareth said.

"We were supposed to be meeting for lunch!" Karen said sourly.

"I had lunch in the snack bar," Gareth said.

"Open your bag," said Drew.

"What?"

"Open it!"

"What *is* this?"

"Drew wants the sphere," said Karen.

Gareth swallowed, unfastened the straps of Bethkahn's shoulder bag, and showed Drew the stabilizer. It had come from the Vehicle Maintenance Department, he said angrily, and he had spent all morning welding it together, for something to do. If Drew wanted the sphere he should have looked in the closet, on the shelf.

"We *have* looked in the closet," Karen said. "We've looked everywhere. We've even checked the toilet tanks in the bathroom."

"So where is it?" asked Drew. "You had it last night in the plastic shopping bag. What have you done with it?"

"It's in the flaming closet!" Gareth said savagely. "I flaming put it there! I tried to give it to the security guards, but they wouldn't listen!" He flung open the closet door, allowed a few seconds to register apparent shock before the contrived reaction. "Flaming hell! It's gone!"

Karen turned to Drew.

Her voice was shrill.

"What did I tell you? If Gareth hasn't taken it then who has? It's *got* to be her!"

"Let's not jump to conclusions," Drew said quickly.

"What's she talking about?" Gareth asked.

"The girl!" shrilled Karen. "The one you saw in the dust storm when Charlie Kunik died! The one from the alien spaceship! She *did* come here last night! She came to your room, Gary, and took back the sphere!"

"Don't talk stupid! I would have seen her!"

"You didn't see anything!" Karen said wildly. "You were asleep! You never heard the second alarm siren! You never heard me come to your room! She could have killed you, and you wouldn't have known!"

Gareth shrugged.

"That's one explanation, I suppose. And what's gone is gone. Now if you don't mind I've got some packing to do."

Quite deliberately Gareth did not look at Drew or Karen. He dragged out his travel bag and closed the closet door. Then he tipped his clothes onto the bed and started to fold them, shirts and sweatshirts, smoothing the creases. Karen started to say something but decided not to, and a moment later Gareth heard the door close behind him. He thought they had gone but when he turned his head Drew was standing there.

"Why didn't you show me the sphere?"

"Because I didn't know what it was."

"Karen says it was a robotic spying device."

"That's only a theory."

"And what about this girl you claimed to have seen?"

"What about her?"

"Jake says he saw her, too."

Gareth bit his lip.

"Is Jake all right?" he asked.

"He will be, providing he can come to terms with the experience," said Drew. "For his sake I have to ask you—was she real? *Is* she real? Is this what we're up against, an alien life form? Is this what I should advise the base commander? This time I take you seriously, Gareth!"

Hunkered on his heels Gareth stayed still. He did not know what to say, how to answer, or how to protect Bethkahn. Truth or lies? Whatever he said Drew was ready to believe him, and Drew was no fool. He was a trained psychologist. One slip of the tongue, one thoughtless mistake, and Drew would be onto it. For Gareth's own sake, as well as for Jake, he had to play safe.

"Last night," said Gareth. "When I came back from the bathroom the security guards were searching. What did they find?"

"Nothing," Drew said evenly.

"What did they hope to find?"

Drew sighed.

"Okay," he said. "I guess I can level with you. That dust storm we encountered on the day Charlie Kunik died was not a straightforward phenomenon. From satellite recordings our computers picked up a faint heat-trace reading, a moving point of energy at the epicenter of the storm. I'm not saying this is evidence and proves you were right, but when the second dust storm happened, and Jake's garbled account told a similar story, it seemed prudent to order a full-scale search. I'm not sure what we expected to find—something or nothing—but we were obligated to check."

"And as it happened you found nothing," Gareth said quietly. "But something, it seems, came here to my room and took the sphere from my closet. So what does that suggest to you, Drew?"

Anxiety showed in Drew's eyes.

"I'll see you later," he said.

23

Gareth stared through the window at the disk of the sun sinking infinitely slowly behind the Lunar Apennines. Nightlong the rim of Mount Conon would eat it away, and before the dawn darkness Bethkahn would return. He had less than twelve hours to make up his mind—whether to go back to Earth or go with her, and both ways he had to be desperate. It was one thing believing he was more than flesh and blood, that there was another side to him indestructible and immortal, but he was not dying to prove it, no more than he was dying to return to Earth. Faced with the choice between life and death Gareth could not decide which he feared most. Drew nudged him, pointed to the steak pie and mashed potatoes on the plate.

"Your food's growing cold."

"What I need is food for my soul," Gareth muttered.

"That's a very peculiar remark," said Drew.

"He's been peculiar all day," Karen said sourly.

"Man shall not live by bread alone," Gareth quoted.

"So what brought this on?" Drew asked.

"Better eat up," J.B. told him. "Russian hospitality is not like ours. All you'll get in the Sinus Iridum is black bread and water."

Gareth scowled at his plate.

"Steak pie or black bread, it's all the same—gut fodder! But there is another deeper hunger that cannot be satisfied, see?"

"Ah," said Drew. "I'm beginning to see."

"I meant to tell you this morning," said J.B.

"How serious is this?" asked Drew.

"He doesn't want to go back," said Karen.

"Nor would you if you had to face my prospects!" Gareth retorted.

"You don't have to go back to Wales," Karen told him. "I've invited you to come to Santa Barbara. Pop will find you a job."

"There you are," J.B. said cheerfully. "The world is your oyster, son. Work hard, save your dollars, invest wisely. You'll be a millionaire by the time you're thirty."

"What good's that?" Gareth said viciously. "The only purpose of money is to buy *things*. Why should I spend the rest of my life scrimping and saving to buy a load of blasted cars and washing machines and a thousand and one consumer goods that I could do without? What a flaming waste of life! There's got to be more than that. There's got to be!"

"Life gets better as you get older," J.B. assured him.

"Not in Aberdare!"

"Even in Aberdare," said Drew. "You can take my word for it. You'll find a meaning."

But words did not help. What was true for Drew and the base commander might not be true for Gareth. He saw things differently, and all he had to go on were his own experiences. They had probably bred, Bethkahn had said of the beings who had once shared her starship, and Gareth was the result. He had a body evolved from the beasts of the Earth, a soul evolved from the stars. He inherited the conflict, torn between spirit and flesh, between Earth's bleak reality and Bethkahn's universe, fear and faith. But the fear was stronger, sheer physicality holding him back, temptation in a dish of lemon sherbet. On Bethkahn's starship, robotic waiters served amber wine in tall glasses. Sensations were not dimmed, she had said, and taste was just as sweet. But words could be lies, and there was only one way for Gareth to find out. Gloomily he picked up the spoon . . . and what he ate was synthetic junk.

"Shall we go for a last swim in the pool?" asked Karen.

"And a last Coke in the moonbase bar?" suggested Drew.

"*You* can," said Gareth. "I'm going to bed."

Karen sighed.

"Do you have to be miserable on our last night?"

"I think you should make an effort," said Drew.

"You have to snap out of it, son," J.B. said kindly.

"Please, Gary, let's have a farewell party," Karen said.

"And here come the guests of honor," said J.B.

White and red, the Russian hopper set down on the landing pad outside, sank and settled in a swirl of dust, looking like a bowlegged beetle with porthole windows along the side, the size of a double-decker bus. The base commander buttoned his Air Force jacket and hurried to greet the Soviet team. Gareth went swimming. And afterward he went to the moonbase bar to join the party. He went because Drew was watching him—gray eyes, with a degree in psychology behind them, summing him up, his dour silence and symptoms of depression. He knew if he was not careful he would end up being analyzed, or drugged into quiescence, dosed with sleeping pills for a night when he needed to stay awake. Ice chinked in his glass, and he fixed a smile on his face.

The room seemed overrun by Russians in gray uniforms, the big promotion scene for East-West relations, handshakes and introductions and background music giving an air of gaiety that was totally false. It was like holding a wake before the funeral, and Gareth was part of it, laughing and talking and playing at being himself—bones and a body with his name attached.

"Mikhail Denovitch," J.B. boomed. "Meet our young visitors. This is Karen. And this is Gareth—the first Welshman on the Moon. If daffodils bloom next spring in the Mare Vaporum it'll be his doing. And you've heard about the bones of the moon beast, of course."

167

The Russian smiled.

"You are the joker, Gareth?"

"Not tonight," said Karen. "Tonight he's pretending he's not one hundred percent miserable."

"You are not drinking the bourbon," Mikhail Denovitch said. "I buy you one, eh?"

"Go on," said Drew. "Have one to drown your sorrows."

"What I need is a permanent solution," said Gareth. "Not a temporary escape route and a thick head. How about a job at the Russian base? Fully qualified, I am. Clean your boots or polish your buggies. Good for nothing, see, with first-class references."

The Russian laughed.

And the base commander's paternal hand rested on Gareth's shoulder. "We're sure going to miss this guy," he said.

But when Gareth slipped away half an hour later no one missed him. Drew was too busy chatting with Valerie Doyle from Communications to notice, and Karen was teaching Mikhail Denovitch to dance. Down empty corridors Gareth walked, and the bright electric lights did not dispel his mood of gloom. And the bare white room with its packed travel bag, closed door, and dull sunset light enhanced it. He felt isolated from everyone, and his sense of unbelonging grew to a kind of terror. The Lunacy Syndrome had its dark side, Drew had said, and solitude was dangerous. What the stars had begun in the first moment of the Moon's morning was now complete. Gareth was meaningless. His stay at the moonbase was over, and on Earth, among the teeming billions of people, his absence would be no loss. Who he was and what he did mattered to no one but himself.

He stood staring out at the darkening landscape, the desert of gray-brown dust and tumbled ridges where nothing lived or moved—only an alien girl who watched and waited, Bethkahn with her amber eyes and drifts of dark hair. He mattered to her. She thought of him and wished for him, not caring about his past or future. She had not said so, but he had felt it, a need in her as deep as his own, her loneliness touching him in the silence. She had not needed to ask why he would help her; that he did was an answer in itself. And he had not needed to ask her what life was like on Khio Three because she too was an answer. She represented it—a beautiful being from a beautiful world. He knew now why men looked up at the stars and called them heaven. A part of them remembered, paradise echoing through generations of human dreams. And Bethkahn with her starship could take him back there, to the land of his fathers that had never been Wales.

Nine thousand light-years, Bethkahn had said.

He would be dead before he got there.

And that was the permanent solution, the final freedom.

But Gareth was convinced he was not just physical.

Like Bethkahn he had an astral body.

The Moon had proved it.

The *Zen Buddhist's Handbook* confirmed it.

Yet the fear remained.

He was afraid of knowing, afraid of extinction, afraid of nothing . . . scared out of his mind. "Help me!" he whispered. But no one came. It was his decision. His and his alone.

Later, as Gareth lay unsleeping fully clothed under the blanket, Drew looked in. Behind him in the lighted corridor Karen giggled and hiccuped and he hushed her to silence and closed the door. There was no sound then but the hum of the air-conditioning and the thud of Gareth's heart as he sat up and waited, watching as the line of light below his door faded at midnight, and the moonbase slept.

He was in no hurry. Time ticked by on his wristwatch, and the fear was gone. A strange calm gripped him, and his stockinged feet made no sound upon the floor tiles when he finally made his move. With the bag containing the stabilizer slung over his shoulder, Gareth opened the door, glanced left and right along the darkened corridor, then hurried away in the direction of the main reception area. Without his weighted training shoes his body felt light and floating, unreal and unbelonging and disconnected from his head. A murmur of voices drifted from the cafeteria, and the Communications room was bright with light, fully staffed, as Gareth went past. No one saw him. And when he turned the corner he waited in the shadows until the guards in the security checkpoint turned their backs, then slipped into the room where the space suits were kept.

There was no one on duty at that time of night—just

rows of silver suits, racks of helmets and oxygen cylinders and strap harnesses on hooks, toilet facilities in the unlit room beyond. Gareth had no plan, but his gaze fixed immediately on the Russian helmets, scarlet and white and bearing the symbols of the Soviet Union. Even from a distance they were unmistakable, quite distinct from the helmets used by the Americans. A few words of Welsh mistaken for Russian, and Gareth would be away. He dressed hurriedly and locked himself in a toilet stall to wait for Bethkahn's approach.

He had to see her again. He had to talk to her. He did not have long to wait—maybe half an hour of sweating inside the insulated suit before the alarm sirens wailed. Then he acted—fitted the oxygen cylinder, buckled the harness, and sealed the Russian helmet. Wrist dials showed green as he picked up the bag and reentered the corridor.

Just as last night, the moonbase was in panic, lights going on and armed guards running in all directions. It was a weird feeling—seeing but not hearing, a goldfish in a bowl staring through the glass at an alien world in which he could not live, could not belong. He felt like a ghost, sitting inside himself and looking out, uninvolved with what went on, not caring about their hopes and fears or the planet they came from. For seventeen years he had been acting out a role in their ghastly pantomime, but now it was over . . . almost.

Gesticulating wildly Gareth approached the checkpoint, a Russian gabbling in some unintelligible language across the suit's transmitter, adding to the general confusion. The two security guards barring his way to the air lock stared at him in alarm. Gareth opened the bag, pointed to the stabilizer and then to the air lock, allowed himself to speak a few words of broken English.

"This," he said. "Into hopper. I go quick."

"You've got to be mad going out there, buddy."

"Orders," said Gareth. "Mikhail Denovitch."

"Okay screwball—it's your life."

"I go?" Gareth said urgently.

"Sure," said the guard. "Carry on."

Gareth did not hesitate. The doors closed behind him. Wall dials in the outer chamber showed zero pressure, and then he was outside. He saw the hopper squatting on the landing pad. He saw the desert stretching out before him, empty, unreal, no one on it. Men would never reach the Moon, never set their feet upon the dust or breathe in the airless spaces. The Moon was a dream, the orbed maiden out of myth and poetry, ruthless and lonely, waiting to kill. But Gareth rounded the corner, crossed the concrete of the loading bay, and went to meet her. Stars blazed, and the sun was half gone behind the rim of Mount Conon. Dust blew in the wind. He thought of peppermint gum and Drew's red hair. He thought of Jake singing, Mom and her lover, and the dull gray streets of Aberdare. But his voice was a cry of joy in the moonwind rising.

"I'm here, Bethkahn!"

24

Karen stood in the reception area in the long, empty minutes before departure. It was dark outside, the shadowy landscape stretching away, desolate below the stars. And the stars were more brilliant than she had ever seen them, gold and glorious in the black depths of space. Their beauty mocked her. They made her feel small and insignificant, without identity. She wanted to go home, back to America where she knew who she was—Karen Angers, her mother's daughter, her kid brother's sister, a pupil at Santa Barbara High School and dating Joey Bellini on Saturday nights. She was meaningless on the Moon. It was lethal and lonely, nothing to do with "Phoebe Unveiled," the imagery of poetry and the essay that had brought her here. More like it was the "Lunacy Syndrome" come to life, a hideous madness. Slow tears trickled down her face as she thought of him. His name was Gareth. It had always been Gareth, and she wanted to scream at him in anger and despair, demand an answer . . . for Pete's sake why? But Gareth was dead, and the hopper was twelve hours late in leaving, and all she could do was cry.

Drew brought her bags.

"They're taking him out now," he said.

The arc lamps switched on, showing the Russian hopper standing on the landing pad, its air lock doors open to receive its passengers. Karen covered her face with her hands. She did not want to see—two corpses sewn in their canvas shrouds, and one of them Gareth. Great sobs shook her body, and Drew held her, smoothing her hair.

"Why did he do it?" Karen wept. "Why did he go outside? He knew what she was—ruthless and lonely. He knew she killed Charlie Kunik, so why did he go? How could he be so stupid?" Drew did not answer, but his touch went on, soothing, comforting, and the words poured from her. "She wasn't even human, so what did he want from her? What did he hope for? He could have come with me to Santa Barbara, but he turned to her, and she murdered him. She *murdered* him, Drew!"

"No," said Drew. "That's not what happened. We have no real proof of this girl's existence and no evidence to suggest that anyone other than Gareth released the seals on his helmet. He died by his own hand, Karen, while the balance of his mind—"

"No! He wouldn't do that! *She* killed him!"

"I think you should face it, sweetheart."

"No! I won't believe it!"

"Listen to me. Listen Karen. Gareth was depressed. He made it quite clear he didn't want to return to Earth. If you have to blame someone then blame me. His death was my fault. I should have realized . . ."

Drew's voice trailed away, and Karen raised her head to look at him. His face was pale beneath the red thatch of his hair, and his gray eyes looked stricken. On a personal level Drew was as much in need of comfort as she was.

"Why should I blame you?" Karen said wretchedly. "He knew what could happen. He was probably trying to hitch a ride on her spaceship. That's the sort of stupid thing he'd try for! I could believe that! But I can't believe in suicide. That's the coward's way out, and Gareth wasn't a coward!"

"No," said Drew. "He was never that."

"So what possible reason could he have had?"

"The permanent solution?" said Drew.

Karen sat heavily on the red padded bench. She could not take it in, could not accept it. She could not wait to get back to Earth, yet Drew said Gareth had died rather than return there, deliberately killed himself. It could not be true! But there was no place on Earth for him, he had said, no reason or purpose working all his life for a load of things he did not want. Suddenly, clear and terrible, Karen saw the world through Gareth's eyes in everything he had talked of—the cruelty and injustice, the squalid streets of Aberdare, his mother living with a man he had not liked. It was all right for

Karen living on the rich West Coast of America. She could remain untouched by it all. But Gareth had despised wealth as much as he had despised poverty. He had turned down the opportunities she had offered because he could not close his eyes to things, could never forgive or forget.

Understanding, Karen hung her head. Gold bangles jangling on her wrists shamed her. She had thought herself lucky to be born American, but now she was ashamed of it, and the tears she cried were different tears, galling, humiliating, guilt mixed with grief. The Moon changed everyone. Gareth had died, and Karen would never be the same again.

"What are we doing?" she sobbed. "What are we thinking of? It's all gone wrong. The whole world's gone wrong. We spend billions of dollars on a useless moonbase, billions more on weapons of destruction, on stupid fashions and cosmetic surgery and so many worthless things. We spend, and others starve, and Gareth could not bear to go back to that. I know how he felt, but he didn't have to die because of it. He could have stayed and fought! He could have fought it much better than me! He could have done so much, and now he can do nothing! So what was the point of it?"

Drew sighed.

"I suppose he saw it as the only way out."

"But he was so alive!" said Karen. "He was the most alive person I ever met. Maddening and infuriating and enough to drive anyone crazy, but he seemed to give out a kind of life. The Moon wasn't dead while he was on it—it was full of bones and daffodils, and pickle factories, silly, ridiculous things. He fooled us, Drew. He was always fooling us. He wouldn't give that up!"

Drew shrugged.

"Maybe he fooled himself," he said bleakly.

"Maybe," Karen said doubtfully. "I know he believed it. He believed in astral bodies and alien spaceships. He believed in the girl too. He believed so much he made me believe also. Why would he believe it if there was no truth in it? Why would he?"

"I think," said Drew, "that we will never know."

"Do you know what I think?" Karen asked. "I think there's something we're not seeing—that he raised his finger to the whole goddam world and is laughing at us."

"Which doesn't alter the fact." Drew sighed.

Karen echoed his sigh, turned to watch the hopper being loaded—an enemy machine, red and white with its symbols of Soviet power. In their silver suits the men worked together, Russian and American, indistinguishable one from another except for their helmets. They were all human beings, all the same underneath.

"I wish I understood," Karen muttered. "I wouldn't mind so much if I knew the reason. It's wasting everything Gareth was, and it just doesn't fit."

Karen leaped to her feet.

The men outside ran for cover.

And a moment later the siren sounded.

177

"It's another dust storm!" Drew said anxiously.

"No," said Karen. "Look over there! It's that volcano! It's an eruption!"

The sky above the Lunar Apennines pulsed red and golden with light and fire. Mount Conon was alive, belching smoke and dust and clouding the stars. But then, in the heart of it, something moved—a vast silver shape among the detritus.

Slowly and ponderously the starship rose, lifting above the crater rim as the siren wailed and moonbase personnel came running and crowding around the windows, their voices shrill with fear and disbelief.

"Is that what I think it is?"

"Some kind of joke?"

"No joke, buddy, it's a flying saucer!"

"It's not true! It can't be!"

"God almighty! Will you look at the size of it!"

"I reckon we've had it! I reckon we don't stand a chance!"

"We're sitting ducks!"

"Someone inform the base commander!"

"We need a nuclear strike, immediately!"

"It's too damned close! We'd be blown to pieces!"

"Lord, into thy hands . . ."

Karen stared at the ship in terror, felt Drew's arm tighten around her. He had not been able to believe what Gareth had said, but everyone believed it now. It was there before them—an alien spaceship hovering hugely above the mountains, then veering toward them. Green, red, blue, yellow, and purple, it flashed its multitude of colored lights as its great bulk sailed across the stars and slowly approached. It hung there, motionless, just a few hundred feet up, seeming to fill the whole sky. The siren ceased, and the lights flashed off and on in the long, terrible seconds of silence. They were waiting to die, spellbound people holding their breaths. But the ship did not kill. Beautiful and spectacular as in a fairy-tale city in space, the colored lights flickered off and on, off and on, as if the starship signaled.

"Screw me!" someone said. "It's moonbase morse!"

Someone else laughed nervously.

"Don't be ridiculous! How the hell would a flying saucer know moonbase morse?"

"By tapping our computers," a security guard said grimly.

"I think it's just random signaling," said Valerie Doyle from Communications. "Gobbledygook. No . . . es . . . da . . . car . . . I . . . ad . . . No . . . es . . . It just keeps repeating it, words with no sense attached. Nos . . . da . . . car-I-ad. Some foreign language perhaps?"

Karen stared at the sky, at the colored lights flashing off and on, off and on. *Nos da, cariad. Nos da.* The colors whispered deep in her mind, glorious with meaning. Gareth had fooled them, just as she had said. Wild with joy, Karen pushed past the security guard and hurled herself at the window. Two hands waved back at him and her voice was screaming.

"*Nos da*, Gareth! *Nos da!*"

"Karen?" said Drew. "What do you think you're doing?"
She turned toward him.

Her eyes were shining in the light.

"It's Welsh," she said. "Good night, darling. *Nos da, cariad.* That's what it means."

"We've no Welsh in our computers," someone said.

"No," said Karen. "But Gareth knows it. He's up there! Saying good-bye . . . to me."

"It's coincidence," said Valerie Doyle.

"Gareth is dead," said Drew.

But Karen would not listen, did not care. She turned back to the window. Click-flash . . . Someone beside her was using her camera, taking pictures of the ship, and the movie camera whirred. But Karen had her memory and would never forget—magical colors, blue, red, yellow, purple, and green, speaking for Gareth, letting her know. He had to go on, not back. The Moon had changed him, and this was the meaning he had talked of—life itself. It was more than the color of a skin, the needs of a body, the wants and greeds of Earth. He had believed it, trusted it, the permanent solution—life, not death. Deep inside herself Karen felt the stirring of her own immortal existence, a surge of power and her soul leaping in joy as she became aware of it. For a trip on a starship and an alien girl Gareth had died and lived, but he had not forgotten Karen. *"Nos da, cariad."* The colors whispered and moondust swirled in the wind as the great ship lifted upward.

"Gee, it's fantastic!" Karen said.

And laughed through her tears.

About the Author

LOUISE LAWRENCE was born in Surrey, England, and now lives in Gloucestershire. Ms. Lawrence has been writing since she was twenty-two, and has since published eight novels for young adults. Her most recent book, CHILDREN OF THE DUST, *was a 1985 ALA Best Book for Young Adults.*